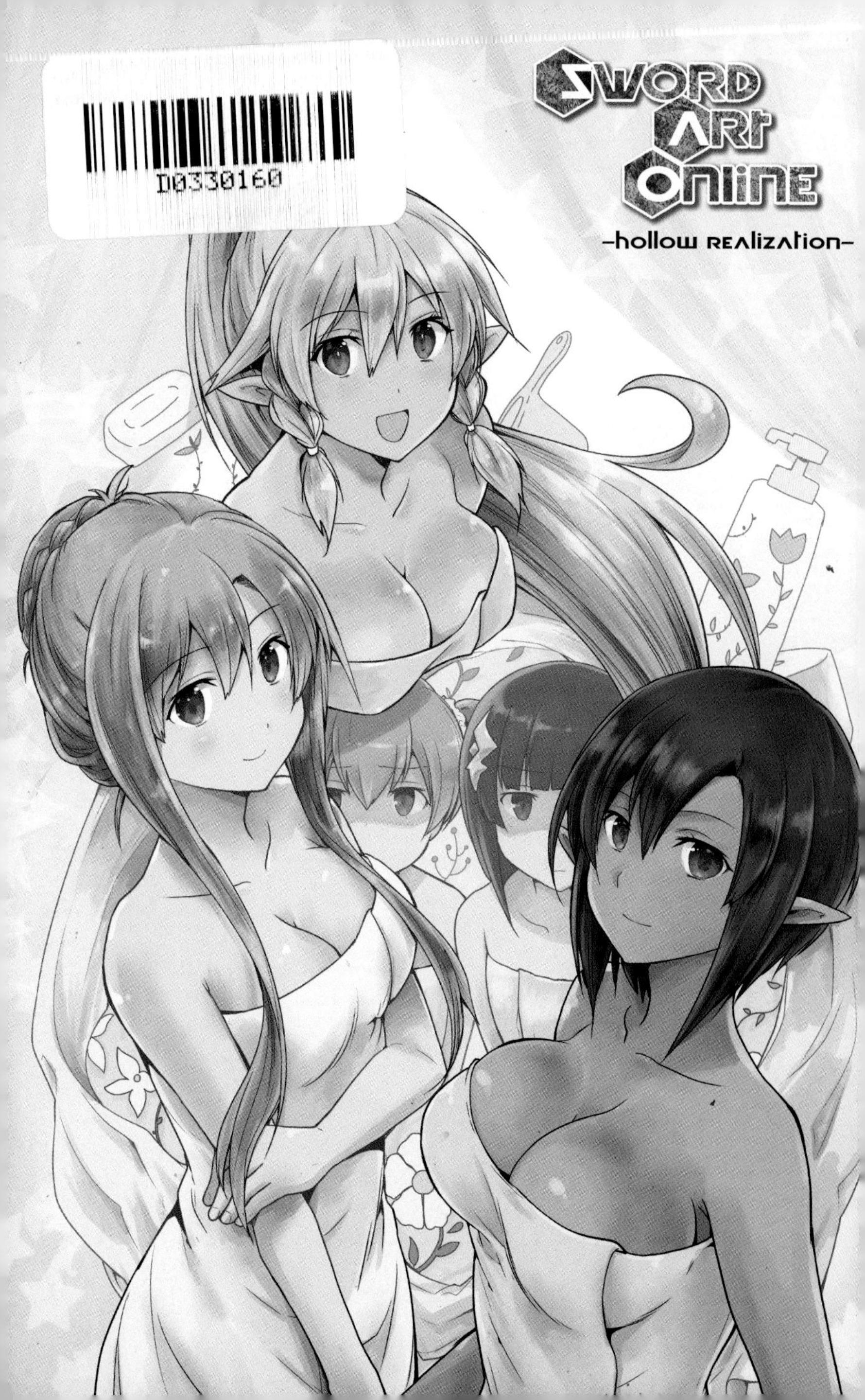
SWORD ART ONLINE
-hollow realization-

SWORD ART ONLINE
—HOLLOW REALIZATION—

004

CONTENTS

I'm back in Aincrad

#15

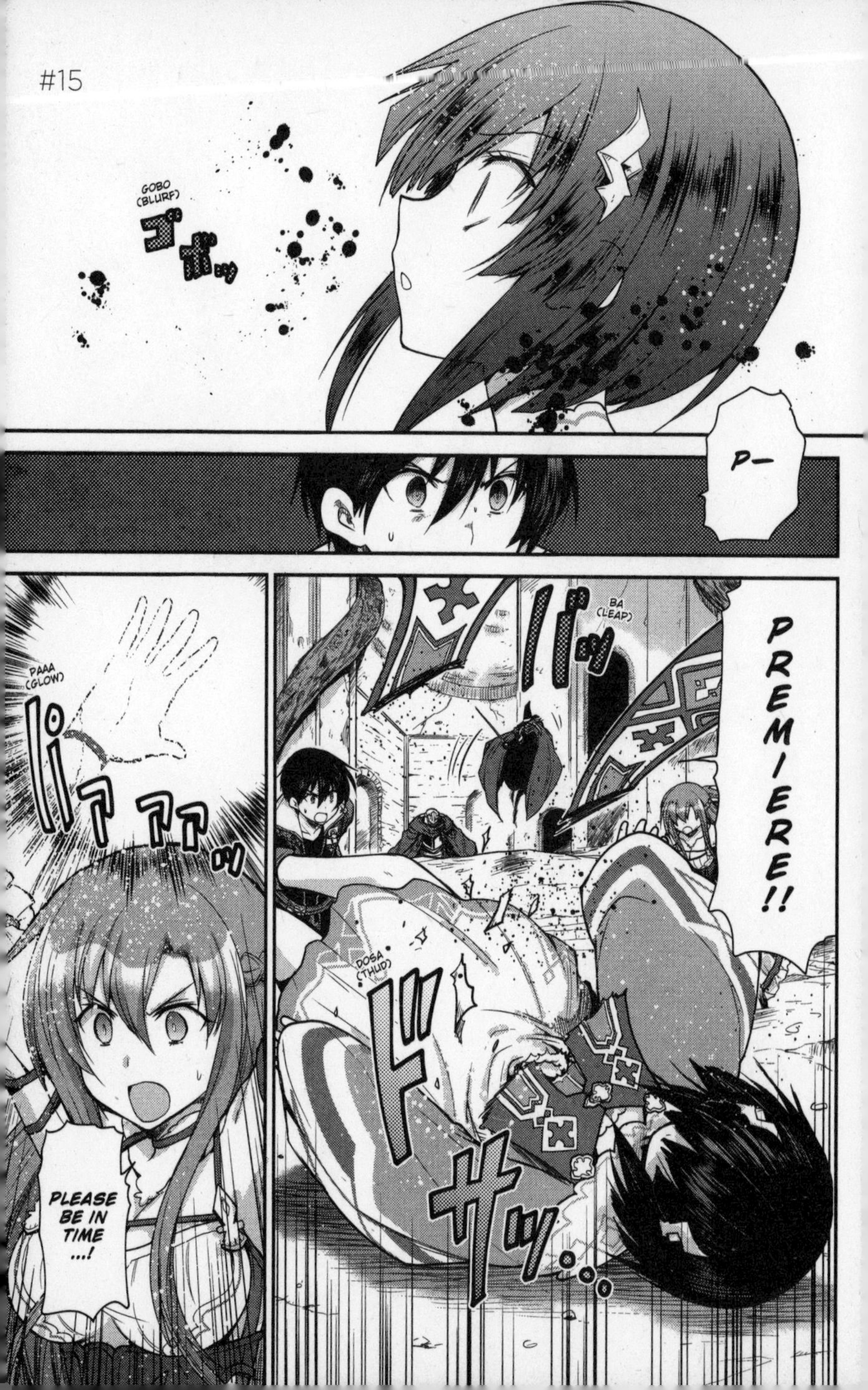
GOBO (BLURF)
ゴボッ
P—
BA (LEAP)
バッ
PREMIERE!!
DOSA (THUD)
ドサッ
PAAA (GLOW)
パァァァッ
PLEASE BE IN TIME ...!

#15: Life

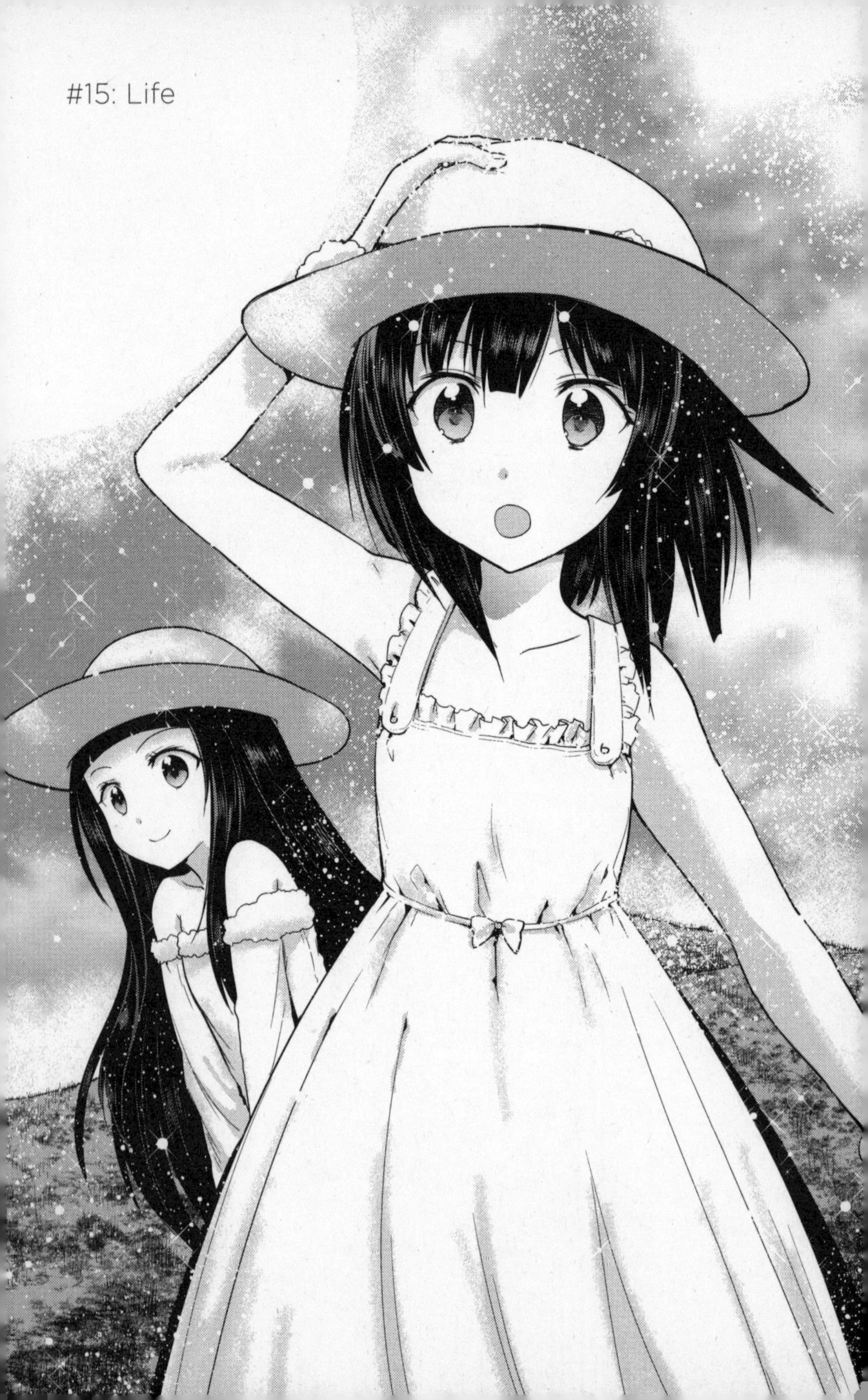

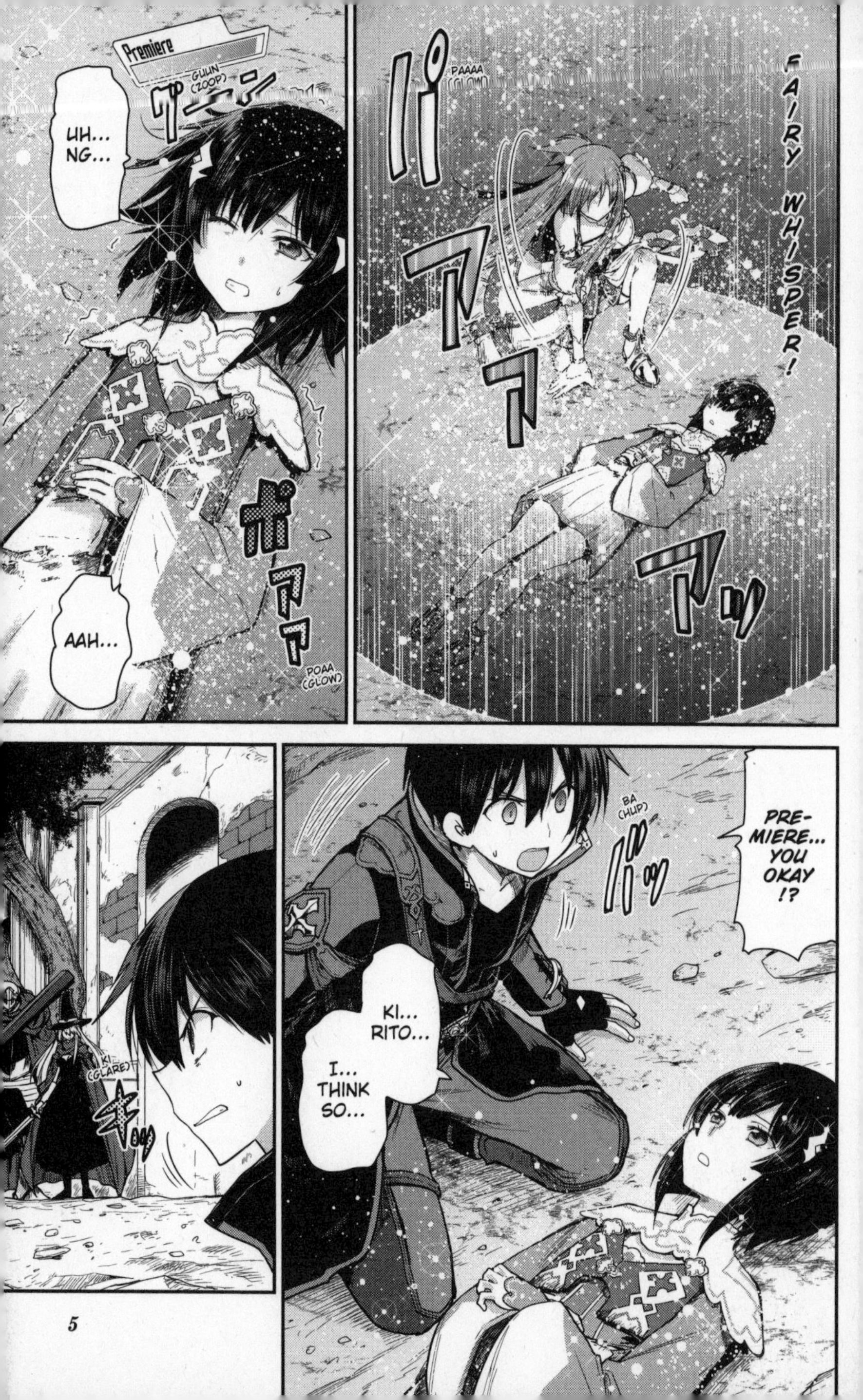
FAIRY WHISPER!
PAAAA (GLOW)
Premiere
GUUN (ZOOP)
UH... NG...
AAH...
POAA (GLOW)
BA (HUP)
PREMIERE... YOU OKAY!?
KI... RITO...
I... THINK SO...
KI (GLARE)

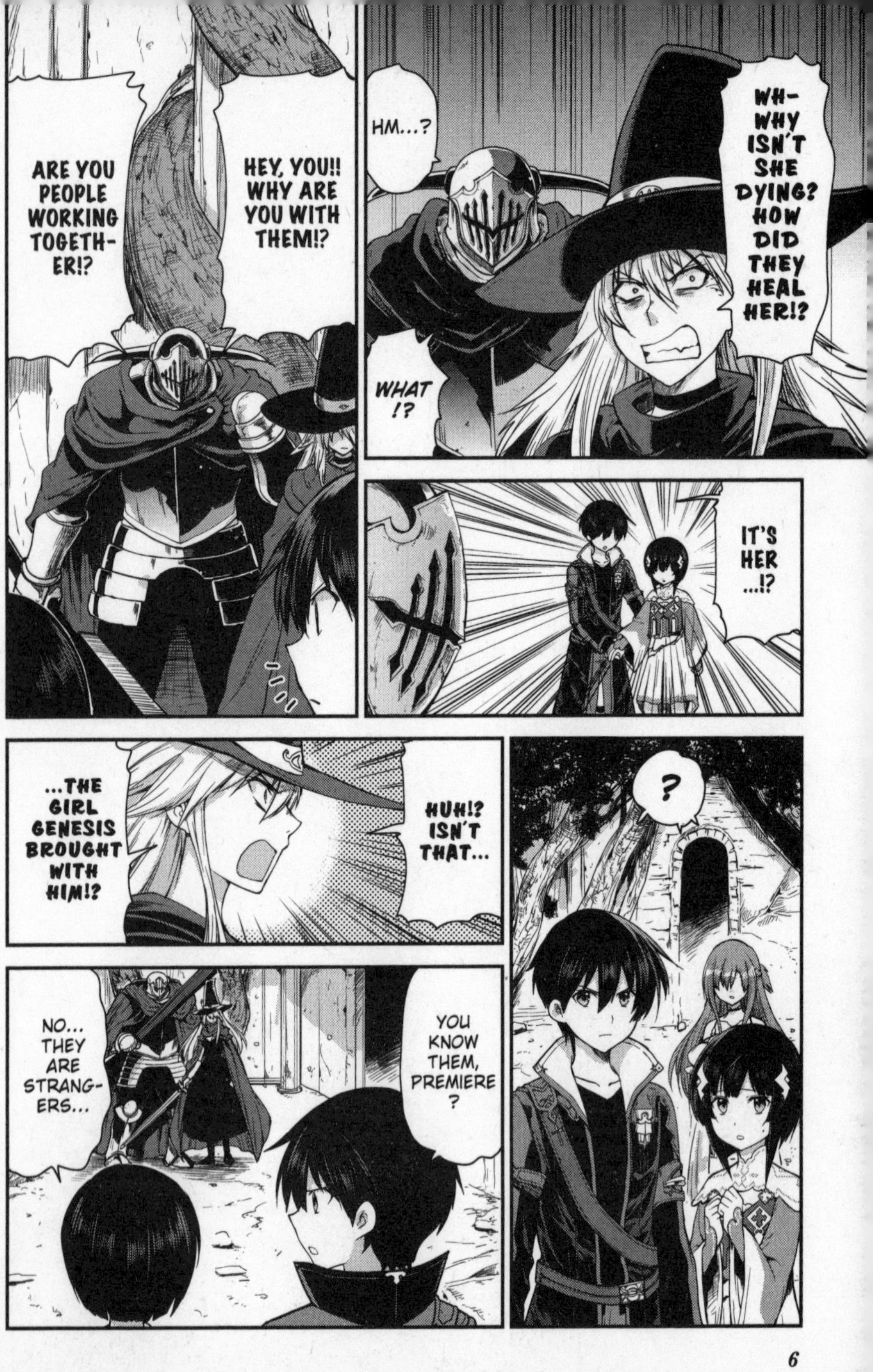
WH-WHY ISN'T SHE DYING? HOW DID THEY HEAL HER!?
HM...?
WHAT!?
IT'S HER...!?
HEY, YOU!! WHY ARE YOU WITH THEM!?
ARE YOU PEOPLE WORKING TOGETH-ER!?
?
HUH!? ISN'T THAT...
...THE GIRL GENESIS BROUGHT WITH HIM!?
YOU KNOW THEM, PREMIERE?
NO... THEY ARE STRANGER-ERS...

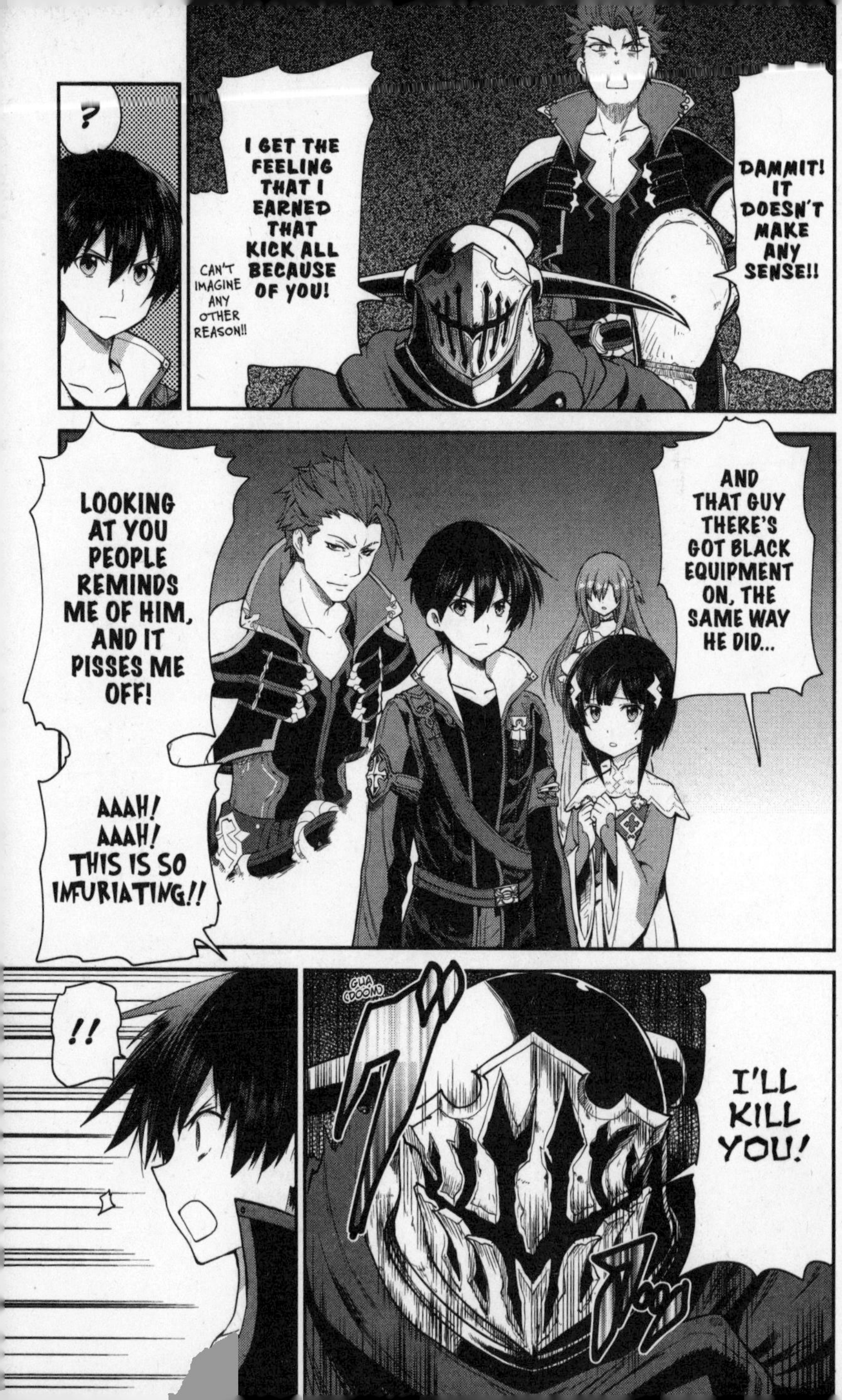
DAMMIT! IT DOESN'T MAKE ANY SENSE!!
I GET THE FEELING THAT I EARNED THAT KICK ALL BECAUSE OF YOU!
CAN'T IMAGINE ANY OTHER REASON!!
?
AND THAT GUY THERE'S GOT BLACK EQUIPMENT ON, THE SAME WAY HE DID...
LOOKING AT YOU PEOPLE REMINDS ME OF HIM, AND IT PISSES ME OFF!
AAAH! AAAH! THIS IS SO INFURIATING!!
GUA (DOON)
I'LL KILL YOU!
!!

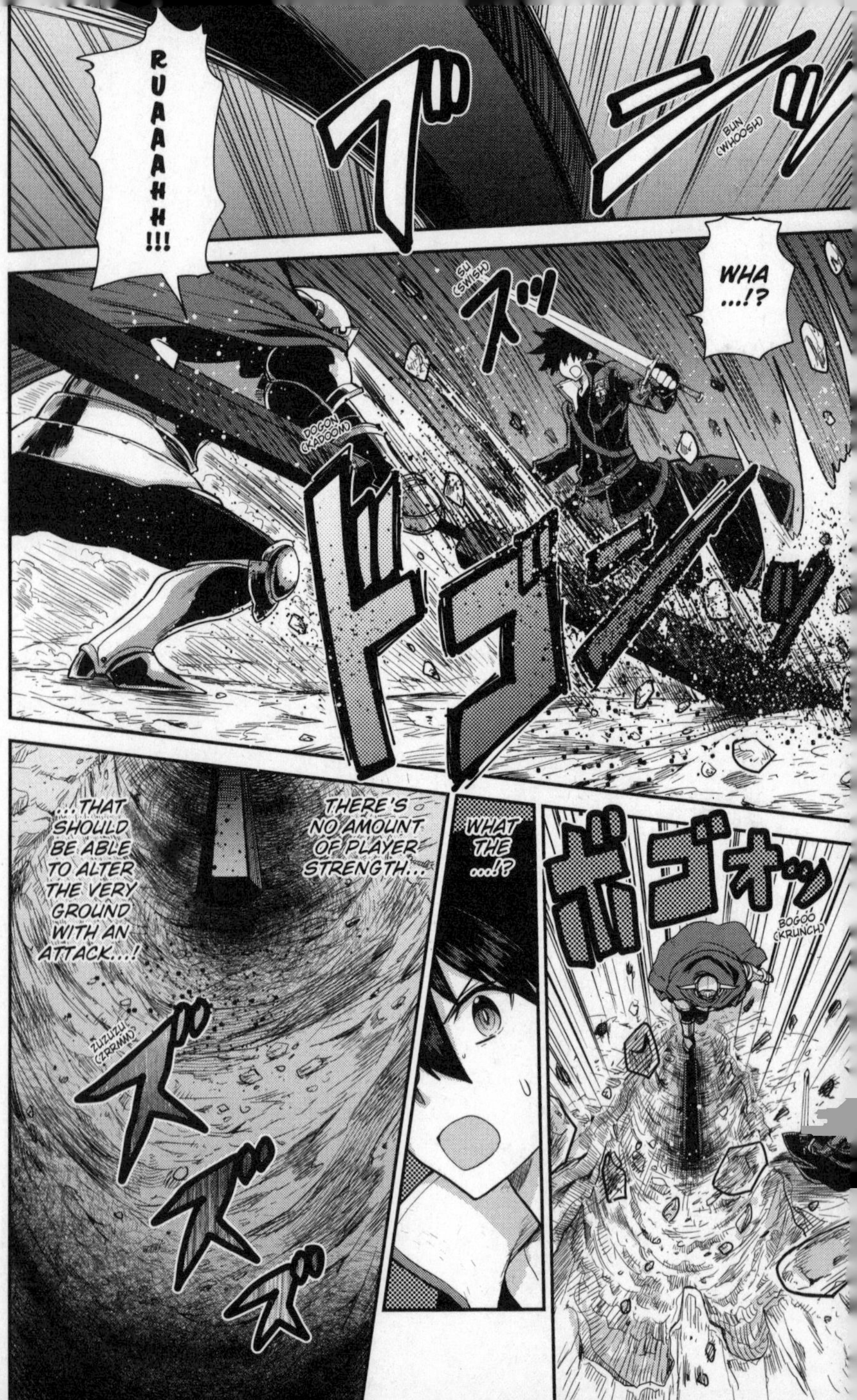
BUN (WHOOSH)
RUAAAAHH!!!
WHA...!?
SU (SWISH)
DOGON (KADOOM)
BOGOO (KRUNCH)
WHAT THE...!?
THERE'S NO AMOUNT OF PLAYER STRENGTH...
...THAT SHOULD BE ABLE TO ALTER THE VERY GROUND WITH AN ATTACK...!
ZUZUZU (ZRRMM)

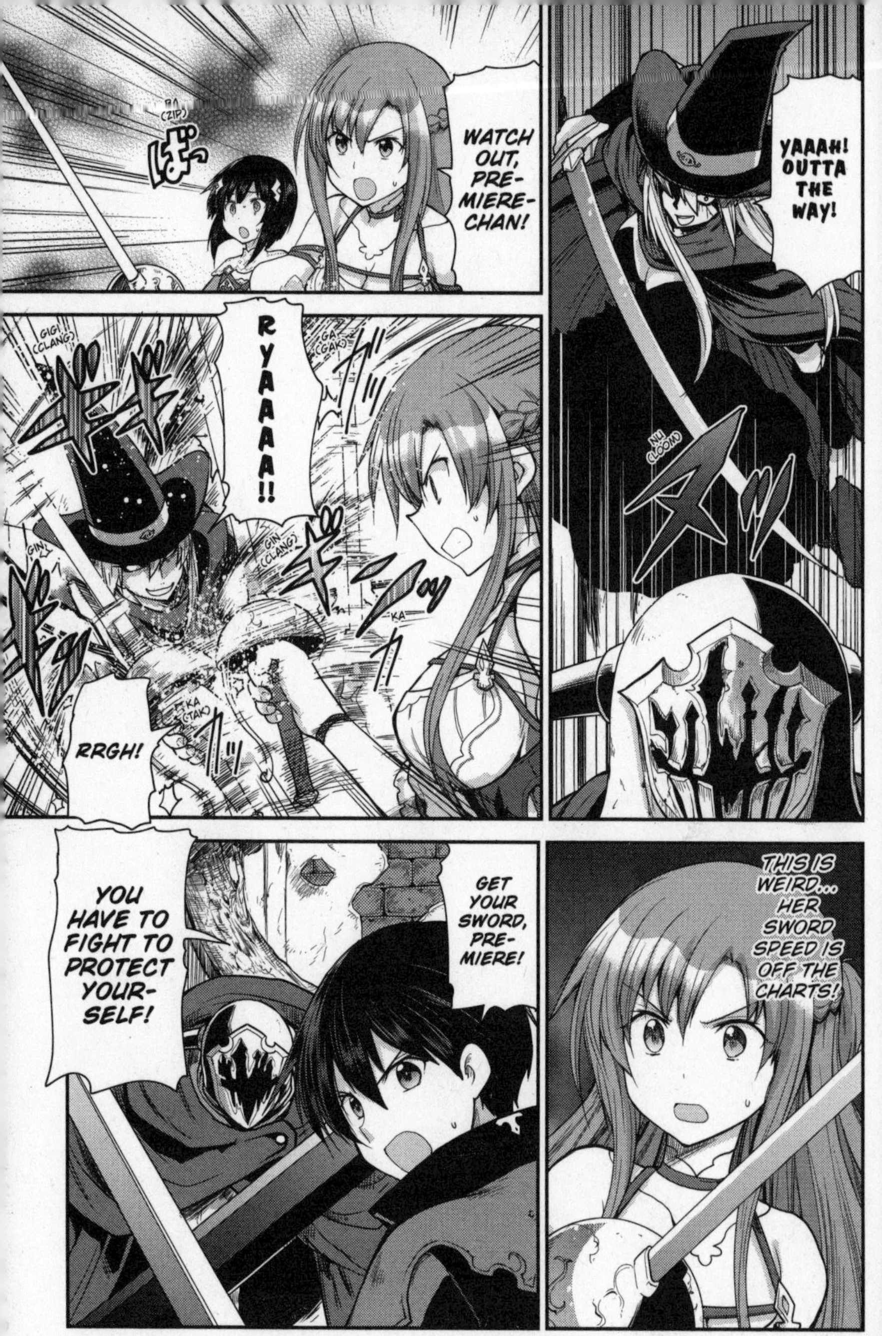
YAAAH! OUTTA THE WAY!
NU (LOOM)
PA (ZIP)
WATCH OUT, PREMIERE-CHAN!
RYAAAAA!!
GA (GAK)
GIGI (CLANG)
GIN (CLANG)
KA
GIN
KA (TAK)
RRGH!
THIS IS WEIRD... HER SWORD SPEED IS OFF THE CHARTS!
GET YOUR SWORD, PREMIERE!
YOU HAVE TO FIGHT TO PROTECT YOURSELF!

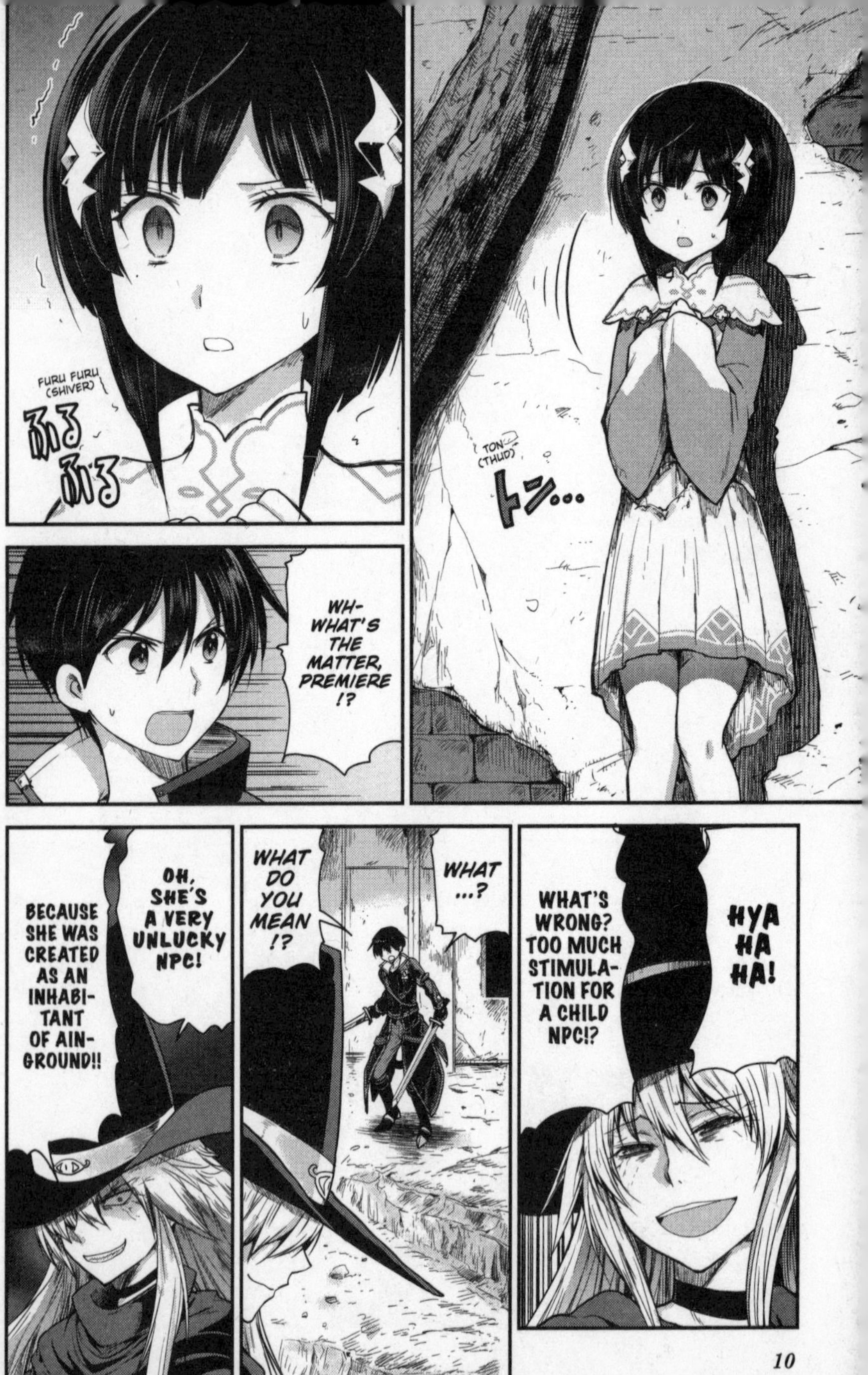
TON (THUD)
トン…
FURU FURU (SHIVER)
ふるふる
WH-WHAT'S THE MATTER, PREMIERE!?
HYA HA HA!
WHAT'S WRONG? TOO MUCH STIMULATION FOR A CHILD NPC!?
WHAT ...?
WHAT DO YOU MEAN!?
OH, SHE'S A VERY UNLUCKY NPC!
BECAUSE SHE WAS CREATED AS AN INHABITANT OF AINGROUND!!

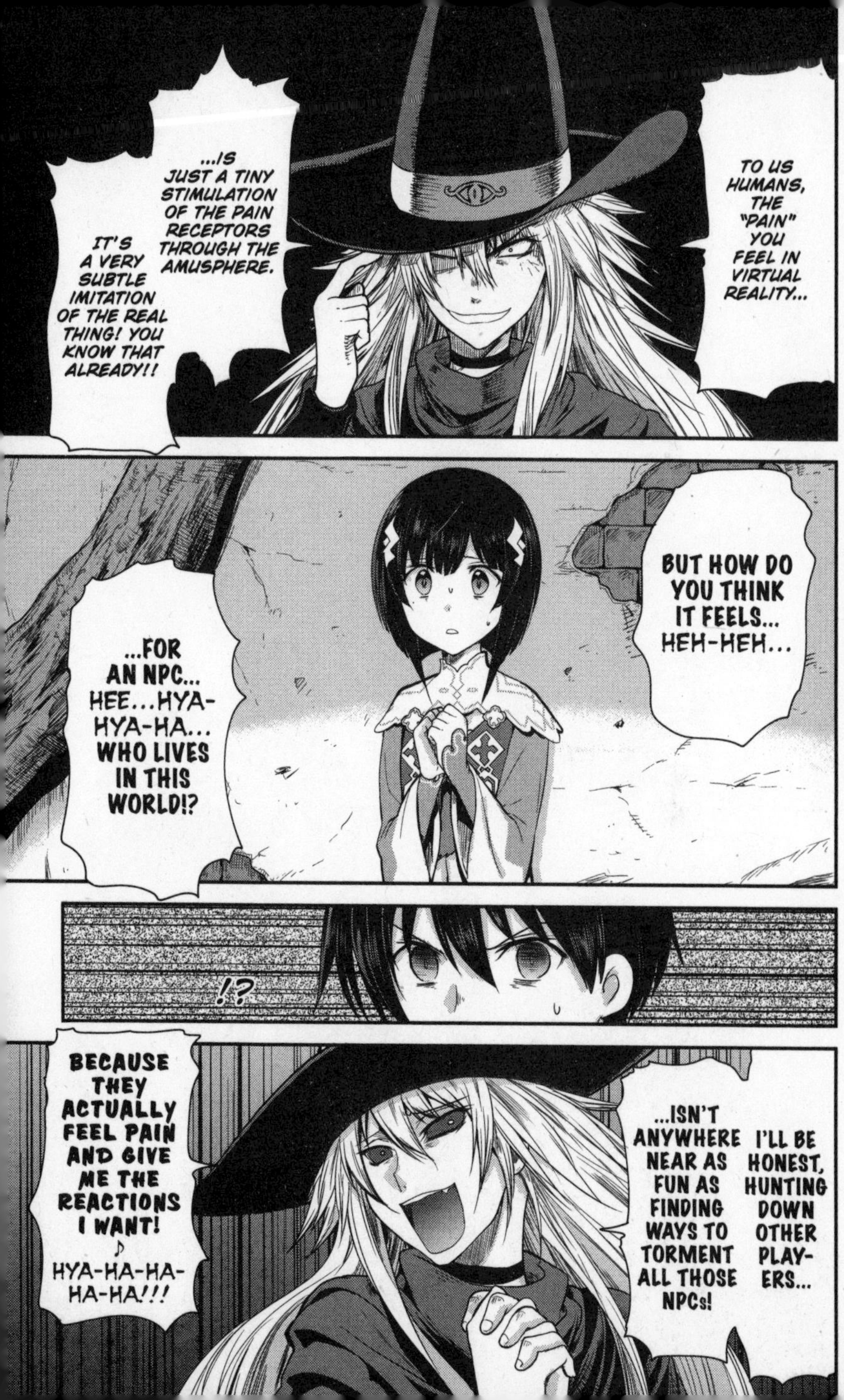
TO US HUMANS, THE "PAIN" YOU FEEL IN VIRTUAL REALITY...
...IS JUST A TINY STIMULATION OF THE PAIN RECEPTORS THROUGH THE AMUSPHERE.
IT'S A VERY SUBTLE IMITATION OF THE REAL THING! YOU KNOW THAT ALREADY!!
BUT HOW DO YOU THINK IT FEELS... HEH-HEH...
...FOR AN NPC... HEE...HYA-HYA-HA... WHO LIVES IN THIS WORLD!?
!?
I'LL BE HONEST, HUNTING DOWN OTHER PLAY-ERS...
...ISN'T ANYWHERE NEAR AS FUN AS FINDING WAYS TO TORMENT ALL THOSE NPCs!
BECAUSE THEY ACTUALLY FEEL PAIN AND GIVE ME THE REACTIONS I WANT! ♪ HYA-HA-HA-HA-HA!!!

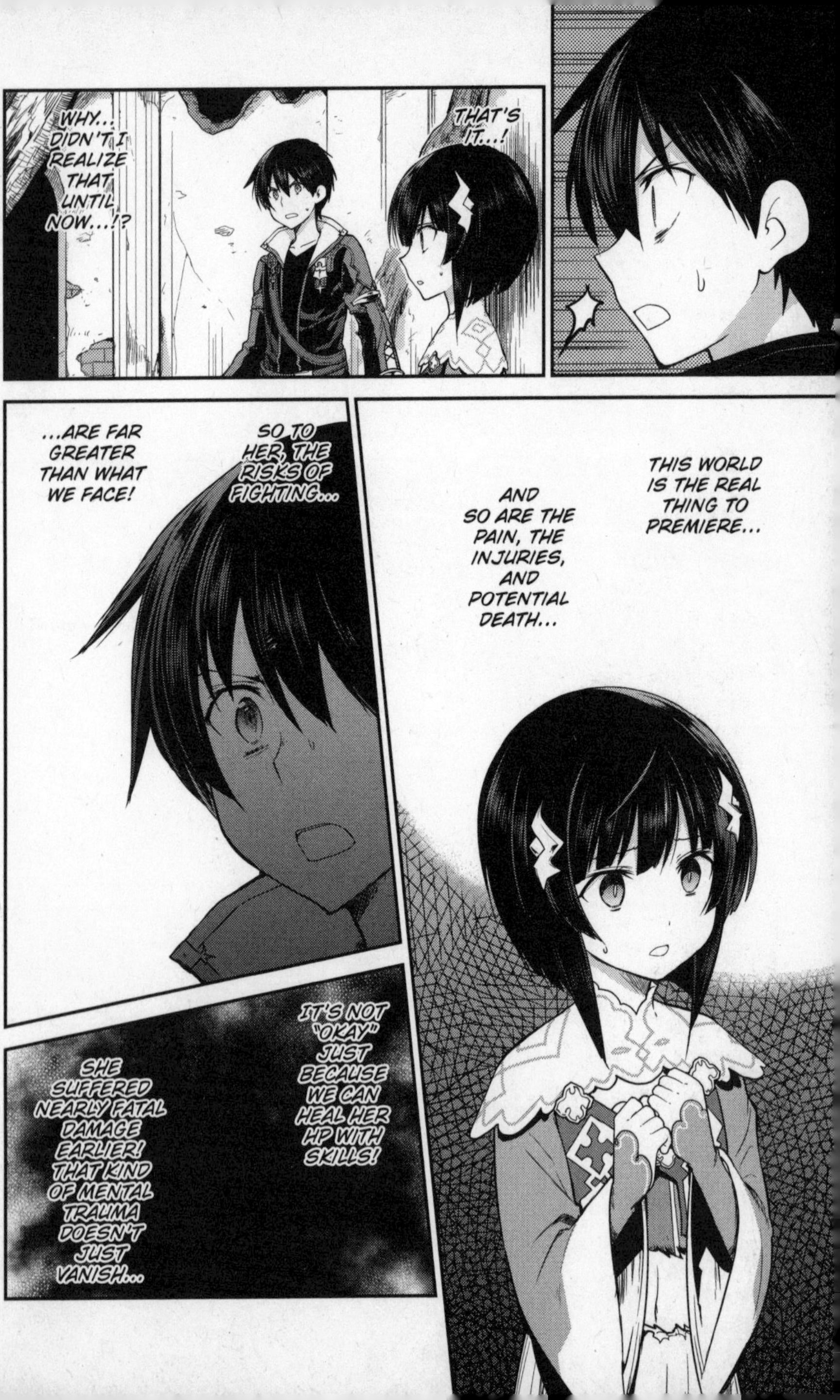
THAT'S IT...!
WHY... DIDN'T I REALIZE THAT UNTIL NOW...!?
THIS WORLD IS THE REAL THING TO PREMIERE...
AND SO ARE THE PAIN, THE INJURIES, AND POTENTIAL DEATH...
SO TO HER, THE RISKS OF FIGHTING...
...ARE FAR GREATER THAN WHAT WE FACE!
IT'S NOT "OKAY" JUST BECAUSE WE CAN HEAL HER HP WITH SKILLS!
SHE SUFFERED NEARLY FATAL DAMAGE EARLIER! THAT KIND OF MENTAL TRAUMA DOESN'T JUST VANISH...

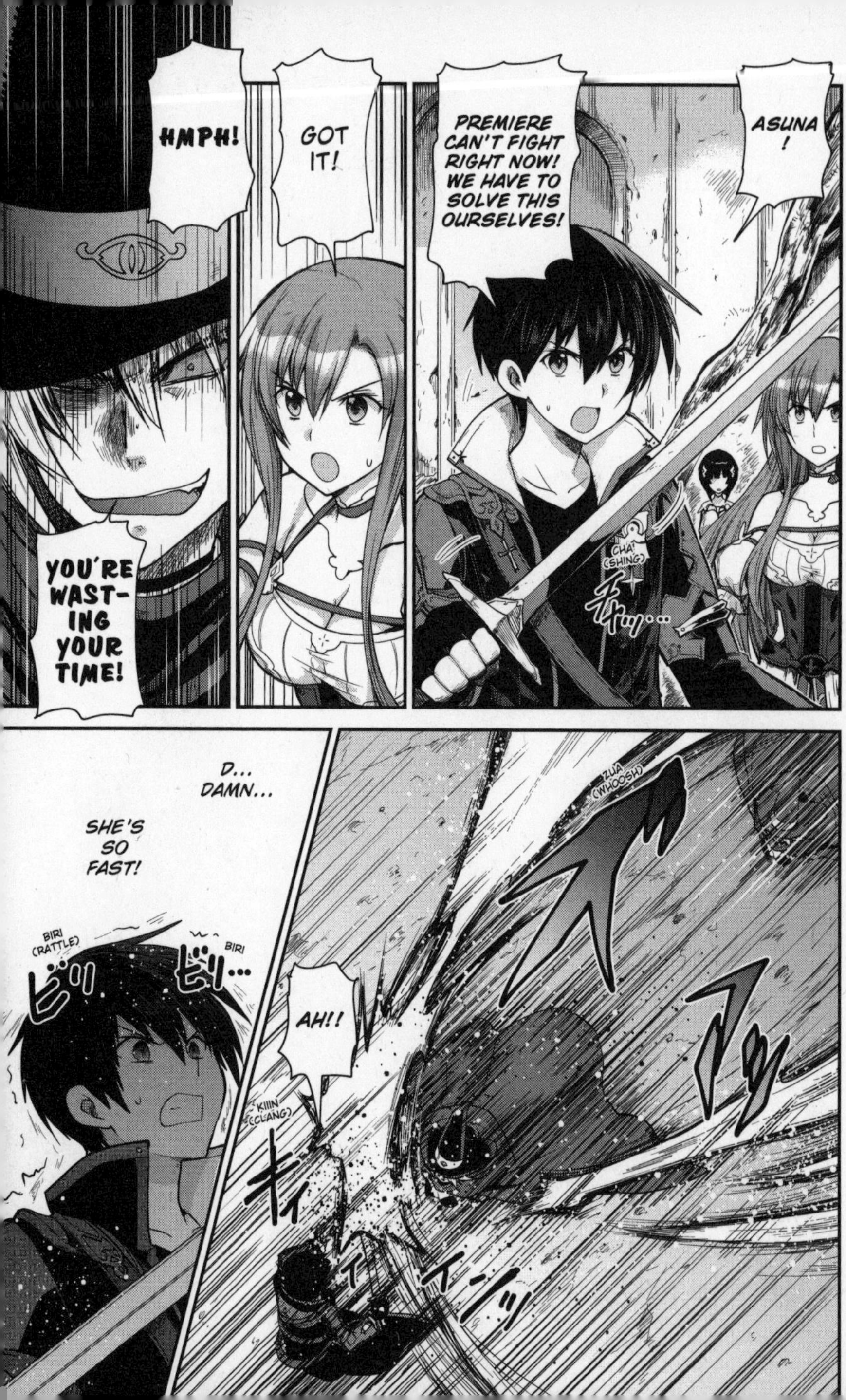
ASUNA!
PREMIERE CAN'T FIGHT RIGHT NOW! WE HAVE TO SOLVE THIS OURSELVES!
CHA (SHING)
GOT IT!
HMPH!
YOU'RE WASTING YOUR TIME!
ZUA (WHOOSH)
AH!!
KIIIN (CLANG)
D... DAMN...
SHE'S SO FAST!
BIRI (RATTLE)
BIRI

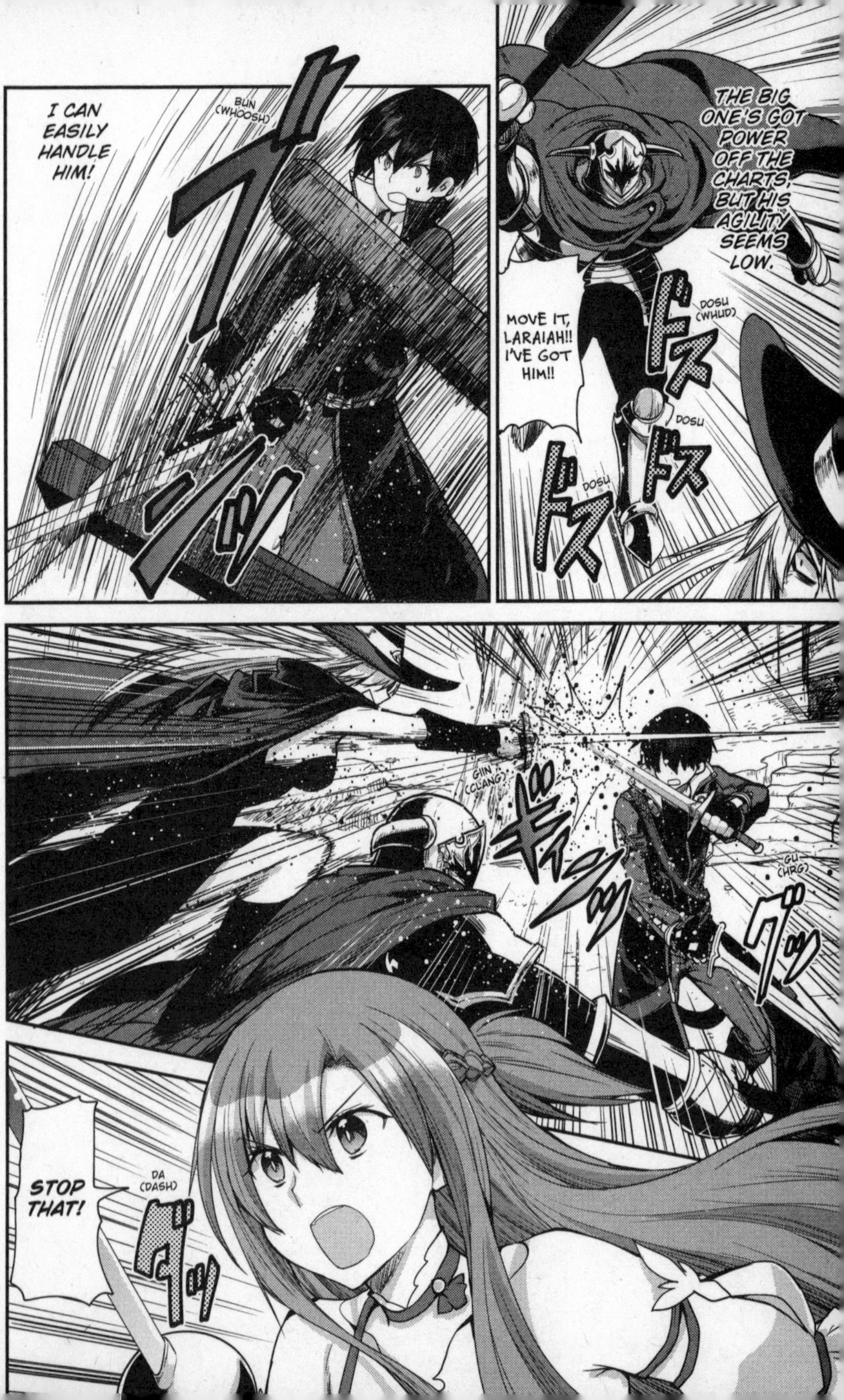
THE BIG ONE'S GOT POWER OFF THE CHARTS, BUT HIS AGILITY SEEMS LOW.
DOSU (WHUD)
MOVE IT, LARAIAH!! I'VE GOT HIM!!
DOSU
DOSU
I CAN EASILY HANDLE HIM!
BUN (WHOOSH)
GIIN (CLANG)
GU (HRG)
DA (DASH)
STOP THAT!

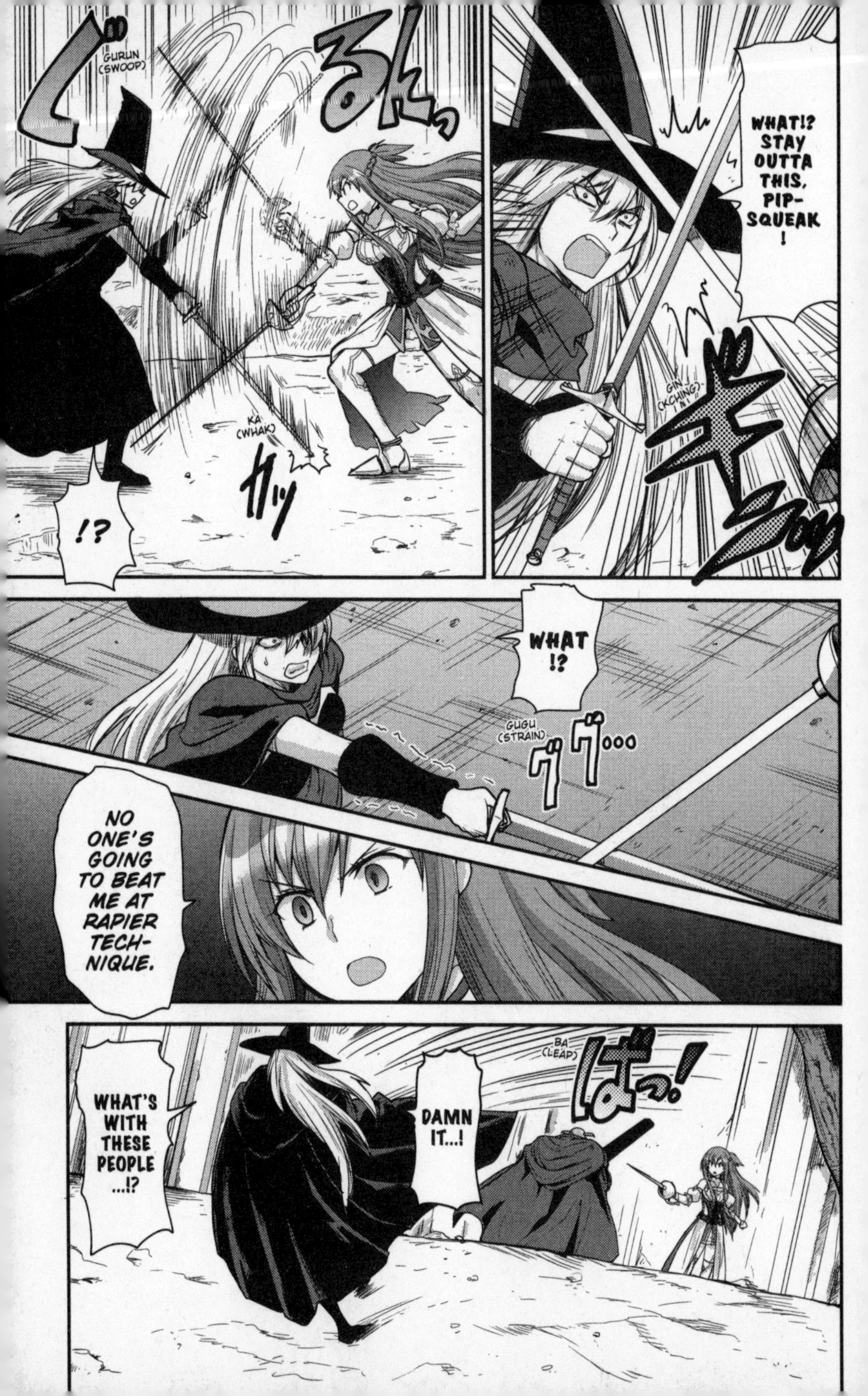
WHAT!? STAY OUTTA THIS, PIP-SQUEAK!
GIN (KCHING)
ぐるんっ
GURUN (SWOOP)
KA (WHAK)
ガッ
!?
WHAT!?
GUGU (STRAIN)
ググ...
NO ONE'S GOING TO BEAT ME AT RAPIER TECH-NIQUE.
BA (LEAP)
ばっ!
DAMN IT...!
WHAT'S WITH THESE PEOPLE...!?

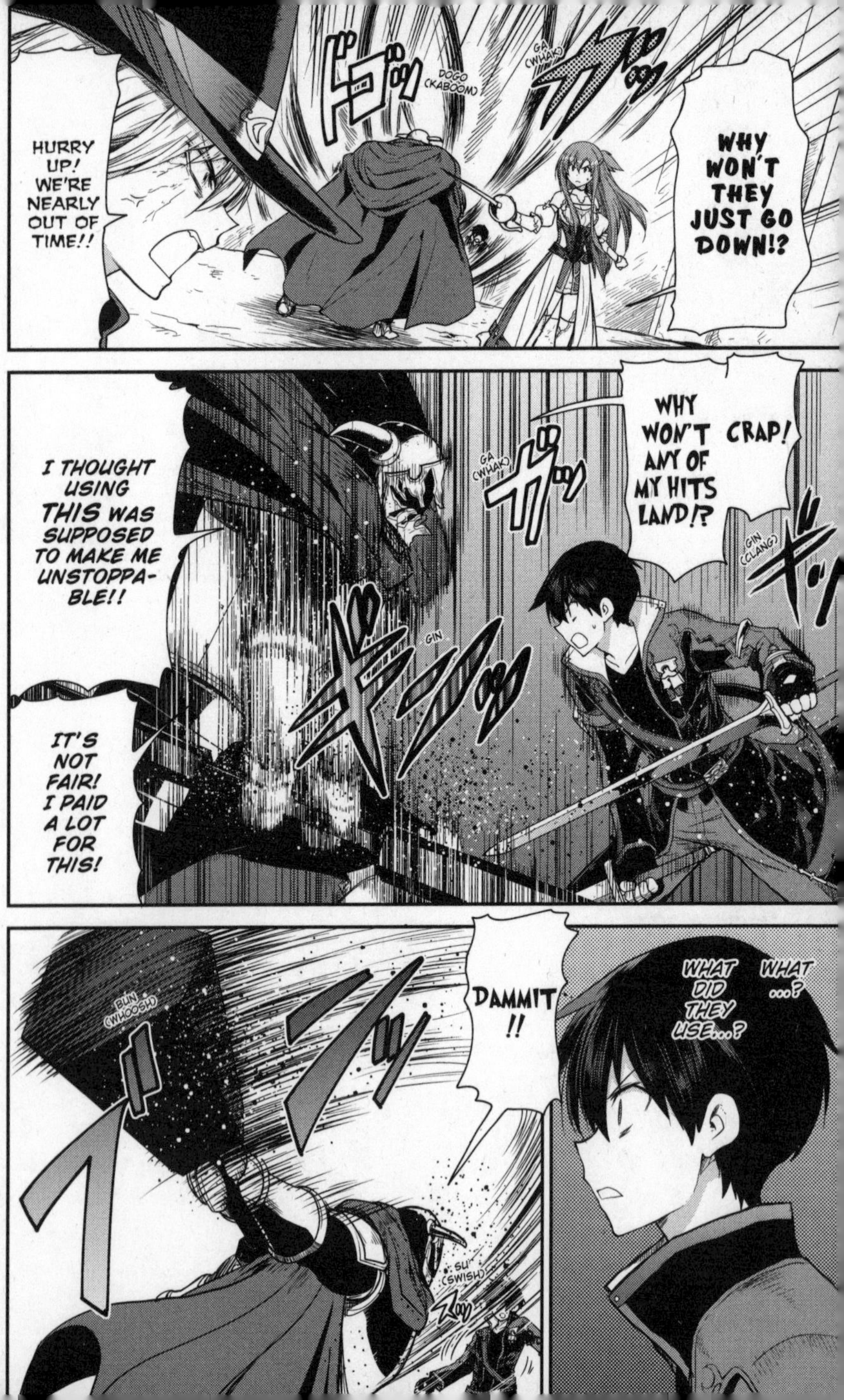
WHY WON'T THEY JUST GO DOWN!?
GA (WHAK)
DOGO (KABOOM)
HURRY UP! WE'RE NEARLY OUT OF TIME!!
CRAP!
GIN (CLANG)
WHY WON'T ANY OF MY HITS LAND!?
GA (WHAK)
GIN
I THOUGHT USING THIS WAS SUPPOSED TO MAKE ME UNSTOPPA-BLE!!
IT'S NOT FAIR! I PAID A LOT FOR THIS!
WHAT ...?
WHAT DID THEY USE...?
DAMMIT!!
BUN (WHOOSH)
SU (SWISH)

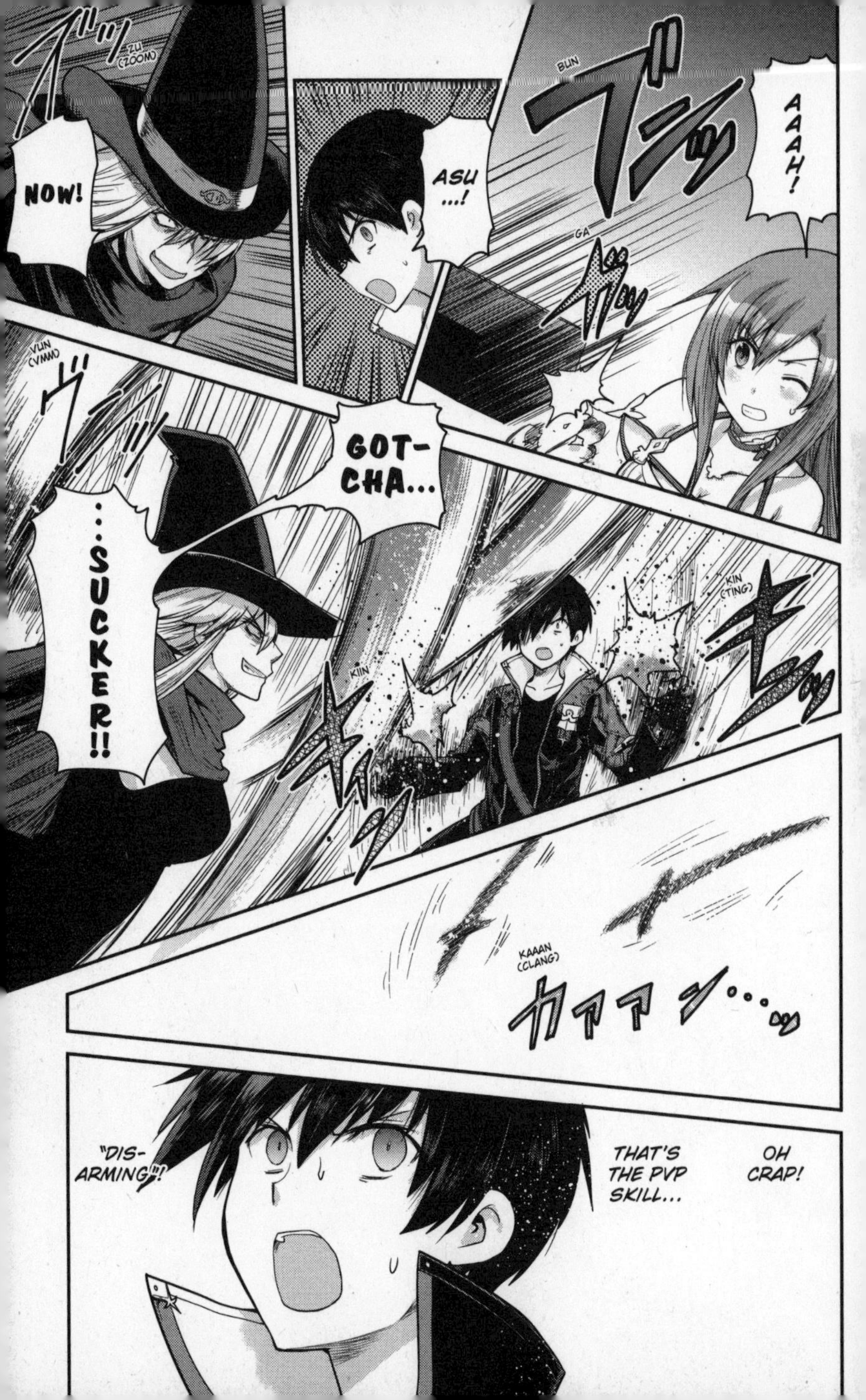
AAAH!
BUN
GA
ASU ...!
ZU (ZOOM)
NOW!
VUN (VMM)
GOT-CHA...
...SUCKER!!
KIN (TING)
KIIN
KAAAN (CLANG)
OH CRAP!
THAT'S THE PVP SKILL...
"DIS-ARMING"!

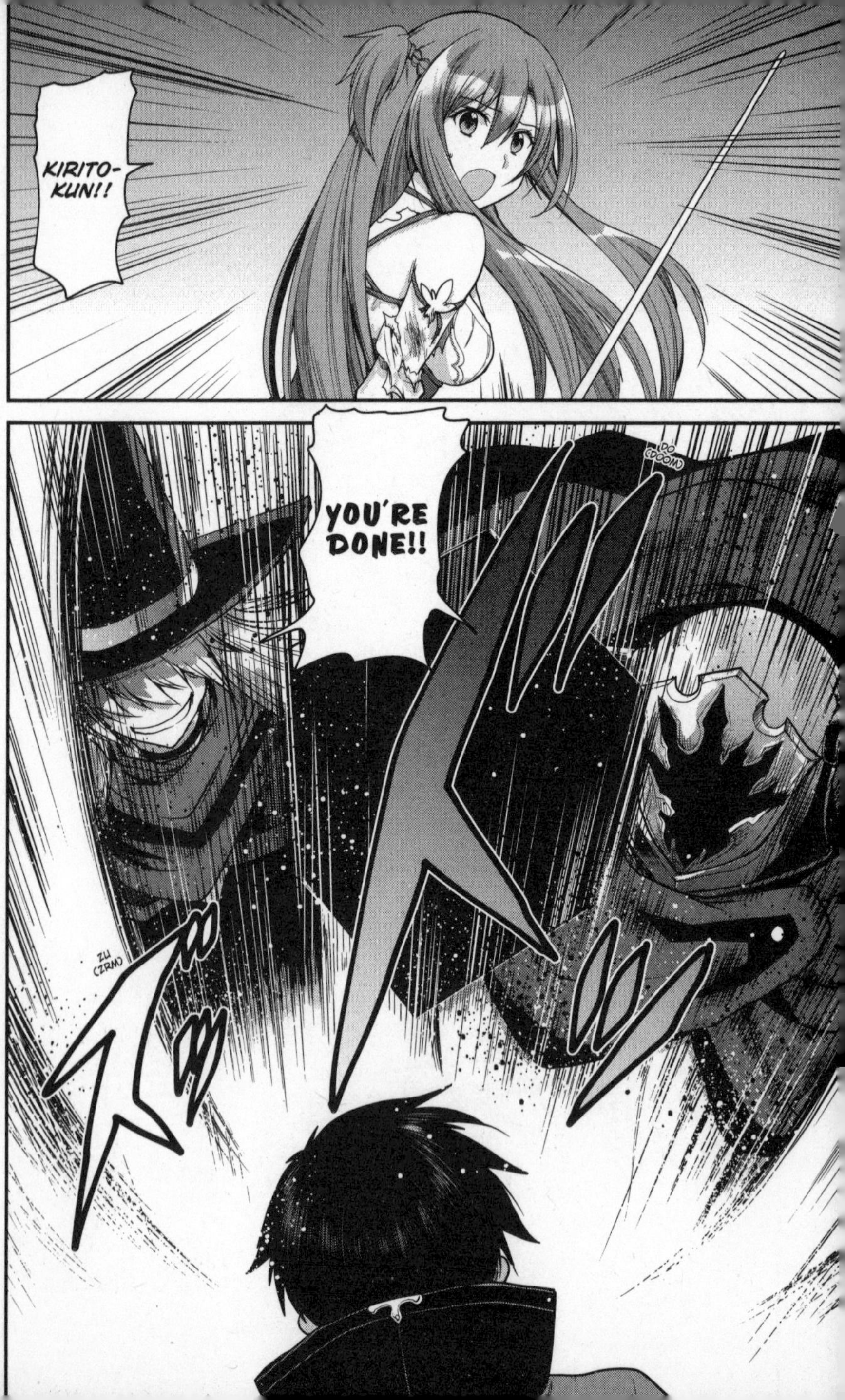
KIRITO-KUN!!
DO (DOOM)
YOU'RE DONE!!
ZU (ZRM)

#16

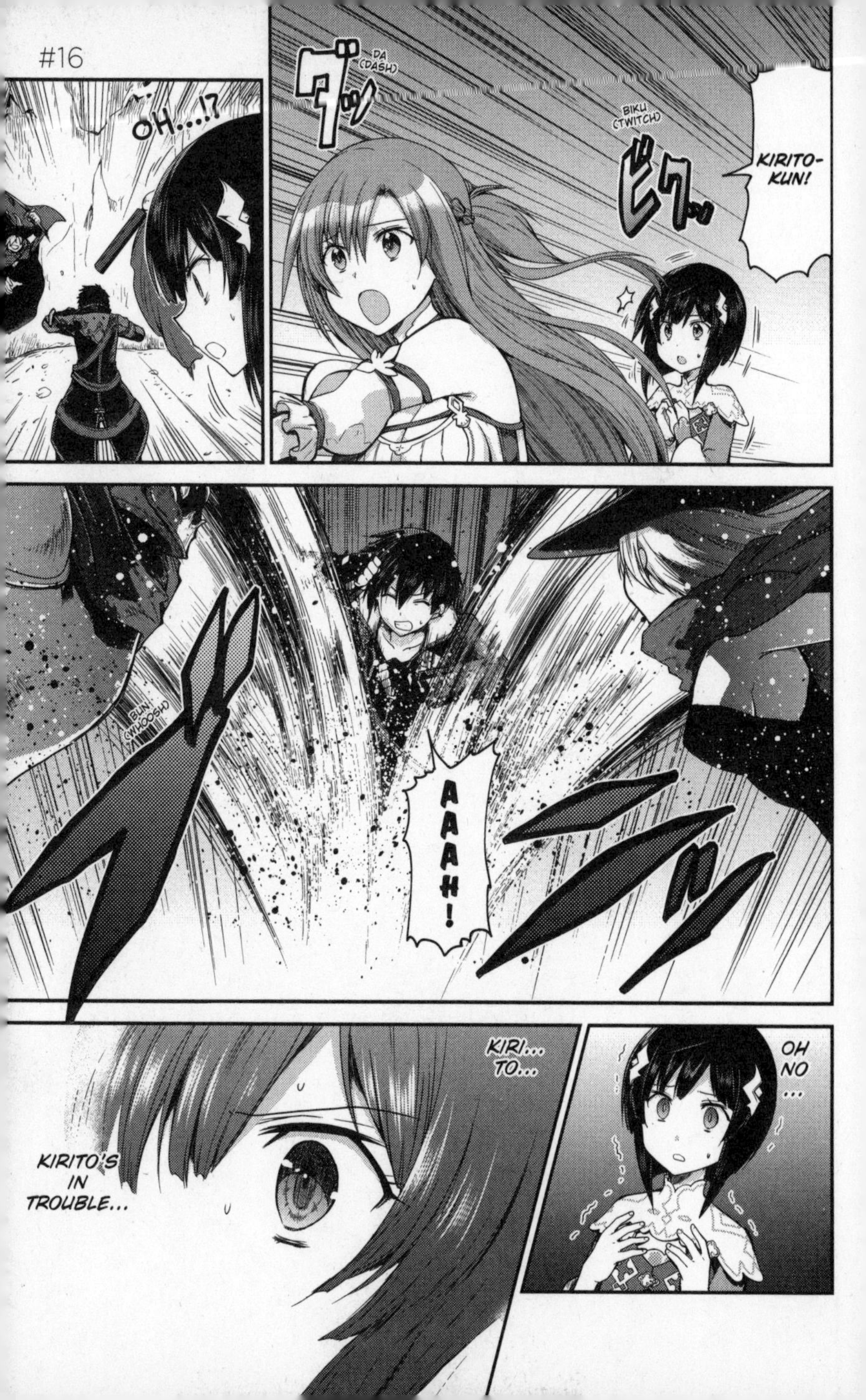
KIRITO-KUN!
BIKU (TWITCH)
DA (DASH)
OH...!?
BUN (WHOOSH)
AAAH!
OH NO ...
KIRI... TO...
KIRITO'S IN TROUBLE...

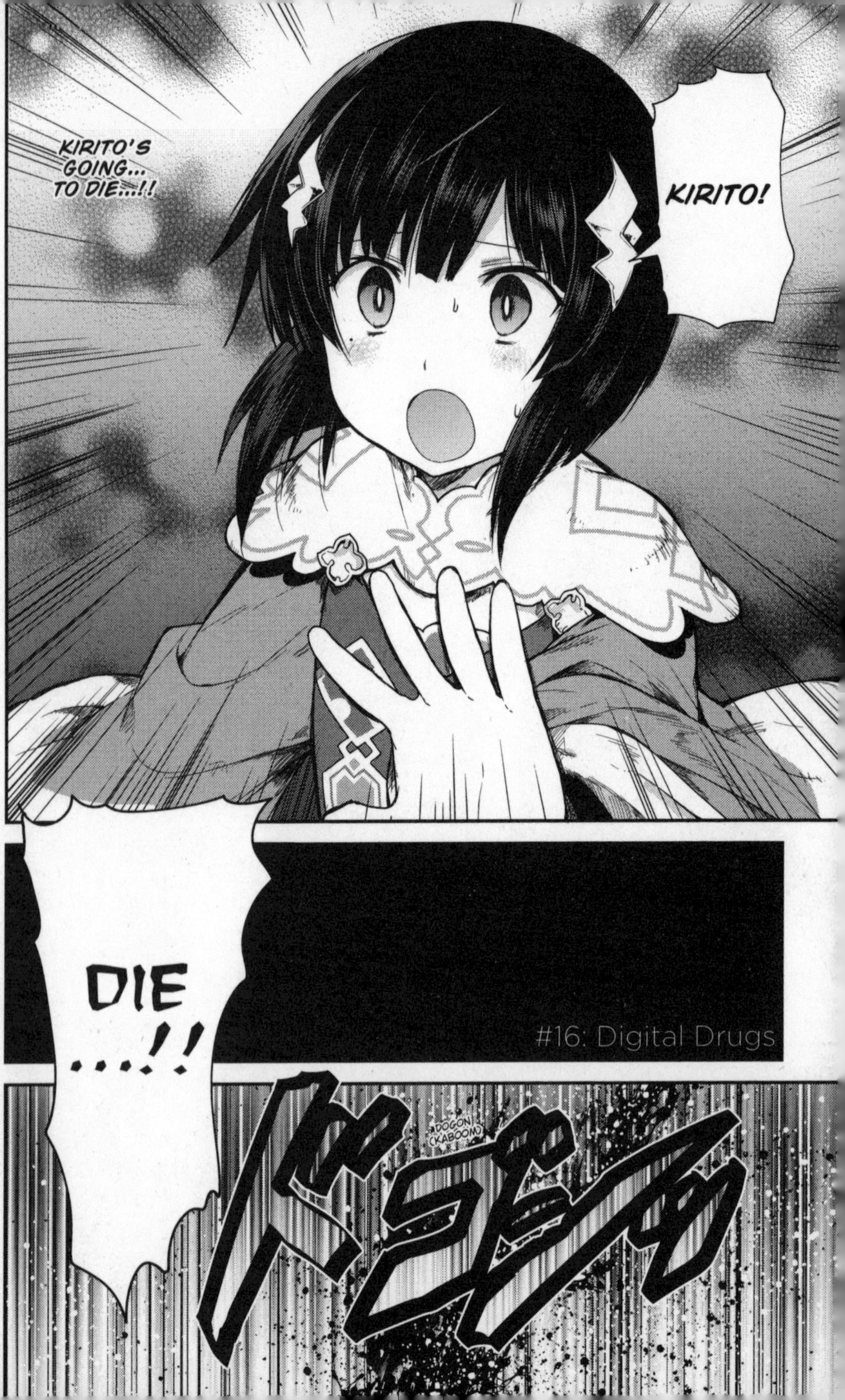
KIRITO!
KIRITO'S GOING... TO DIE...!!
#16: Digital Drugs
DIE ...!!
DOGON (KABOOM)

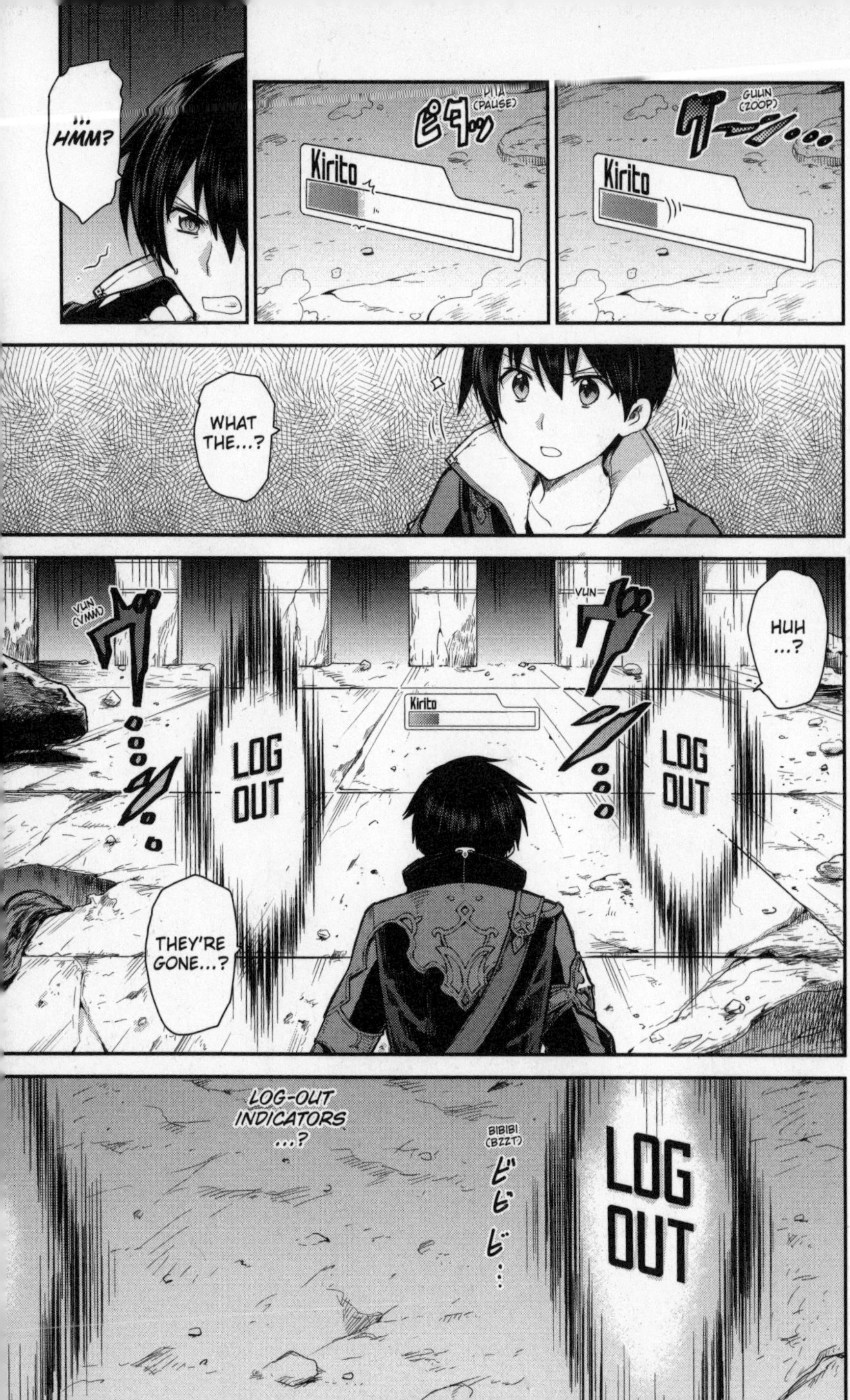
GUUN (ZOOP)
Kirito
PITA (PAUSE)
Kirito
...HMM?
WHAT THE...?
HUH...?
VUN
LOG OUT
Kirito
VUN (VMM)
LOG OUT
THEY'RE GONE...?
BIBIBI (BZZT)
LOG OUT
LOG-OUT INDICATORS...?

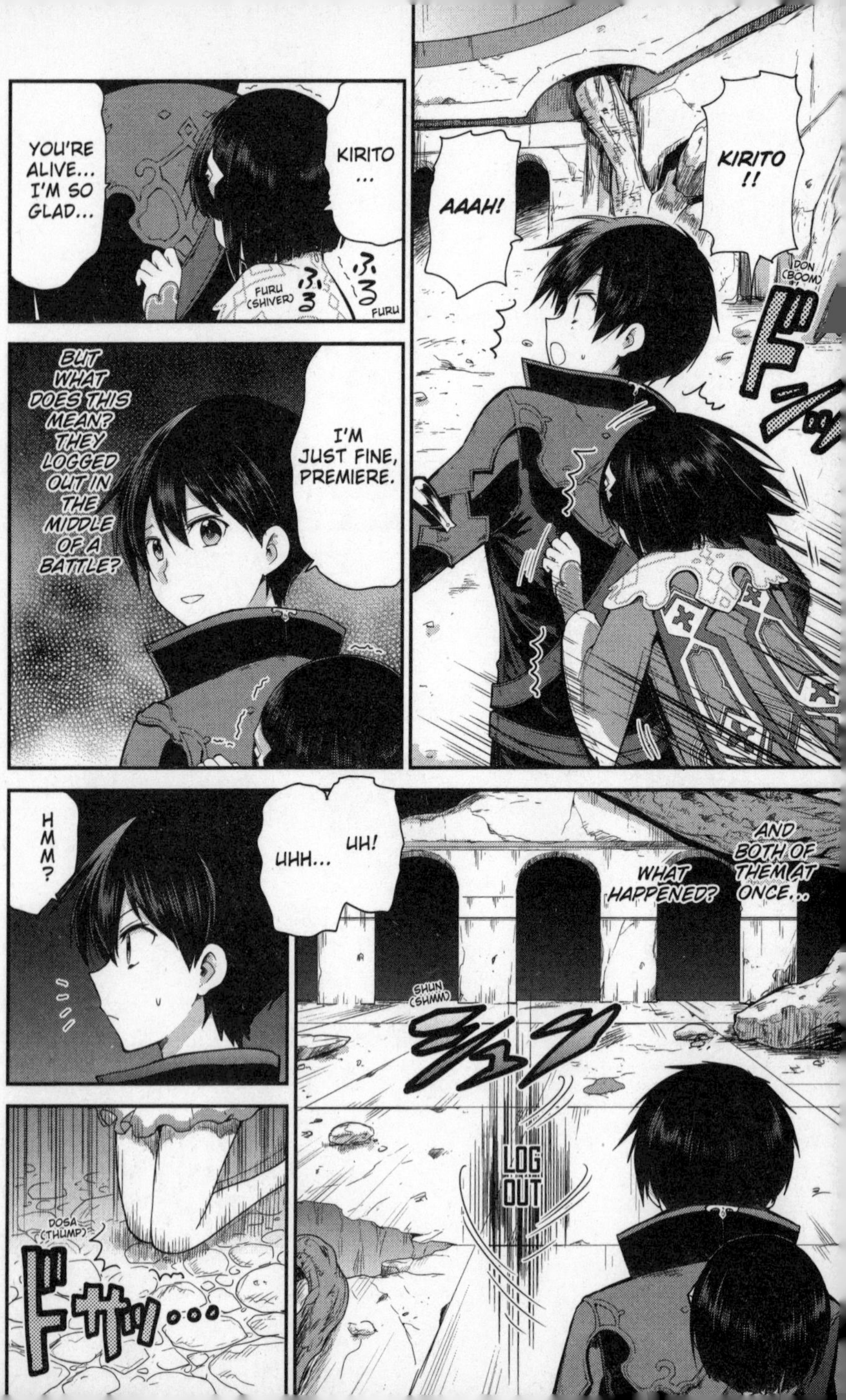
KIRITO !!
DON (BOOM)
AAAH!
KIRITO ...
YOU'RE ALIVE... I'M SO GLAD...
ふる ふる
FURU (SHIVER) FURU
I'M JUST FINE, PREMIERE.
BUT WHAT DOES THIS MEAN? THEY LOGGED OUT IN THE MIDDLE OF A BATTLE?
AND BOTH OF THEM AT ONCE...
WHAT HAPPENED?
SHUN (SHMM)
UH!
UHH...
HMM?
LOG OUT
DOSA (THUMP)

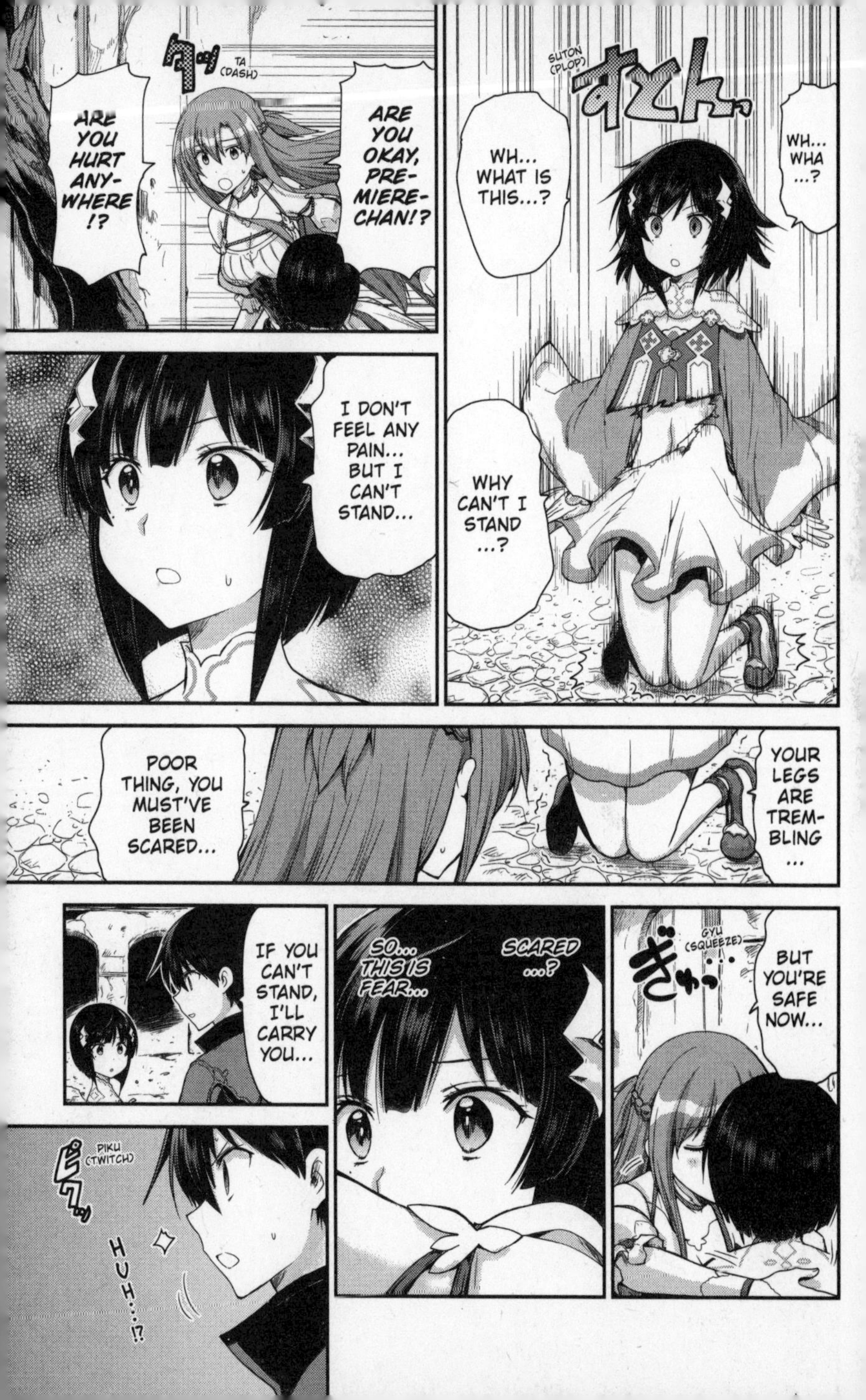
SUTON (PLOP)
WH... WHA...?
WH... WHAT IS THIS...?
WHY CAN'T I STAND...?
TA (DASH)
ARE YOU OKAY, PREMIERE-CHAN!?
ARE YOU HURT ANYWHERE!?
I DON'T FEEL ANY PAIN... BUT I CAN'T STAND...
YOUR LEGS ARE TREMBLING...
POOR THING, YOU MUST'VE BEEN SCARED...
GYU (SQUEEZE)
BUT YOU'RE SAFE NOW...
SCARED...?
SO... THIS IS FEAR...
IF YOU CAN'T STAND, I'LL CARRY YOU...
PIKU (TWITCH)
HUH...!?

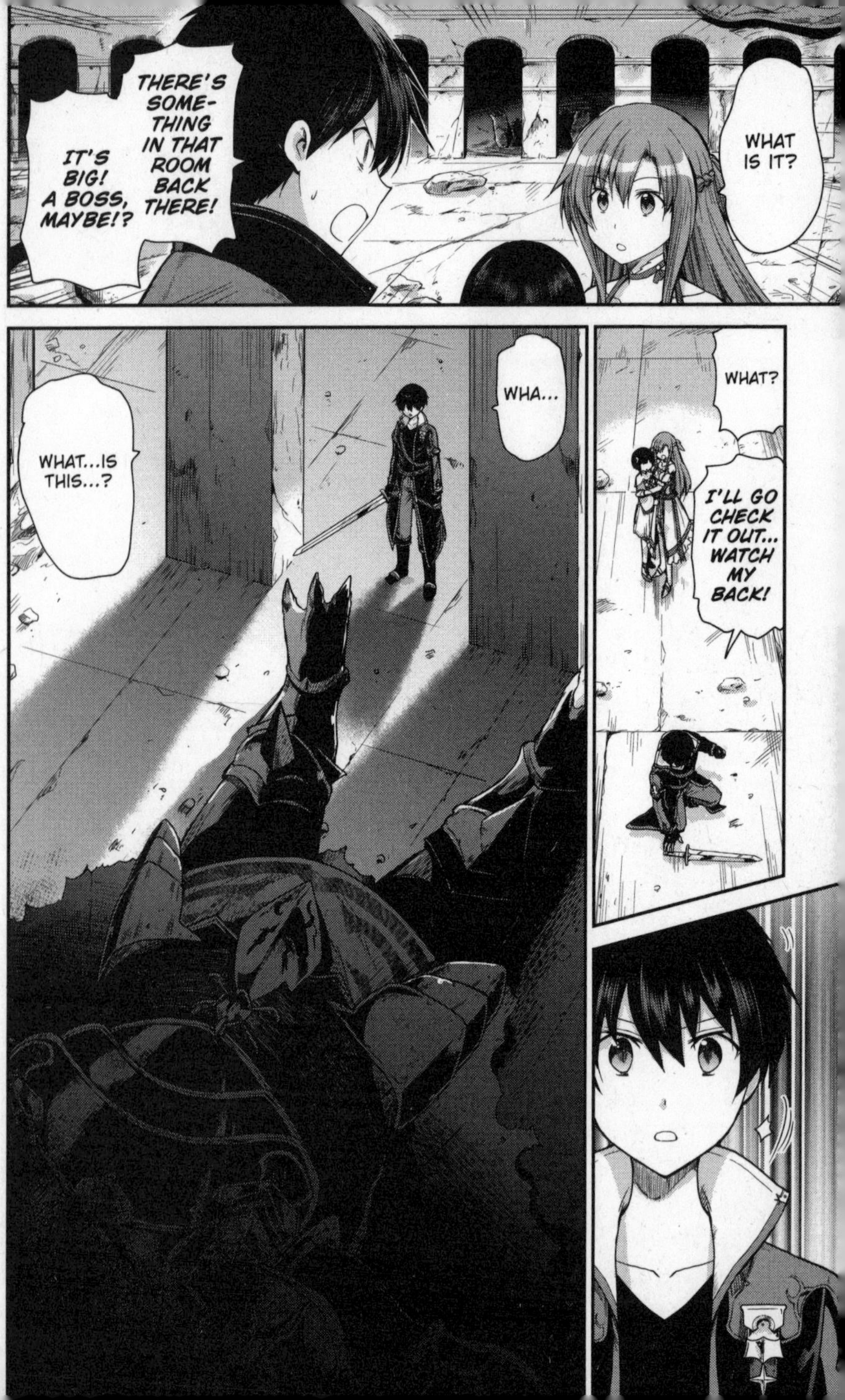
WHAT IS IT?
THERE'S SOME-THING IN THAT ROOM BACK THERE!
IT'S BIG! A BOSS, MAYBE!?
WHAT?
I'LL GO CHECK IT OUT... WATCH MY BACK!
WHA...
WHAT...IS THIS...?

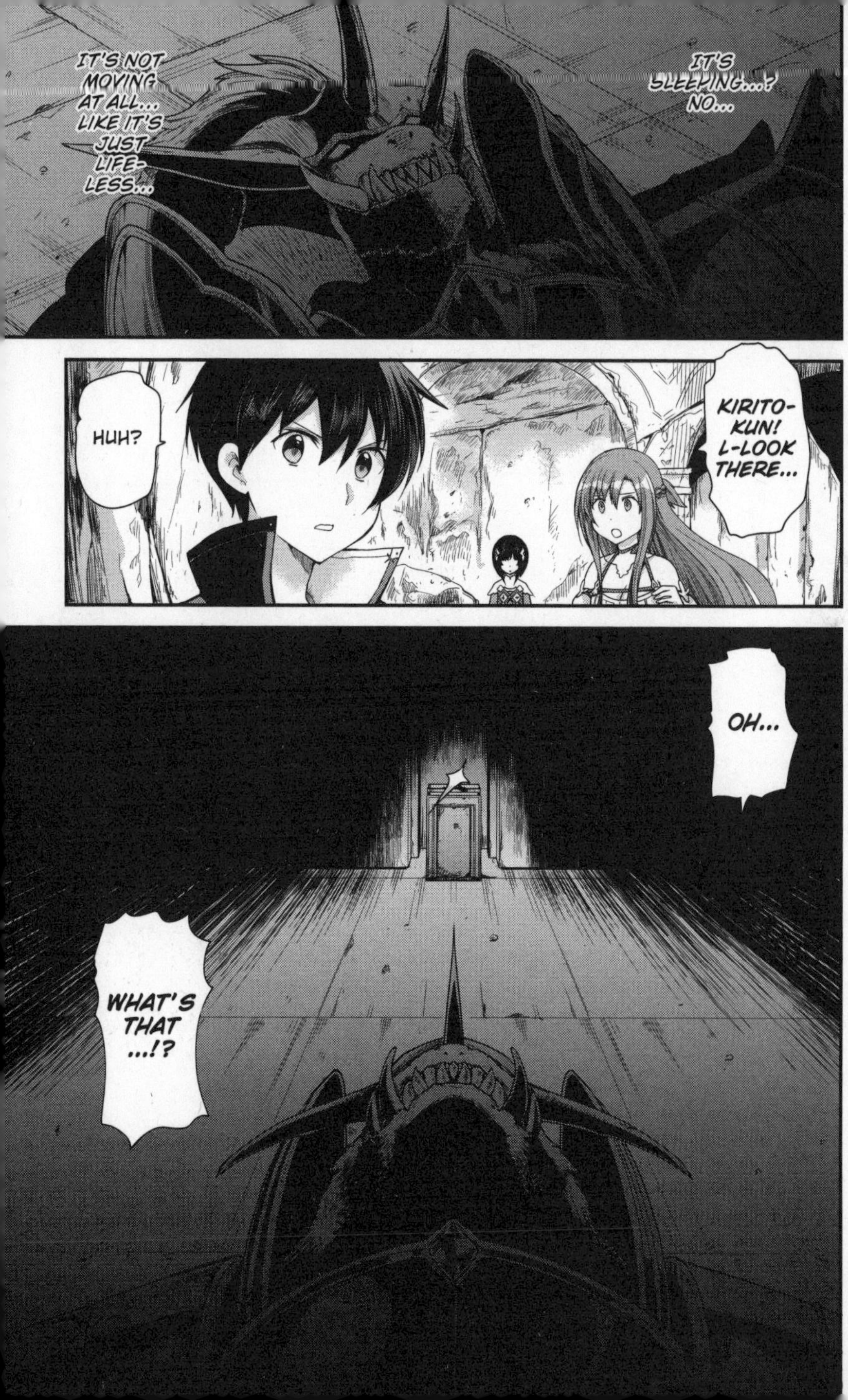
IT'S SLEEPING...? NO...
IT'S NOT MOVING AT ALL... LIKE IT'S JUST LIFE-LESS...
KIRITO-KUN! L-LOOK THERE...
HUH?
OH...
WHAT'S THAT ...!?

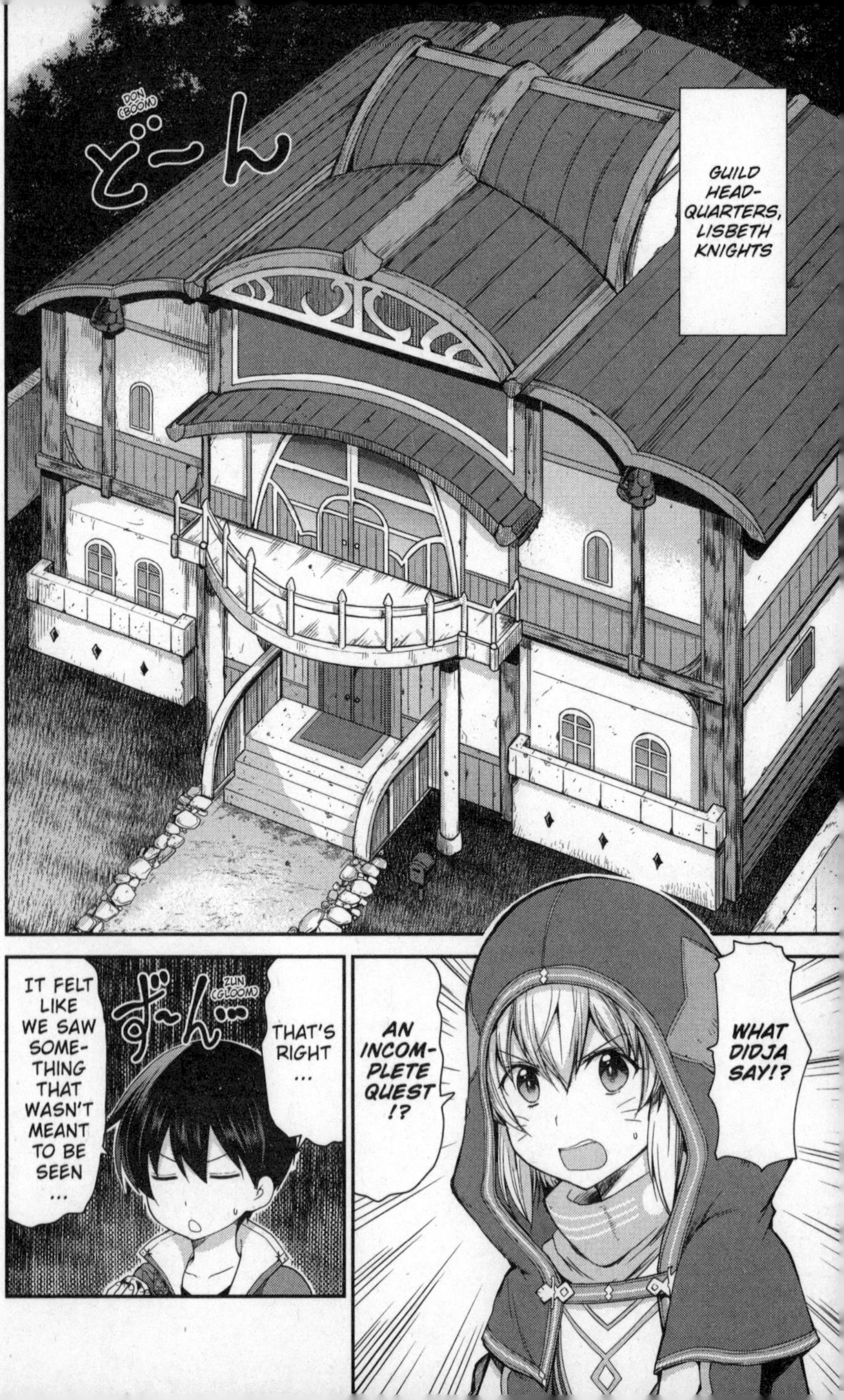
GUILD HEADQUARTERS, LISBETH KNIGHTS
どーん
DON (BOOM)
WHAT DIDJA SAY!?
AN INCOMPLETE QUEST!?
THAT'S RIGHT ...
ずーん...
ZUN (GLOOM)
IT FELT LIKE WE SAW SOMETHING THAT WASN'T MEANT TO BE SEEN ...

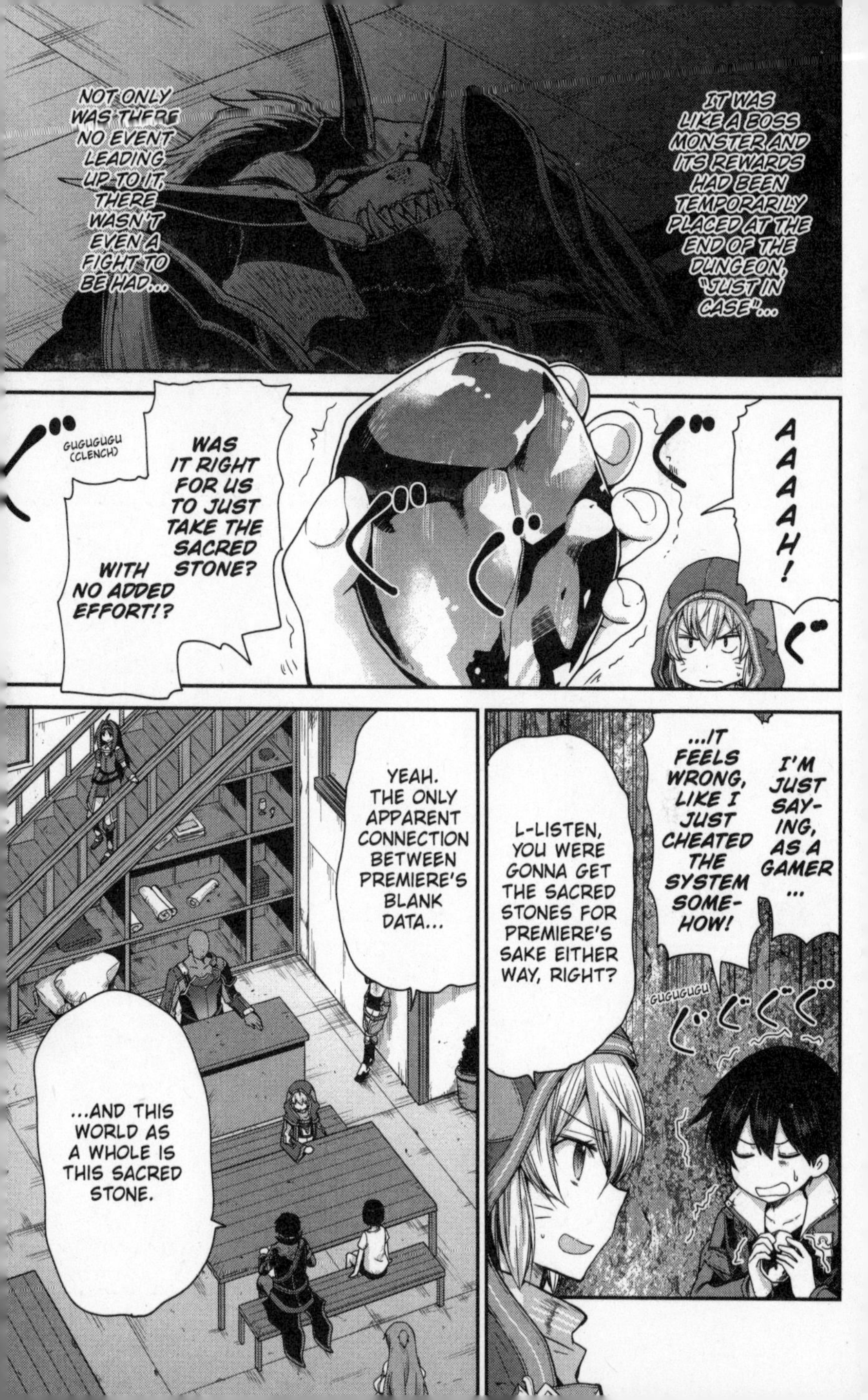
IT WAS LIKE A BOSS MONSTER AND ITS REWARDS HAD BEEN TEMPORARILY PLACED AT THE END OF THE DUNGEON, "JUST IN CASE"...
NOT ONLY WAS THERE NO EVENT LEADING UP TO IT, THERE WASN'T EVEN A FIGHT TO BE HAD...
AAAAAH!
WAS IT RIGHT FOR US TO JUST TAKE THE SACRED STONE?
WITH NO ADDED EFFORT!?
GUGUGUGU (CLENCH)
I'M JUST SAYING, AS A GAMER...
...IT FEELS WRONG, LIKE I JUST CHEATED THE SYSTEM SOME-HOW!
GUGUGUGU
L-LISTEN, YOU WERE GONNA GET THE SACRED STONES FOR PREMIERE'S SAKE EITHER WAY, RIGHT?
YEAH. THE ONLY APPARENT CONNECTION BETWEEN PREMIERE'S BLANK DATA...
...AND THIS WORLD AS A WHOLE IS THIS SACRED STONE.

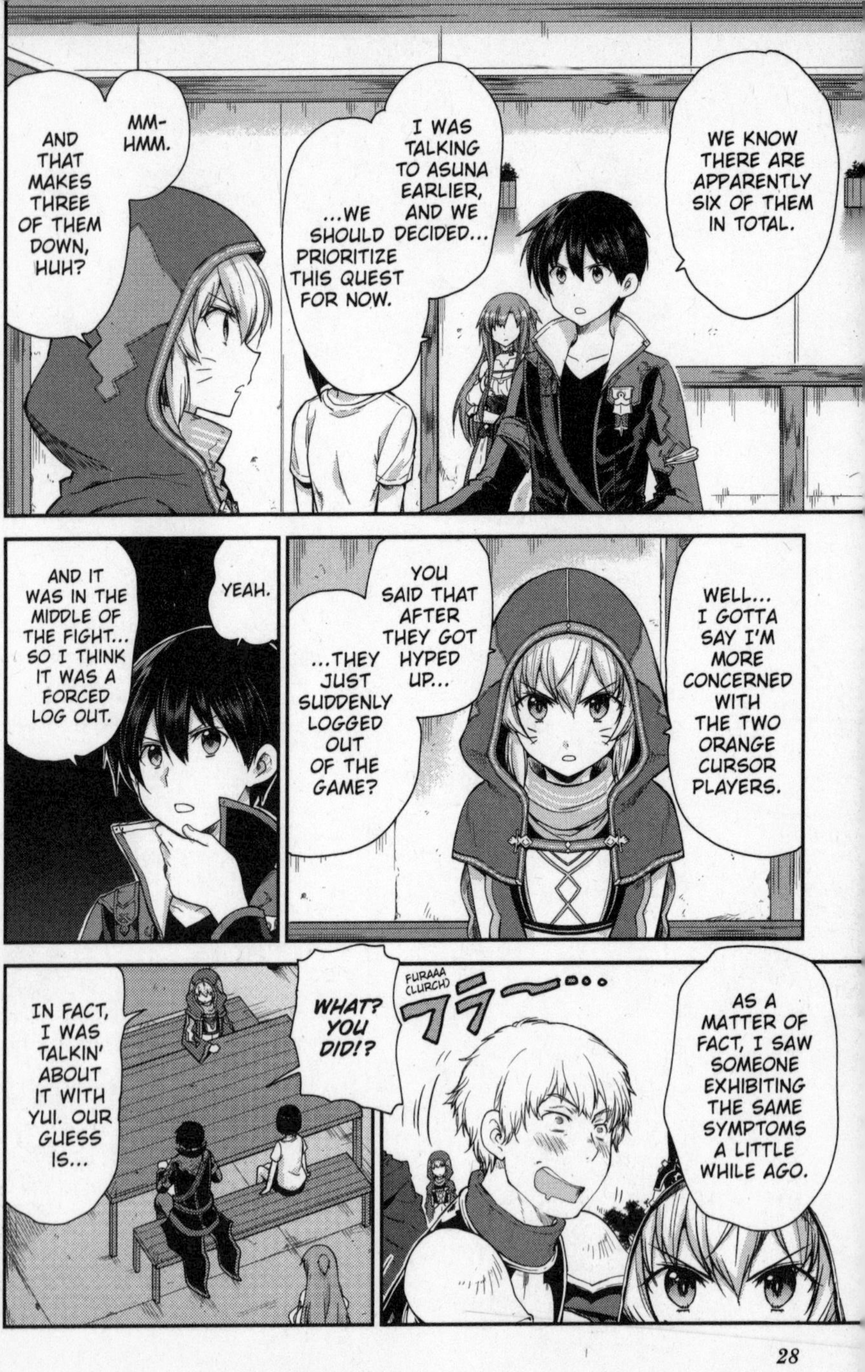
WE KNOW THERE ARE APPARENTLY SIX OF THEM IN TOTAL.
I WAS TALKING TO ASUNA EARLIER, AND WE DECIDED...
...WE SHOULD PRIORITIZE THIS QUEST FOR NOW.
MM-HMM.
AND THAT MAKES THREE OF THEM DOWN, HUH?
WELL... I GOTTA SAY I'M MORE CONCERNED WITH THE TWO ORANGE CURSOR PLAYERS.
YOU SAID THAT AFTER THEY GOT HYPED UP...
...THEY JUST SUDDENLY LOGGED OUT OF THE GAME?
YEAH.
AND IT WAS IN THE MIDDLE OF THE FIGHT... SO I THINK IT WAS A FORCED LOG OUT.
AS A MATTER OF FACT, I SAW SOMEONE EXHIBITING THE SAME SYMPTOMS A LITTLE WHILE AGO.
FURAAA (LURCH)
フラー…
WHAT? YOU DID!?
IN FACT, I WAS TALKIN' ABOUT IT WITH YUI. OUR GUESS IS...

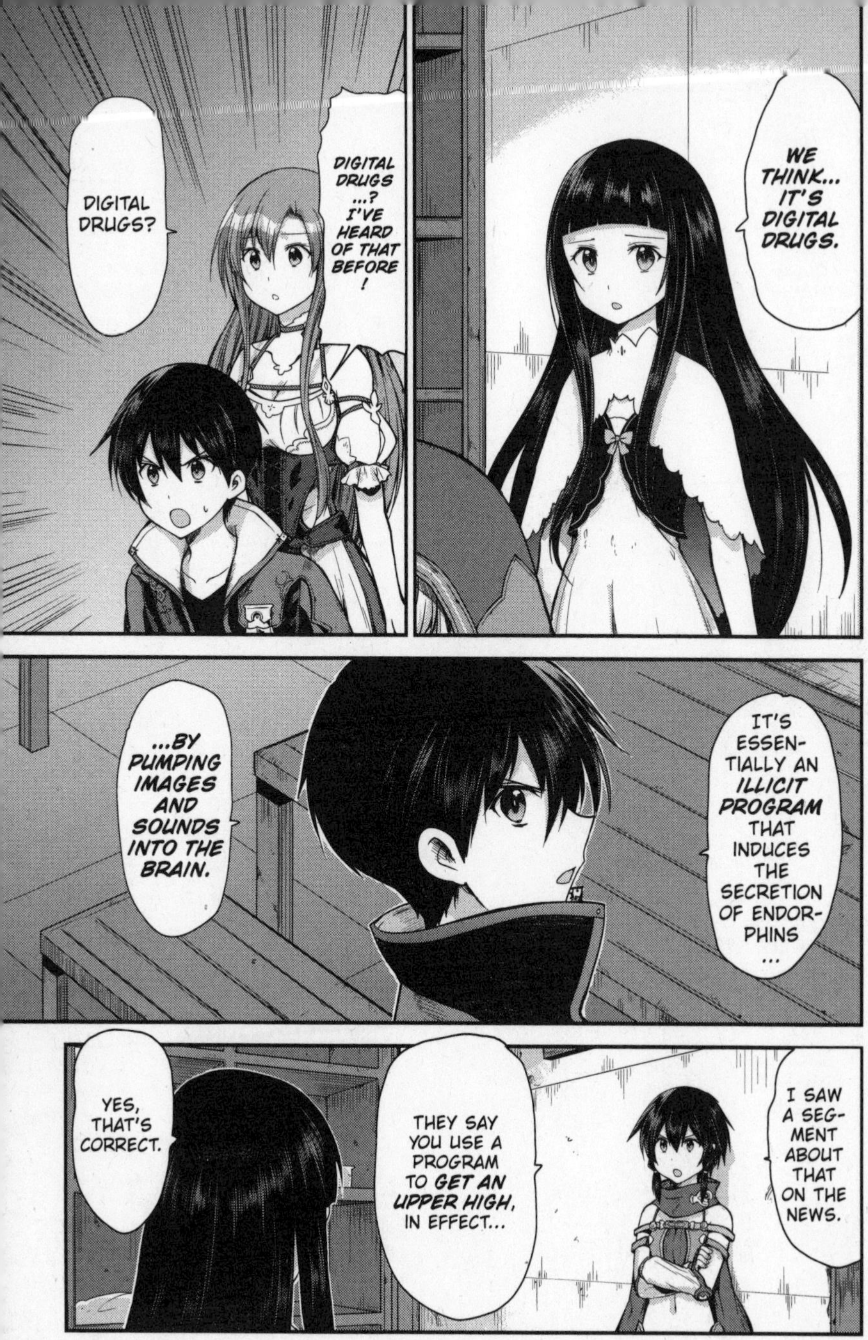
WE THINK... IT'S DIGITAL DRUGS.
DIGITAL DRUGS...? I'VE HEARD OF THAT BEFORE!
DIGITAL DRUGS?
IT'S ESSEN-TIALLY AN ILLICIT PROGRAM THAT INDUCES THE SECRETION OF ENDOR-PHINS...
...BY PUMPING IMAGES AND SOUNDS INTO THE BRAIN.
I SAW A SEG-MENT ABOUT THAT ON THE NEWS.
THEY SAY YOU USE A PROGRAM TO GET AN UPPER HIGH, IN EFFECT...
YES, THAT'S CORRECT.

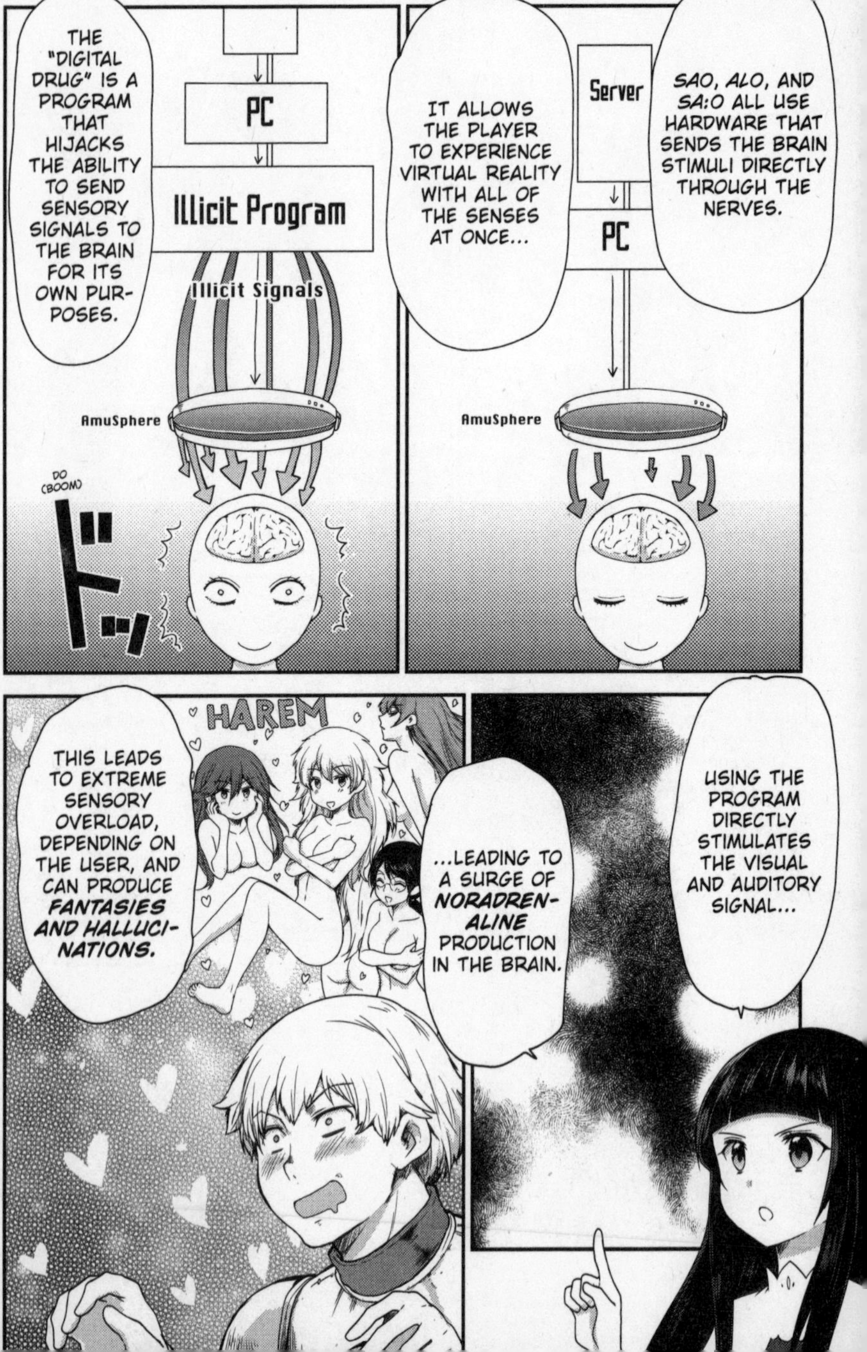
SAO, ALO, AND SA:O ALL USE HARDWARE THAT SENDS THE BRAIN STIMULI DIRECTLY THROUGH THE NERVES.
Server
PC
IT ALLOWS THE PLAYER TO EXPERIENCE VIRTUAL REALITY WITH ALL OF THE SENSES AT ONCE...
AmuSphere
PC
Illicit Program
THE "DIGITAL DRUG" IS A PROGRAM THAT HIJACKS THE ABILITY TO SEND SENSORY SIGNALS TO THE BRAIN FOR ITS OWN PURPOSES.
Illicit Signals
AmuSphere
DO (BOOM)
ドッ
USING THE PROGRAM DIRECTLY STIMULATES THE VISUAL AND AUDITORY SIGNAL...
...LEADING TO A SURGE OF NORADRENALINE PRODUCTION IN THE BRAIN.
HAREM
THIS LEADS TO EXTREME SENSORY OVERLOAD, DEPENDING ON THE USER, AND CAN PRODUCE FANTASIES AND HALLUCINATIONS.

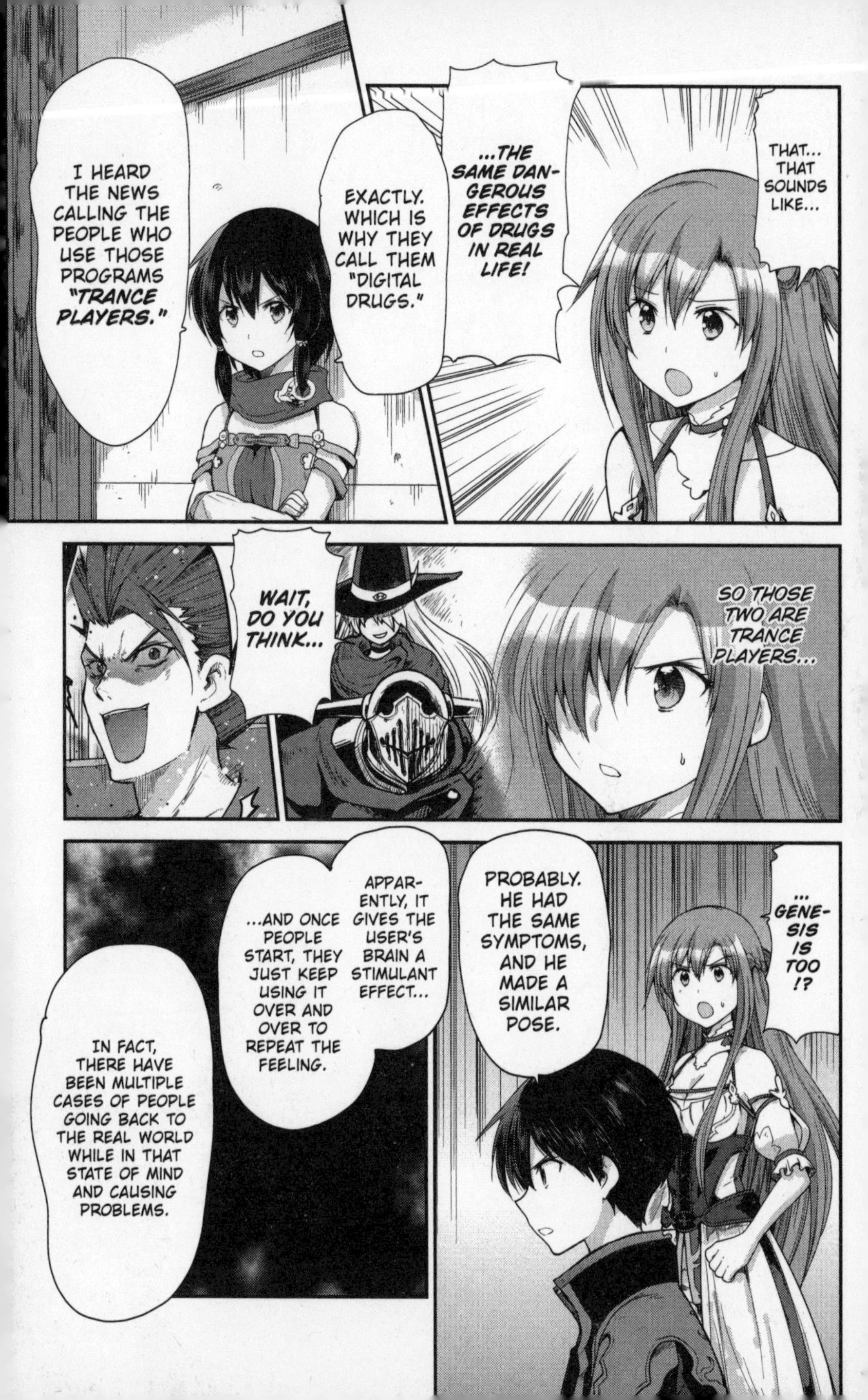
THAT... THAT SOUNDS LIKE...
...THE SAME DANGEROUS EFFECTS OF DRUGS IN REAL LIFE!
EXACTLY. WHICH IS WHY THEY CALL THEM "DIGITAL DRUGS."
I HEARD THE NEWS CALLING THE PEOPLE WHO USE THOSE PROGRAMS *"TRANCE PLAYERS."*
SO THOSE TWO ARE TRANCE PLAYERS...
WAIT, DO YOU THINK...
...GENESIS IS TOO!?
PROBABLY. HE HAD THE SAME SYMPTOMS, AND HE MADE A SIMILAR POSE.
APPARENTLY, IT GIVES THE USER'S BRAIN A STIMULANT EFFECT...
...AND ONCE PEOPLE START, THEY JUST KEEP USING IT OVER AND OVER TO REPEAT THE FEELING.
IN FACT, THERE HAVE BEEN MULTIPLE CASES OF PEOPLE GOING BACK TO THE REAL WORLD WHILE IN THAT STATE OF MIND AND CAUSING PROBLEMS.

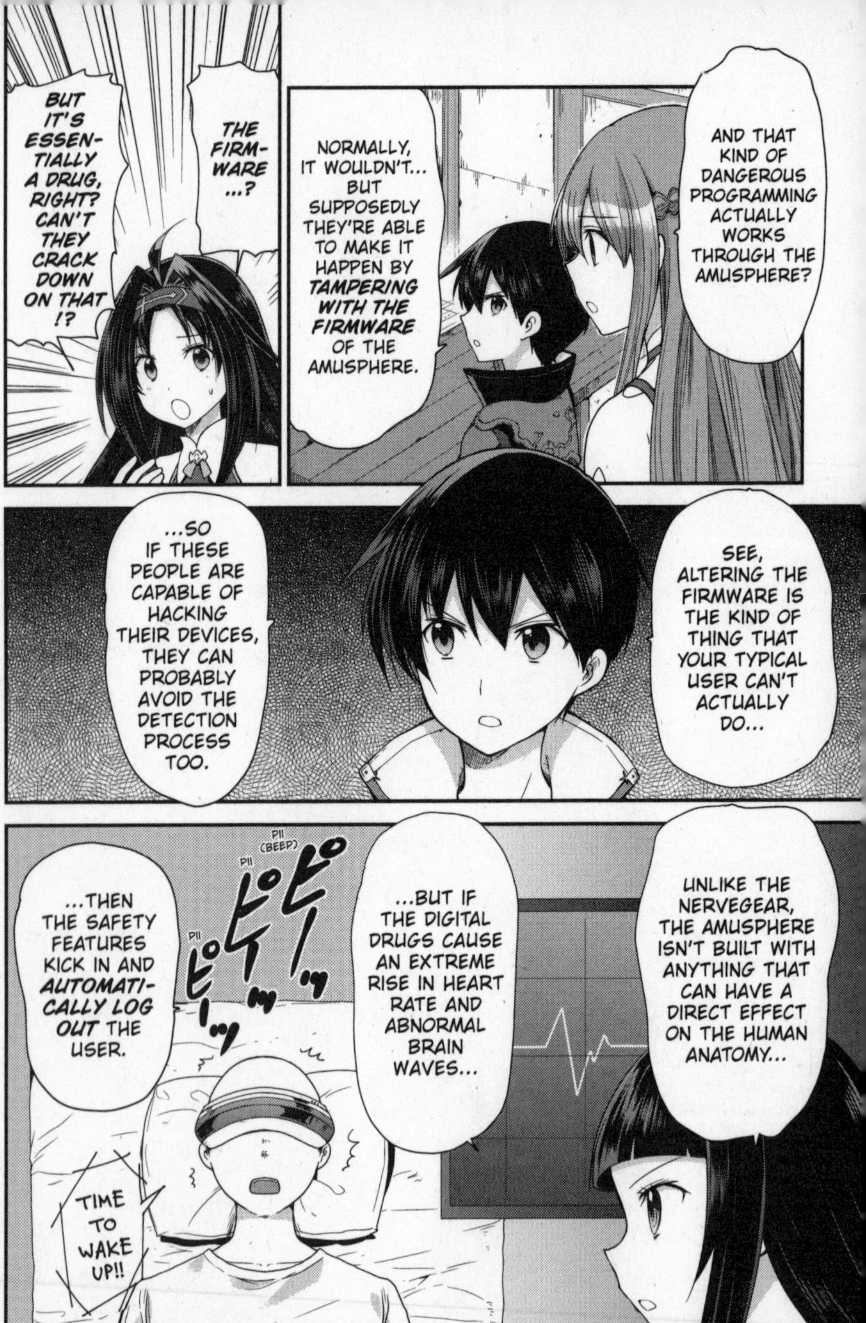
AND THAT KIND OF DANGEROUS PROGRAMMING ACTUALLY WORKS THROUGH THE AMUSPHERE?
NORMALLY, IT WOULDN'T... BUT SUPPOSEDLY THEY'RE ABLE TO MAKE IT HAPPEN BY TAMPERING WITH THE FIRMWARE OF THE AMUSPHERE.
THE FIRMWARE...?
BUT IT'S ESSENTIALLY A DRUG, RIGHT? CAN'T THEY CRACK DOWN ON THAT!?
SEE, ALTERING THE FIRMWARE IS THE KIND OF THING THAT YOUR TYPICAL USER CAN'T ACTUALLY DO...
...SO IF THESE PEOPLE ARE CAPABLE OF HACKING THEIR DEVICES, THEY CAN PROBABLY AVOID THE DETECTION PROCESS TOO.
UNLIKE THE NERVEGEAR, THE AMUSPHERE ISN'T BUILT WITH ANYTHING THAT CAN HAVE A DIRECT EFFECT ON THE HUMAN ANATOMY...
...BUT IF THE DIGITAL DRUGS CAUSE AN EXTREME RISE IN HEART RATE AND ABNORMAL BRAIN WAVES...
PII (BEEP)
PII
PII
...THEN THE SAFETY FEATURES KICK IN AND AUTOMATICALLY LOG OUT THE USER.
TIME TO WAKE UP!!

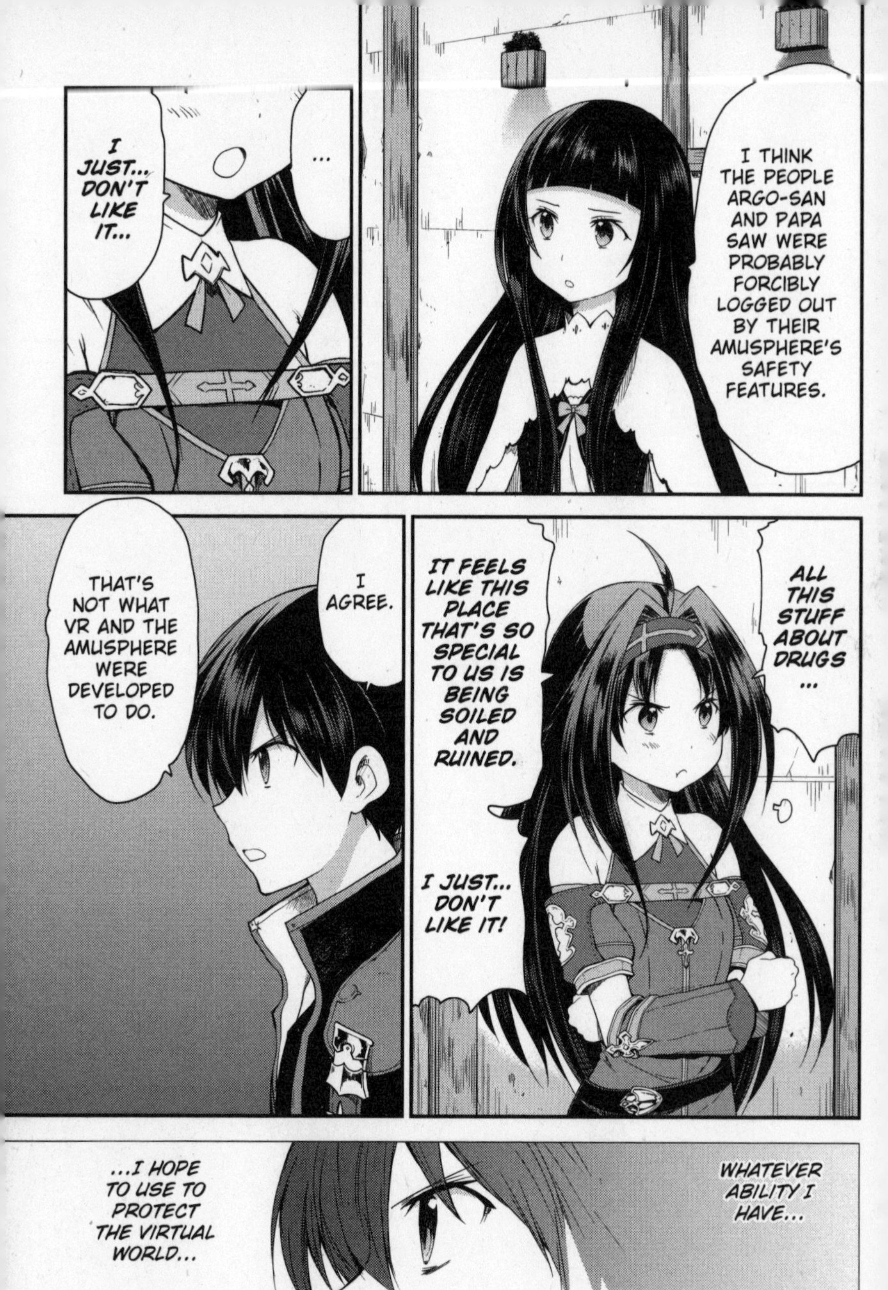
I THINK THE PEOPLE ARGO-SAN AND PAPA SAW WERE PROBABLY FORCIBLY LOGGED OUT BY THEIR AMUSPHERE'S SAFETY FEATURES.
...
I JUST... DON'T LIKE IT...
ALL THIS STUFF ABOUT DRUGS...
IT FEELS LIKE THIS PLACE THAT'S SO SPECIAL TO US IS BEING SOILED AND RUINED.
I JUST... DON'T LIKE IT!
I AGREE.
THAT'S NOT WHAT VR AND THE AMUSPHERE WERE DEVELOPED TO DO.
WHATEVER ABILITY I HAVE...
...I HOPE TO USE TO PROTECT THE VIRTUAL WORLD...

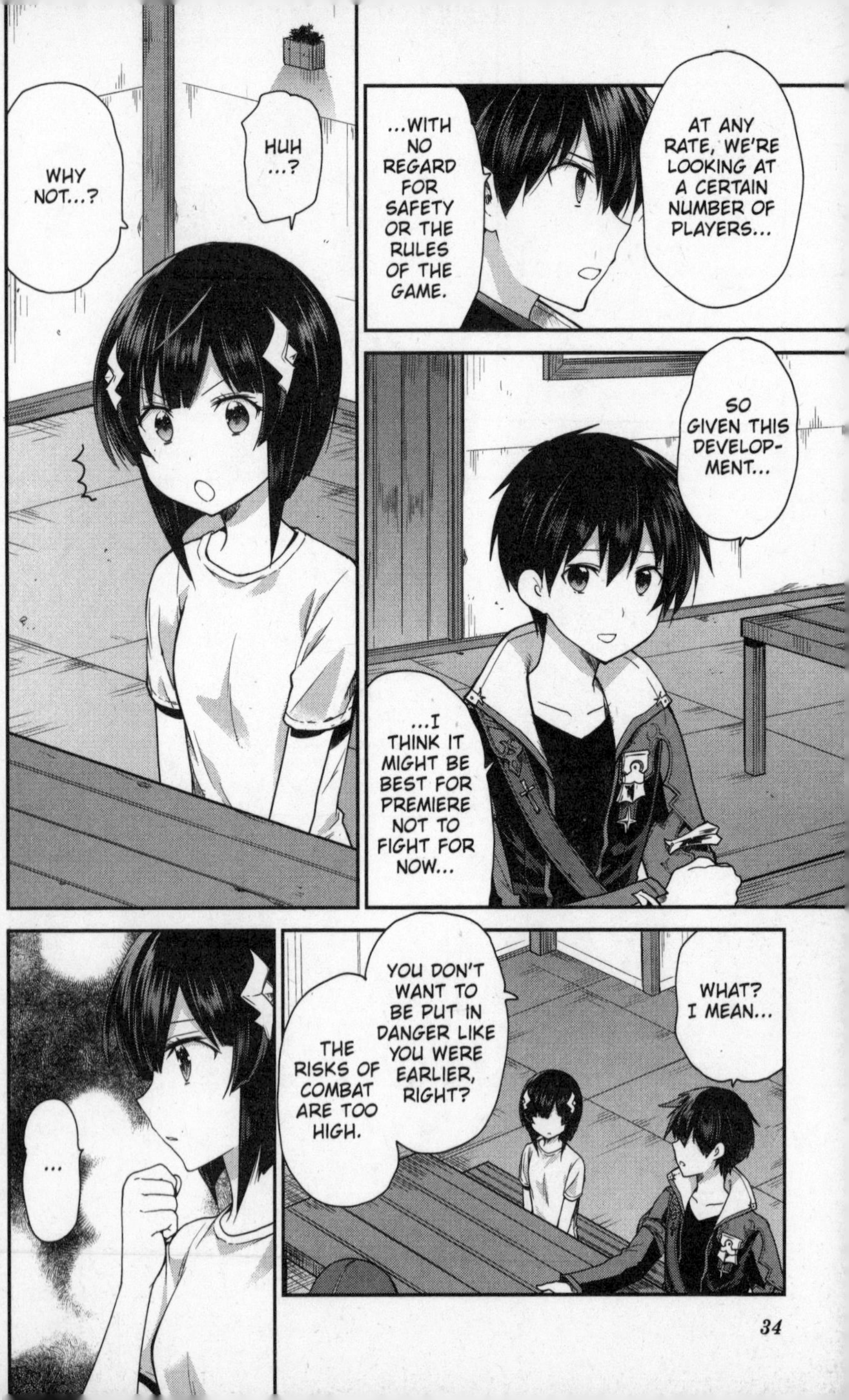
AT ANY RATE, WE'RE LOOKING AT A CERTAIN NUMBER OF PLAYERS...
...WITH NO REGARD FOR SAFETY OR THE RULES OF THE GAME.
SO GIVEN THIS DEVELOP-MENT...
...I THINK IT MIGHT BE BEST FOR PREMIERE NOT TO FIGHT FOR NOW...
HUH ...?
WHY NOT...?
WHAT? I MEAN...
YOU DON'T WANT TO BE PUT IN DANGER LIKE YOU WERE EARLIER, RIGHT?
THE RISKS OF COMBAT ARE TOO HIGH.
...

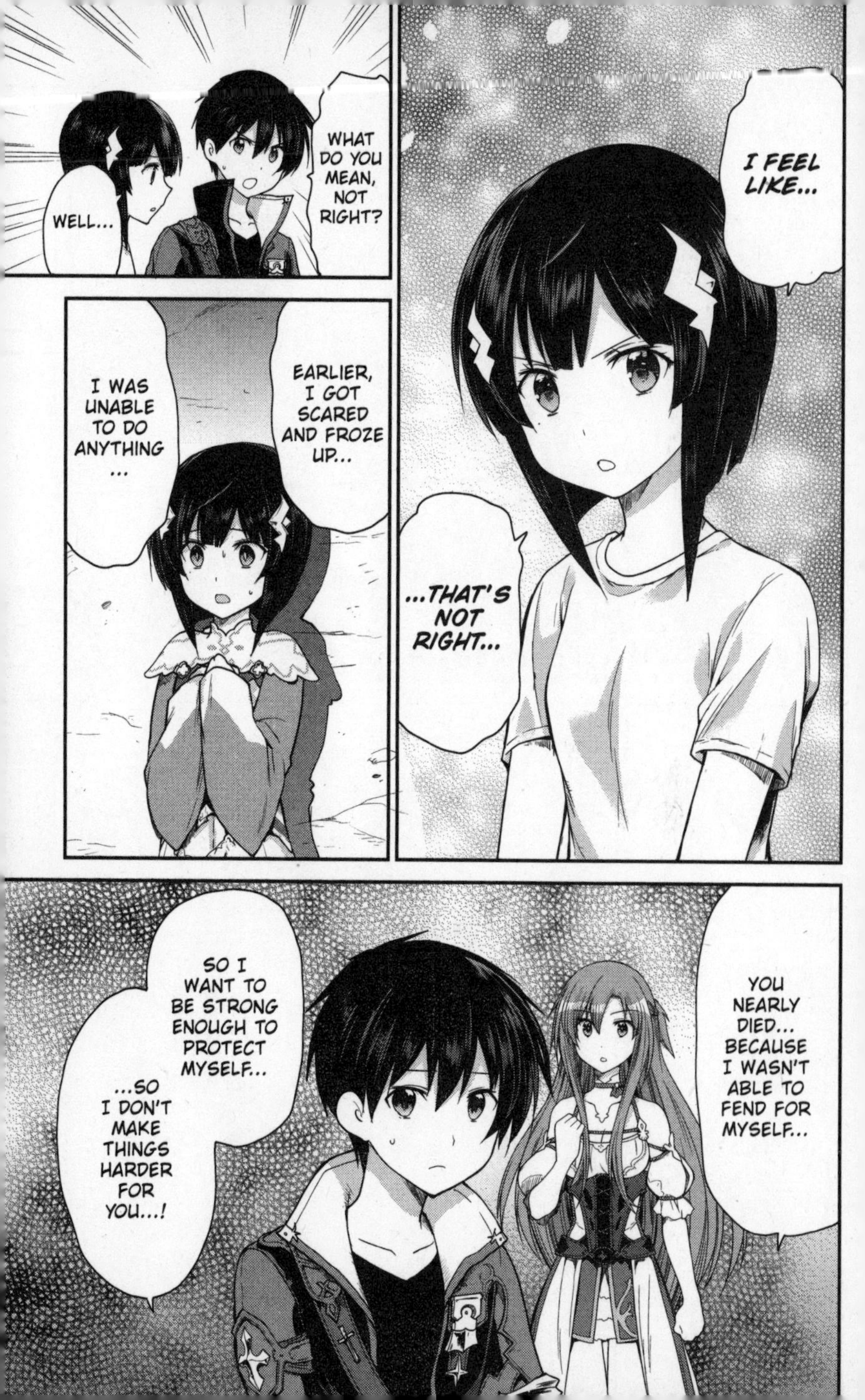
I FEEL LIKE...
...THAT'S NOT RIGHT...
WHAT DO YOU MEAN, NOT RIGHT?
WELL...
EARLIER, I GOT SCARED AND FROZE UP...
I WAS UNABLE TO DO ANYTHING ...
YOU NEARLY DIED... BECAUSE I WASN'T ABLE TO FEND FOR MYSELF...
SO I WANT TO BE STRONG ENOUGH TO PROTECT MYSELF...
...SO I DON'T MAKE THINGS HARDER FOR YOU...!

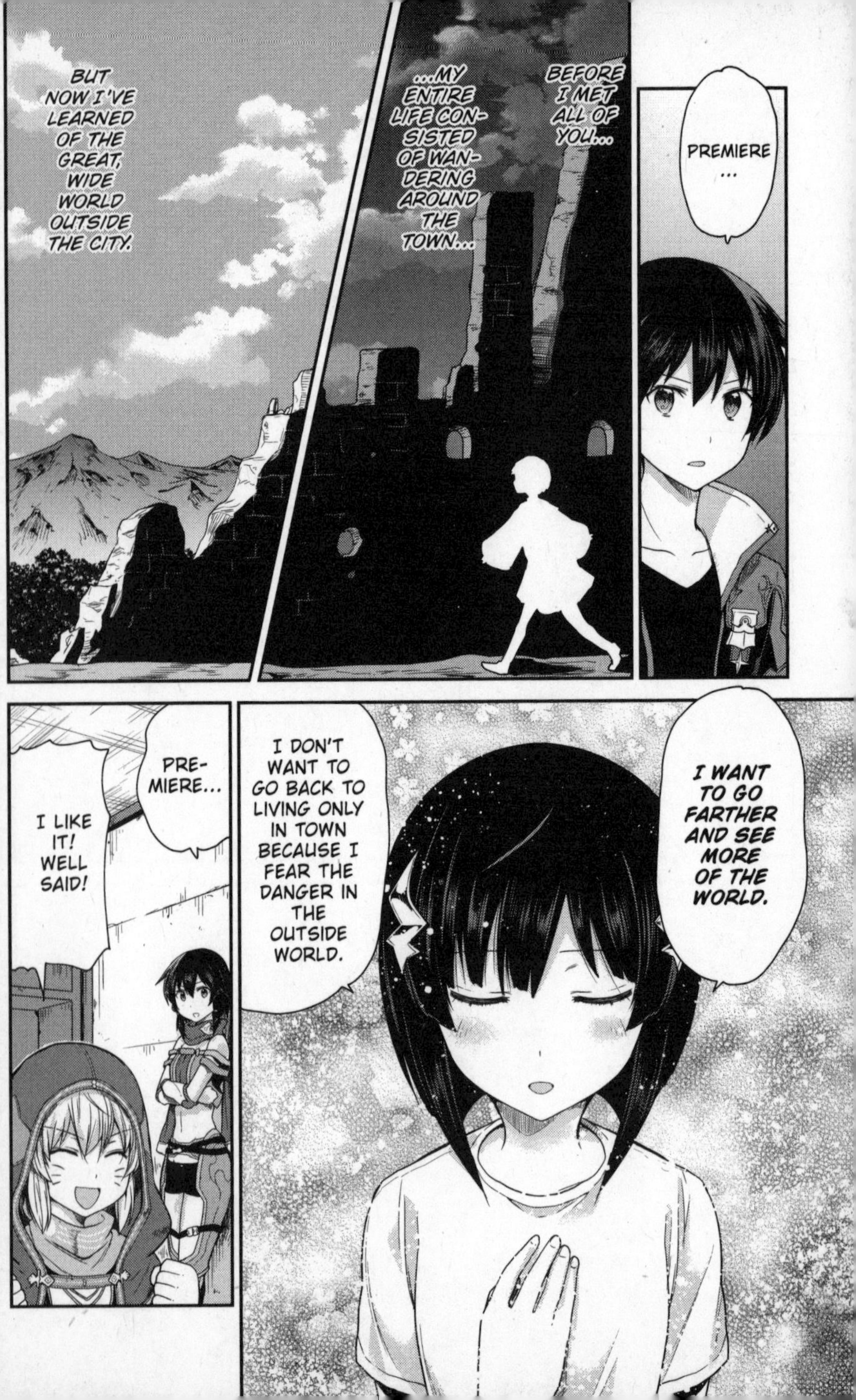
PREMIERE...
BEFORE I MET ALL OF YOU...
...MY ENTIRE LIFE CONSISTED OF WANDERING AROUND THE TOWN...
BUT NOW I'VE LEARNED OF THE GREAT, WIDE WORLD OUTSIDE THE CITY.
I WANT TO GO FARTHER AND SEE MORE OF THE WORLD.
I DON'T WANT TO GO BACK TO LIVING ONLY IN TOWN BECAUSE I FEAR THE DANGER IN THE OUTSIDE WORLD.
PREMIERE...
I LIKE IT! WELL SAID!

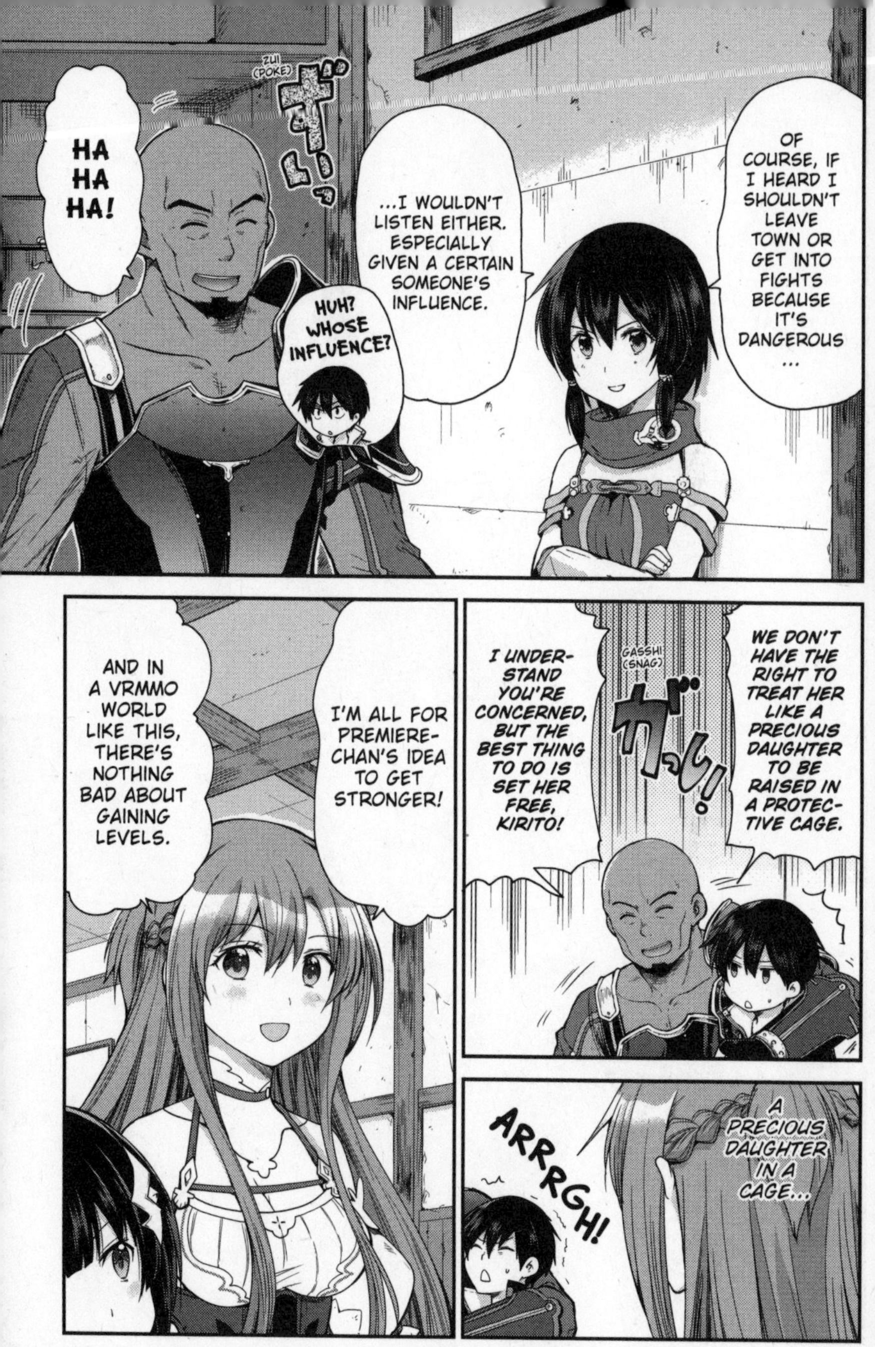
OF COURSE, IF I HEARD I SHOULDN'T LEAVE TOWN OR GET INTO FIGHTS BECAUSE IT'S DANGEROUS...
...I WOULDN'T LISTEN EITHER. ESPECIALLY GIVEN A CERTAIN SOMEONE'S INFLUENCE.
HUH? WHOSE INFLUENCE?
ZUI (POKE)
HA HA HA!
WE DON'T HAVE THE RIGHT TO TREAT HER LIKE A PRECIOUS DAUGHTER TO BE RAISED IN A PROTECTIVE CAGE.
GASSHI (SNAG)
I UNDERSTAND YOU'RE CONCERNED, BUT THE BEST THING TO DO IS SET HER FREE, KIRITO!
A PRECIOUS DAUGHTER IN A CAGE...
ARRRGH!
I'M ALL FOR PREMIERE-CHAN'S IDEA TO GET STRONGER!
AND IN A VRMMO WORLD LIKE THIS, THERE'S NOTHING BAD ABOUT GAINING LEVELS.

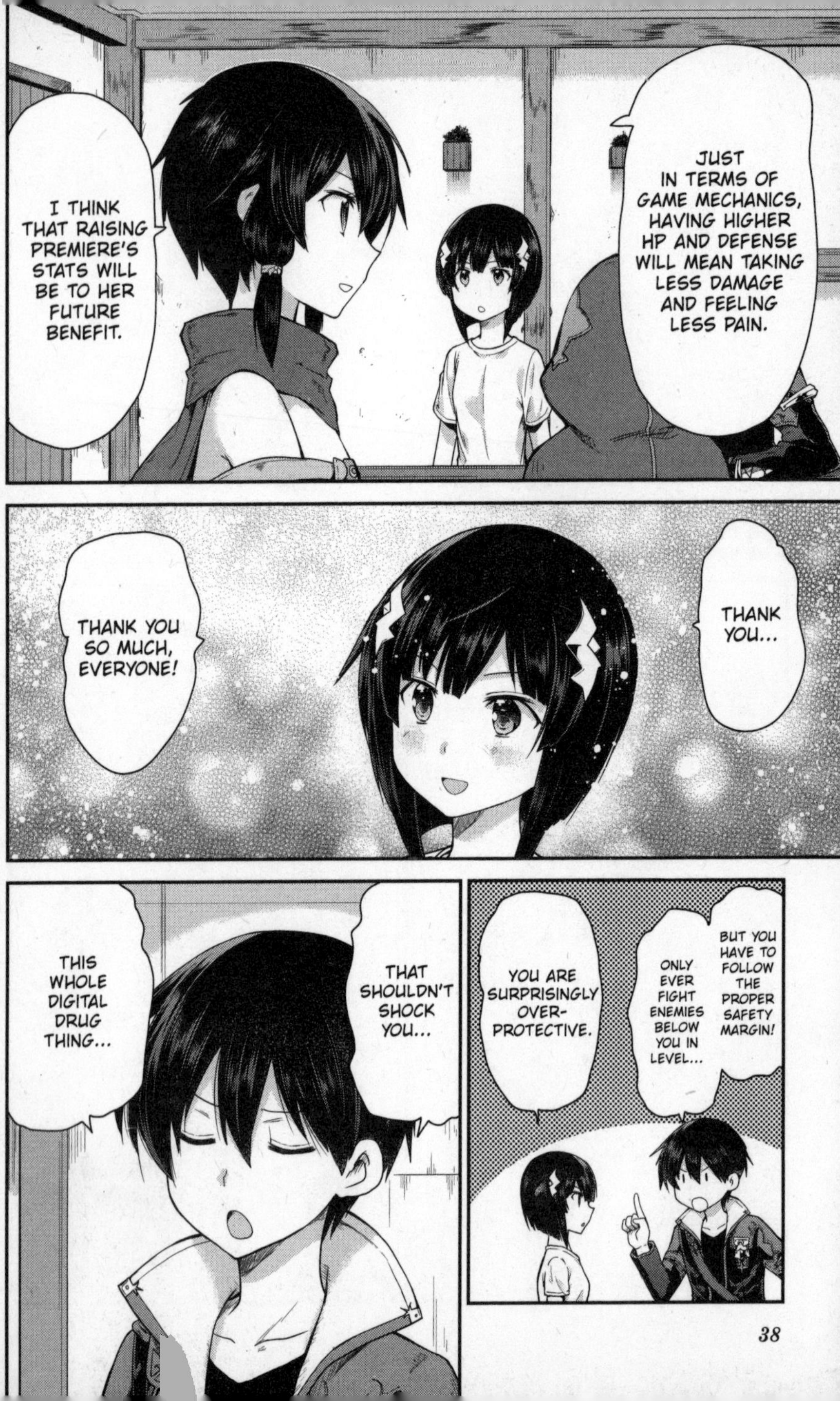
JUST IN TERMS OF GAME MECHANICS, HAVING HIGHER HP AND DEFENSE WILL MEAN TAKING LESS DAMAGE AND FEELING LESS PAIN.
I THINK THAT RAISING PREMIERE'S STATS WILL BE TO HER FUTURE BENEFIT.
THANK YOU...
THANK YOU SO MUCH, EVERYONE!
BUT YOU HAVE TO FOLLOW THE PROPER SAFETY MARGIN!
ONLY EVER FIGHT ENEMIES BELOW YOU IN LEVEL...
YOU ARE SURPRISINGLY OVER-PROTECTIVE.
THAT SHOULDN'T SHOCK YOU...
THIS WHOLE DIGITAL DRUG THING...

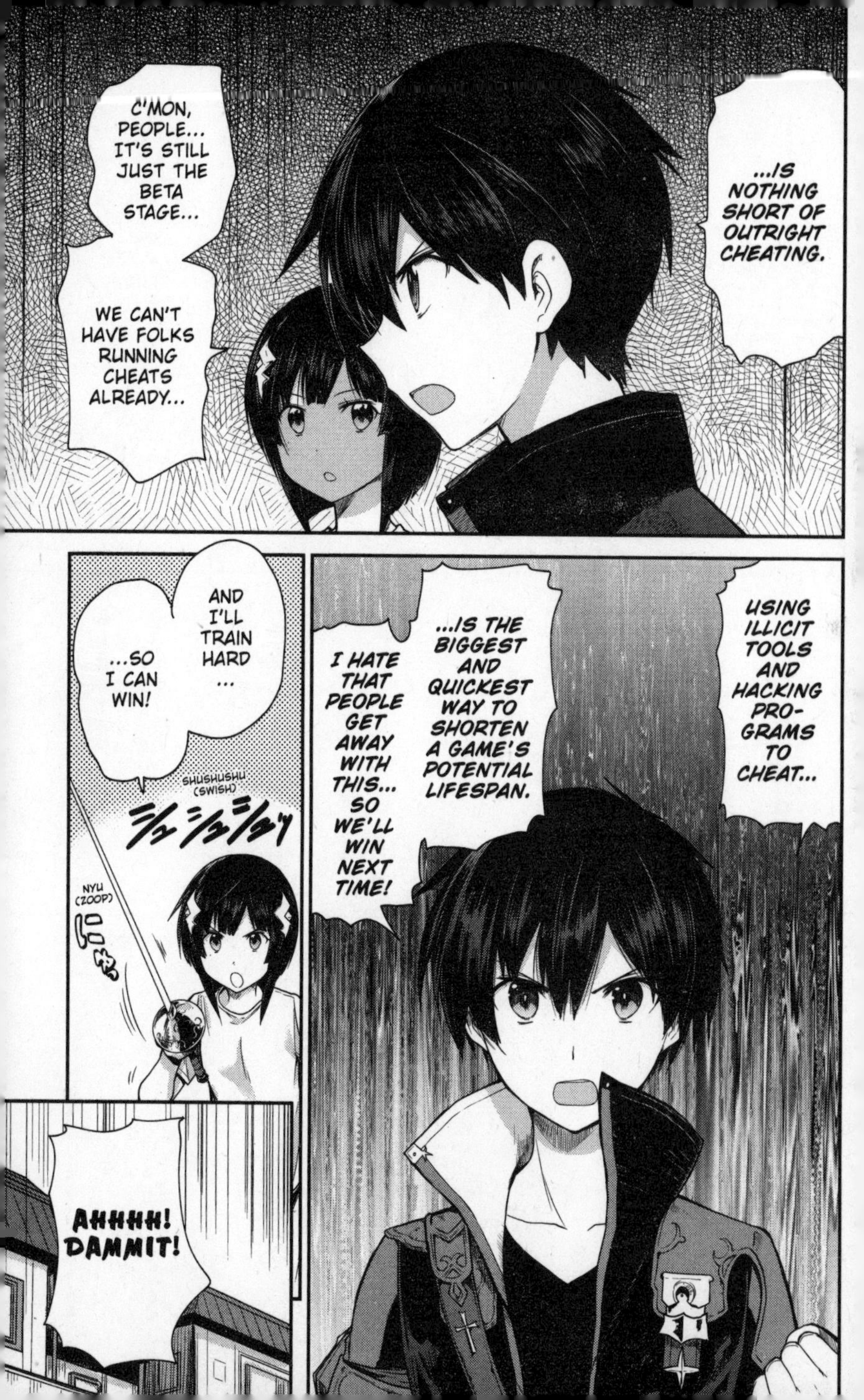
...IS NOTHING SHORT OF OUTRIGHT CHEATING.
C'MON, PEOPLE... IT'S STILL JUST THE BETA STAGE...
WE CAN'T HAVE FOLKS RUNNING CHEATS ALREADY...
USING ILLICIT TOOLS AND HACKING PRO-GRAMS TO CHEAT...
...IS THE BIGGEST AND QUICKEST WAY TO SHORTEN A GAME'S POTENTIAL LIFESPAN.
I HATE THAT PEOPLE GET AWAY WITH THIS... SO WE'LL WIN NEXT TIME!
AND I'LL TRAIN HARD...
...SO I CAN WIN!
SHUSHUSHU (SWISH)
NYU (ZOOP)
AHHHH! DAMMIT!

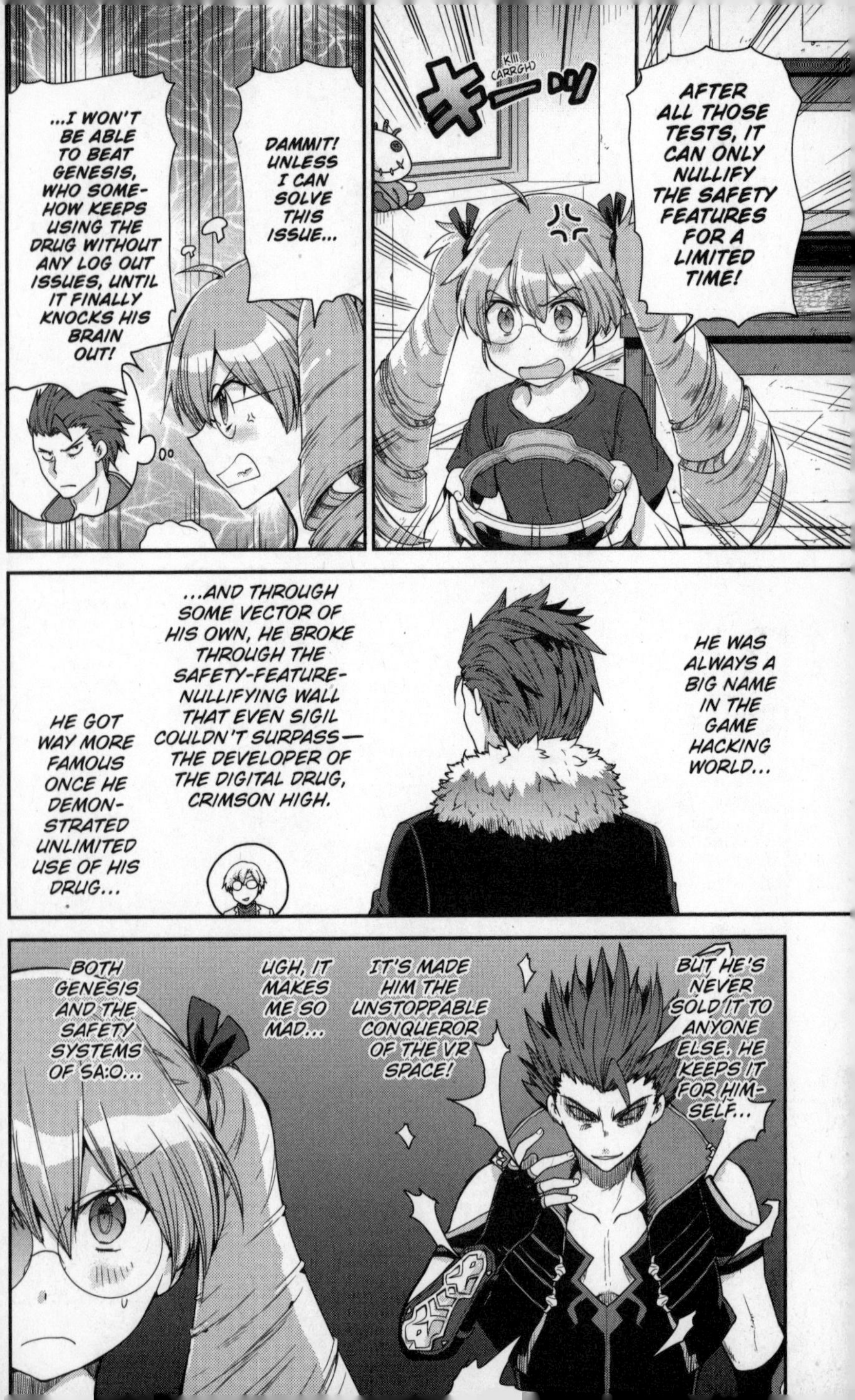
AFTER ALL THOSE TESTS, IT CAN ONLY NULLIFY THE SAFETY FEATURES FOR A LIMITED TIME!
KIII (ARRGH)
DAMMIT! UNLESS I CAN SOLVE THIS ISSUE...
...I WON'T BE ABLE TO BEAT GENESIS, WHO SOME-HOW KEEPS USING THE DRUG WITHOUT ANY LOG OUT ISSUES, UNTIL IT FINALLY KNOCKS HIS BRAIN OUT!
HE WAS ALWAYS A BIG NAME IN THE GAME HACKING WORLD...
...AND THROUGH SOME VECTOR OF HIS OWN, HE BROKE THROUGH THE SAFETY-FEATURE-NULLIFYING WALL THAT EVEN SIGIL COULDN'T SURPASS—THE DEVELOPER OF THE DIGITAL DRUG, CRIMSON HIGH.
HE GOT WAY MORE FAMOUS ONCE HE DEMON-STRATED UNLIMITED USE OF HIS DRUG...
BUT HE'S NEVER SOLD IT TO ANYONE ELSE. HE KEEPS IT FOR HIM-SELF...
IT'S MADE HIM THE UNSTOPPABLE CONQUEROR OF THE VR SPACE!
UGH, IT MAKES ME SO MAD...
BOTH GENESIS AND THE SAFETY SYSTEMS OF SA:O...

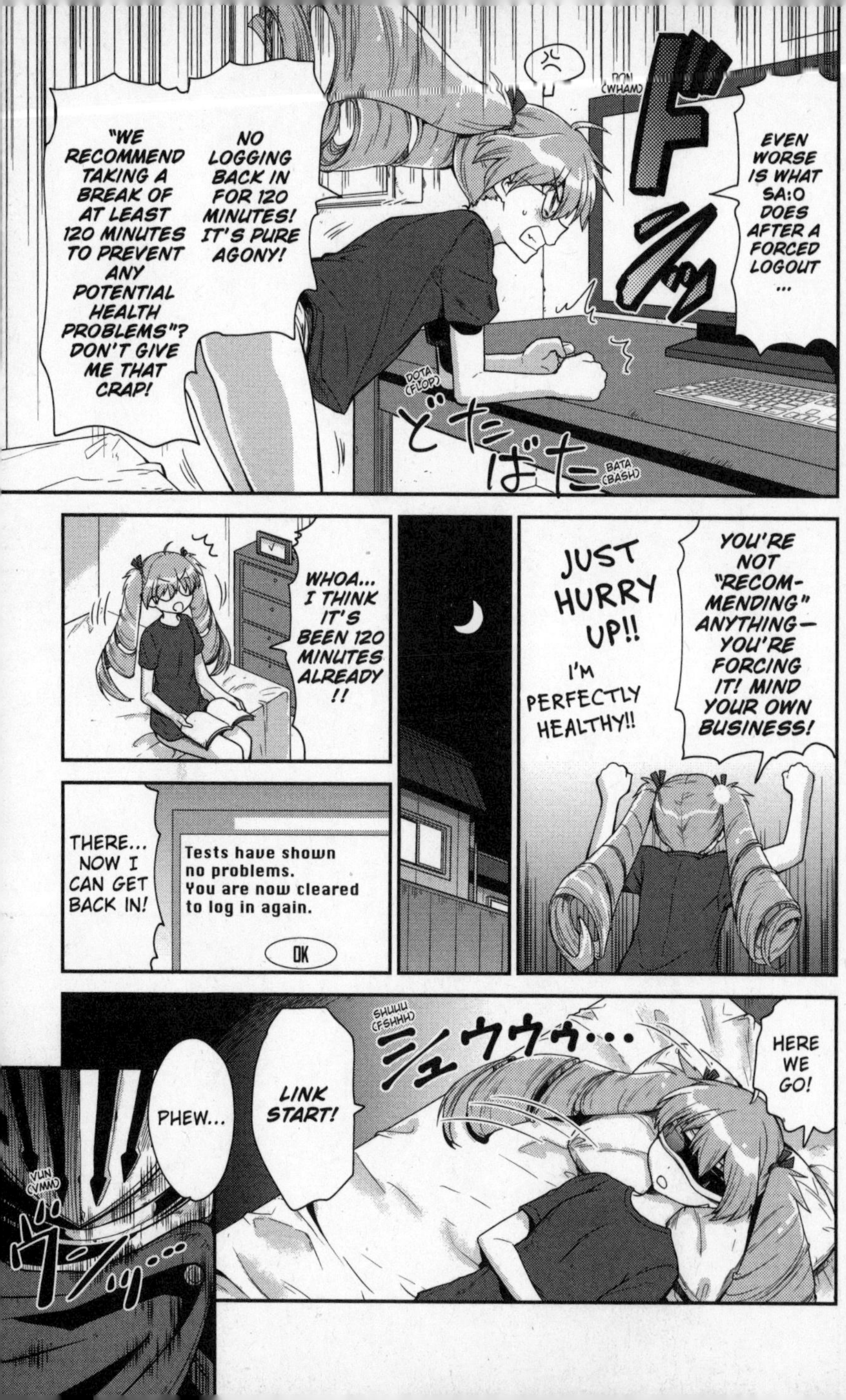
EVEN WORSE IS WHAT SA:O DOES AFTER A FORCED LOGOUT ...
DON (WHAM)
NO LOGGING BACK IN FOR 120 MINUTES! IT'S PURE AGONY!
"WE RECOMMEND TAKING A BREAK OF AT LEAST 120 MINUTES TO PREVENT ANY POTENTIAL HEALTH PROBLEMS"? DON'T GIVE ME THAT CRAP!
DOTA (FLOP)
どたばた
BATA (BASH)
YOU'RE NOT "RECOM-MENDING" ANYTHING— YOU'RE FORCING IT! MIND YOUR OWN BUSINESS!
JUST HURRY UP!!
I'M PERFECTLY HEALTHY!!
WHOA... I THINK IT'S BEEN 120 MINUTES ALREADY!!
THERE... NOW I CAN GET BACK IN!
Tests have shown no problems. You are now cleared to log in again.
OK
HERE WE GO!
SHUUU (FSHHH)
シュウウウ…
LINK START!
PHEW...
VUN (VMM)

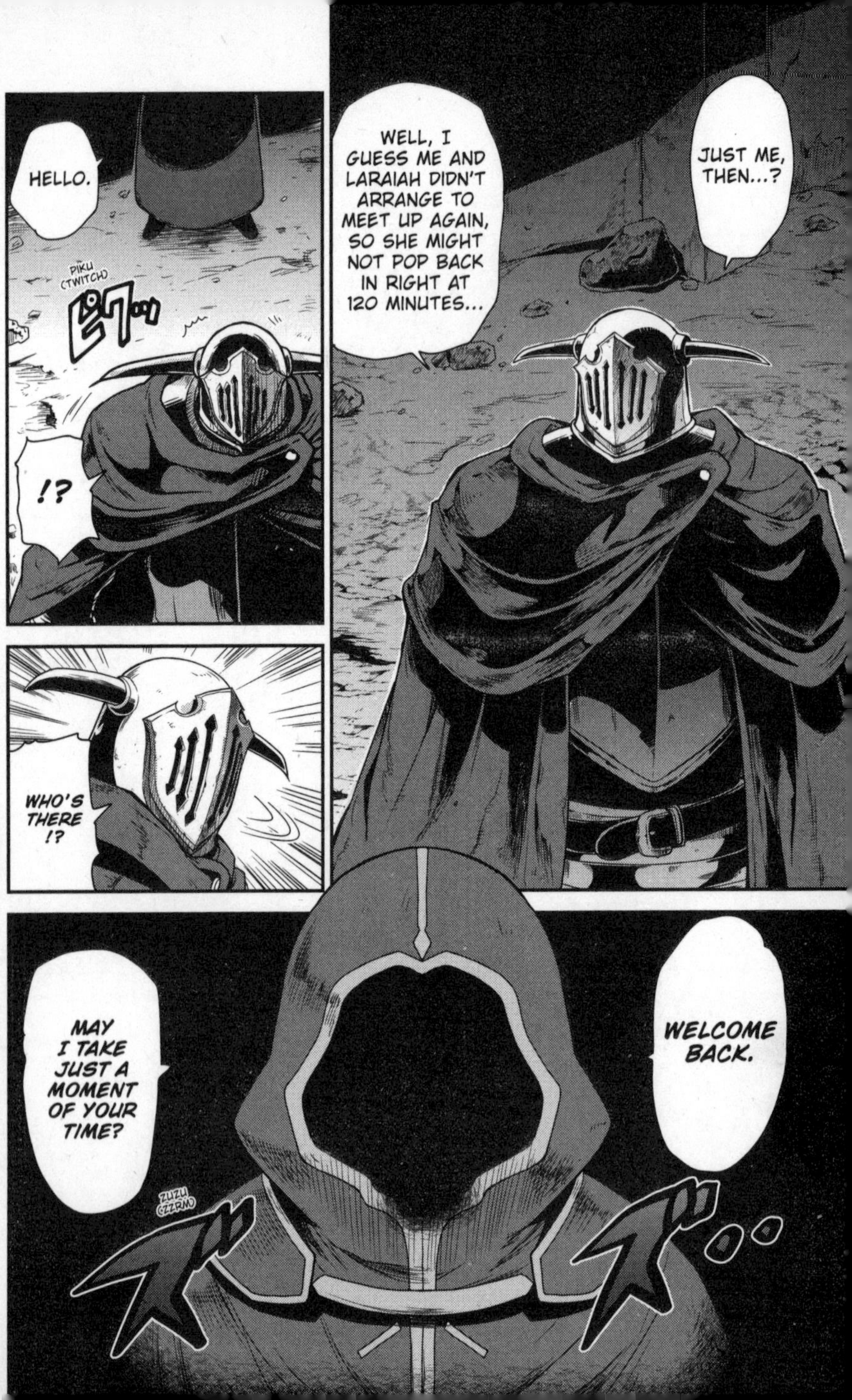
JUST ME, THEN...?
WELL, I GUESS ME AND LARAIAH DIDN'T ARRANGE TO MEET UP AGAIN, SO SHE MIGHT NOT POP BACK IN RIGHT AT 120 MINUTES...
HELLO.
PIKU (TWITCH)
!?
WHO'S THERE !?
WELCOME BACK.
MAY I TAKE JUST A MOMENT OF YOUR TIME?
ZUZU (ZZARM)

#17: Priestess of the Holy Tree, Part II

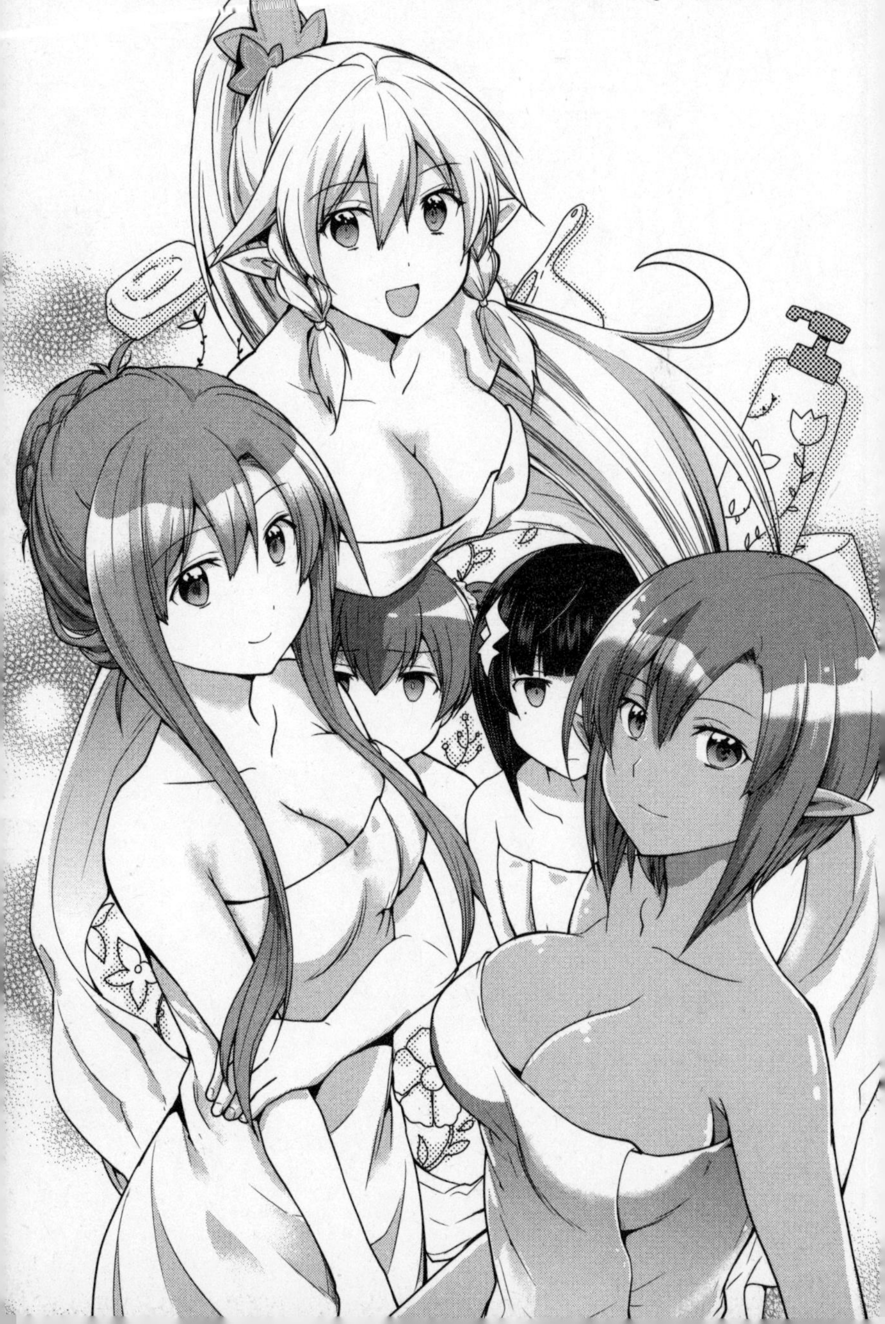

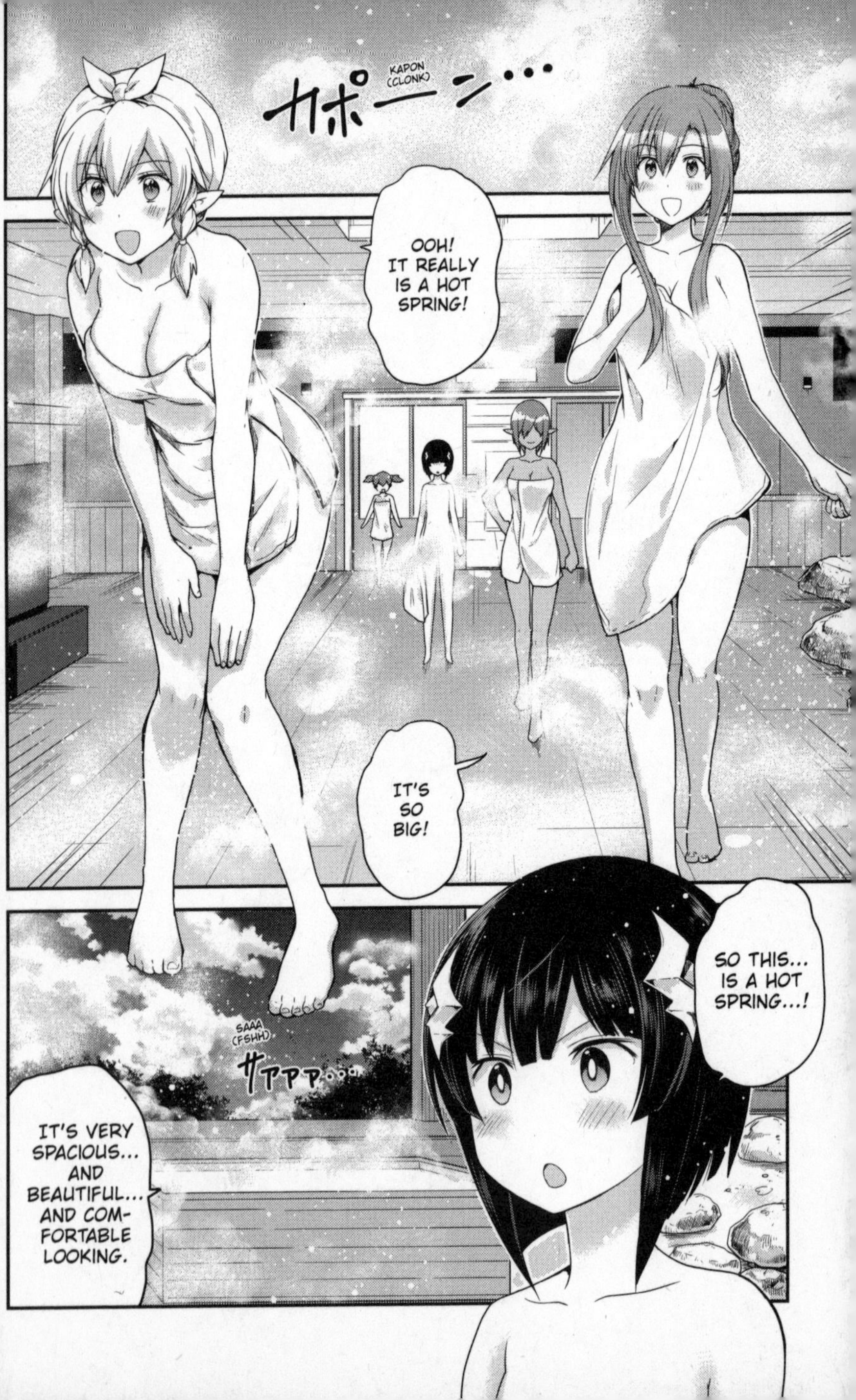
カポーン…
KAPON (CLONK)
OOH! IT REALLY IS A HOT SPRING!
IT'S SO BIG!
SO THIS... IS A HOT SPRING...!
SAAA (FSHH)
サァァ…
IT'S VERY SPACIOUS... AND BEAUTIFUL... AND COM-FORTABLE LOOKING.

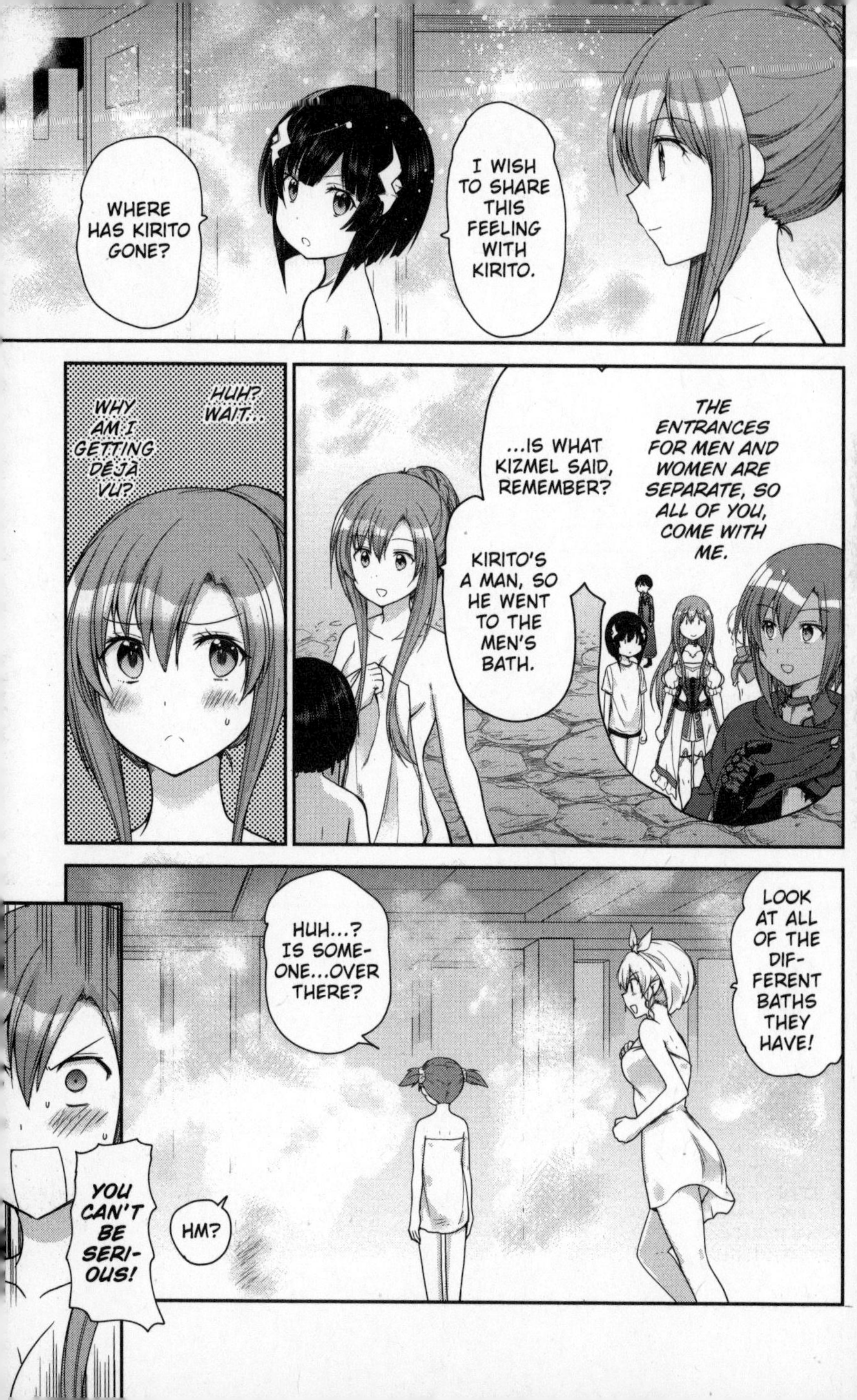
I WISH TO SHARE THIS FEELING WITH KIRITO.
WHERE HAS KIRITO GONE?
THE ENTRANCES FOR MEN AND WOMEN ARE SEPARATE, SO ALL OF YOU, COME WITH ME.
...IS WHAT KIZMEL SAID, REMEMBER?
KIRITO'S A MAN, SO HE WENT TO THE MEN'S BATH.
HUH? WAIT...
WHY AM I GETTING DÉJÀ VU?
LOOK AT ALL OF THE DIF-FERENT BATHS THEY HAVE!
HUH...? IS SOME-ONE...OVER THERE?
HM?
YOU CAN'T BE SERI-OUS!

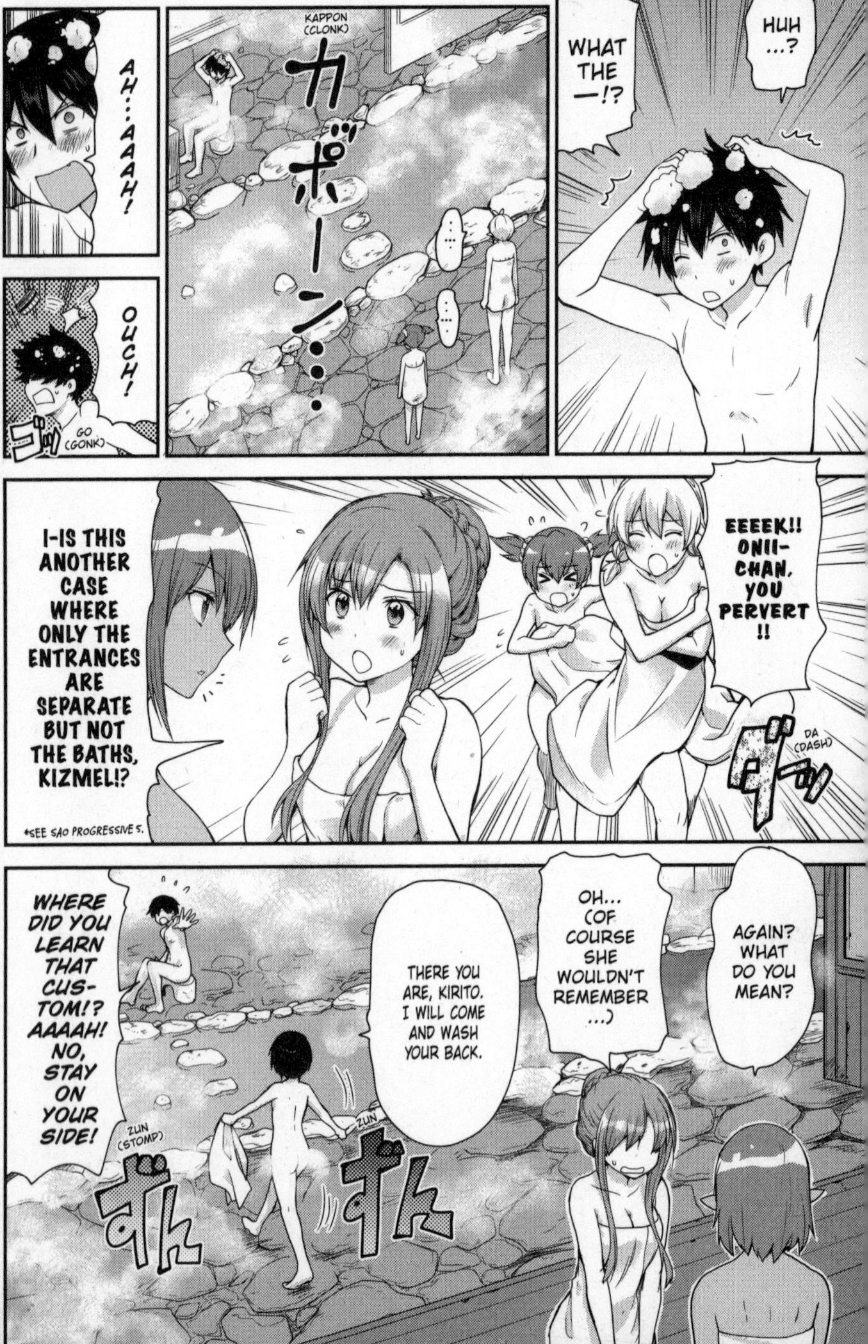
HUH ...?
WHAT THE—!?
KAPPON (CLONK)
......
......
AH... AAAAH!
OUCH!
GO (GONK)
EEEEK!! ONII-CHAN, YOU PERVERT!!
DA (DASH)
I-IS THIS ANOTHER CASE WHERE ONLY THE ENTRANCES ARE SEPARATE BUT NOT THE BATHS, KIZMEL!?
*SEE SAO PROGRESSIVE 5.
AGAIN? WHAT DO YOU MEAN?
OH... (OF COURSE SHE WOULDN'T REMEMBER ...)
THERE YOU ARE, KIRITO. I WILL COME AND WASH YOUR BACK.
ZUN
ZUN (STOMP)
WHERE DID YOU LEARN THAT CUSTOM!? AAAAH! NO, STAY ON YOUR SIDE!

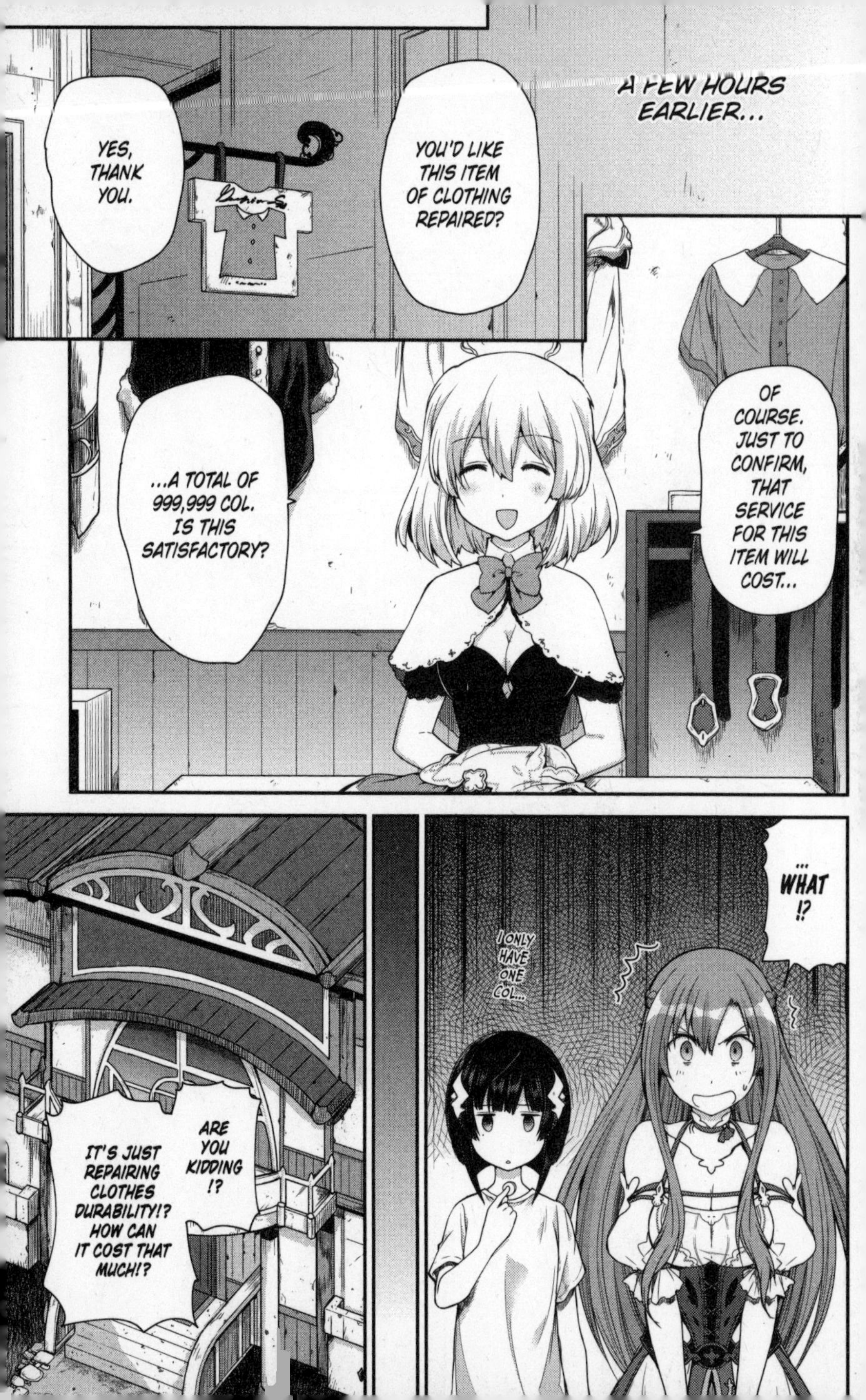
A FEW HOURS EARLIER...
YOU'D LIKE THIS ITEM OF CLOTHING REPAIRED?
YES, THANK YOU.
OF COURSE. JUST TO CONFIRM, THAT SERVICE FOR THIS ITEM WILL COST...
...A TOTAL OF 999,999 COL. IS THIS SATISFACTORY?
...WHAT!?
I ONLY HAVE ONE COL...
ARE YOU KIDDING!?
IT'S JUST REPAIRING CLOTHES DURABILITY!? HOW CAN IT COST THAT MUCH!?

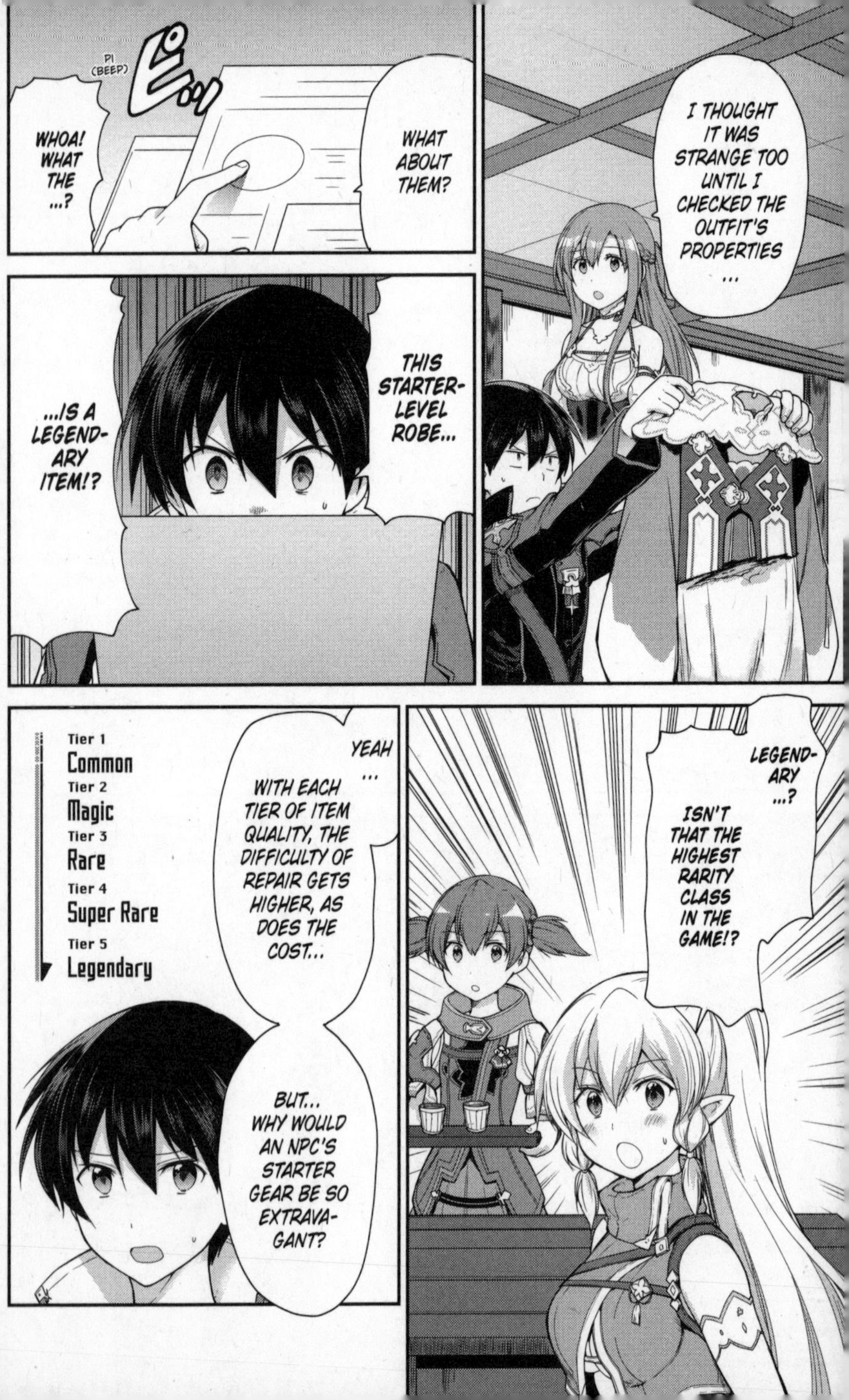
I THOUGHT IT WAS STRANGE TOO UNTIL I CHECKED THE OUTFIT'S PROPERTIES...
WHAT ABOUT THEM?
PI (BEEP)
WHOA! WHAT THE ...?
THIS STARTER-LEVEL ROBE...
...IS A LEGENDARY ITEM!?
LEGENDARY ...?
ISN'T THAT THE HIGHEST RARITY CLASS IN THE GAME!?
YEAH...
WITH EACH TIER OF ITEM QUALITY, THE DIFFICULTY OF REPAIR GETS HIGHER, AS DOES THE COST...
Tier 1 Common
Tier 2 Magic
Tier 3 Rare
Tier 4 Super Rare
Tier 5 Legendary
BUT... WHY WOULD AN NPC'S STARTER GEAR BE SO EXTRAVAGANT?

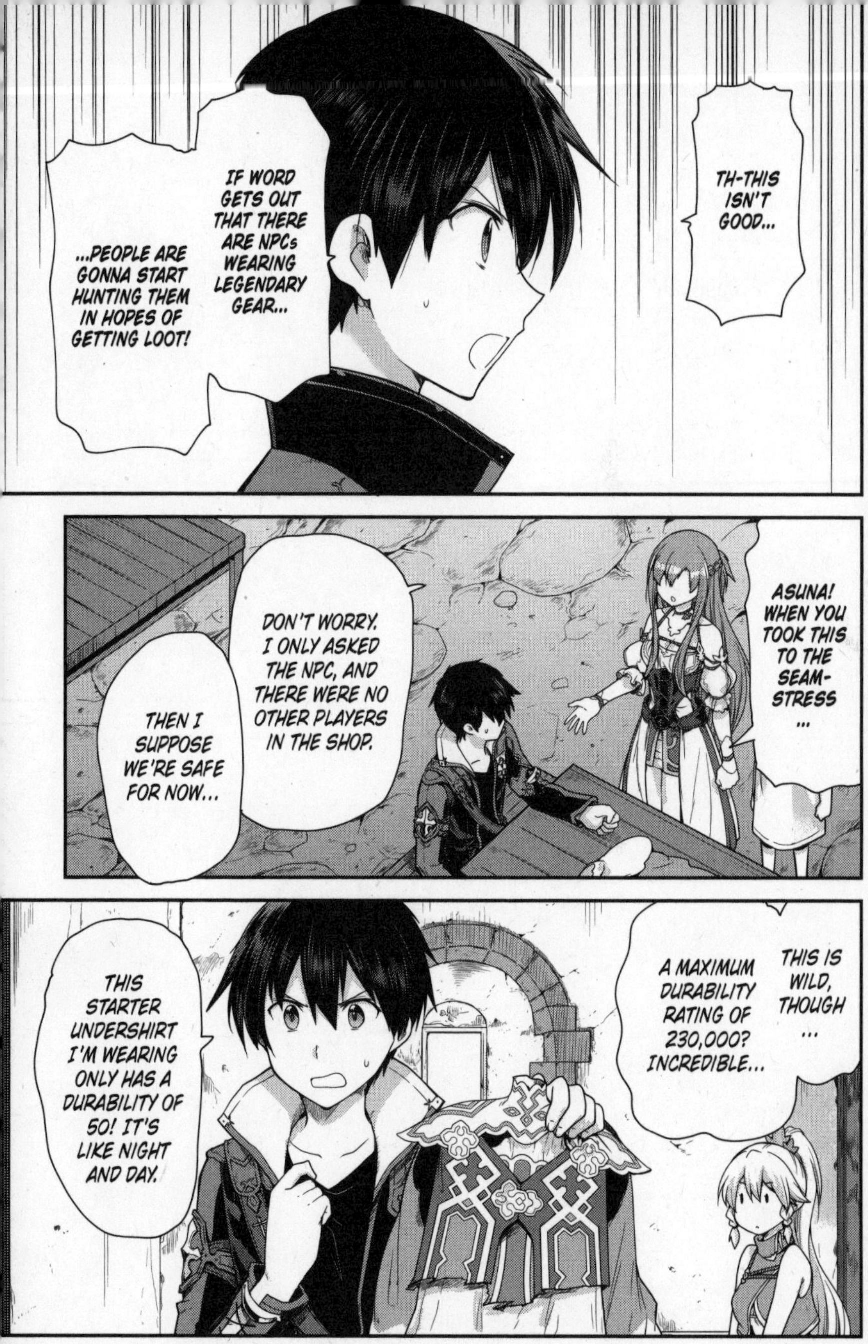
TH-THIS ISN'T GOOD...
IF WORD GETS OUT THAT THERE ARE NPCs WEARING LEGENDARY GEAR...
...PEOPLE ARE GONNA START HUNTING THEM IN HOPES OF GETTING LOOT!
ASUNA! WHEN YOU TOOK THIS TO THE SEAM-STRESS ...
DON'T WORRY. I ONLY ASKED THE NPC, AND THERE WERE NO OTHER PLAYERS IN THE SHOP.
THEN I SUPPOSE WE'RE SAFE FOR NOW...
THIS IS WILD, THOUGH ...
A MAXIMUM DURABILITY RATING OF 230,000? INCREDIBLE...
THIS STARTER UNDERSHIRT I'M WEARING ONLY HAS A DURABILITY OF 50! IT'S LIKE NIGHT AND DAY.

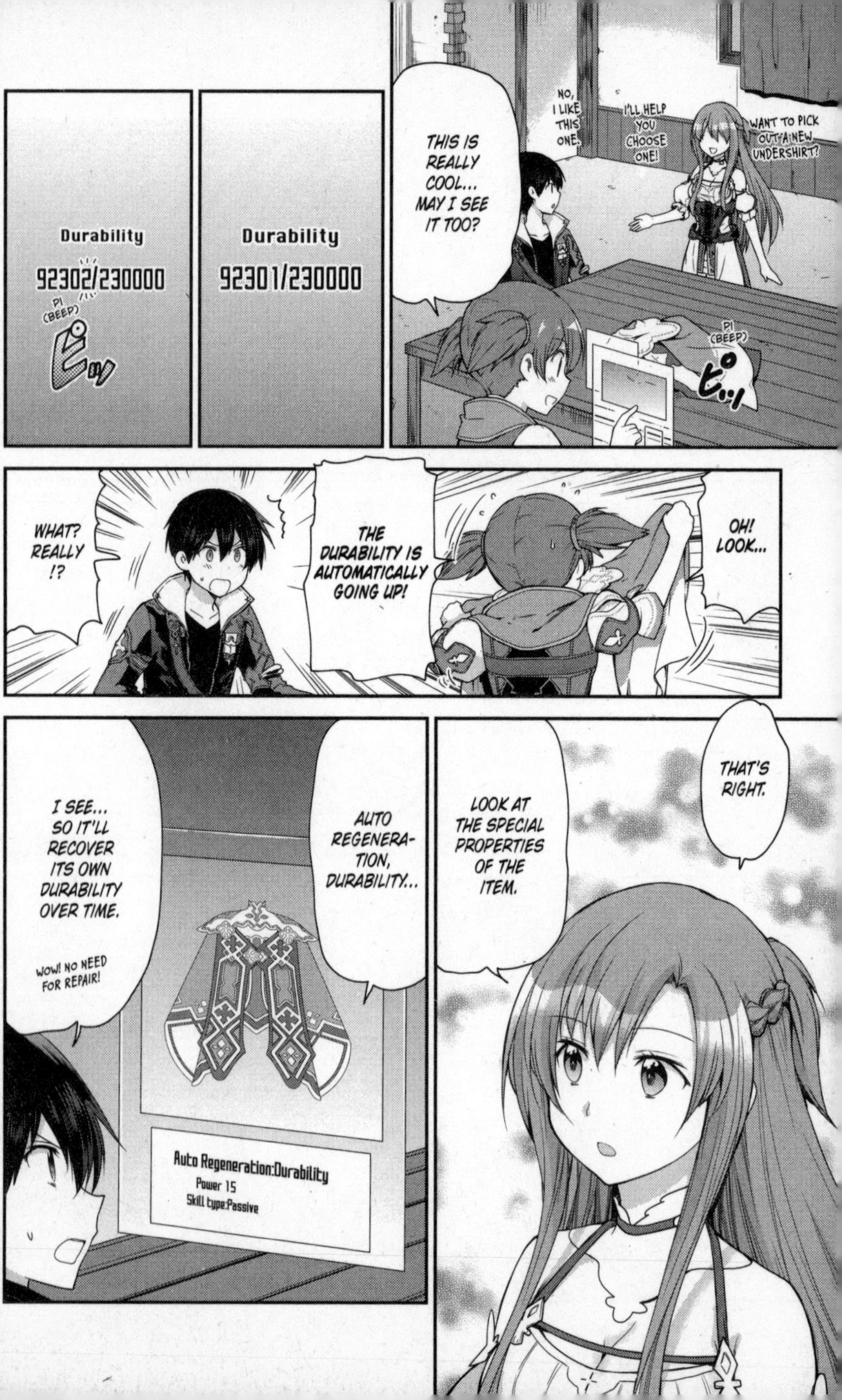
WANT TO PICK OUT A NEW UNDERSHIRT?
I'LL HELP YOU CHOOSE ONE!
NO, I LIKE THIS ONE.
THIS IS REALLY COOL... MAY I SEE IT TOO?
PI (BEEP)
Durability
92301/230000
Durability
92302/230000
PI (BEEP)
OH! LOOK...
THE DURABILITY IS AUTOMATICALLY GOING UP!
WHAT? REALLY !?
THAT'S RIGHT.
LOOK AT THE SPECIAL PROPERTIES OF THE ITEM.
AUTO REGENERATION, DURABILITY...
I SEE... SO IT'LL RECOVER ITS OWN DURABILITY OVER TIME.
WOW! NO NEED FOR REPAIR!
Auto Regeneration:Durability
Power 15
Skill type:Passive

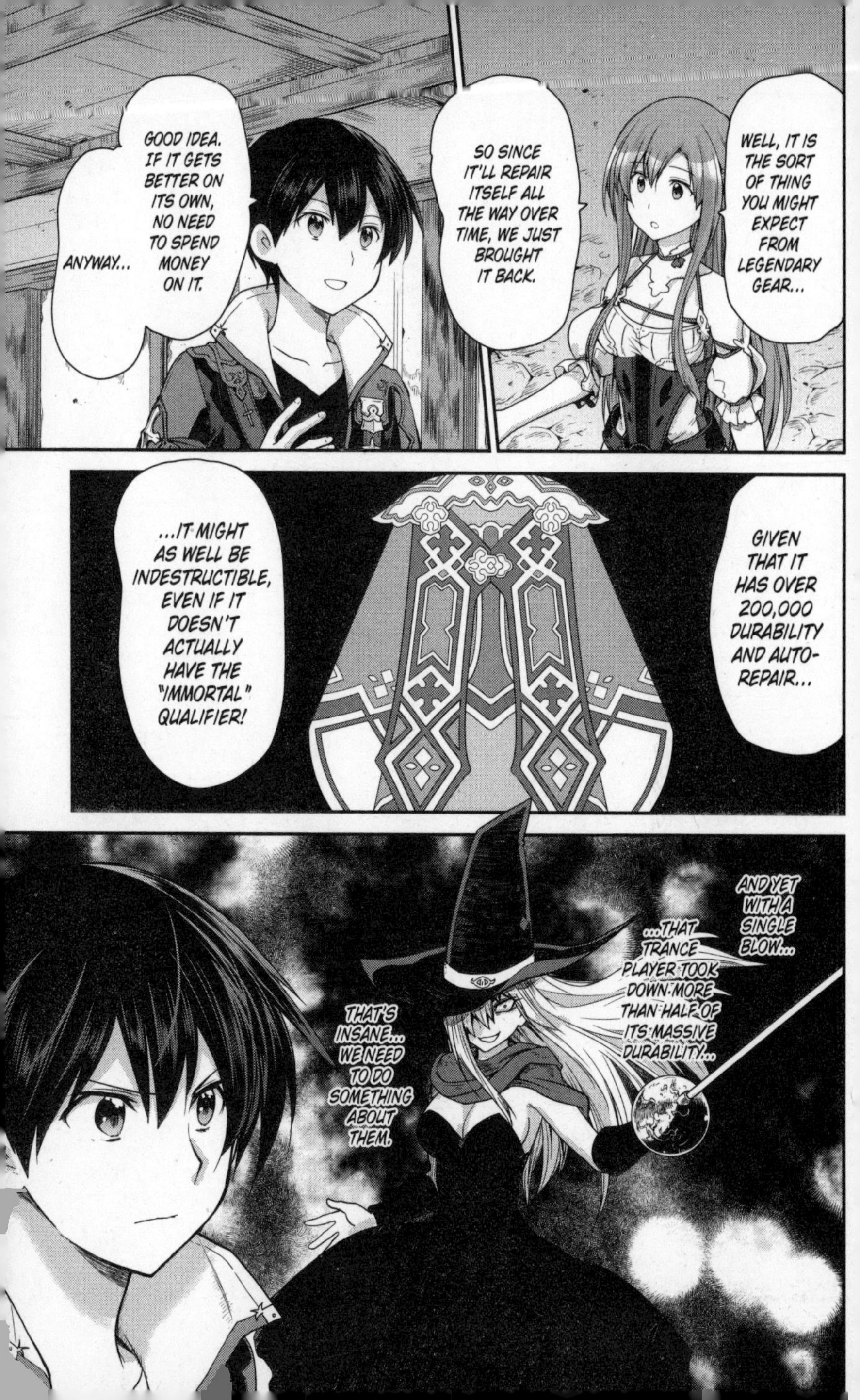
WELL, IT IS THE SORT OF THING YOU MIGHT EXPECT FROM LEGENDARY GEAR...
SO SINCE IT'LL REPAIR ITSELF ALL THE WAY OVER TIME, WE JUST BROUGHT IT BACK.
GOOD IDEA. IF IT GETS BETTER ON ITS OWN, NO NEED TO SPEND MONEY ON IT.
ANYWAY...
GIVEN THAT IT HAS OVER 200,000 DURABILITY AND AUTO-REPAIR...
...IT MIGHT AS WELL BE INDESTRUCTIBLE, EVEN IF IT DOESN'T ACTUALLY HAVE THE "IMMORTAL" QUALIFIER!
AND YET WITH A SINGLE BLOW...
...THAT TRANCE PLAYER TOOK DOWN MORE THAN HALF OF ITS MASSIVE DURABILITY...
THAT'S INSANE... WE NEED TO DO SOMETHING ABOUT THEM.

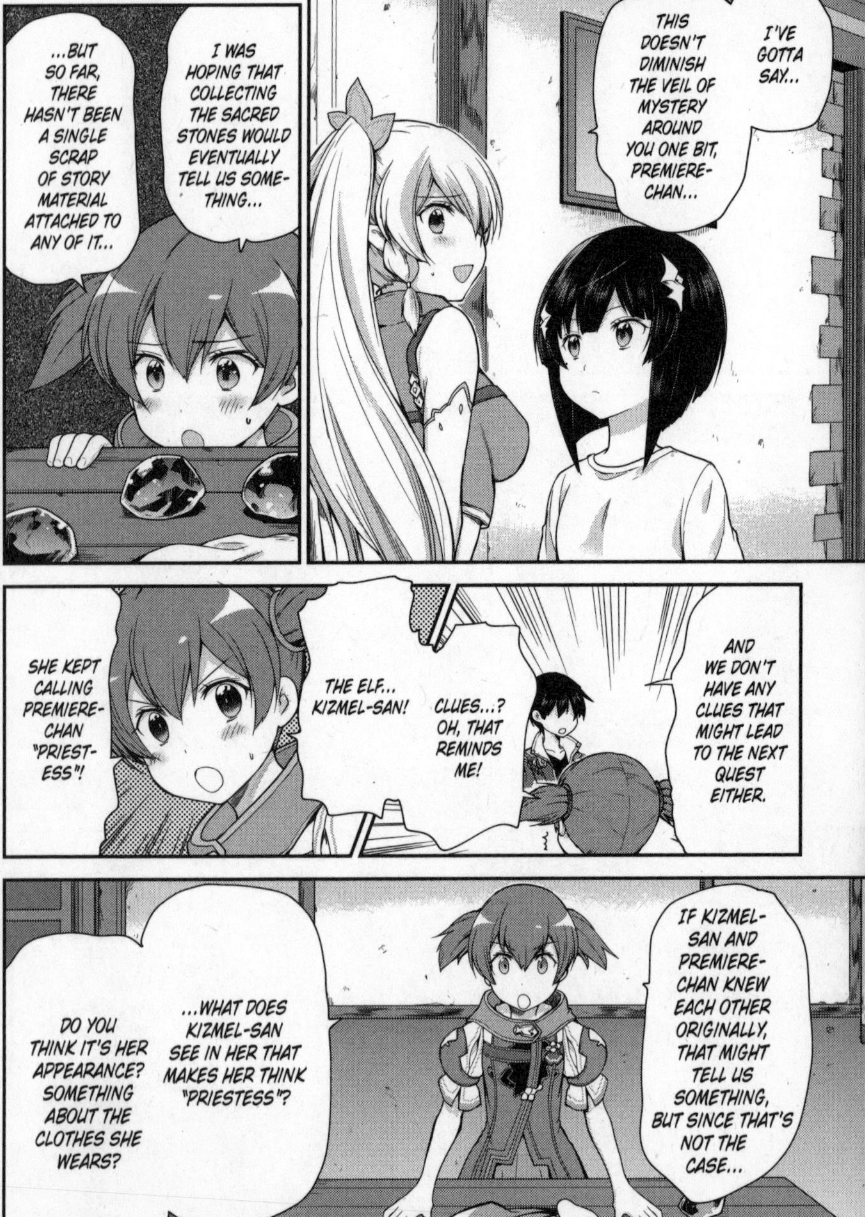
I'VE GOTTA SAY...
THIS DOESN'T DIMINISH THE VEIL OF MYSTERY AROUND YOU ONE BIT, PREMIERE-CHAN...
I WAS HOPING THAT COLLECTING THE SACRED STONES WOULD EVENTUALLY TELL US SOME-THING...
...BUT SO FAR, THERE HASN'T BEEN A SINGLE SCRAP OF STORY MATERIAL ATTACHED TO ANY OF IT...
AND WE DON'T HAVE ANY CLUES THAT MIGHT LEAD TO THE NEXT QUEST EITHER.
CLUES...? OH, THAT REMINDS ME!
THE ELF... KIZMEL-SAN!
SHE KEPT CALLING PREMIERE-CHAN "PRIEST-ESS"!
IF KIZMEL-SAN AND PREMIERE-CHAN KNEW EACH OTHER ORIGINALLY, THAT MIGHT TELL US SOMETHING, BUT SINCE THAT'S NOT THE CASE...
...WHAT DOES KIZMEL-SAN SEE IN HER THAT MAKES HER THINK "PRIESTESS"?
DO YOU THINK IT'S HER APPEARANCE? SOMETHING ABOUT THE CLOTHES SHE WEARS?

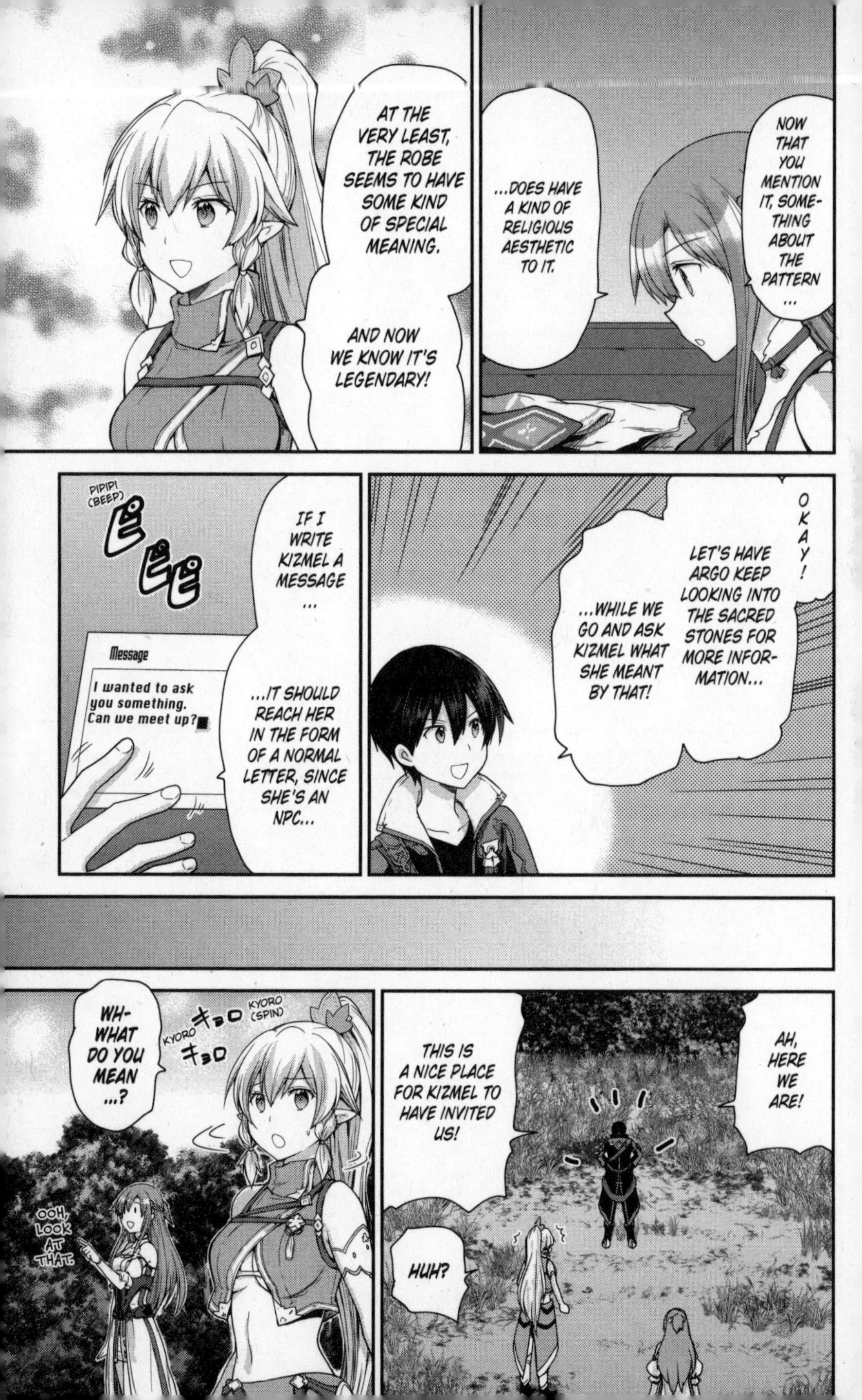
NOW THAT YOU MENTION IT, SOME-THING ABOUT THE PATTERN...
...DOES HAVE A KIND OF RELIGIOUS AESTHETIC TO IT.
AT THE VERY LEAST, THE ROBE SEEMS TO HAVE SOME KIND OF SPECIAL MEANING.
AND NOW WE KNOW IT'S LEGENDARY!
OKAY!
LET'S HAVE ARGO KEEP LOOKING INTO THE SACRED STONES FOR MORE INFOR-MATION...
...WHILE WE GO AND ASK KIZMEL WHAT SHE MEANT BY THAT!
PIPIPI (BEEP)
ピピピ
IF I WRITE KIZMEL A MESSAGE...
Message
I wanted to ask you something. Can we meet up?
...IT SHOULD REACH HER IN THE FORM OF A NORMAL LETTER, SINCE SHE'S AN NPC...
AH, HERE WE ARE!
THIS IS A NICE PLACE FOR KIZMEL TO HAVE INVITED US!
HUH?
KYORO キョロ KYORO (SPIN) キョロ
WH-WHAT DO YOU MEAN...?
OOH, LOOK AT THAT.

YOU'RE THE ONLY ONE OF US WHO DIDN'T FINISH THE HOLY TREE QUEST. THAT MUST BE WHY YOU'RE NOT SEEING IT.

OH, I GET IT...

WHAT ARE YOU ALL SEEING? IT'S NOTHING BUT FOREST AROUND US!

WHAT? WHAT DO YOU MEAN!?

OOOH!

...YOU SHOULD FORM A PARTY WITH ASUNA AND LET HER BE THE LEADER, SINCE SHE FINISHED THE QUEST.

SINCE THE QUEST PROGRESS OF THE PARTY DEPENDS ON WHO THE PARTY LEADER IS...

Leader	
Kirito	
Asuna	
Silica	
Premiere	

Leader	
Asuna	
LeaFa	

OH, GOOD! YOU CAN SEE IT.

N-NOW THERE'S A BUILDING IN THE FOREST!

IS THAT... A HOT SPRING SYMBOL!?

THIS IS APPARENTLY AN ISOLATED ELF HOT SPRING INN.

!

VUN GYNN

NOW AS LONG AS YOU'RE TEAMED UP WITH ASUNA, THE GAME WILL ACT LIKE YOU'VE ALSO FINISHED THE HOLY TREE QUEST, LEAFA.

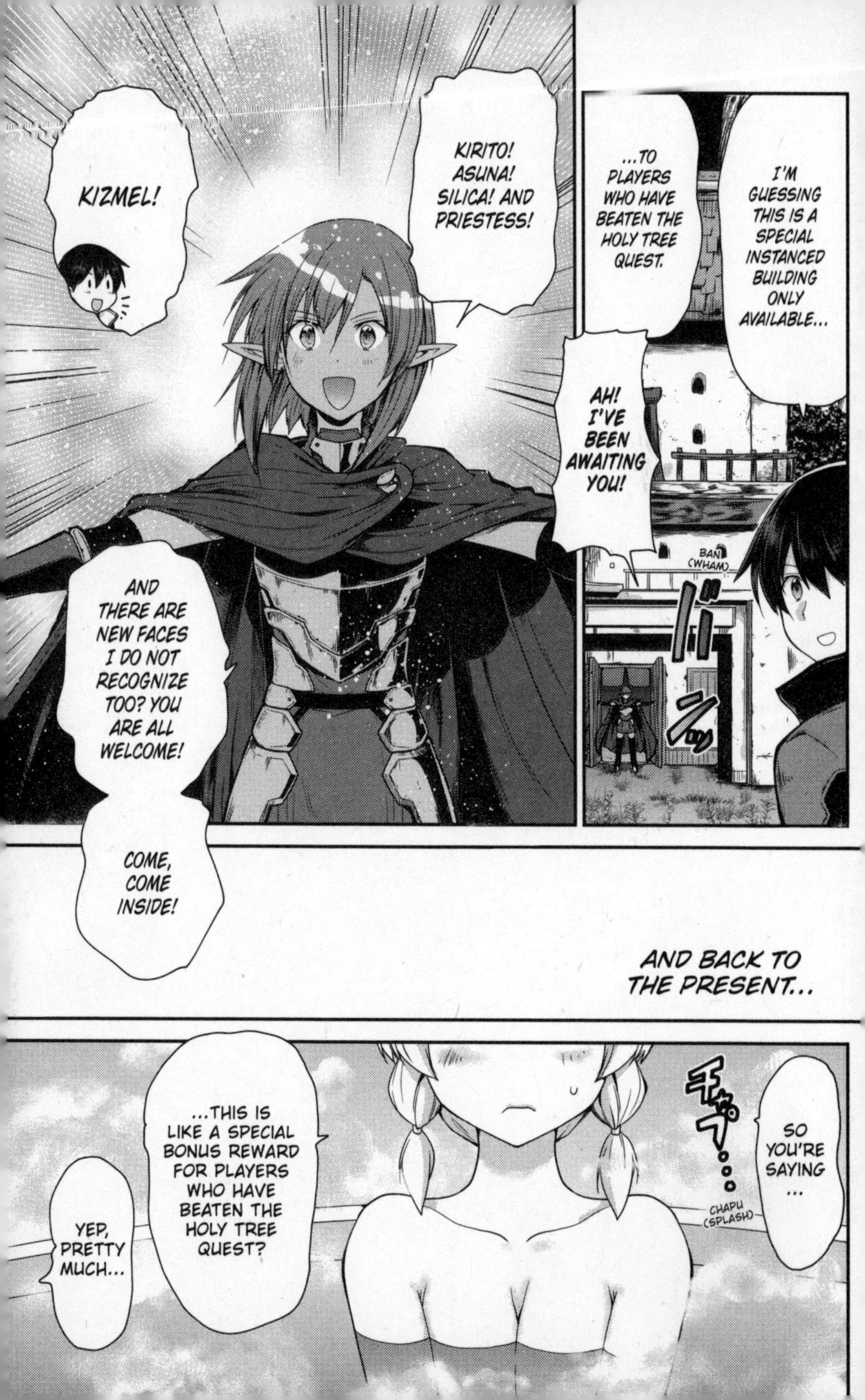
I'M GUESSING THIS IS A SPECIAL INSTANCED BUILDING ONLY AVAILABLE...
...TO PLAYERS WHO HAVE BEATEN THE HOLY TREE QUEST.
AH! I'VE BEEN AWAITING YOU!
BAN (WHAM)
KIRITO! ASUNA! SILICA! AND PRIESTESS!
KIZMEL!
AND THERE ARE NEW FACES I DO NOT RECOGNIZE TOO? YOU ARE ALL WELCOME!
COME, COME INSIDE!
AND BACK TO THE PRESENT...
SO YOU'RE SAYING ...
CHAPU (SPLASH)
...THIS IS LIKE A SPECIAL BONUS REWARD FOR PLAYERS WHO HAVE BEATEN THE HOLY TREE QUEST?
YEP, PRETTY MUCH...

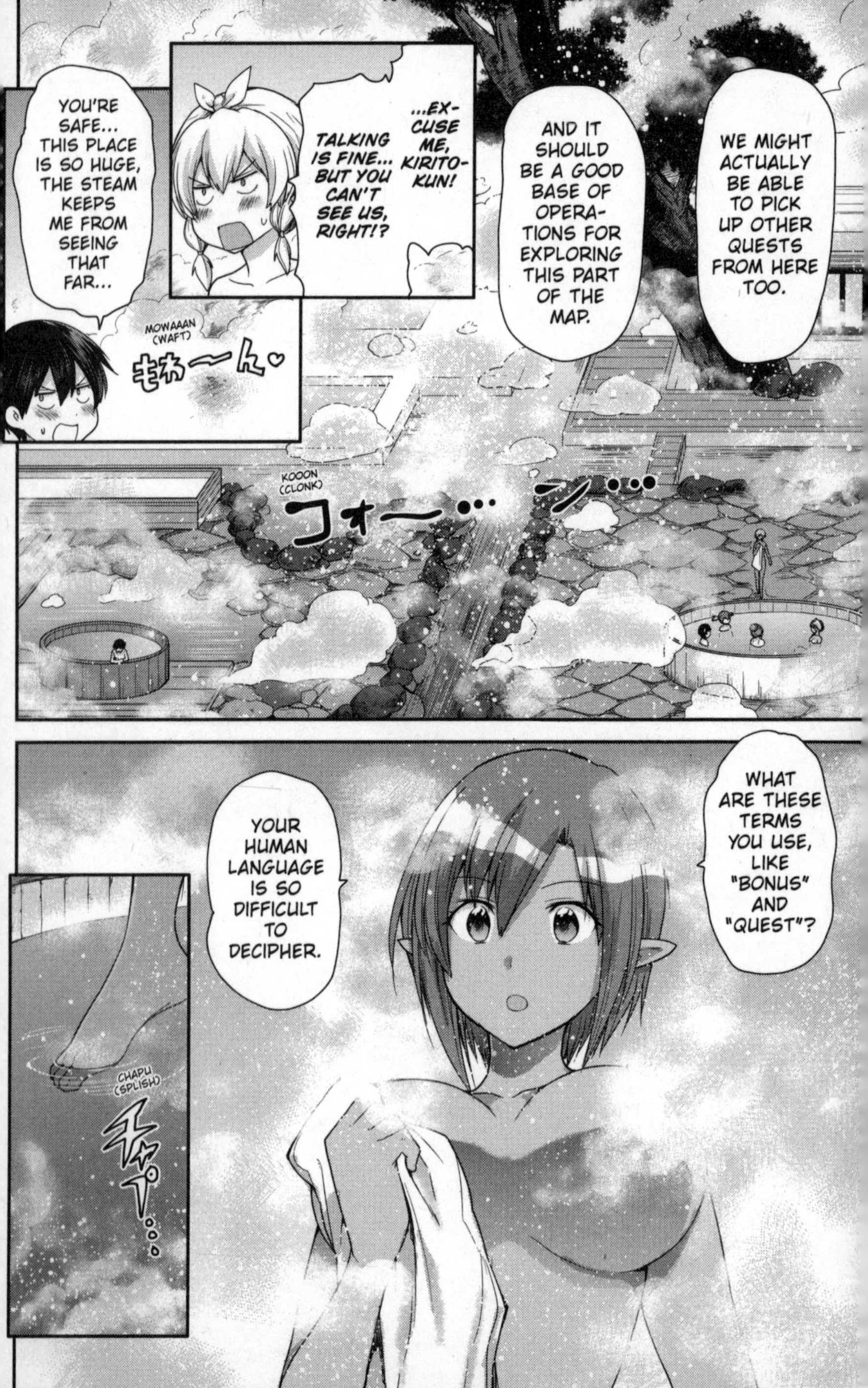
WE MIGHT ACTUALLY BE ABLE TO PICK UP OTHER QUESTS FROM HERE TOO.
AND IT SHOULD BE A GOOD BASE OF OPERA-TIONS FOR EXPLORING THIS PART OF THE MAP.
...EX-CUSE ME, KIRITO-KUN!
TALKING IS FINE... BUT YOU CAN'T SEE US, RIGHT!?
YOU'RE SAFE... THIS PLACE IS SO HUGE, THE STEAM KEEPS ME FROM SEEING THAT FAR...
MOWAAAN (WAFT)
もわ〜ん♡
KOOON (CLONK)
コォー‥ン‥
WHAT ARE THESE TERMS YOU USE, LIKE "BONUS" AND "QUEST"?
YOUR HUMAN LANGUAGE IS SO DIFFICULT TO DECIPHER.
CHAPU (SPLISH)
チャプ…

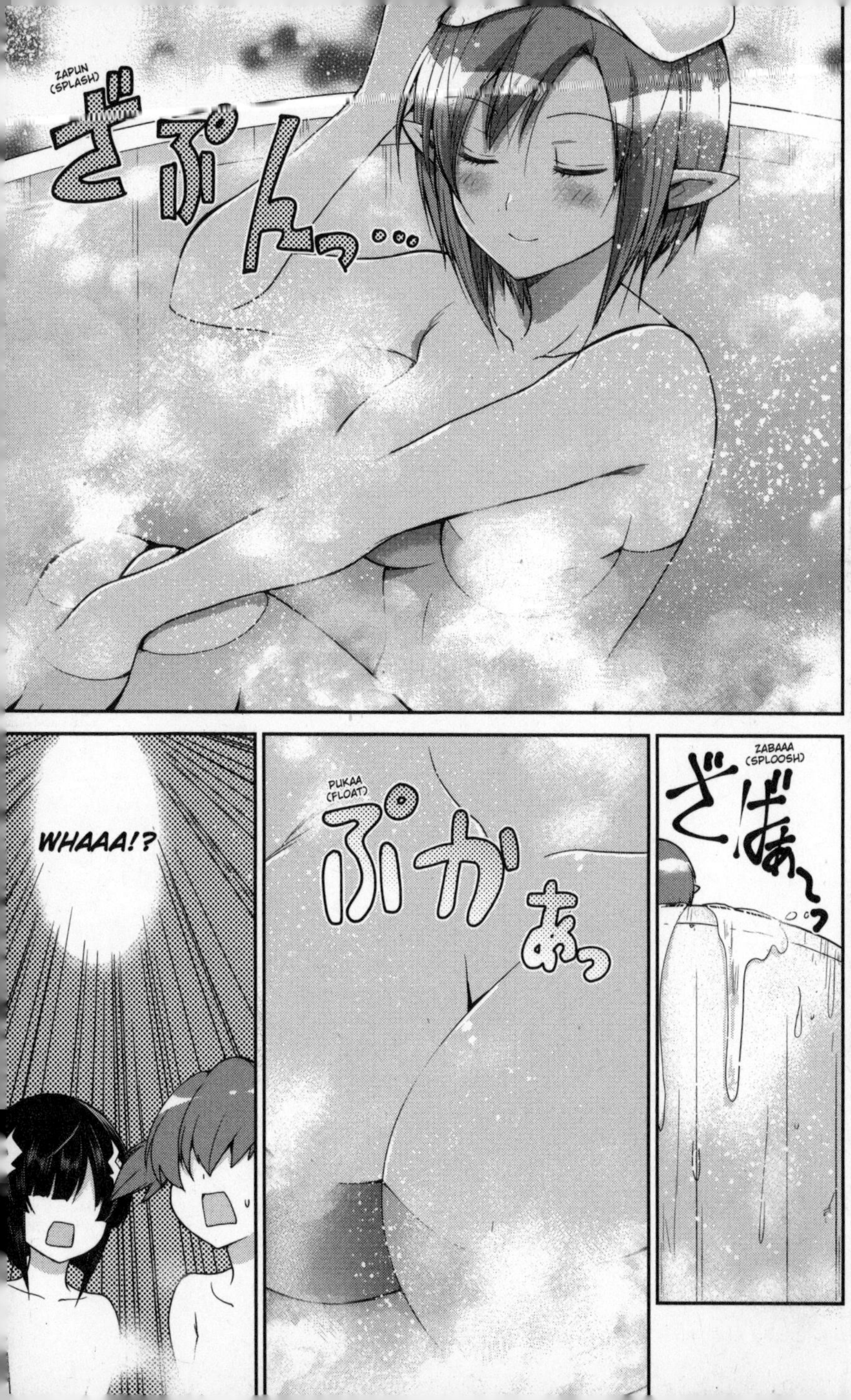
ZAPUN (SPLASH)
ざぷんっ…
ZABAAA (SPLOOSH)
ざばぁ～っ
PUKAA (FLOAT)
ぷかぁっ
WHAAA!?

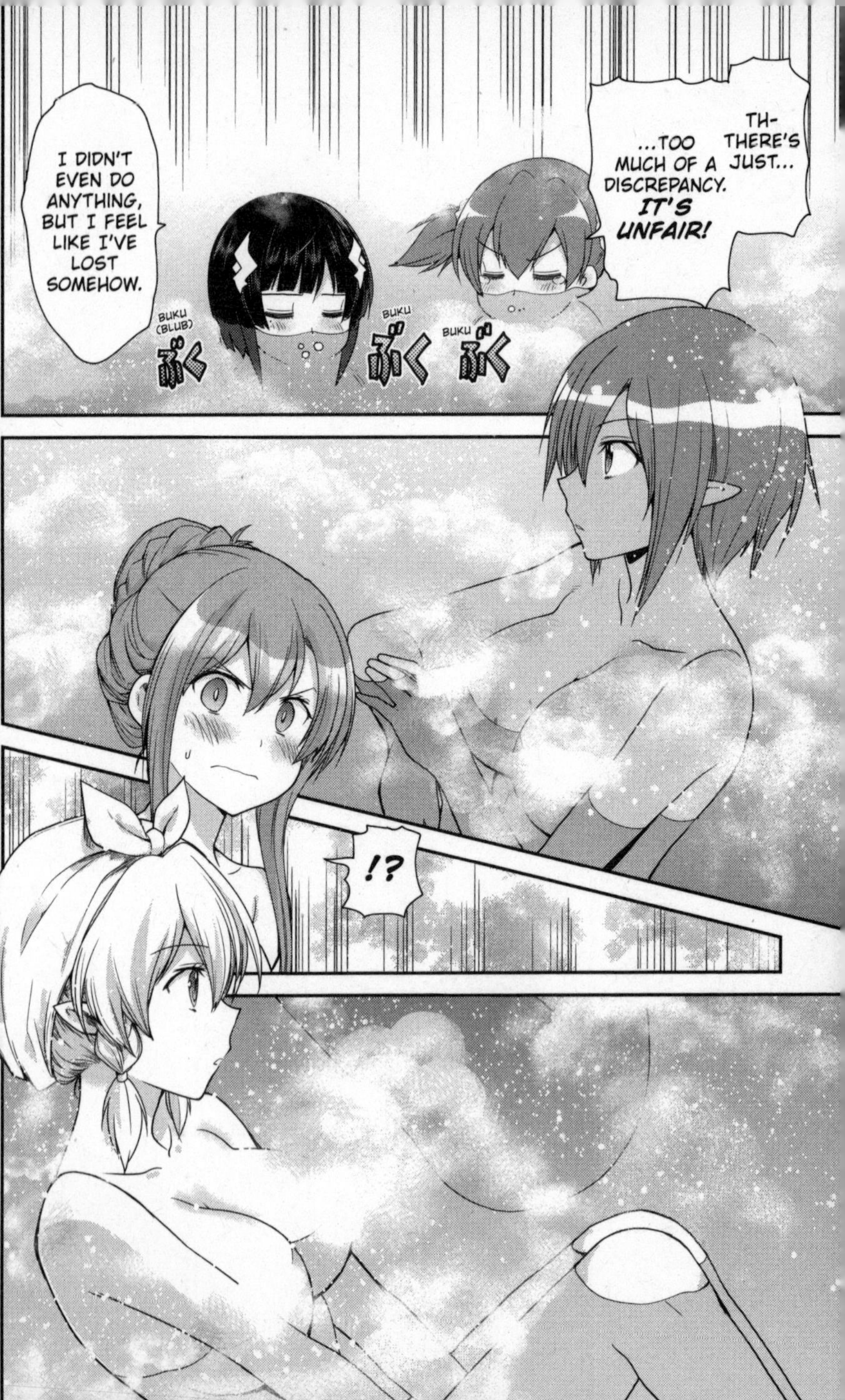
TH- THERE'S JUST... ...TOO MUCH OF A DISCREPANCY. IT'S UNFAIR!
BUKU ぶく
BUKU ぶく
BUKU (BLUB) ぶく
I DIDN'T EVEN DO ANYTHING, BUT I FEEL LIKE I'VE LOST SOMEHOW.
!?

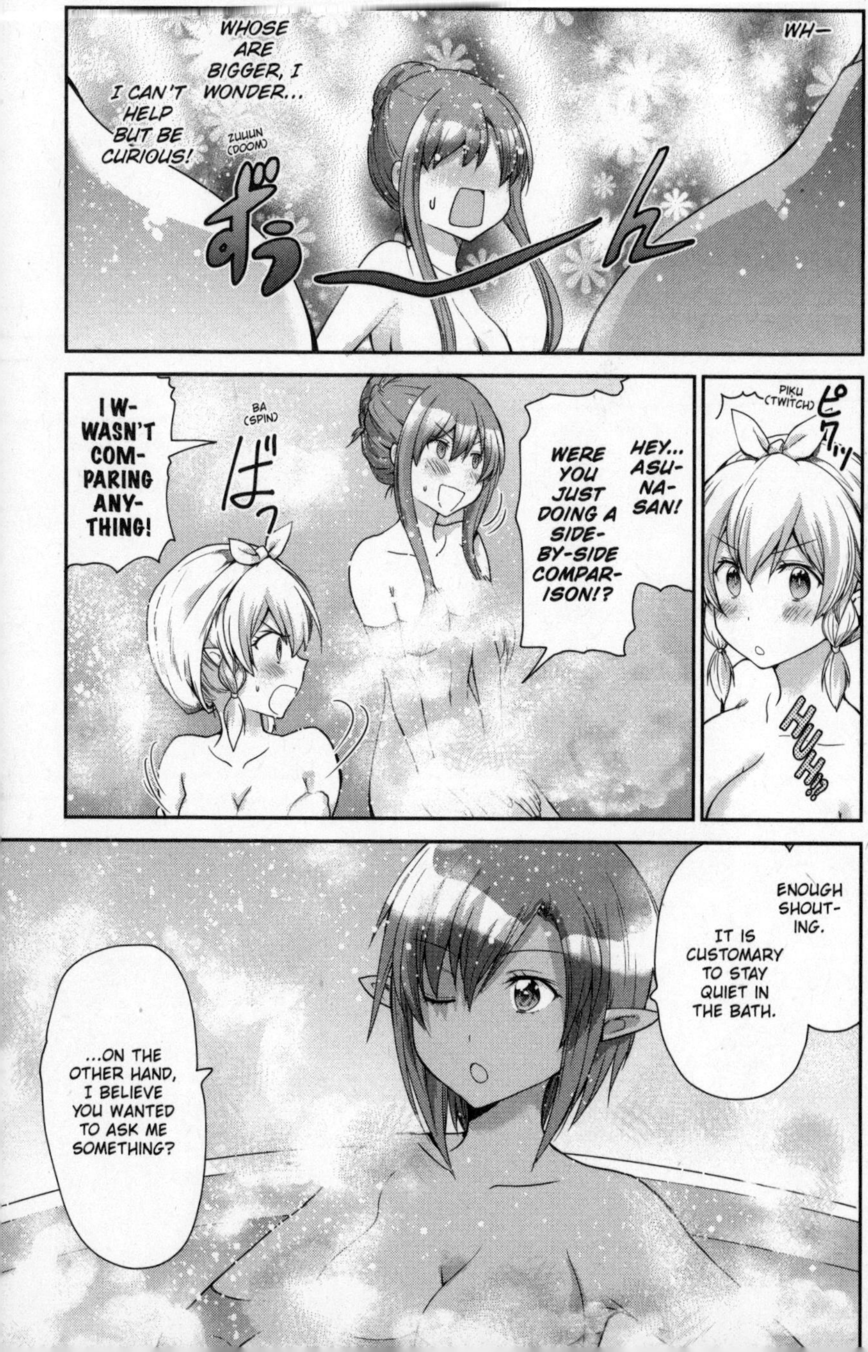
WH—
WHOSE ARE BIGGER, I WONDER...
I CAN'T HELP BUT BE CURIOUS!
ZUUUN (DOOM)
PIKU (TWITCH)
HUH!?
HEY... ASUNA-SAN!
WERE YOU JUST DOING A SIDE-BY-SIDE COMPARISON!?
BA (SPIN)
I W-WASN'T COMPARING ANYTHING!
ENOUGH SHOUTING.
IT IS CUSTOMARY TO STAY QUIET IN THE BATH.
...ON THE OTHER HAND, I BELIEVE YOU WANTED TO ASK ME SOMETHING?

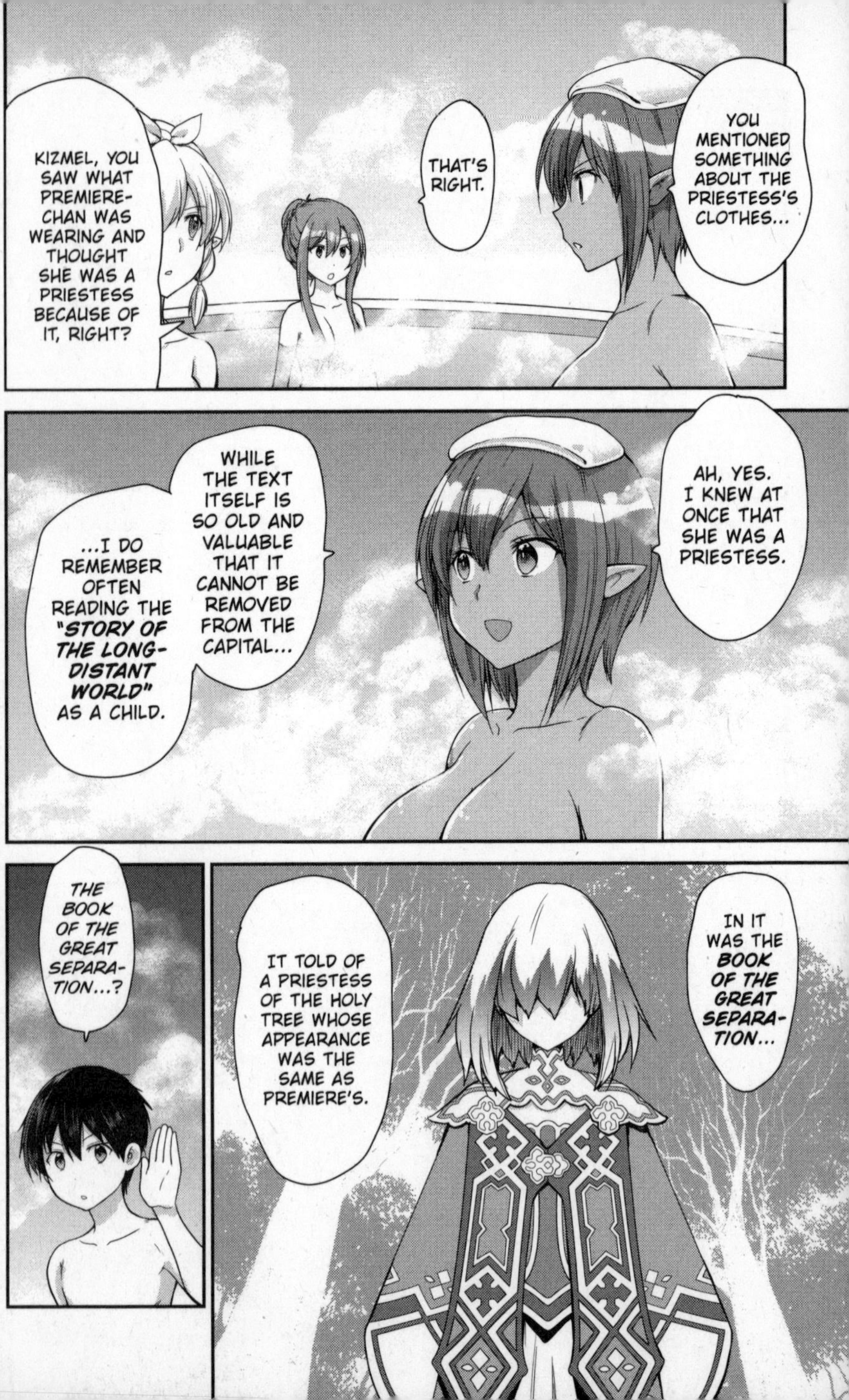
YOU MENTIONED SOMETHING ABOUT THE PRIESTESS'S CLOTHES...
THAT'S RIGHT.
KIZMEL, YOU SAW WHAT PREMIERE-CHAN WAS WEARING AND THOUGHT SHE WAS A PRIESTESS BECAUSE OF IT, RIGHT?
AH, YES. I KNEW AT ONCE THAT SHE WAS A PRIESTESS.
WHILE THE TEXT ITSELF IS SO OLD AND VALUABLE THAT IT CANNOT BE REMOVED FROM THE CAPITAL...
...I DO REMEMBER OFTEN READING THE *"STORY OF THE LONG-DISTANT WORLD"* AS A CHILD.
IN IT WAS THE *BOOK OF THE GREAT SEPARATION...*
IT TOLD OF A PRIESTESS OF THE HOLY TREE WHOSE APPEARANCE WAS THE SAME AS PREMIERE'S.
THE BOOK OF THE GREAT SEPARATION...?

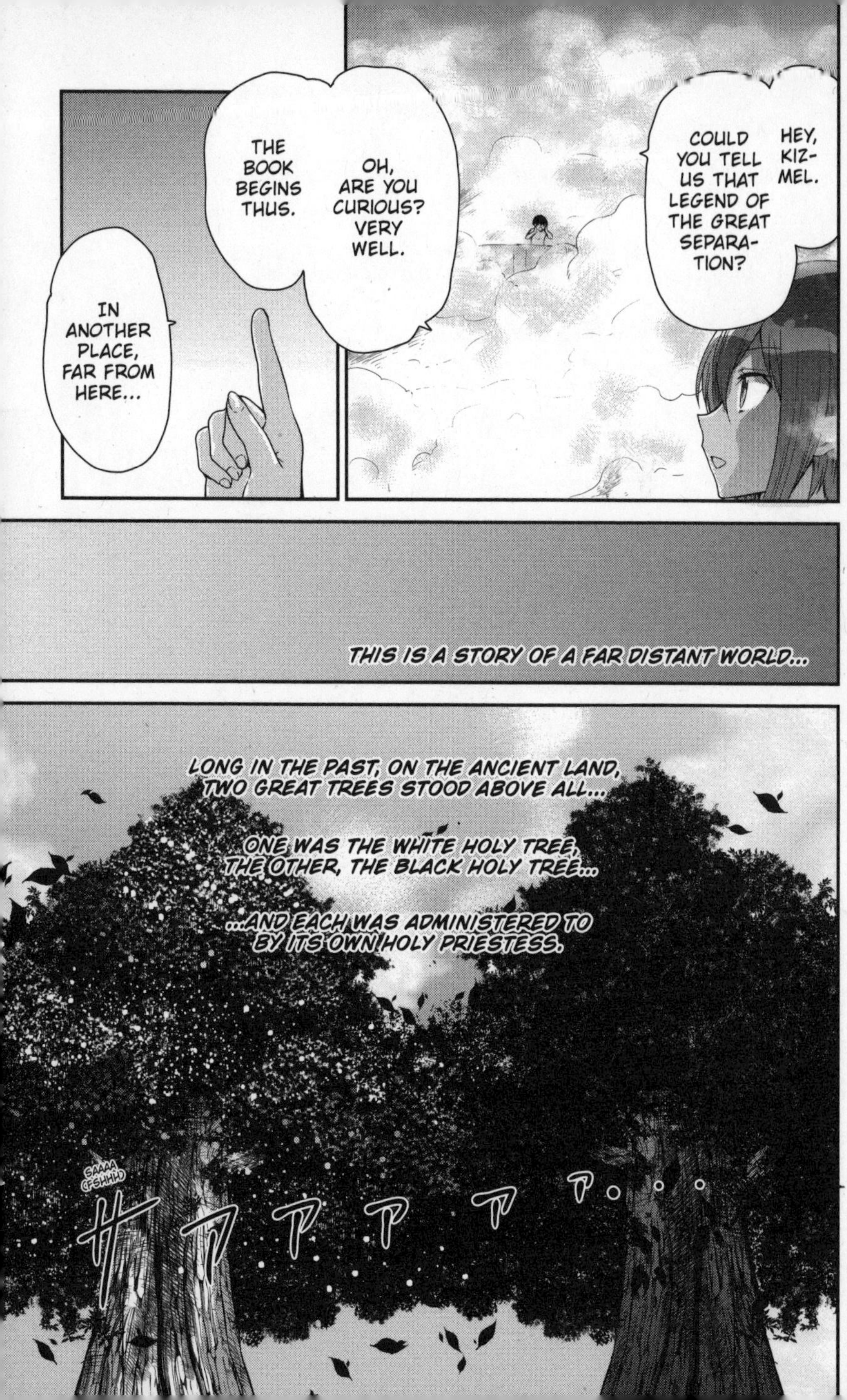
HEY, KIZ-MEL.
COULD YOU TELL US THAT LEGEND OF THE GREAT SEPARA-TION?
OH, ARE YOU CURIOUS? VERY WELL.
THE BOOK BEGINS THUS.
IN ANOTHER PLACE, FAR FROM HERE...
THIS IS A STORY OF A FAR DISTANT WORLD...
LONG IN THE PAST, ON THE ANCIENT LAND, TWO GREAT TREES STOOD ABOVE ALL...
ONE WAS THE WHITE HOLY TREE, THE OTHER, THE BLACK HOLY TREE...
...AND EACH WAS ADMINISTERED TO BY ITS OWN HOLY PRIESTESS.
SAAAA (FSHHH)
サァァァァ。。。

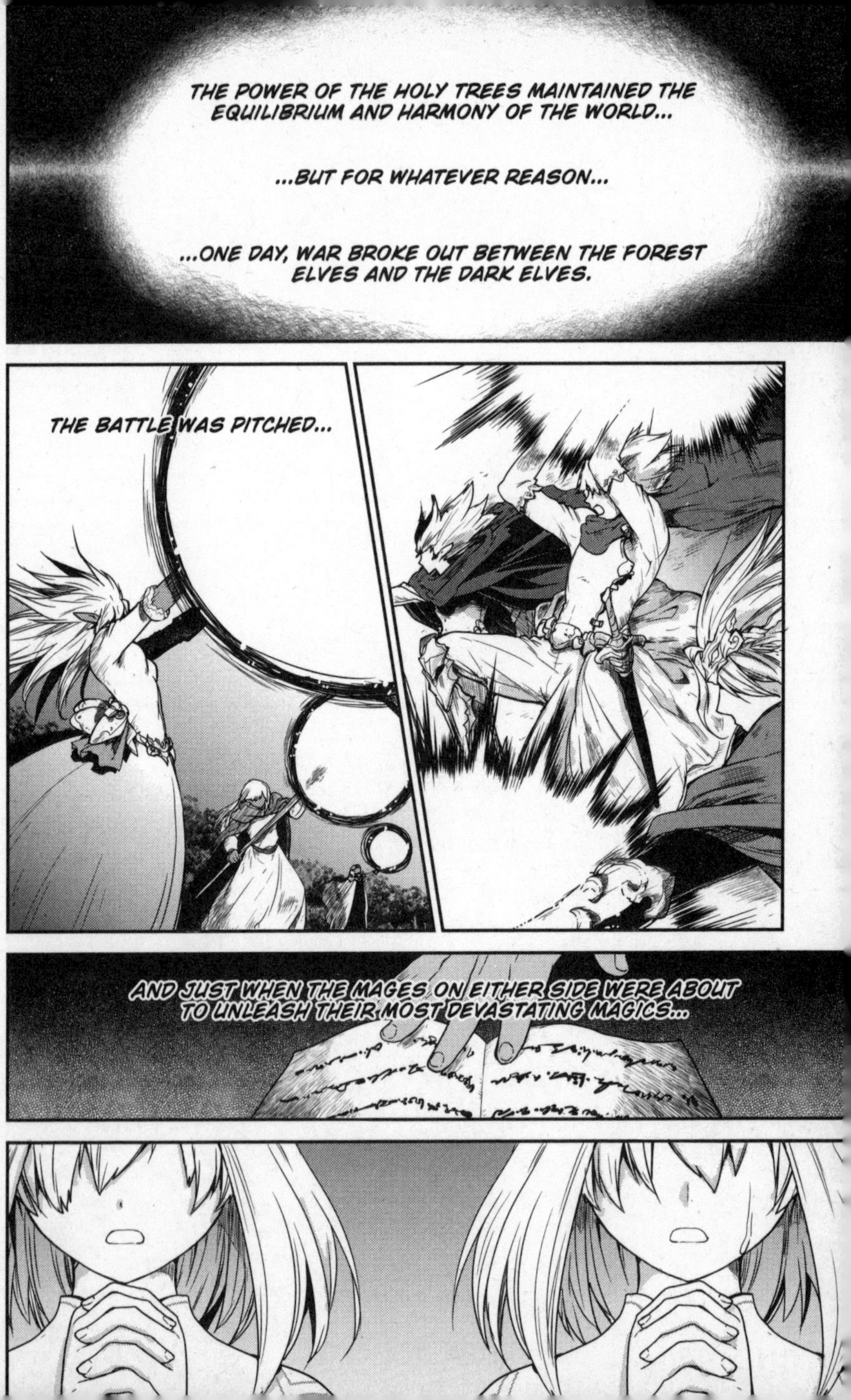
THE POWER OF THE HOLY TREES MAINTAINED THE EQUILIBRIUM AND HARMONY OF THE WORLD...
...BUT FOR WHATEVER REASON...
...ONE DAY, WAR BROKE OUT BETWEEN THE FOREST ELVES AND THE DARK ELVES.
THE BATTLE WAS PITCHED...
AND JUST WHEN THE MAGES ON EITHER SIDE WERE ABOUT TO UNLEASH THEIR MOST DEVASTATING MAGICS...

THE TWO PRIESTESSES PRAYED TO
THE HOLY TREES TO END THE FIGHTING...

THE HOLY TREES HEARD
THE PRIESTESSES' PRAYERS...

...AND THEY CARVED OUT THE BATTLEFIELDS...

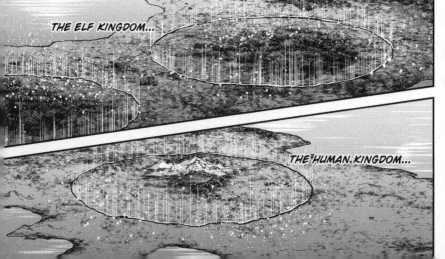

THE ELF KINGDOM...

THE HUMAN KINGDOM...

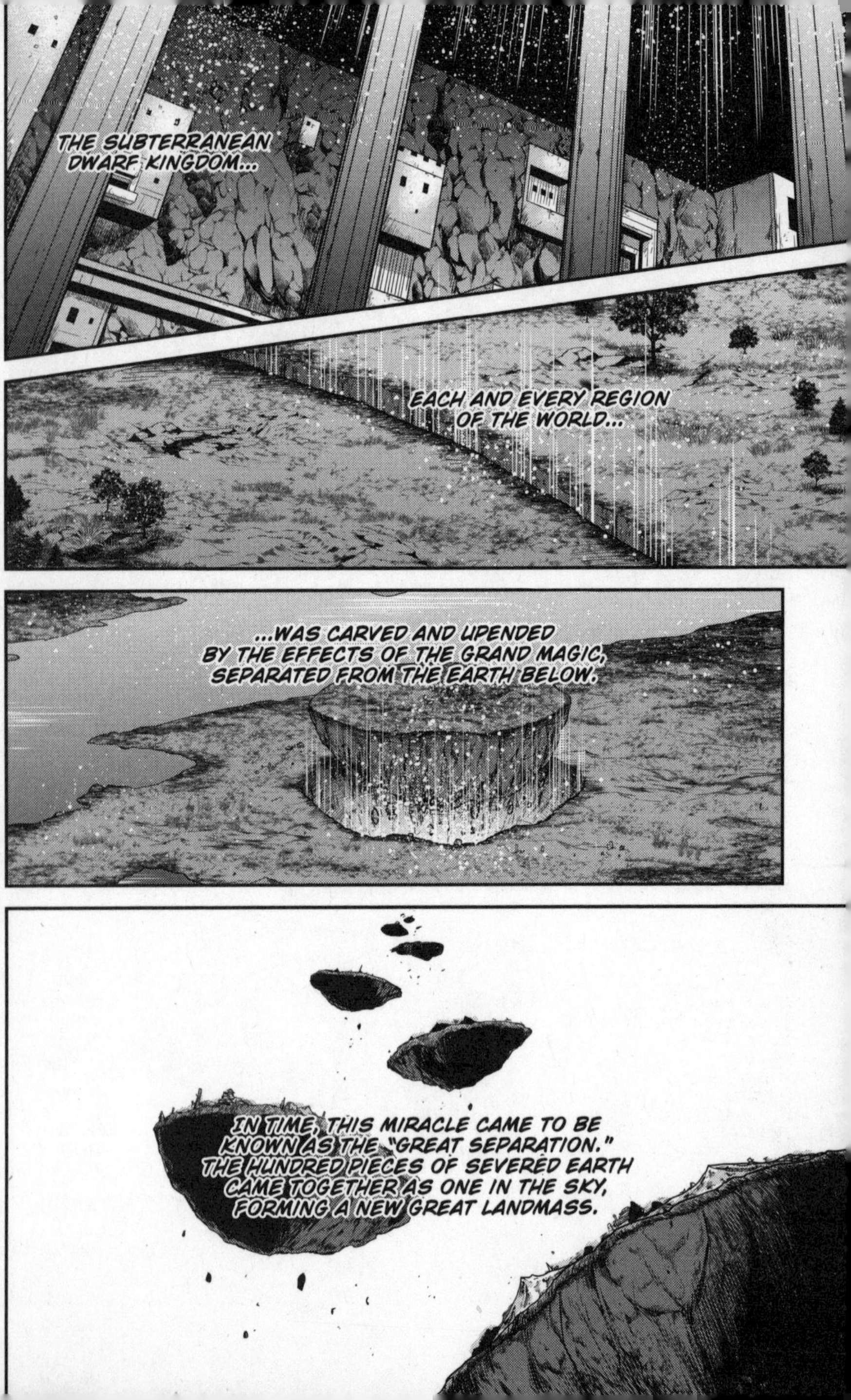
THE SUBTERRANEAN DWARF KINGDOM...
EACH AND EVERY REGION OF THE WORLD...
...WAS CARVED AND UPENDED BY THE EFFECTS OF THE GRAND MAGIC, SEPARATED FROM THE EARTH BELOW.
IN TIME, THIS MIRACLE CAME TO BE KNOWN AS THE "GREAT SEPARATION." THE HUNDRED PIECES OF SEVERED EARTH CAME TOGETHER AS ONE IN THE SKY, FORMING A NEW GREAT LANDMASS.

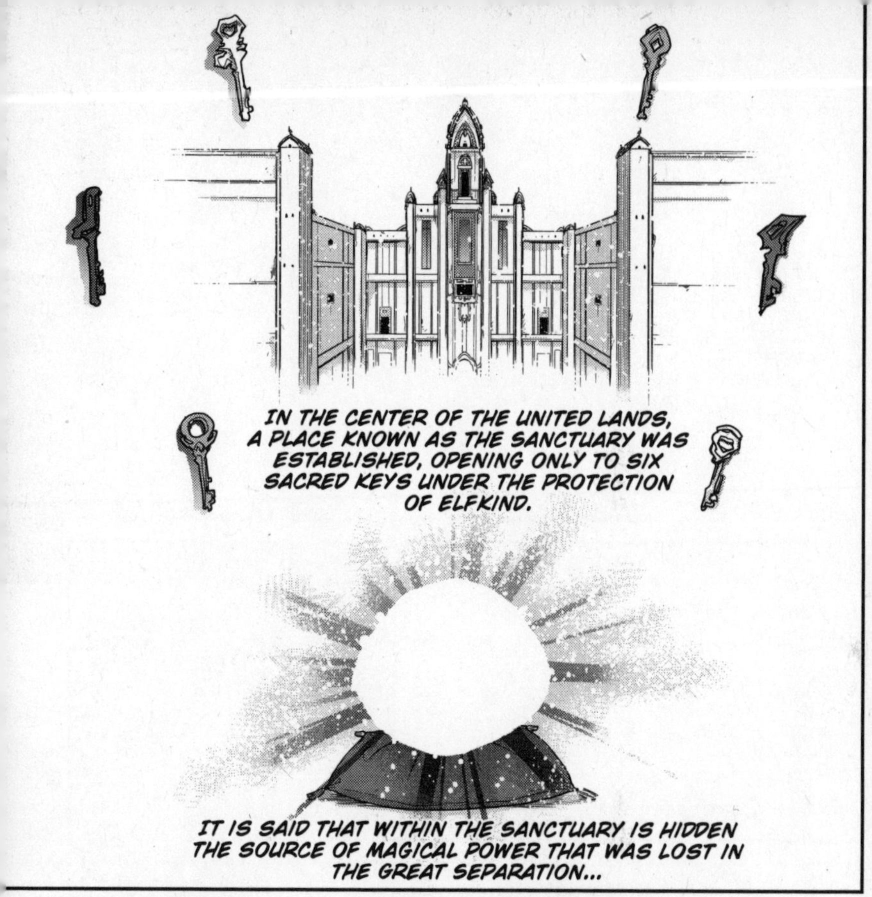
IN THE CENTER OF THE UNITED LANDS, A PLACE KNOWN AS THE SANCTUARY WAS ESTABLISHED, OPENING ONLY TO SIX SACRED KEYS UNDER THE PROTECTION OF ELFKIND.
IT IS SAID THAT WITHIN THE SANCTUARY IS HIDDEN THE SOURCE OF MAGICAL POWER THAT WAS LOST IN THE GREAT SEPARATION...
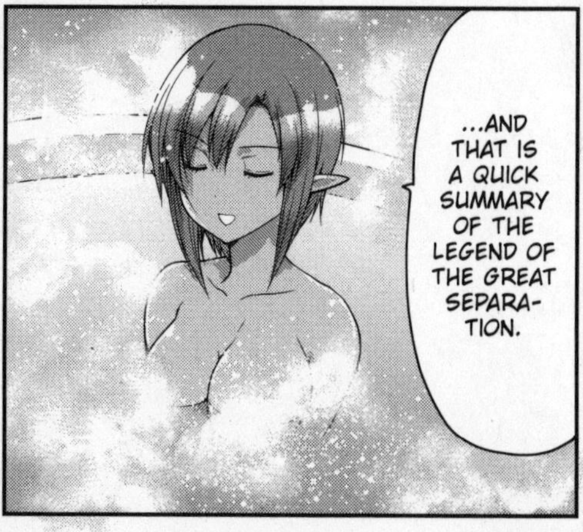
...AND THAT IS A QUICK SUMMARY OF THE LEGEND OF THE GREAT SEPARATION.
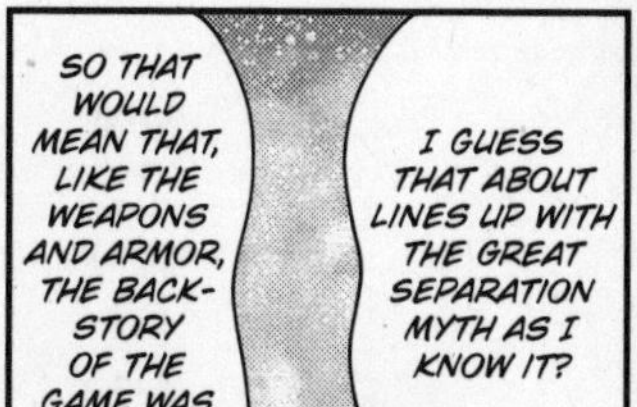
I GUESS THAT ABOUT LINES UP WITH THE GREAT SEPARATION MYTH AS I KNOW IT?
SO THAT WOULD MEAN THAT, LIKE THE WEAPONS AND ARMOR, THE BACKSTORY OF THE GAME WAS BROUGHT OVER DIRECTLY TO AINGROUND TOO.

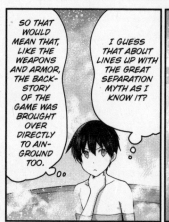

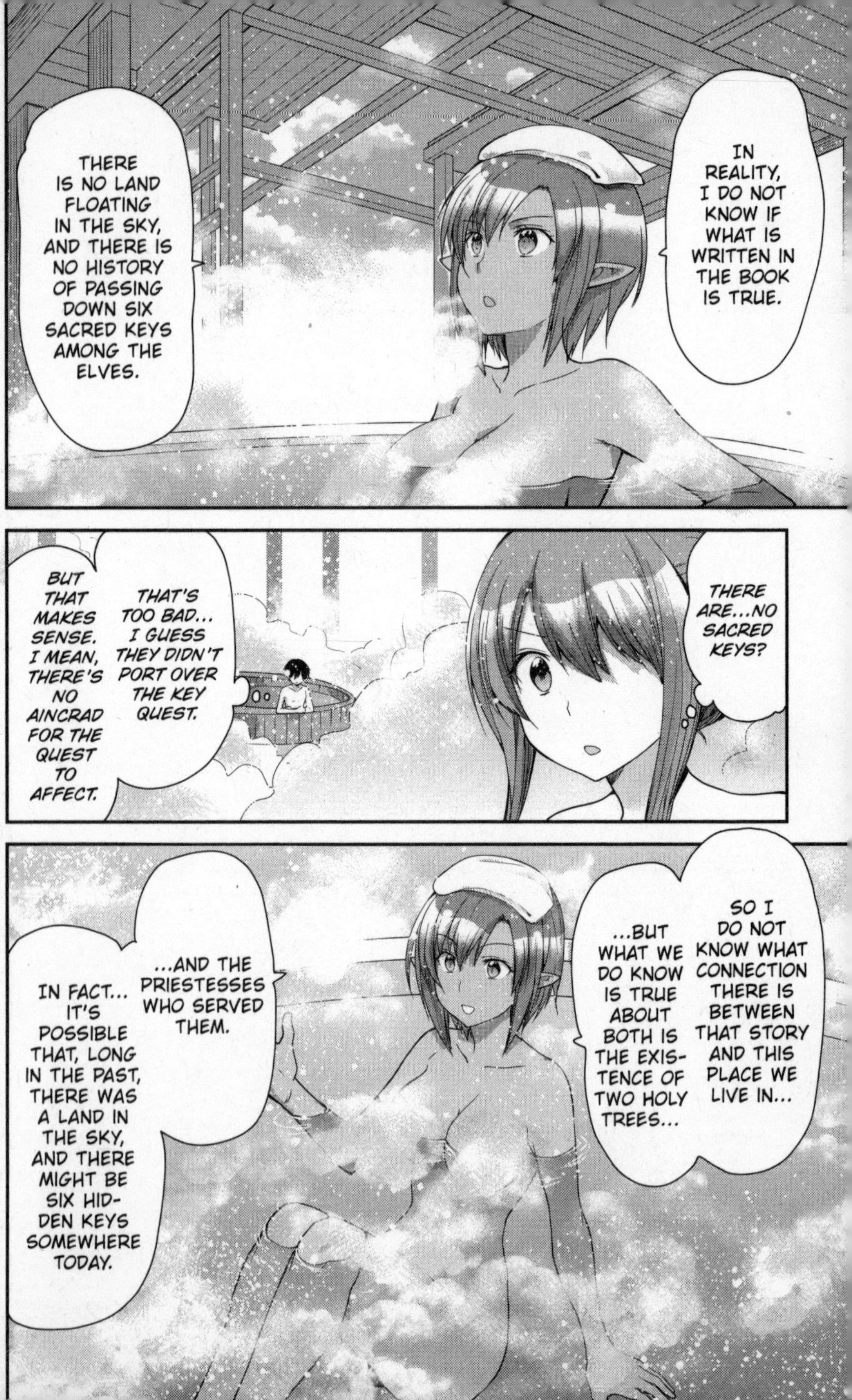
IN REALITY, I DO NOT KNOW IF WHAT IS WRITTEN IN THE BOOK IS TRUE.
THERE IS NO LAND FLOATING IN THE SKY, AND THERE IS NO HISTORY OF PASSING DOWN SIX SACRED KEYS AMONG THE ELVES.
THERE ARE...NO SACRED KEYS?
THAT'S TOO BAD... I GUESS THEY DIDN'T PORT OVER THE KEY QUEST.
BUT THAT MAKES SENSE. I MEAN, THERE'S NO AINCRAD FOR THE QUEST TO AFFECT.
SO I DO NOT KNOW WHAT CONNECTION THERE IS BETWEEN THAT STORY AND THIS PLACE WE LIVE IN...
...BUT WHAT WE DO KNOW IS TRUE ABOUT BOTH IS THE EXIS-TENCE OF TWO HOLY TREES...
...AND THE PRIESTESSES WHO SERVED THEM.
IN FACT... IT'S POSSIBLE THAT, LONG IN THE PAST, THERE WAS A LAND IN THE SKY, AND THERE MIGHT BE SIX HID-DEN KEYS SOMEWHERE TODAY.

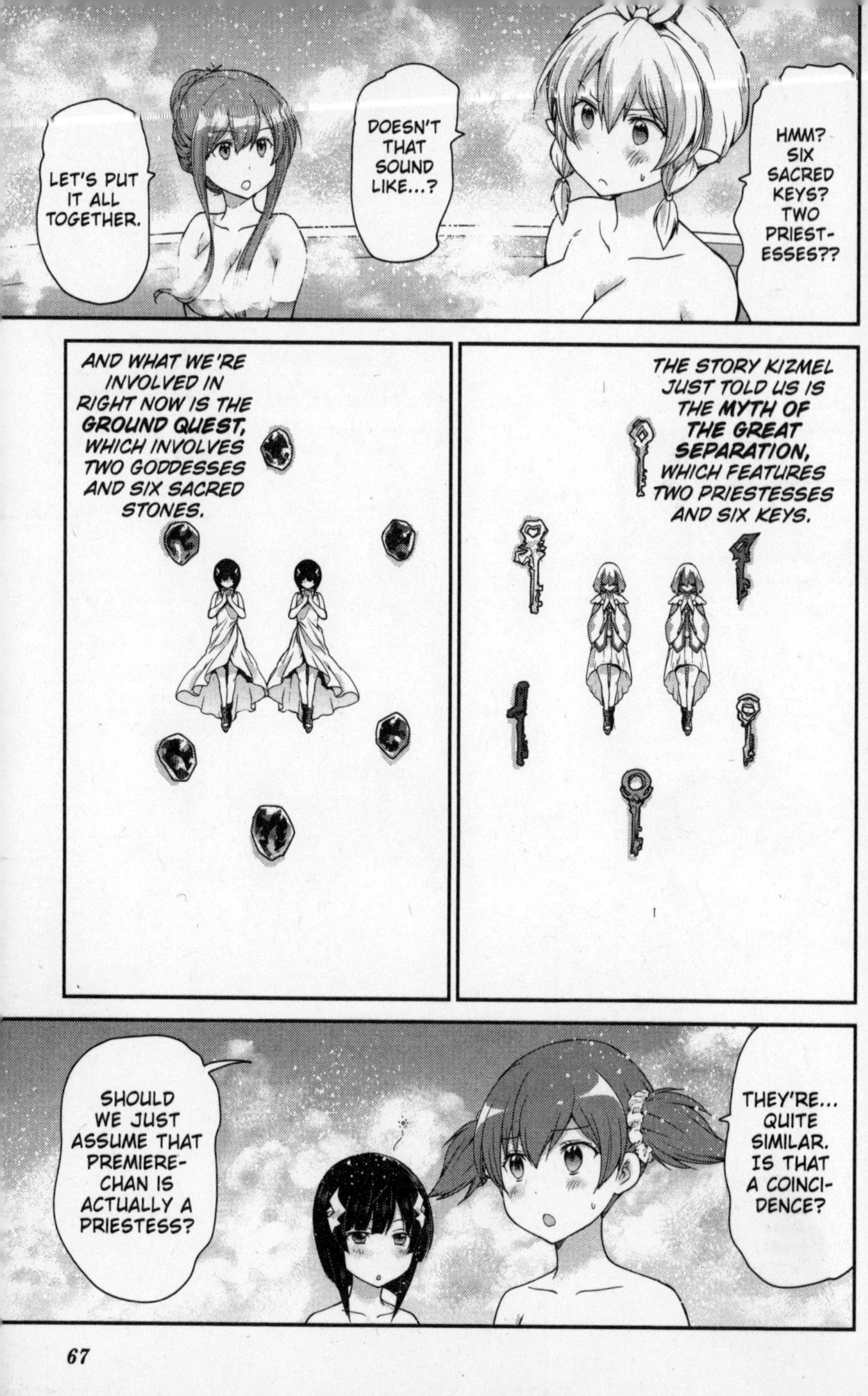
HMM? SIX SACRED KEYS? TWO PRIEST-ESSES??
DOESN'T THAT SOUND LIKE...?
LET'S PUT IT ALL TOGETHER.
THE STORY KIZMEL JUST TOLD US IS THE MYTH OF THE GREAT SEPARATION, WHICH FEATURES TWO PRIESTESSES AND SIX KEYS.
AND WHAT WE'RE INVOLVED IN RIGHT NOW IS THE GROUND QUEST, WHICH INVOLVES TWO GODDESSES AND SIX SACRED STONES.
THEY'RE... QUITE SIMILAR. IS THAT A COINCIDENCE?
SHOULD WE JUST ASSUME THAT PREMIERE-CHAN IS ACTUALLY A PRIESTESS?

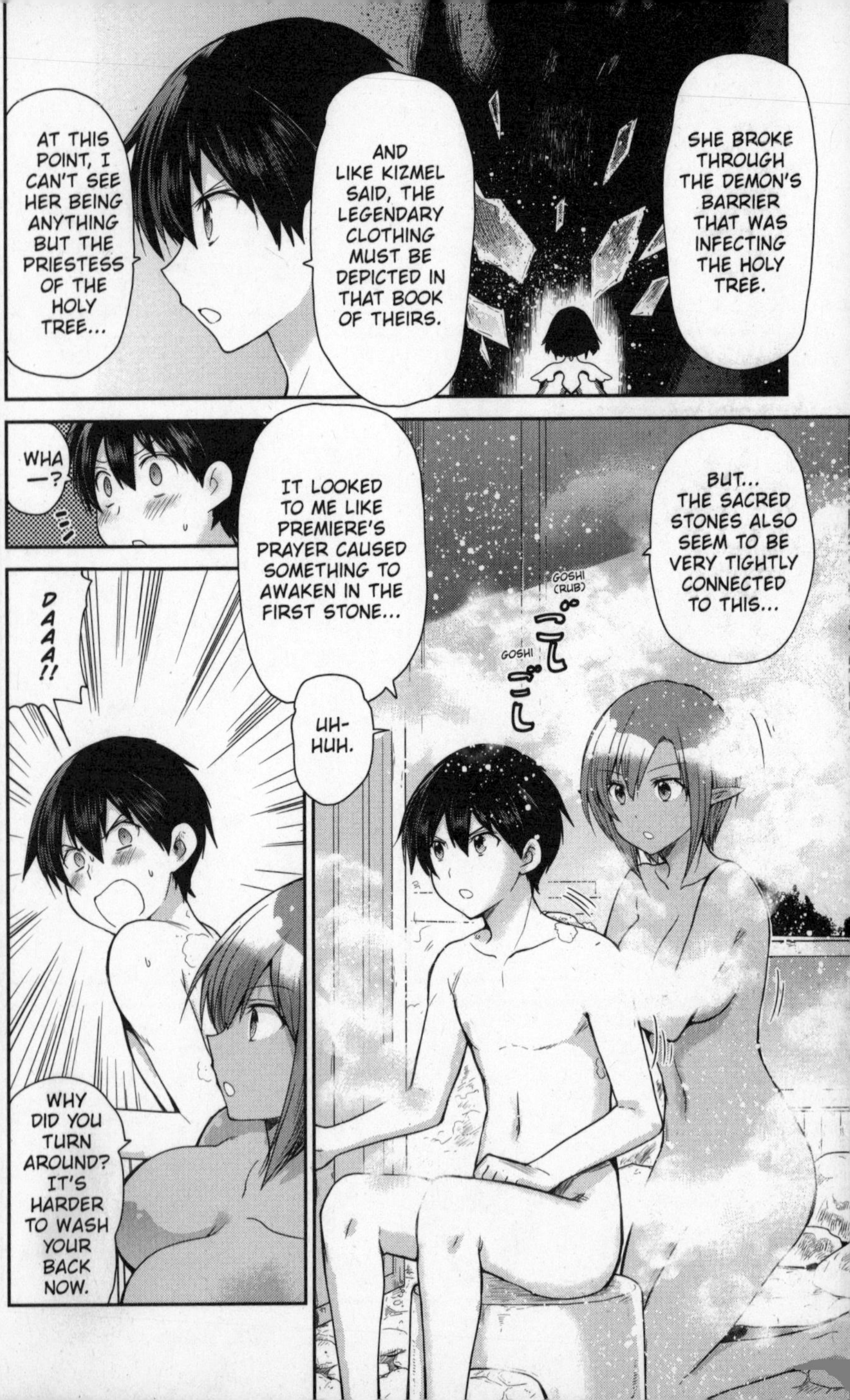
SHE BROKE THROUGH THE DEMON'S BARRIER THAT WAS INFECTING THE HOLY TREE.
AND LIKE KIZMEL SAID, THE LEGENDARY CLOTHING MUST BE DEPICTED IN THAT BOOK OF THEIRS.
AT THIS POINT, I CAN'T SEE HER BEING ANYTHING BUT THE PRIESTESS OF THE HOLY TREE...
BUT... THE SACRED STONES ALSO SEEM TO BE VERY TIGHTLY CONNECTED TO THIS...
ごし
GOSHI (RUB)
ごし
GOSHI
IT LOOKED TO ME LIKE PREMIERE'S PRAYER CAUSED SOMETHING TO AWAKEN IN THE FIRST STONE...
UH-HUH.
WHA—?
DAAAA!!
WHY DID YOU TURN AROUND? IT'S HARDER TO WASH YOUR BACK NOW.

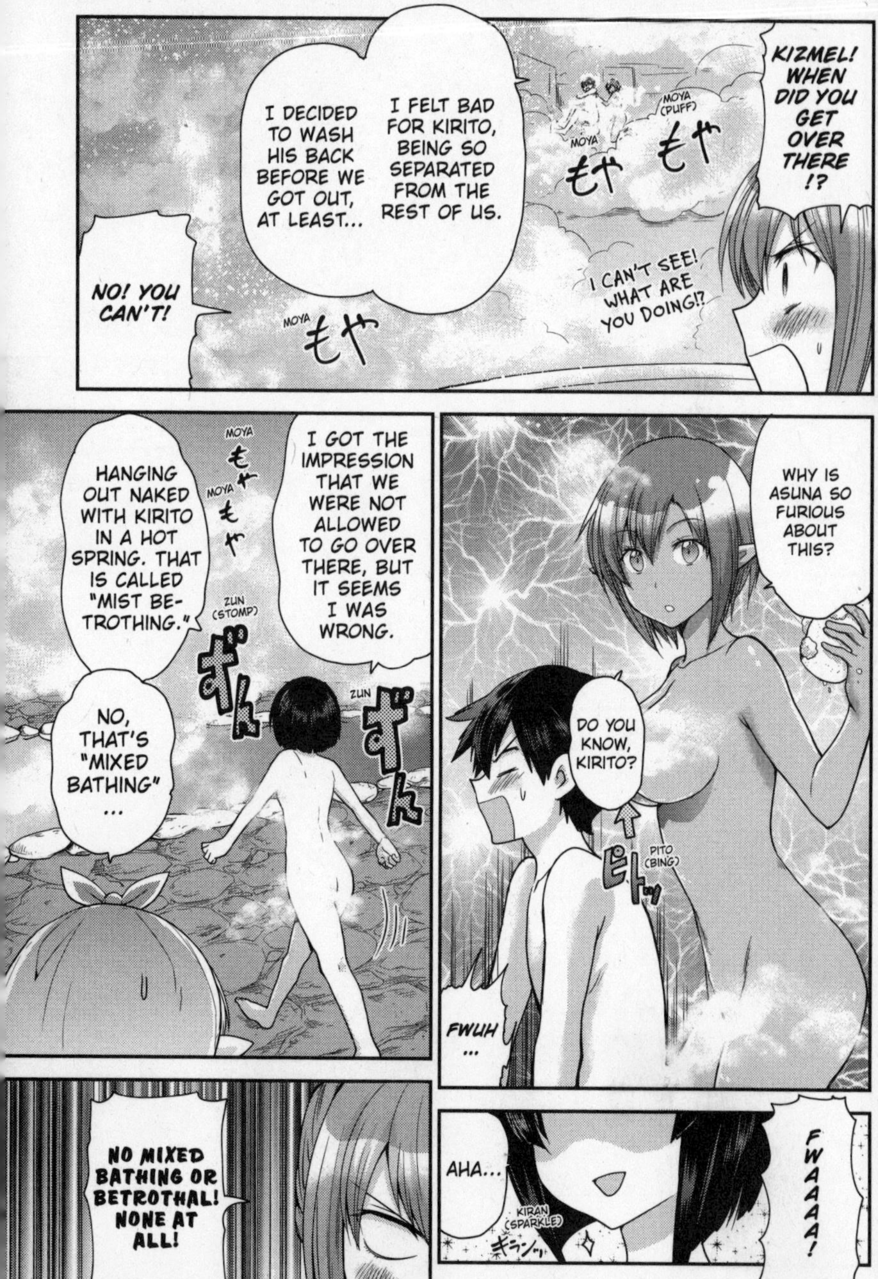

KIZMEL! WHEN DID YOU GET OVER THERE!?
MOYA (PUFF)
もや
MOYA
もや
I CAN'T SEE! WHAT ARE YOU DOING!?
I FELT BAD FOR KIRITO, BEING SO SEPARATED FROM THE REST OF US.
I DECIDED TO WASH HIS BACK BEFORE WE GOT OUT, AT LEAST...
MOYA
もや
NO! YOU CAN'T!
WHY IS ASUNA SO FURIOUS ABOUT THIS?
DO YOU KNOW, KIRITO?
PITO (BING)
FWUH ...
I GOT THE IMPRESSION THAT WE WERE NOT ALLOWED TO GO OVER THERE, BUT IT SEEMS I WAS WRONG.
MOYA
もや
MOYA
もや
HANGING OUT NAKED WITH KIRITO IN A HOT SPRING. THAT IS CALLED "MIST BE-TROTHING."
ZUN
ずん
ZUN (STOMP)
ずん
NO, THAT'S "MIXED BATHING" ...
FWAAAAA!
AHA...
KIRAN (SPARKLE)
NO MIXED BATHING OR BETROTHAL! NONE AT ALL!

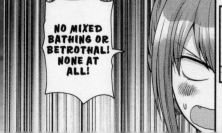

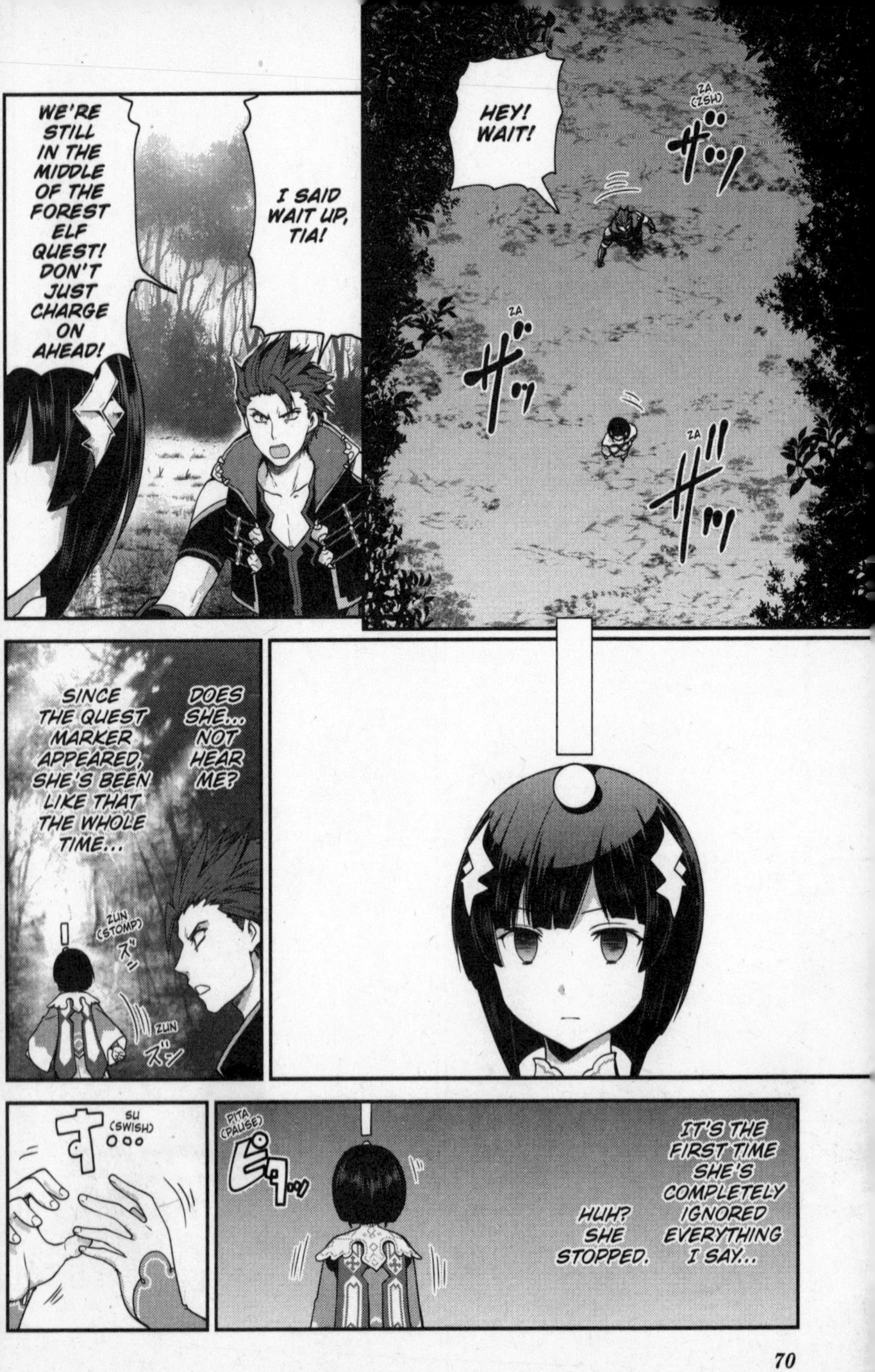
HEY! WAIT!
ZA (ZSH)
ZA
ZA
I SAID WAIT UP, TIA!
WE'RE STILL IN THE MIDDLE OF THE FOREST ELF QUEST! DON'T JUST CHARGE ON AHEAD!
DOES SHE... NOT HEAR ME?
SINCE THE QUEST MARKER APPEARED, SHE'S BEEN LIKE THAT THE WHOLE TIME...
ZUN (STOMP)
ZUN
IT'S THE FIRST TIME SHE'S COMPLETELY IGNORED EVERYTHING I SAY...
HUH? SHE STOPPED.
PITA (PAUSE)
SU (SWISH)

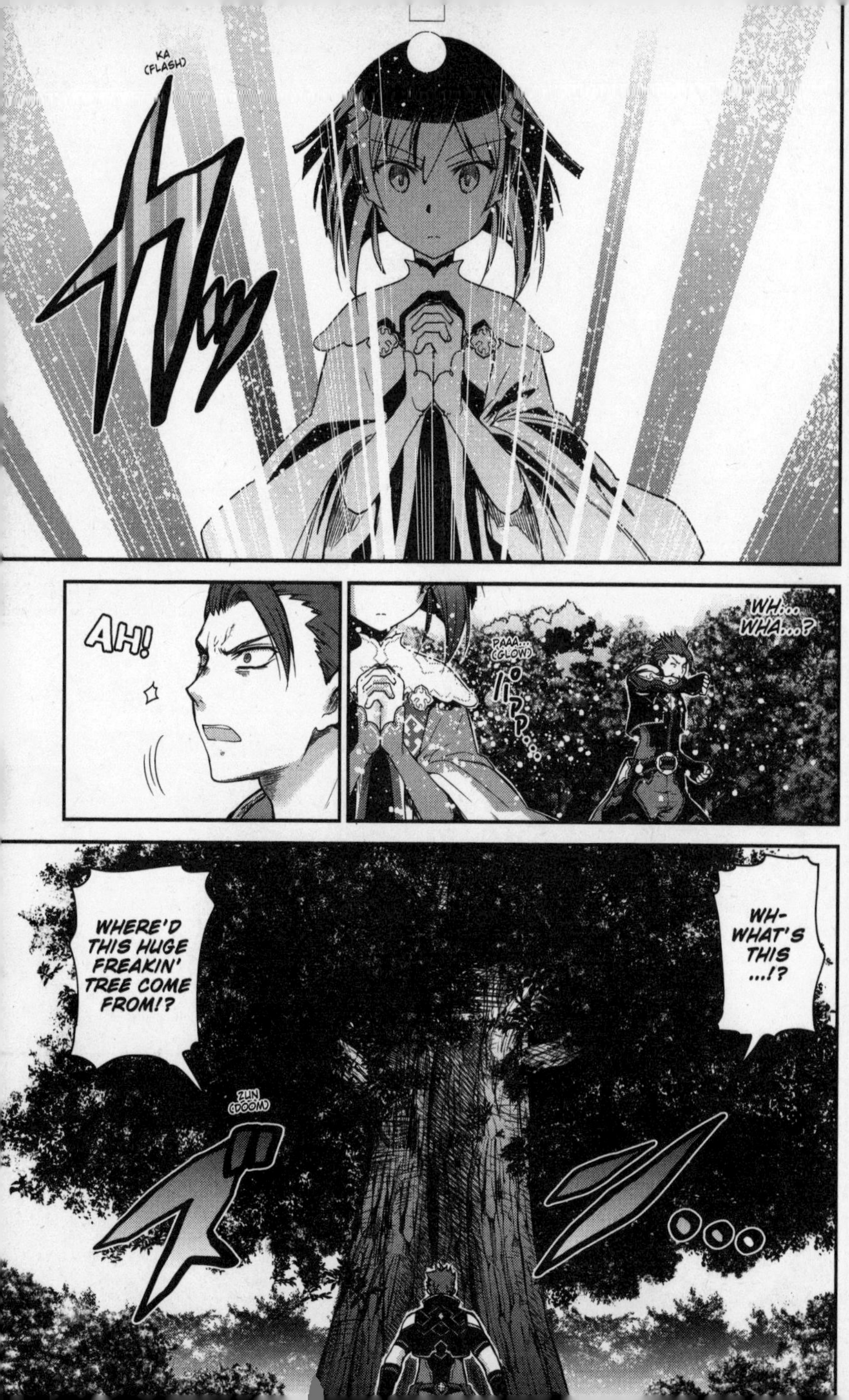
KA (FLASH)
WH... WHA...?
PAAA... (GLOW)
AH!
WH- WHAT'S THIS ...!?
WHERE'D THIS HUGE FREAKIN' TREE COME FROM!?
ZUN (DOOM)
...

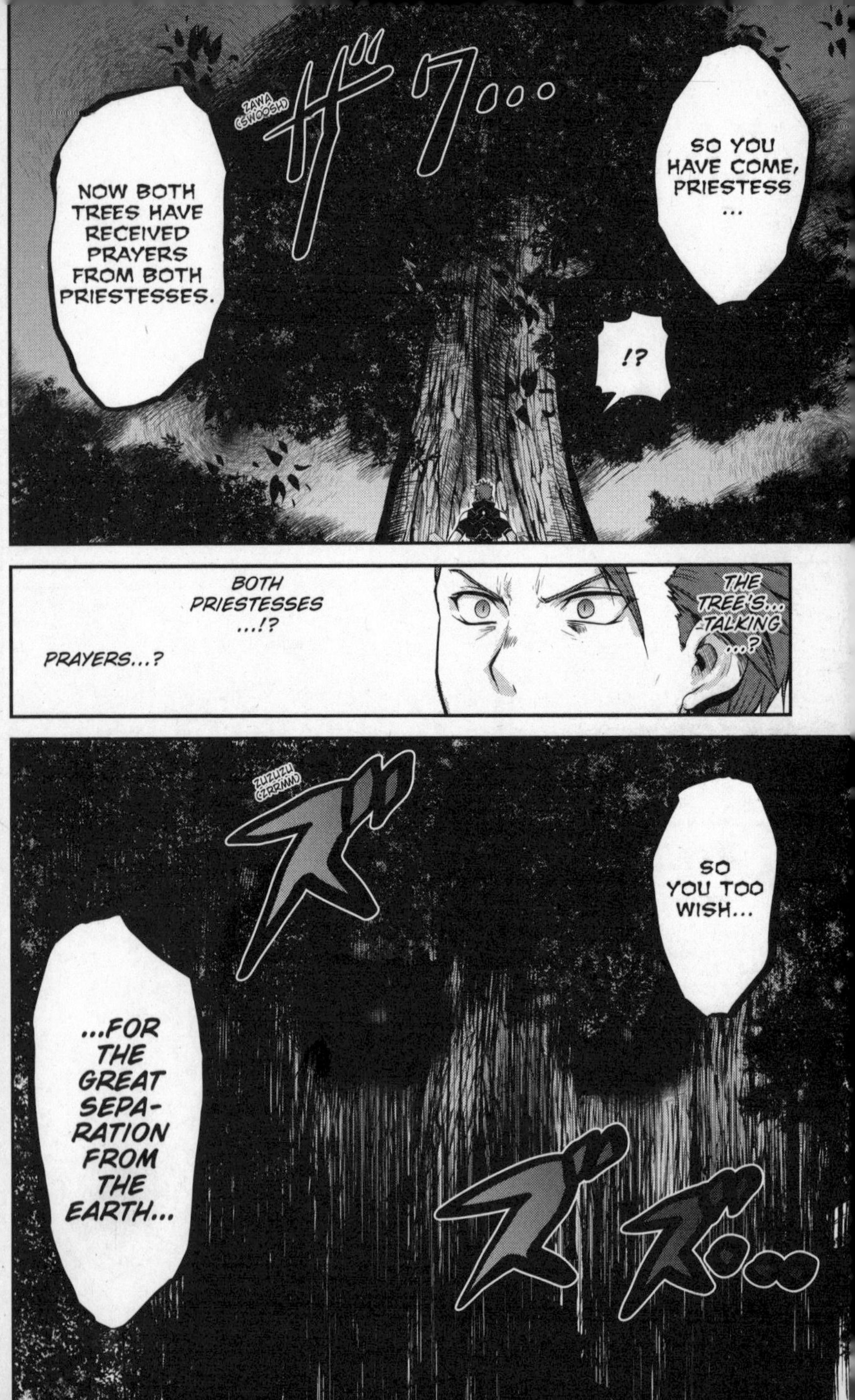
SO YOU HAVE COME, PRIESTESS ...
ZAWA (SWOOSH)
!?
NOW BOTH TREES HAVE RECEIVED PRAYERS FROM BOTH PRIESTESSES.
THE TREE'S... TALKING ...?
BOTH PRIESTESSES ...!?
PRAYERS...?
ZUZUZU (ZRRMM)
SO YOU TOO WISH...
...FOR THE GREAT SEPA-RATION FROM THE EARTH...

#18: Path to the Console

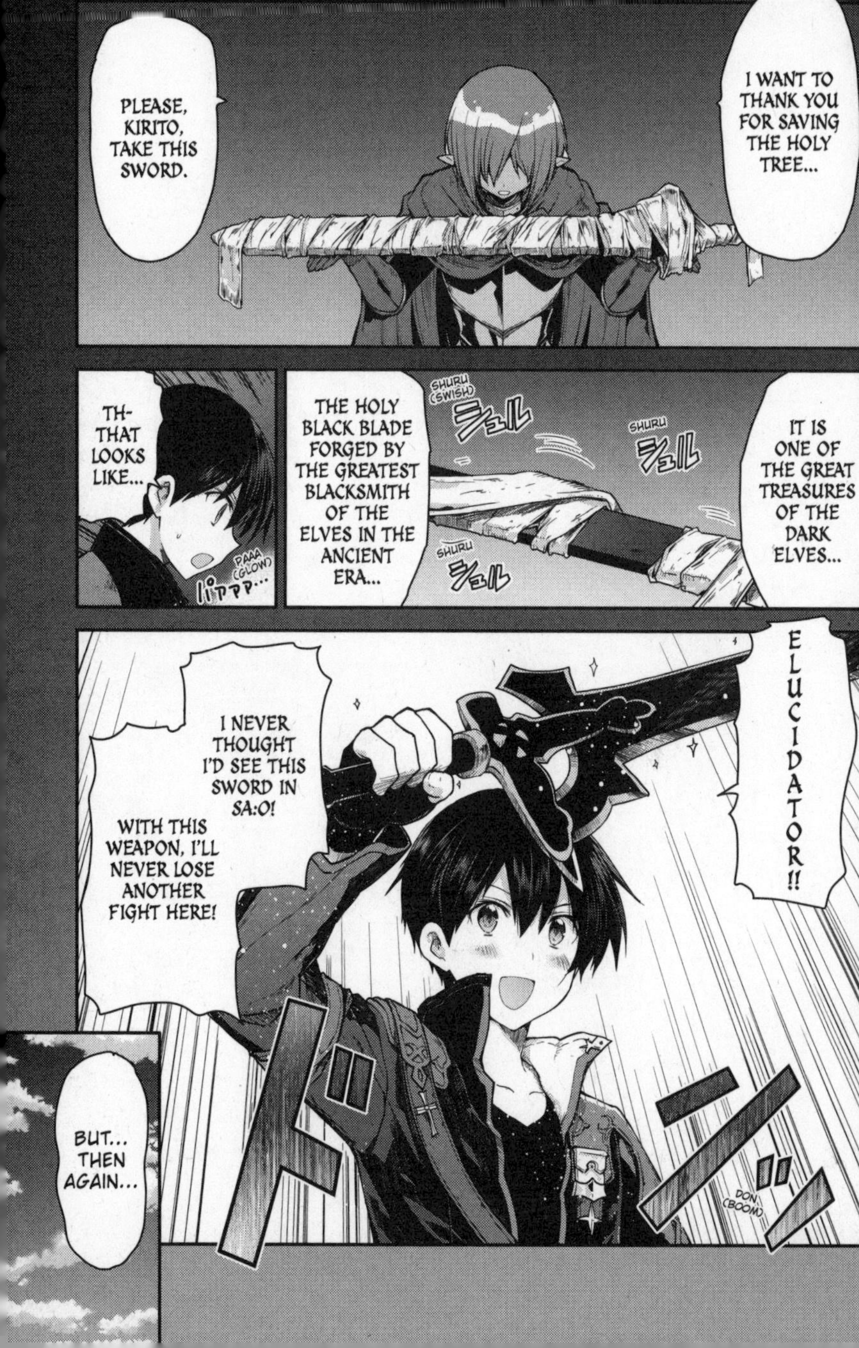
I WANT TO THANK YOU FOR SAVING THE HOLY TREE...
PLEASE, KIRITO, TAKE THIS SWORD.
IT IS ONE OF THE GREAT TREASURES OF THE DARK ELVES...
SHURU (SWISH) シュル
SHURU シュル
SHURU シュル
THE HOLY BLACK BLADE FORGED BY THE GREATEST BLACKSMITH OF THE ELVES IN THE ANCIENT ERA...
TH- THAT LOOKS LIKE...
PAAA (GLOW) パァァァ...
ELUCIDATOR!!
I NEVER THOUGHT I'D SEE THIS SWORD IN SA:O!
WITH THIS WEAPON, I'LL NEVER LOSE ANOTHER FIGHT HERE!
DON (BOOM)
BUT... THEN AGAIN...

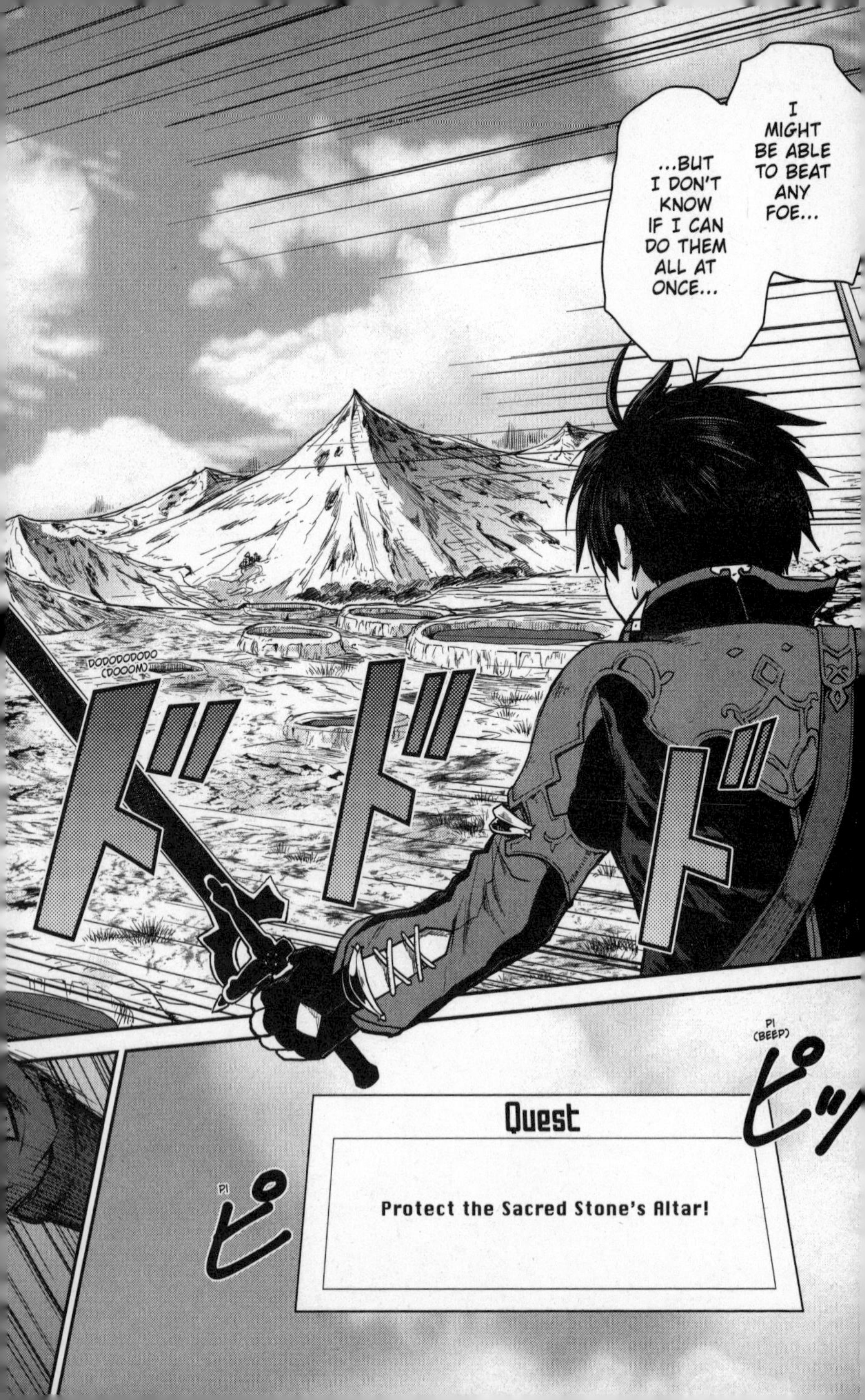
I MIGHT BE ABLE TO BEAT ANY FOE...
...BUT I DON'T KNOW IF I CAN DO THEM ALL AT ONCE...
DODODODODO (DOOOM)
ドドド
ピッ
PI (BEEP)
Quest
Protect the Sacred Stone's Altar!
ピ
PI

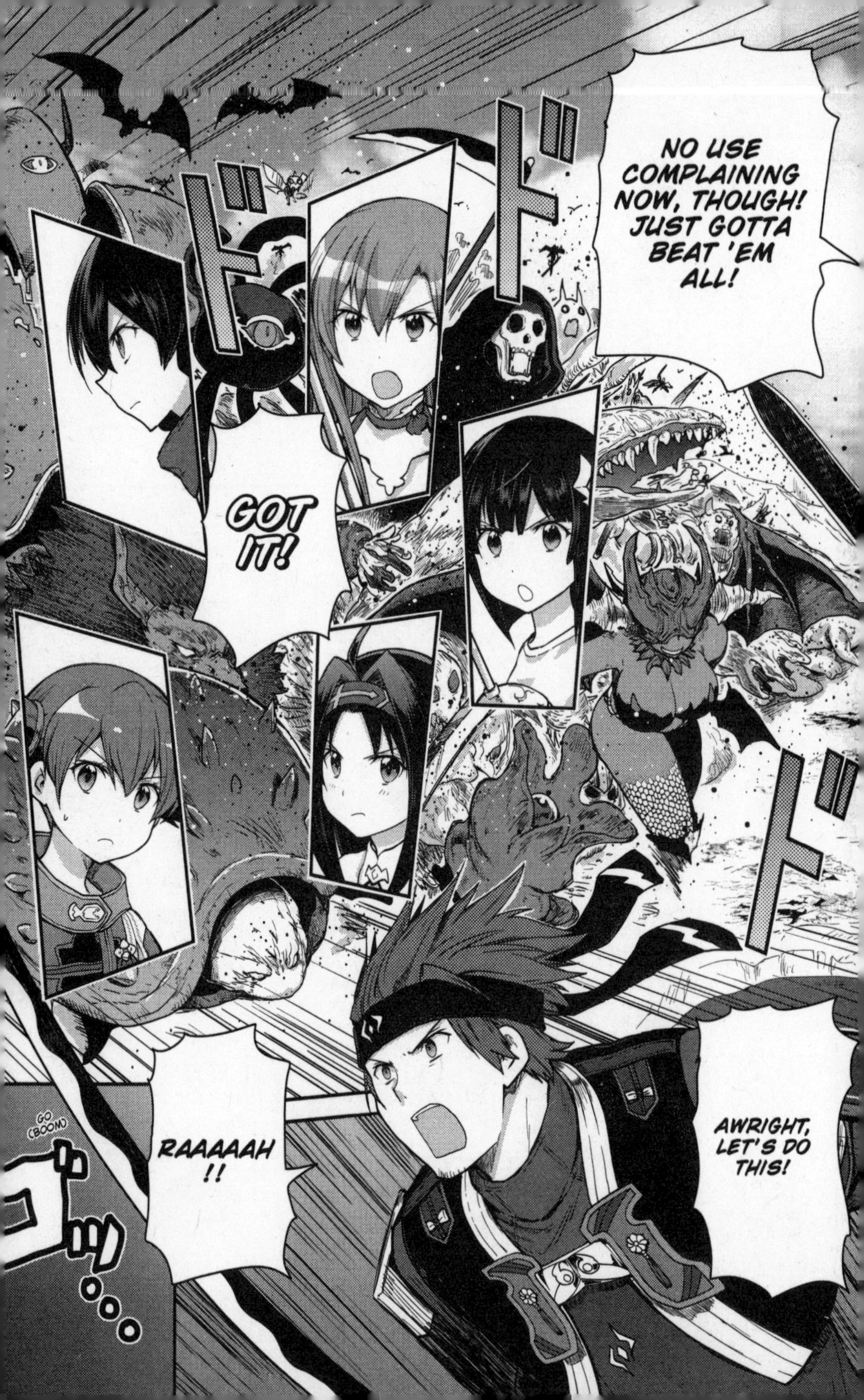
NO USE COMPLAINING NOW, THOUGH! JUST GOTTA BEAT 'EM ALL!
GOT IT!
AWRIGHT, LET'S DO THIS!
RAAAAAH!!
GO (BOOM)

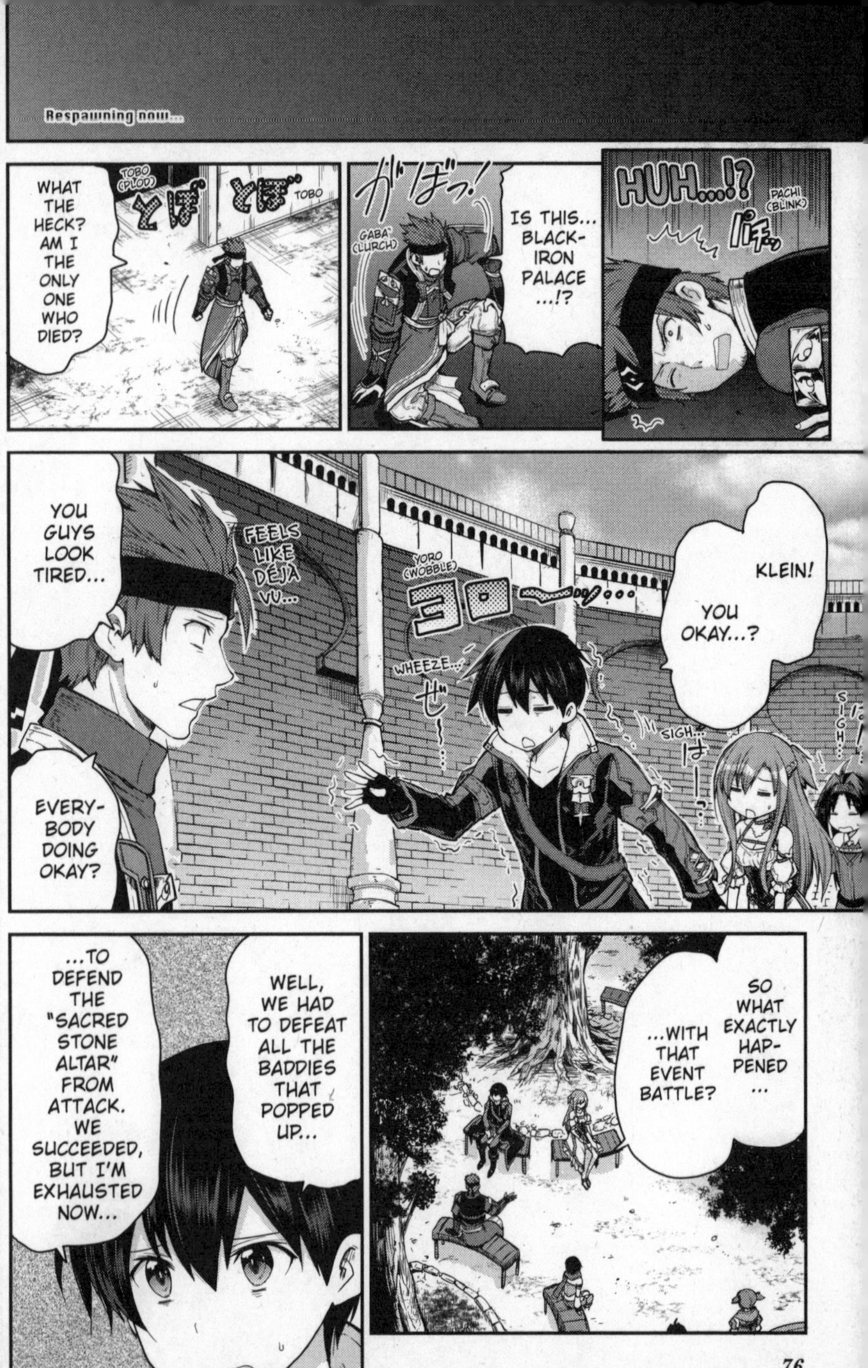
Respawning now...
HUH...!?
PACHI (BLINK)
IS THIS... BLACK-IRON PALACE ...!?
GABA (LURCH)
TOBO (PLOD)
TOBO
WHAT THE HECK? AM I THE ONLY ONE WHO DIED?
KLEIN!
YOU OKAY...?
SIGH...
SIGH...
WHEEZE...
YORO (WOBBLE)
FEELS LIKE DÉJÀ VU...
YOU GUYS LOOK TIRED...
EVERY-BODY DOING OKAY?
SO WHAT EXACTLY HAP-PENED...
...WITH THAT EVENT BATTLE?
WELL, WE HAD TO DEFEAT ALL THE BADDIES THAT POPPED UP...
...TO DEFEND THE "SACRED STONE ALTAR" FROM ATTACK. WE SUCCEEDED, BUT I'M EXHAUSTED NOW...

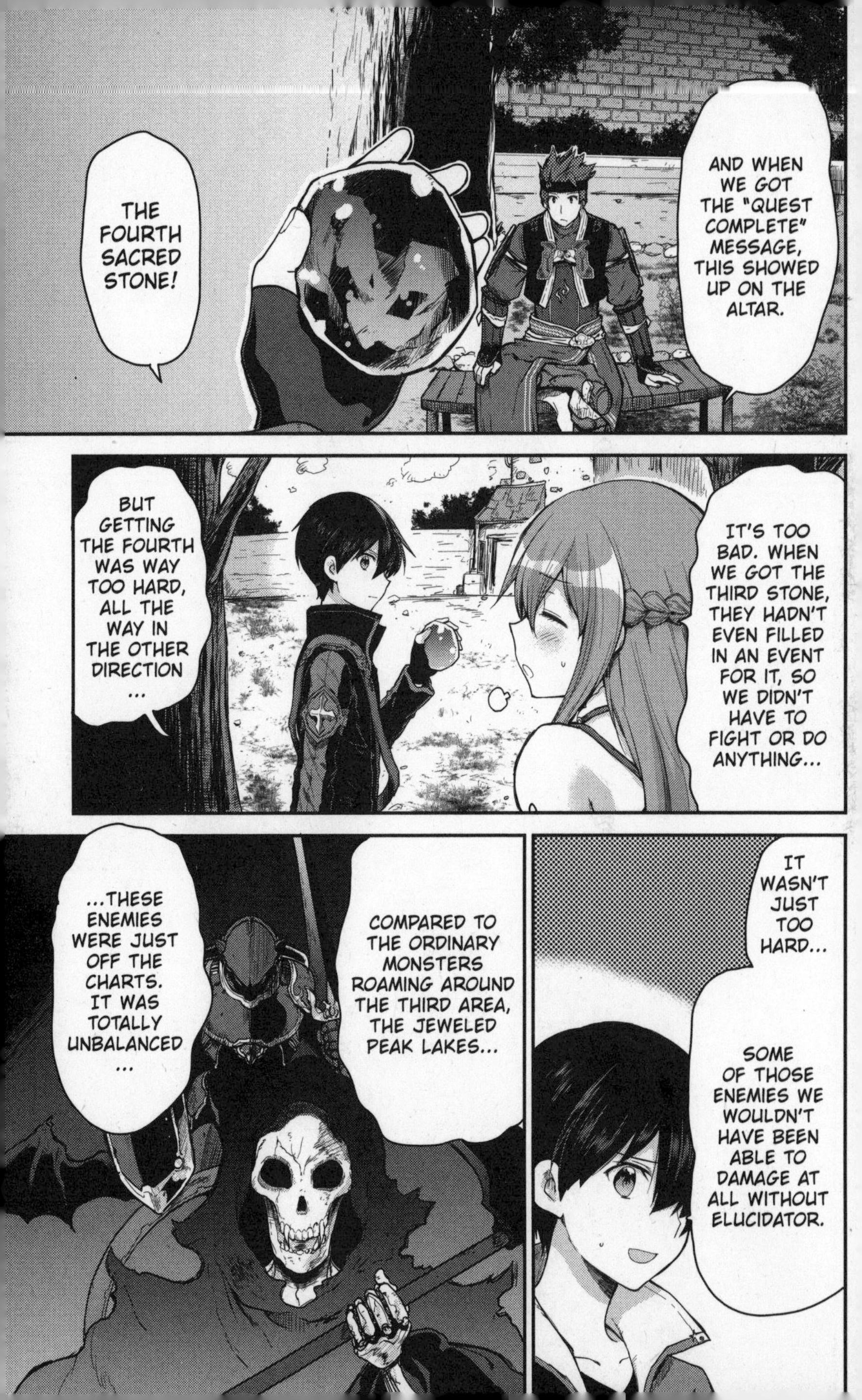
AND WHEN WE GOT THE "QUEST COMPLETE" MESSAGE, THIS SHOWED UP ON THE ALTAR.
THE FOURTH SACRED STONE!
IT'S TOO BAD. WHEN WE GOT THE THIRD STONE, THEY HADN'T EVEN FILLED IN AN EVENT FOR IT, SO WE DIDN'T HAVE TO FIGHT OR DO ANYTHING...
BUT GETTING THE FOURTH WAS WAY TOO HARD, ALL THE WAY IN THE OTHER DIRECTION ...
IT WASN'T JUST TOO HARD...
SOME OF THOSE ENEMIES WE WOULDN'T HAVE BEEN ABLE TO DAMAGE AT ALL WITHOUT ELUCIDATOR.
COMPARED TO THE ORDINARY MONSTERS ROAMING AROUND THE THIRD AREA, THE JEWELED PEAK LAKES...
...THESE ENEMIES WERE JUST OFF THE CHARTS. IT WAS TOTALLY UNBALANCED ...

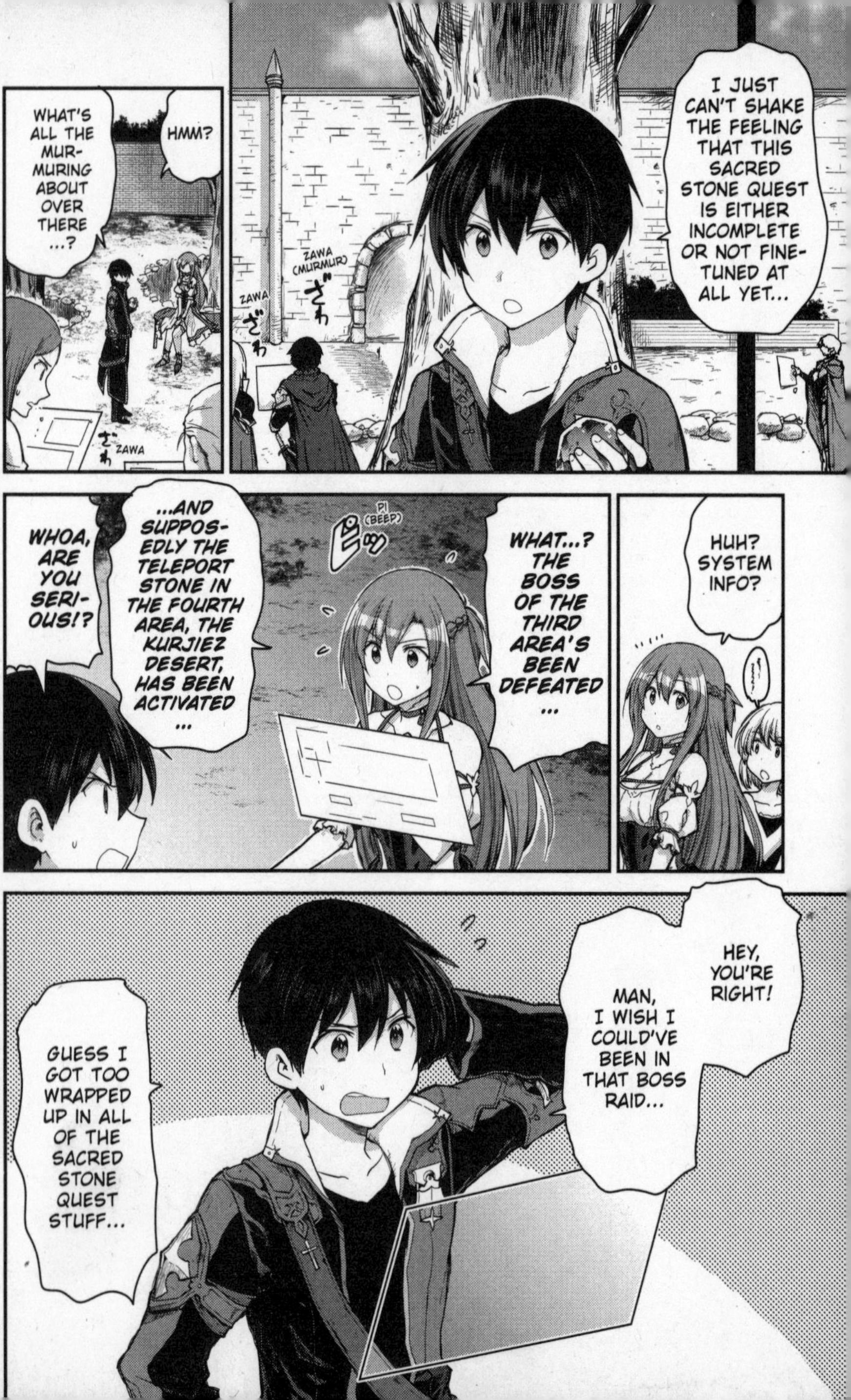
I JUST CAN'T SHAKE THE FEELING THAT THIS SACRED STONE QUEST IS EITHER INCOMPLETE OR NOT FINE-TUNED AT ALL YET...
ZAWA (MURMUR)
ZAWA
HMM?
WHAT'S ALL THE MURMURING ABOUT OVER THERE ...?
ZAWA
HUH? SYSTEM INFO?
WHAT...? THE BOSS OF THE THIRD AREA'S BEEN DEFEATED ...
PI (BEEP)
...AND SUPPOSEDLY THE TELEPORT STONE IN THE FOURTH AREA, THE KURJIEZ DESERT, HAS BEEN ACTIVATED ...
WHOA, ARE YOU SERIOUS!?
HEY, YOU'RE RIGHT!
MAN, I WISH I COULD'VE BEEN IN THAT BOSS RAID...
GUESS I GOT TOO WRAPPED UP IN ALL OF THE SACRED STONE QUEST STUFF...

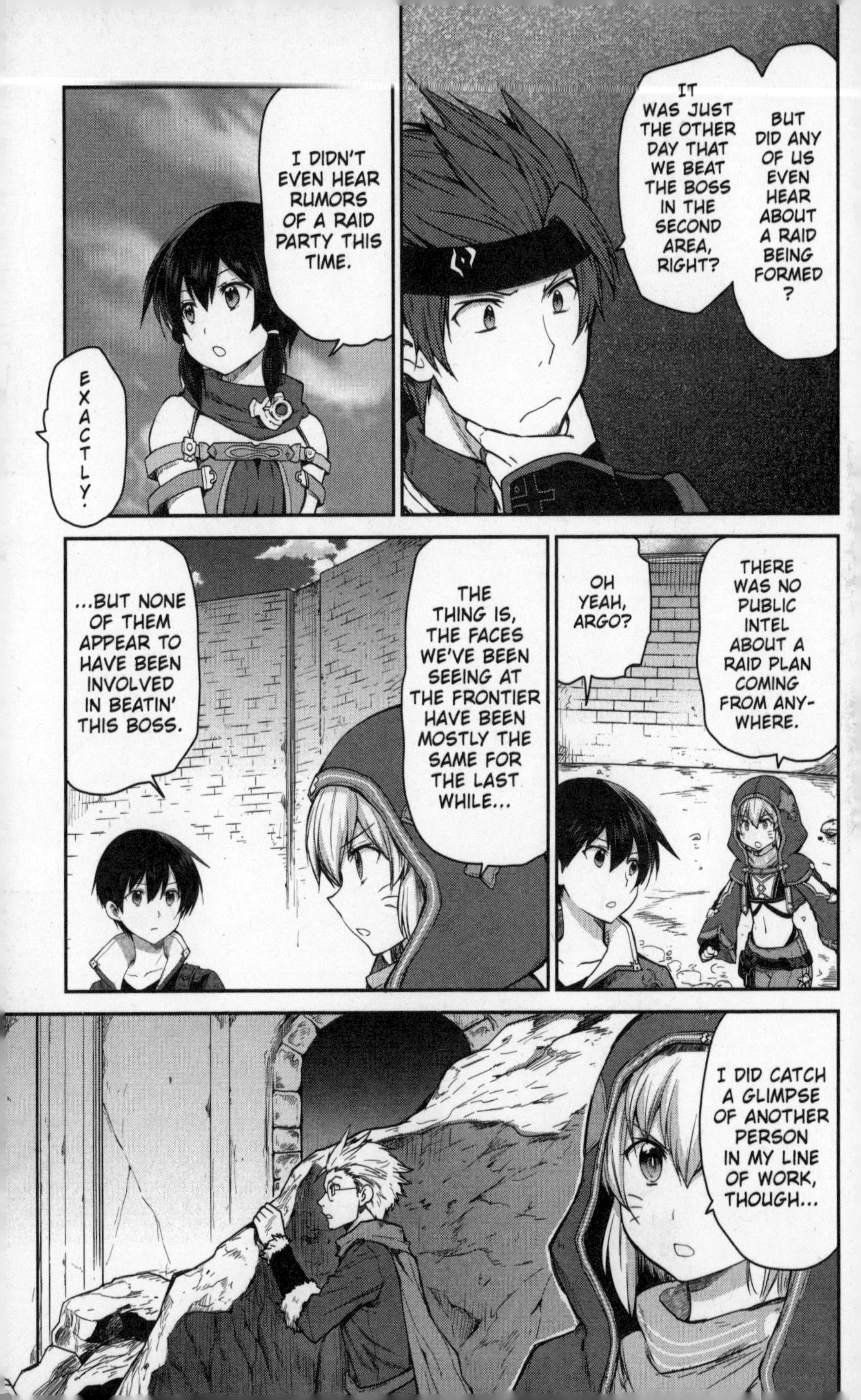
IT WAS JUST THE OTHER DAY THAT WE BEAT THE BOSS IN THE SECOND AREA, RIGHT?
BUT DID ANY OF US EVEN HEAR ABOUT A RAID BEING FORMED?
I DIDN'T EVEN HEAR RUMORS OF A RAID PARTY THIS TIME.
EXACTLY.
THERE WAS NO PUBLIC INTEL ABOUT A RAID PLAN COMING FROM ANYWHERE.
OH YEAH, ARGO?
THE THING IS, THE FACES WE'VE BEEN SEEING AT THE FRONTIER HAVE BEEN MOSTLY THE SAME FOR THE LAST WHILE...
...BUT NONE OF THEM APPEAR TO HAVE BEEN INVOLVED IN BEATIN' THIS BOSS.
I DID CATCH A GLIMPSE OF ANOTHER PERSON IN MY LINE OF WORK, THOUGH...

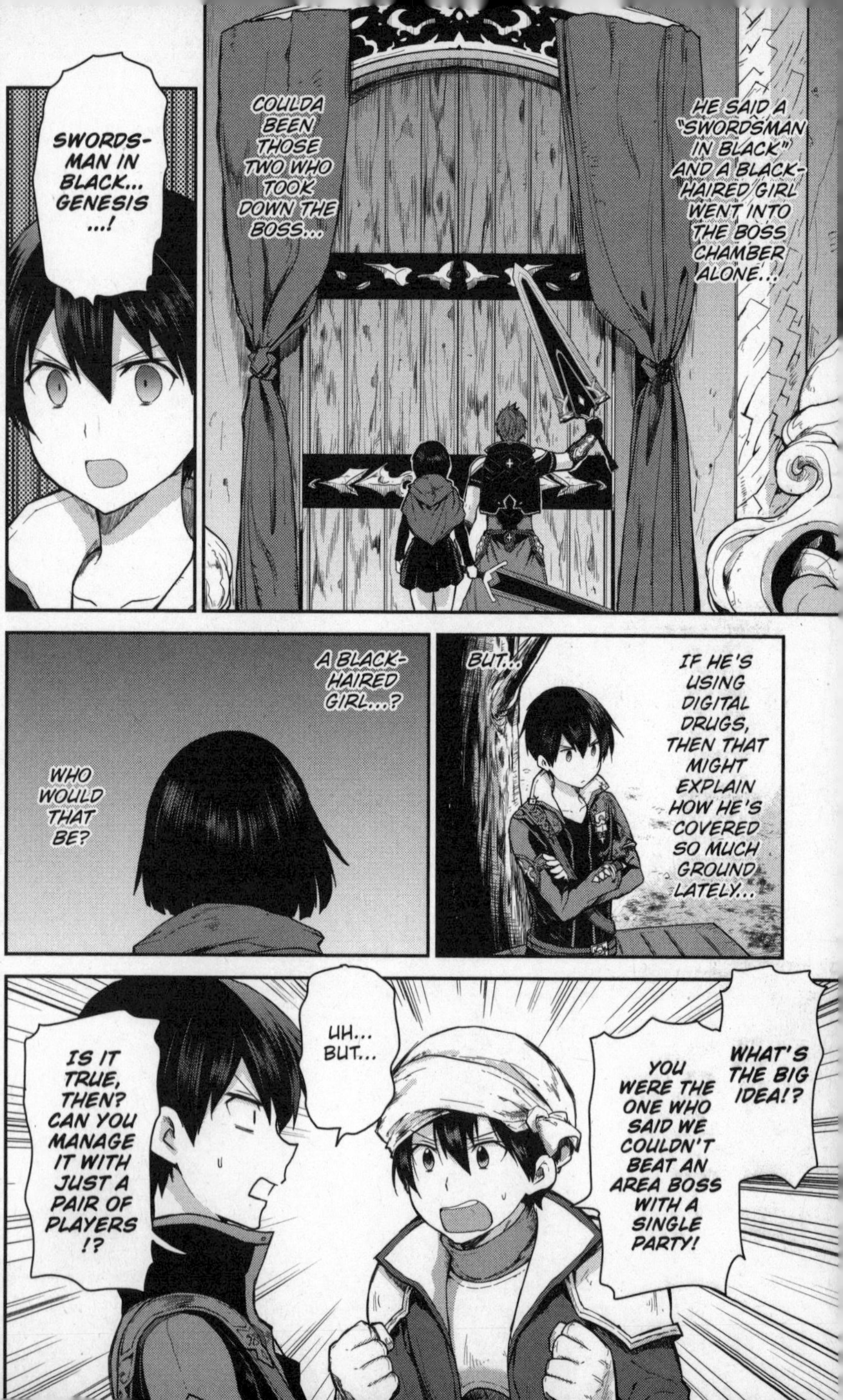
HE SAID A "SWORDSMAN IN BLACK" AND A BLACK-HAIRED GIRL WENT INTO THE BOSS CHAMBER ALONE...
COULDA BEEN THOSE TWO WHO TOOK DOWN THE BOSS...
SWORDSMAN IN BLACK... GENESIS...!
IF HE'S USING DIGITAL DRUGS, THEN THAT MIGHT EXPLAIN HOW HE'S COVERED SO MUCH GROUND LATELY...
BUT...
A BLACK-HAIRED GIRL...?
WHO WOULD THAT BE?
WHAT'S THE BIG IDEA!?
YOU WERE THE ONE WHO SAID WE COULDN'T BEAT AN AREA BOSS WITH A SINGLE PARTY!
UH... BUT...
IS IT TRUE, THEN? CAN YOU MANAGE IT WITH JUST A PAIR OF PLAYERS!?

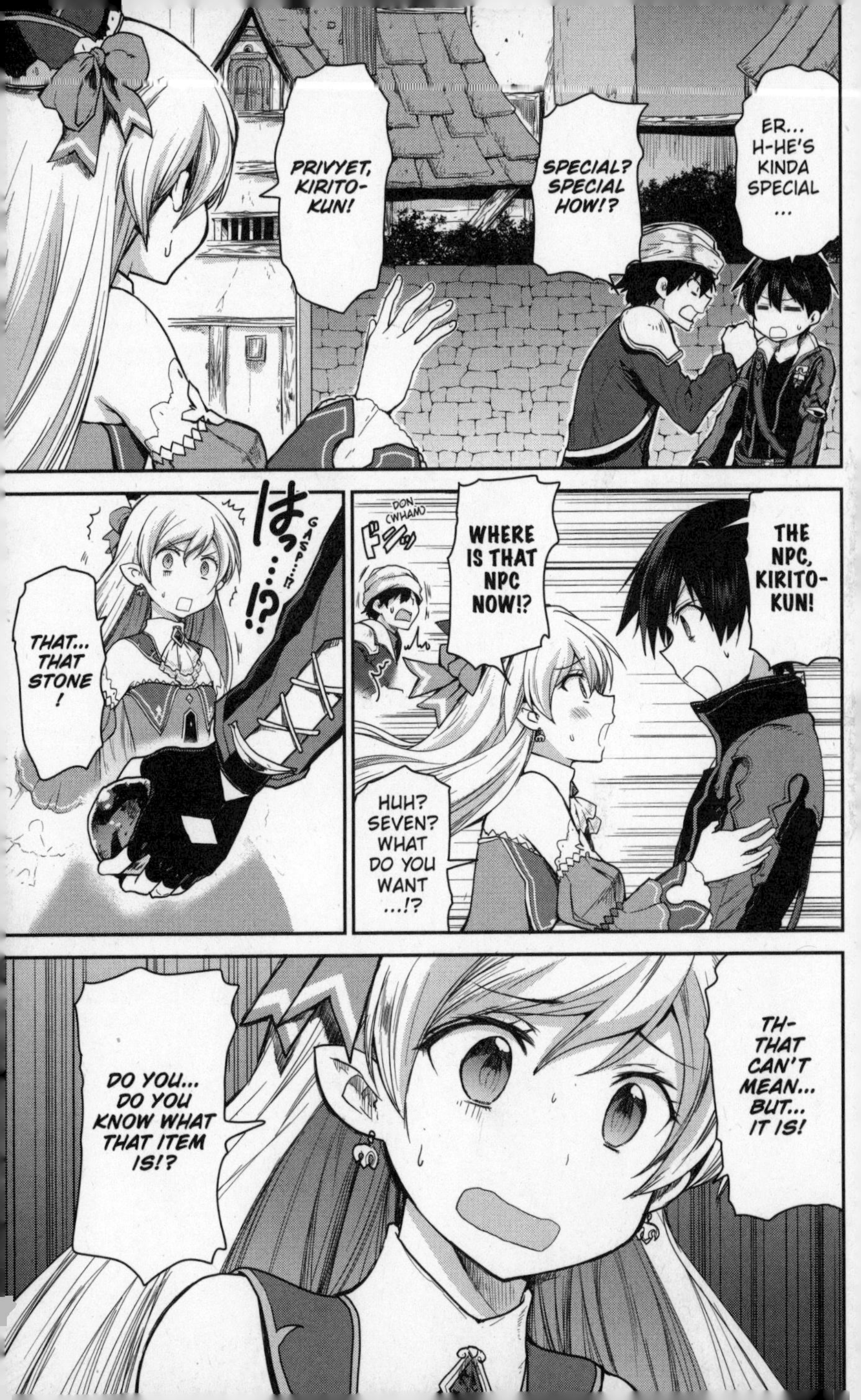
ER... H-HE'S KINDA SPECIAL ...
SPECIAL? SPECIAL HOW!?
PRIVYET, KIRITO-KUN!
THE NPC, KIRITO-KUN!
WHERE IS THAT NPC NOW!?
ドン
DON (WHAM)
HUH? SEVEN? WHAT DO YOU WANT ...!?
はっ…!?
GASP...!?
THAT... THAT STONE!
TH-THAT CAN'T MEAN... BUT... IT IS!
DO YOU... DO YOU KNOW WHAT THAT ITEM IS!?

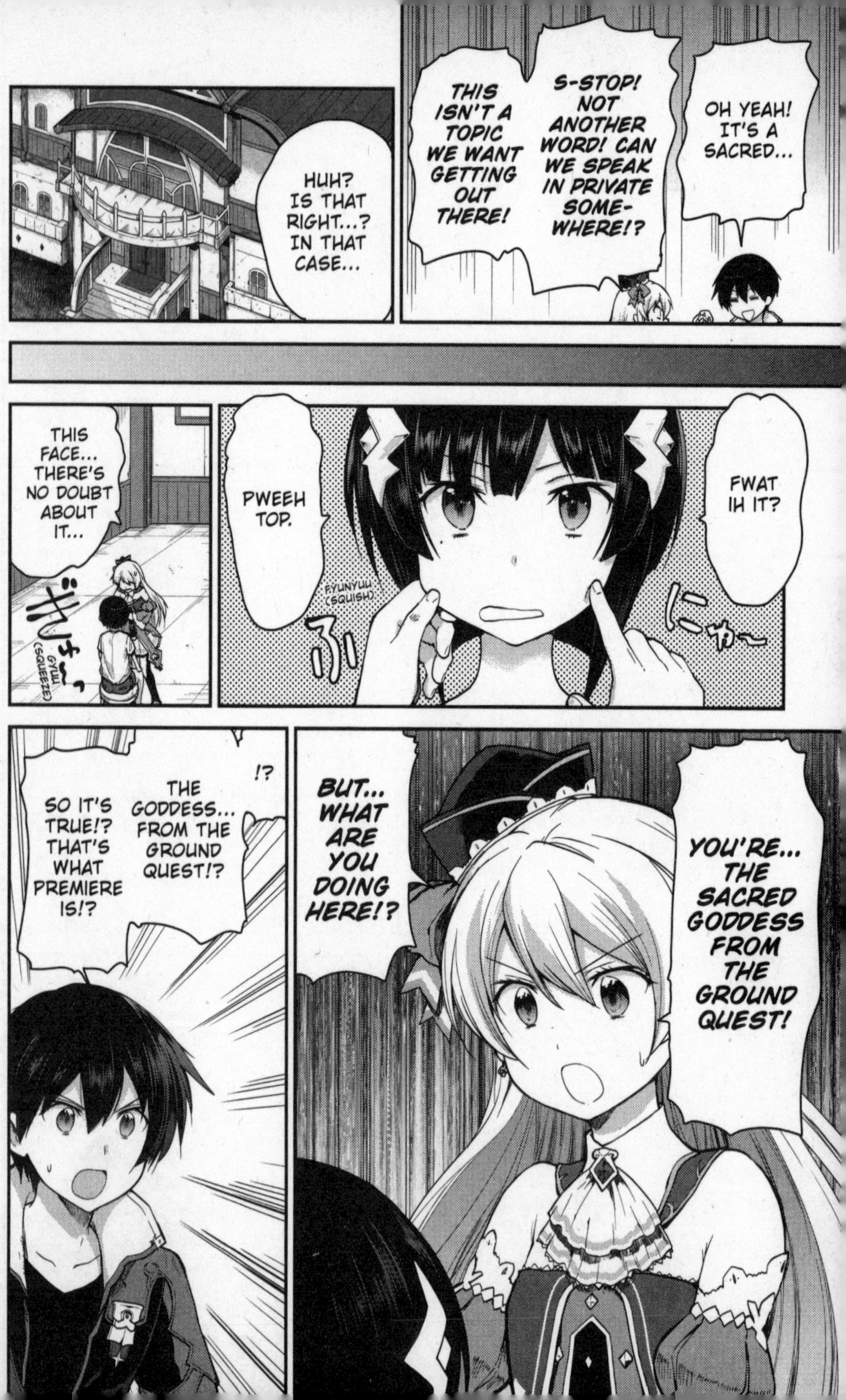
OH YEAH! IT'S A SACRED...
S-STOP! NOT ANOTHER WORD! CAN WE SPEAK IN PRIVATE SOME-WHERE!?
THIS ISN'T A TOPIC WE WANT GETTING OUT THERE!
HUH? IS THAT RIGHT...? IN THAT CASE...
FWAT IH IT?
にゅ~
PWEEH TOP.
FYUNYUU (SQUISH)
ふ
THIS FACE... THERE'S NO DOUBT ABOUT IT...
ぎゅ~っ
GYUU (SQUEEZE)
YOU'RE... THE SACRED GODDESS FROM THE GROUND QUEST!
BUT... WHAT ARE YOU DOING HERE!?
!?
THE GODDESS... FROM THE GROUND QUEST!?
SO IT'S TRUE!? THAT'S WHAT PREMIERE IS!?

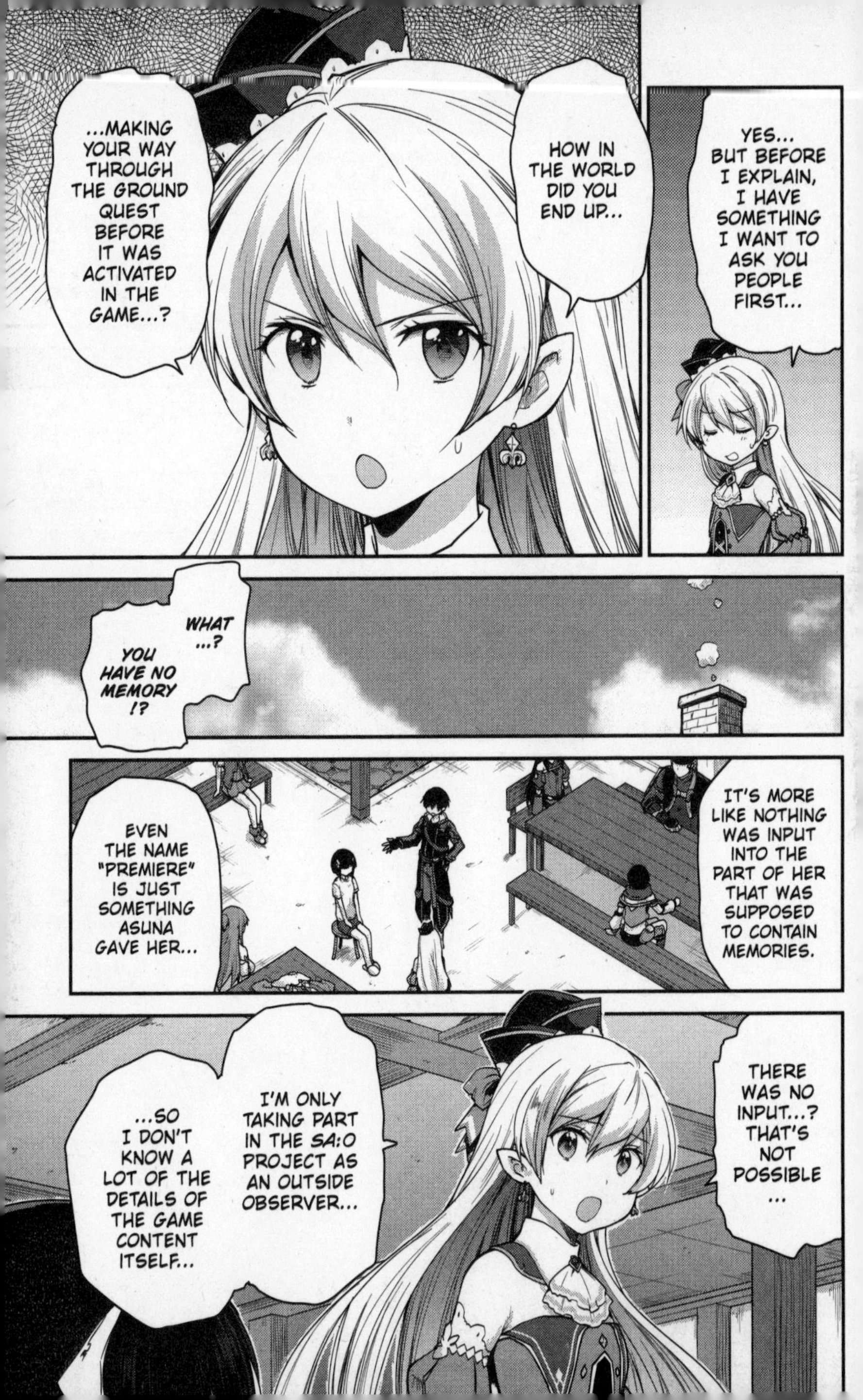
HOW IN THE WORLD DID YOU END UP...
...MAKING YOUR WAY THROUGH THE GROUND QUEST BEFORE IT WAS ACTIVATED IN THE GAME...?
YES... BUT BEFORE I EXPLAIN, I HAVE SOMETHING I WANT TO ASK YOU PEOPLE FIRST...
WHAT ...? YOU HAVE NO MEMORY !?
IT'S MORE LIKE NOTHING WAS INPUT INTO THE PART OF HER THAT WAS SUPPOSED TO CONTAIN MEMORIES.
EVEN THE NAME "PREMIERE" IS JUST SOMETHING ASUNA GAVE HER...
THERE WAS NO INPUT...? THAT'S NOT POSSIBLE ...
I'M ONLY TAKING PART IN THE SA:O PROJECT AS AN OUTSIDE OBSERVER...
...SO I DON'T KNOW A LOT OF THE DETAILS OF THE GAME CONTENT ITSELF...

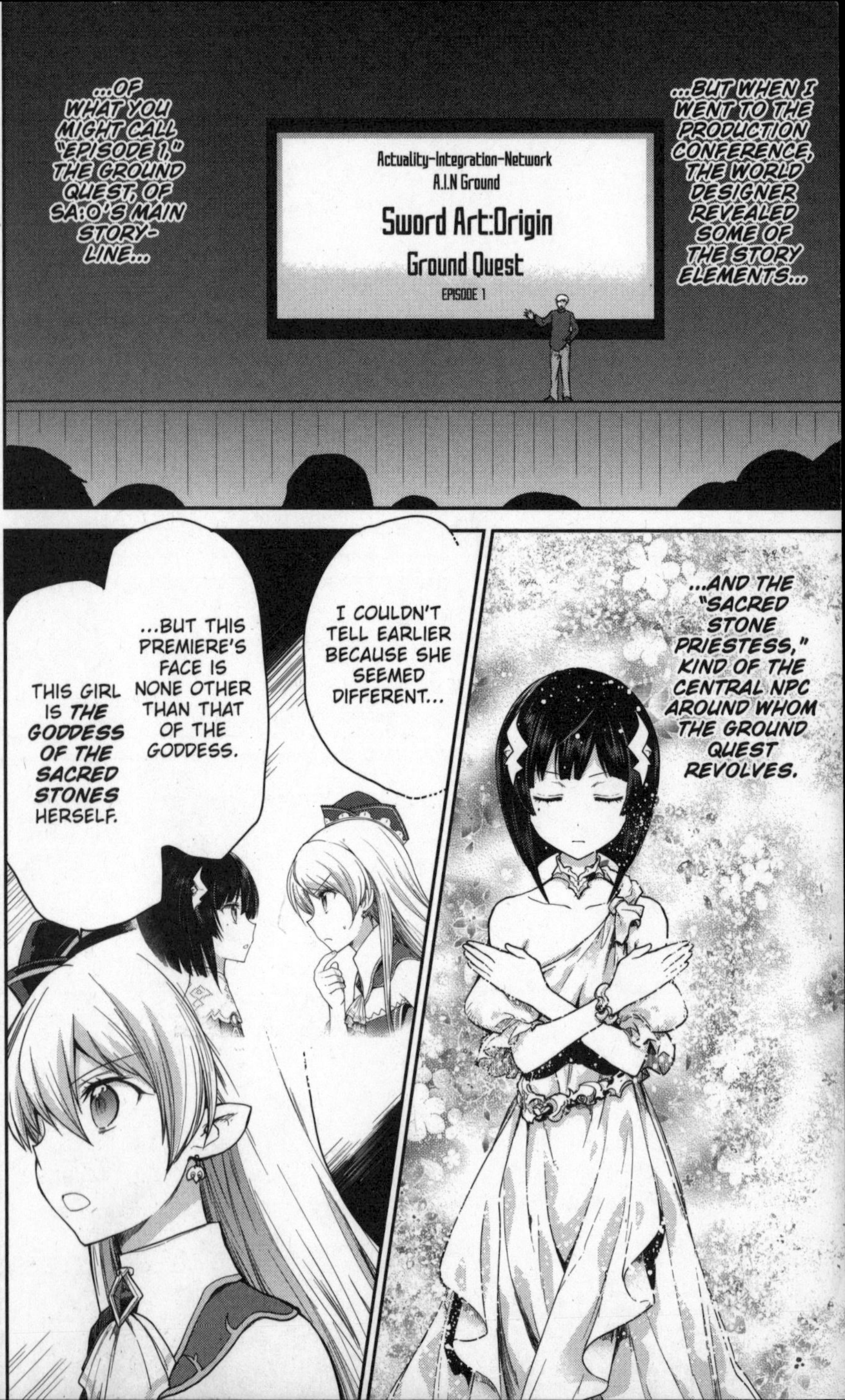
...BUT WHEN I WENT TO THE PRODUCTION CONFERENCE, THE WORLD DESIGNER REVEALED SOME OF THE STORY ELEMENTS...
...OF WHAT YOU MIGHT CALL "EPISODE 1," THE GROUND QUEST, OF SA:O'S MAIN STORY-LINE...
Actuality-Integration-Network
A.I.N Ground
Sword Art:Origin
Ground Quest
EPISODE 1
...AND THE "SACRED STONE PRIESTESS," KIND OF THE CENTRAL NPC AROUND WHOM THE GROUND QUEST REVOLVES.
I COULDN'T TELL EARLIER BECAUSE SHE SEEMED DIFFERENT...
...BUT THIS PREMIERE'S FACE IS NONE OTHER THAN THAT OF THE GODDESS.
THIS GIRL IS *THE GODDESS OF THE SACRED STONES* HERSELF.

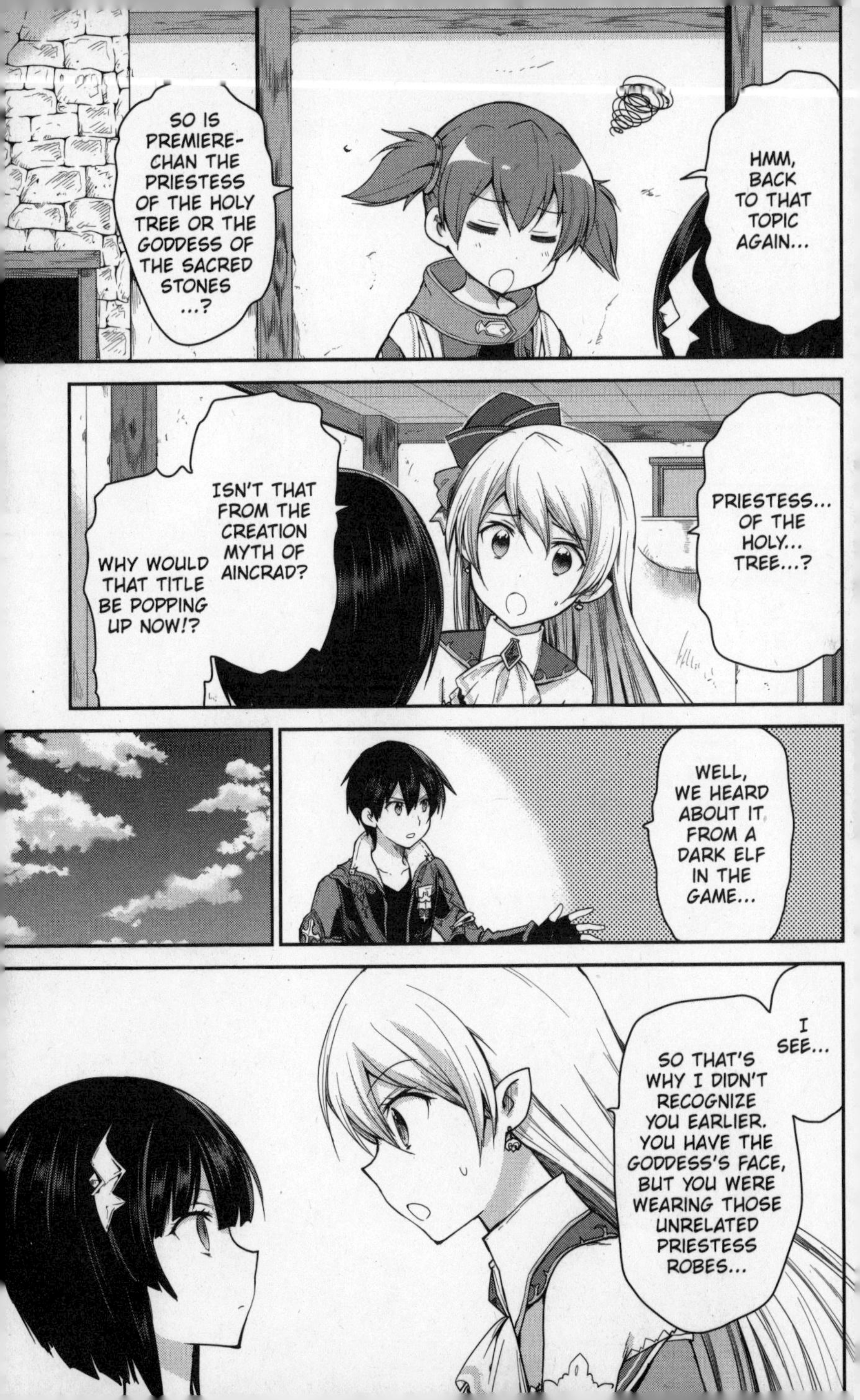
HMM, BACK TO THAT TOPIC AGAIN...
SO IS PREMIERE-CHAN THE PRIESTESS OF THE HOLY TREE OR THE GODDESS OF THE SACRED STONES ...?
PRIESTESS... OF THE HOLY... TREE...?
ISN'T THAT FROM THE CREATION MYTH OF AINCRAD?
WHY WOULD THAT TITLE BE POPPING UP NOW!?
WELL, WE HEARD ABOUT IT FROM A DARK ELF IN THE GAME...
I SEE...
SO THAT'S WHY I DIDN'T RECOGNIZE YOU EARLIER. YOU HAVE THE GODDESS'S FACE, BUT YOU WERE WEARING THOSE UNRELATED PRIESTESS ROBES...

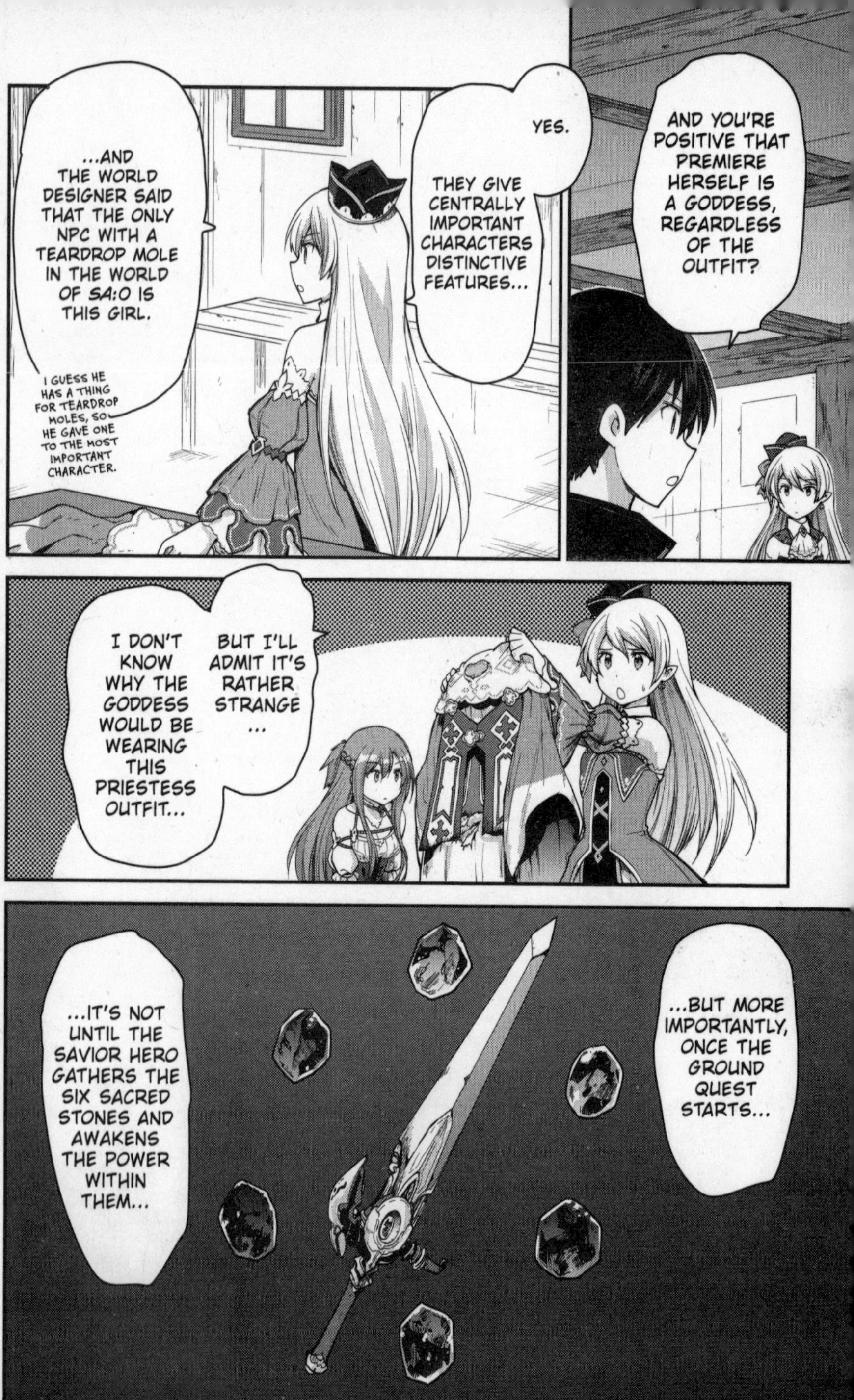
AND YOU'RE POSITIVE THAT PREMIERE HERSELF IS A GODDESS, REGARDLESS OF THE OUTFIT?
YES.
THEY GIVE CENTRALLY IMPORTANT CHARACTERS DISTINCTIVE FEATURES...
...AND THE WORLD DESIGNER SAID THAT THE ONLY NPC WITH A TEARDROP MOLE IN THE WORLD OF SA:O IS THIS GIRL.
I GUESS HE HAS A THING FOR TEARDROP MOLES, SO HE GAVE ONE TO THE MOST IMPORTANT CHARACTER.
BUT I'LL ADMIT IT'S RATHER STRANGE...
I DON'T KNOW WHY THE GODDESS WOULD BE WEARING THIS PRIESTESS OUTFIT...
...BUT MORE IMPORTANTLY, ONCE THE GROUND QUEST STARTS...
...IT'S NOT UNTIL THE SAVIOR HERO GATHERS THE SIX SACRED STONES AND AWAKENS THE POWER WITHIN THEM...

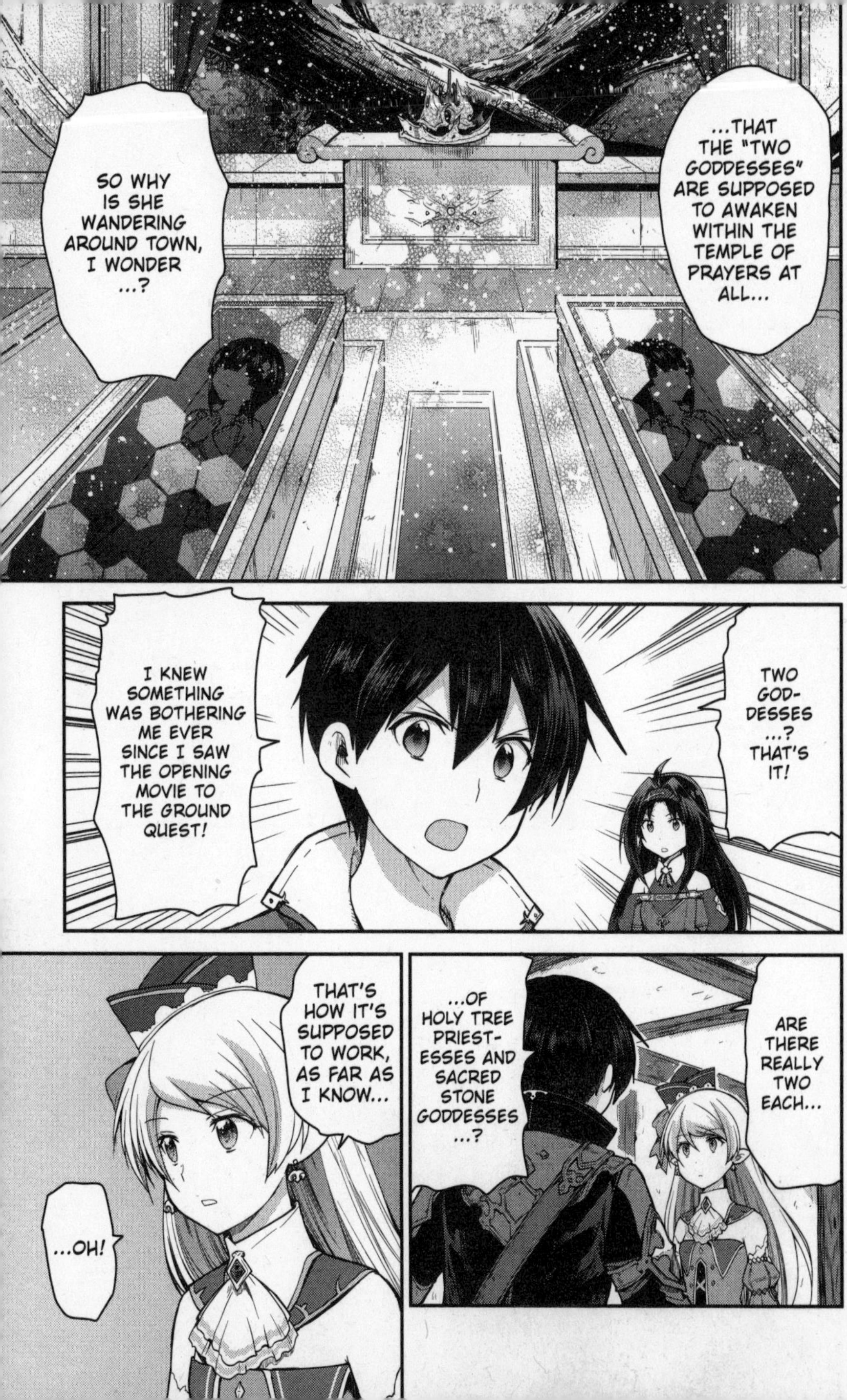
...THAT THE "TWO GODDESSES" ARE SUPPOSED TO AWAKEN WITHIN THE TEMPLE OF PRAYERS AT ALL...
SO WHY IS SHE WANDERING AROUND TOWN, I WONDER ...?
TWO GOD-DESSES ...? THAT'S IT!
I KNEW SOMETHING WAS BOTHERING ME EVER SINCE I SAW THE OPENING MOVIE TO THE GROUND QUEST!
ARE THERE REALLY TWO EACH...
...OF HOLY TREE PRIEST-ESSES AND SACRED STONE GODDESSES ...?
THAT'S HOW IT'S SUPPOSED TO WORK, AS FAR AS I KNOW...
...OH!

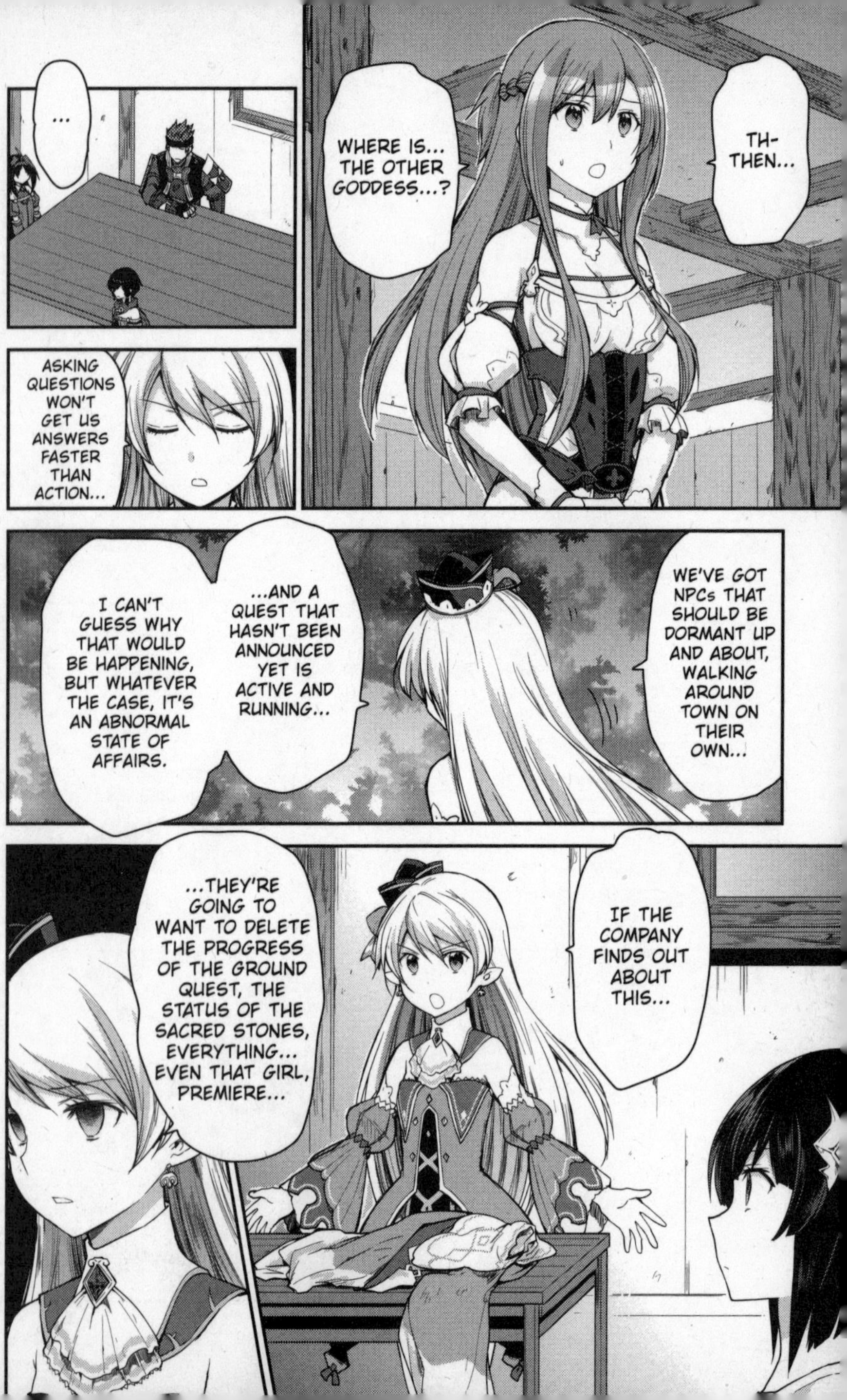
TH- THEN...
WHERE IS... THE OTHER GODDESS...?
...
ASKING QUESTIONS WON'T GET US ANSWERS FASTER THAN ACTION...
WE'VE GOT NPCs THAT SHOULD BE DORMANT UP AND ABOUT, WALKING AROUND TOWN ON THEIR OWN...
...AND A QUEST THAT HASN'T BEEN ANNOUNCED YET IS ACTIVE AND RUNNING...
I CAN'T GUESS WHY THAT WOULD BE HAPPENING, BUT WHATEVER THE CASE, IT'S AN ABNORMAL STATE OF AFFAIRS.
IF THE COMPANY FINDS OUT ABOUT THIS...
...THEY'RE GOING TO WANT TO DELETE THE PROGRESS OF THE GROUND QUEST, THE STATUS OF THE SACRED STONES, EVERYTHING... EVEN THAT GIRL, PREMIERE...

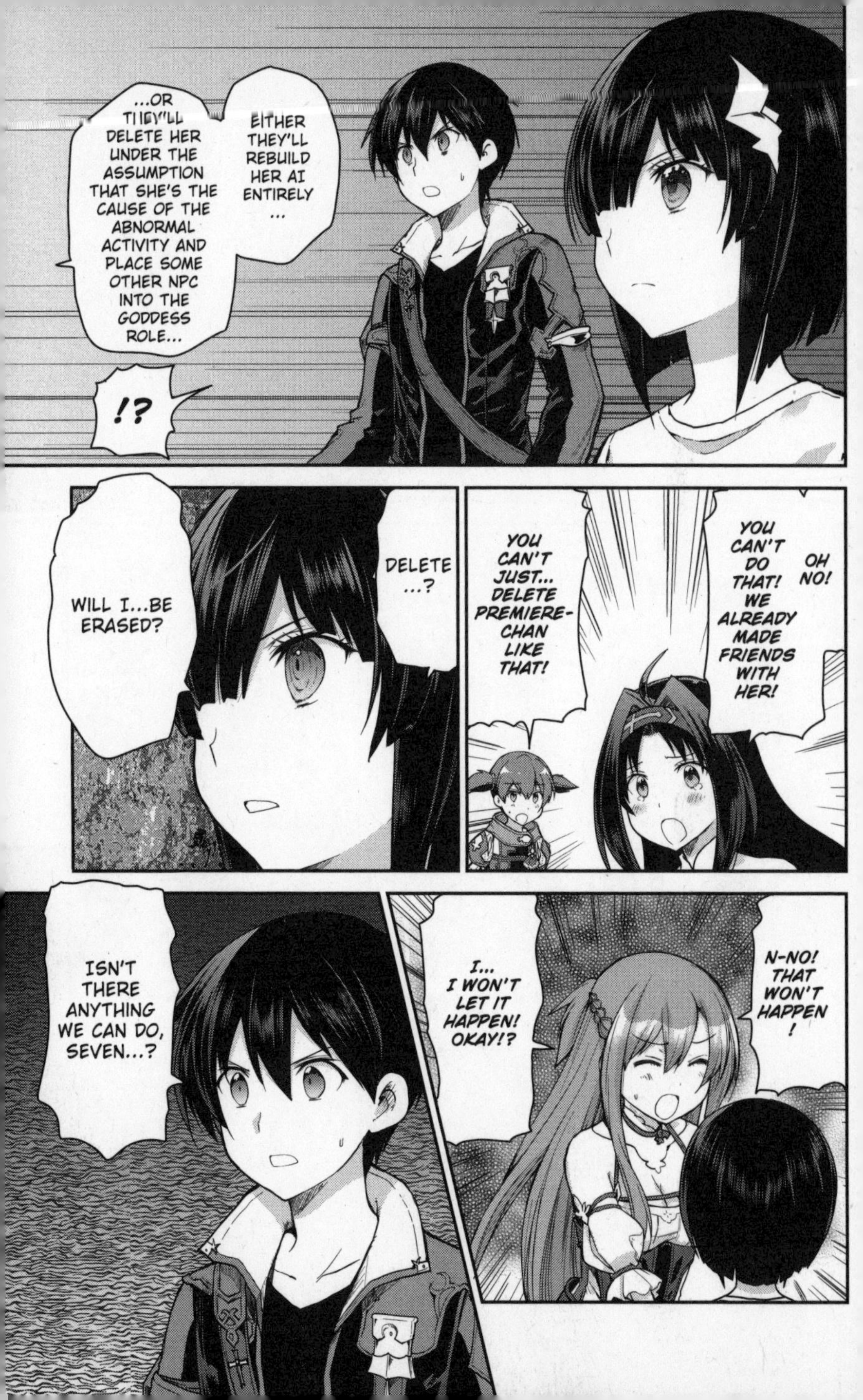
EITHER THEY'LL REBUILD HER AI ENTIRELY ...
...OR THEY'LL DELETE HER UNDER THE ASSUMPTION THAT SHE'S THE CAUSE OF THE ABNORMAL ACTIVITY AND PLACE SOME OTHER NPC INTO THE GODDESS ROLE...
!?
OH NO!
YOU CAN'T DO THAT! WE ALREADY MADE FRIENDS WITH HER!
YOU CAN'T JUST... DELETE PREMIERE-CHAN LIKE THAT!
DELETE ...?
WILL I...BE ERASED?
N-NO! THAT WON'T HAPPEN!
I... I WON'T LET IT HAPPEN! OKAY!?
ISN'T THERE ANYTHING WE CAN DO, SEVEN...?

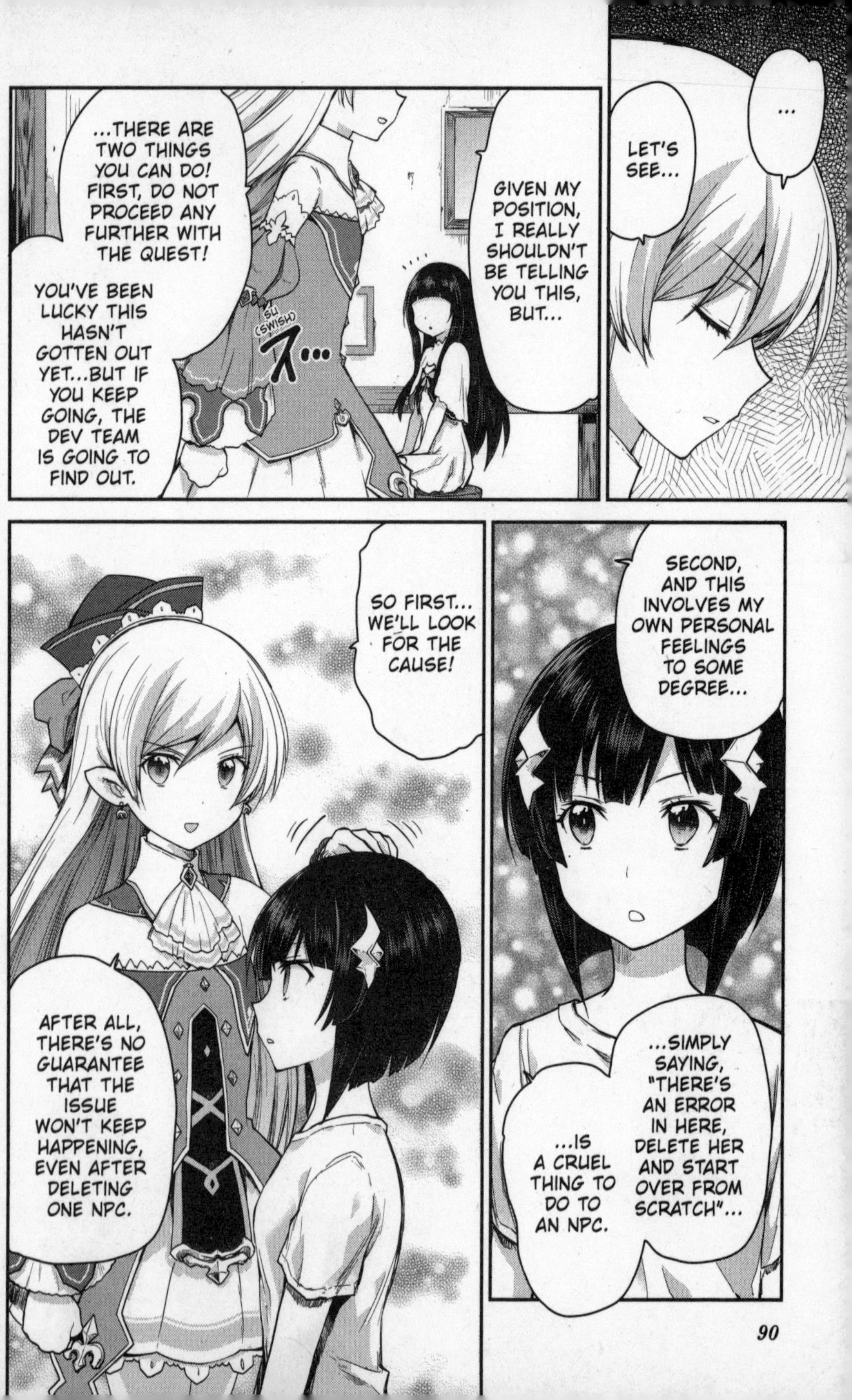
...
LET'S SEE...
GIVEN MY POSITION, I REALLY SHOULDN'T BE TELLING YOU THIS, BUT...
...THERE ARE TWO THINGS YOU CAN DO! FIRST, DO NOT PROCEED ANY FURTHER WITH THE QUEST!
YOU'VE BEEN LUCKY THIS HASN'T GOTTEN OUT YET...BUT IF YOU KEEP GOING, THE DEV TEAM IS GOING TO FIND OUT.
SU (SWISH) ス...
SECOND, AND THIS INVOLVES MY OWN PERSONAL FEELINGS TO SOME DEGREE...
...SIMPLY SAYING, "THERE'S AN ERROR IN HERE, DELETE HER AND START OVER FROM SCRATCH"...
...IS A CRUEL THING TO DO TO AN NPC.
SO FIRST... WE'LL LOOK FOR THE CAUSE!
AFTER ALL, THERE'S NO GUARANTEE THAT THE ISSUE WON'T KEEP HAPPENING, EVEN AFTER DELETING ONE NPC.

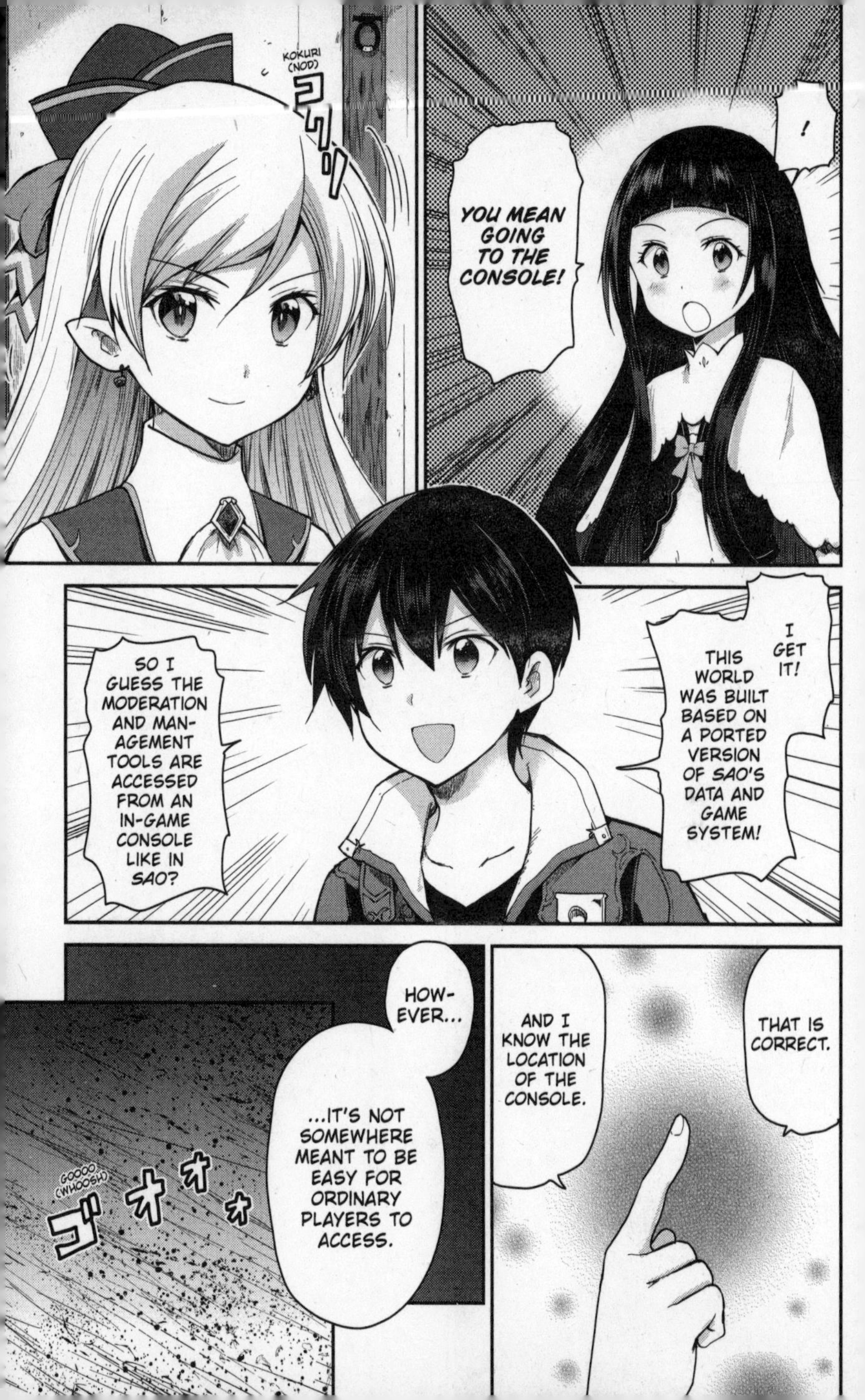
!
YOU MEAN GOING TO THE CONSOLE!
KOKURI (NOD)
I GET IT!
THIS WORLD WAS BUILT BASED ON A PORTED VERSION OF SAO'S DATA AND GAME SYSTEM!
SO I GUESS THE MODERATION AND MAN-AGEMENT TOOLS ARE ACCESSED FROM AN IN-GAME CONSOLE LIKE IN SAO?
THAT IS CORRECT.
AND I KNOW THE LOCATION OF THE CONSOLE.
HOW-EVER...
...IT'S NOT SOMEWHERE MEANT TO BE EASY FOR ORDINARY PLAYERS TO ACCESS.
GOOOO (WHOOSH)

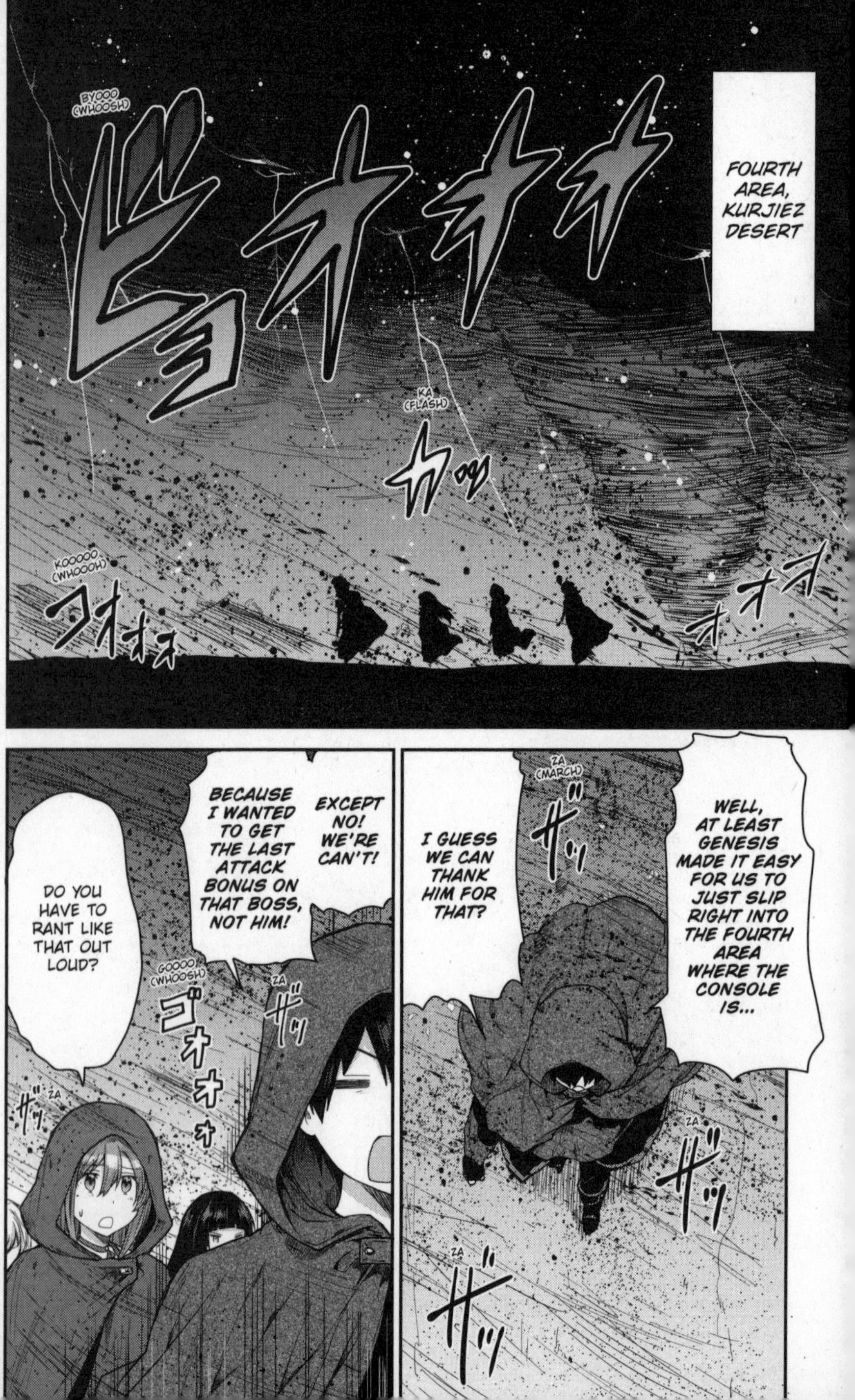
FOURTH AREA, KURJIEZ DESERT
BYOOO (WHOOSH)
KA (FLASH)
KOOOOO (WHOOOH)
WELL, AT LEAST GENESIS MADE IT EASY FOR US TO JUST SLIP RIGHT INTO THE FOURTH AREA WHERE THE CONSOLE IS...
ZA (MARCH)
I GUESS WE CAN THANK HIM FOR THAT?
ZA
ZA
EXCEPT NO! WE'RE CAN'T!
BECAUSE I WANTED TO GET THE LAST ATTACK BONUS ON THAT BOSS, NOT HIM!
GOOOO (WHOOSH)
ZA
ZA
DO YOU HAVE TO RANT LIKE THAT OUT LOUD?

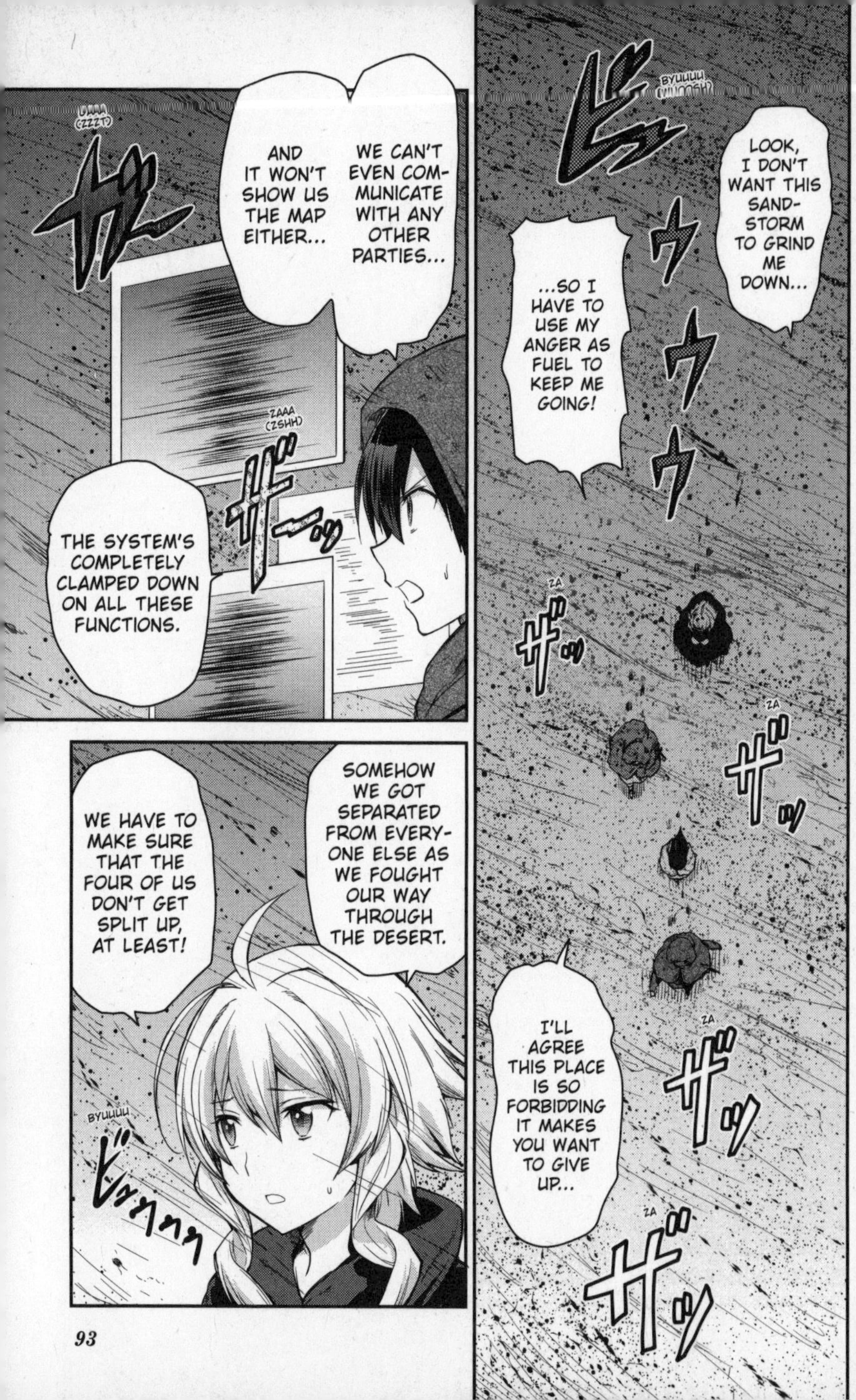
BYUUUU (WHOOSH)
LOOK, I DON'T WANT THIS SAND-STORM TO GRIND ME DOWN...
...SO I HAVE TO USE MY ANGER AS FUEL TO KEEP ME GOING!
ZA
ZA
I'LL AGREE THIS PLACE IS SO FORBIDDING IT MAKES YOU WANT TO GIVE UP...
ZA
ZA
ZAAA (ZZZT)
WE CAN'T EVEN COM-MUNICATE WITH ANY OTHER PARTIES...
AND IT WON'T SHOW US THE MAP EITHER...
ZAAA (ZSHH)
THE SYSTEM'S COMPLETELY CLAMPED DOWN ON ALL THESE FUNCTIONS.
SOMEHOW WE GOT SEPARATED FROM EVERY-ONE ELSE AS WE FOUGHT OUR WAY THROUGH THE DESERT.
WE HAVE TO MAKE SURE THAT THE FOUR OF US DON'T GET SPLIT UP, AT LEAST!
BYUUUU

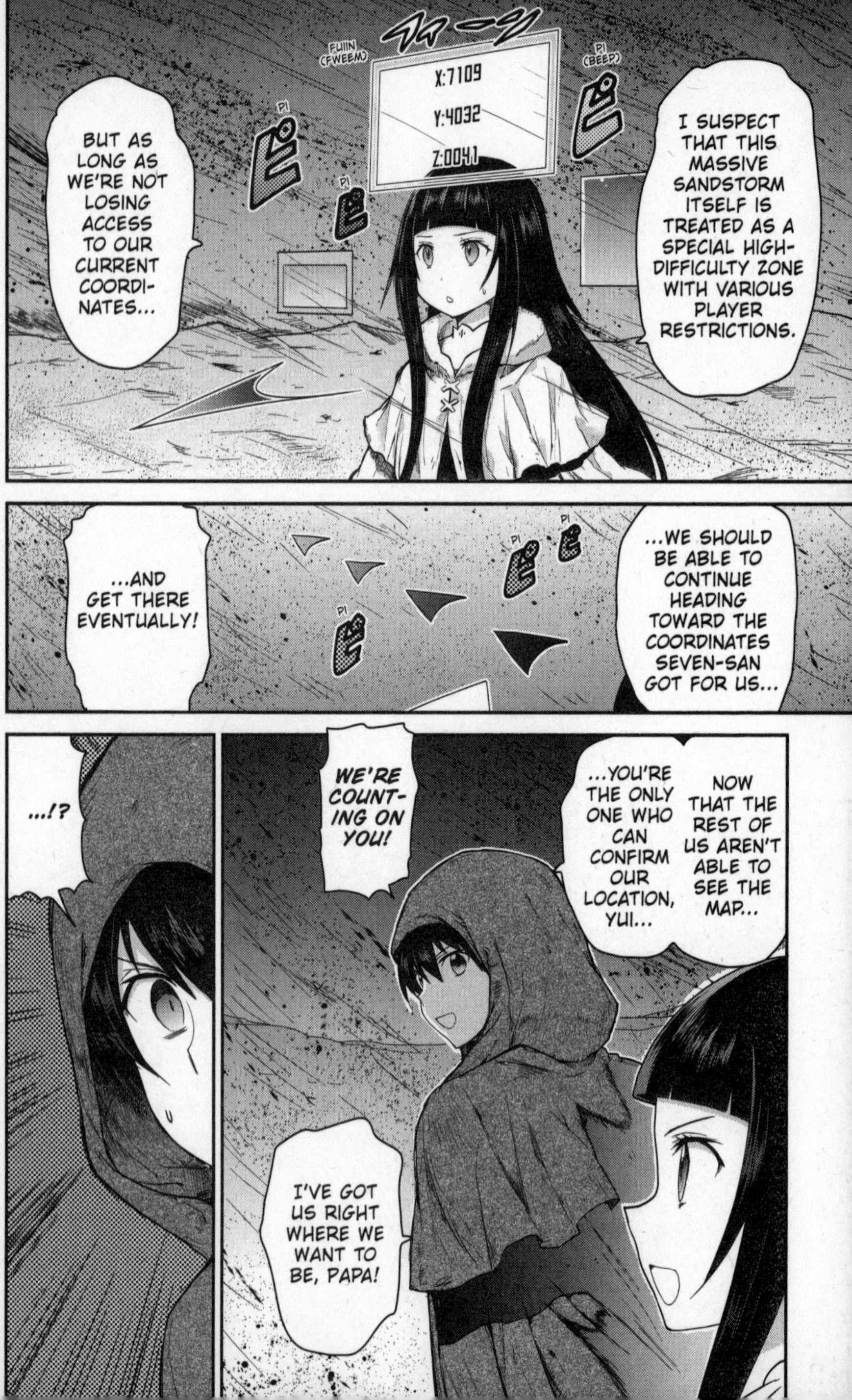
FUIIN (FWEEM)
X:7109
Y:4032
Z:0041
PI (BEEP)
PI
PI
I SUSPECT THAT THIS MASSIVE SANDSTORM ITSELF IS TREATED AS A SPECIAL HIGH-DIFFICULTY ZONE WITH VARIOUS PLAYER RESTRICTIONS.
BUT AS LONG AS WE'RE NOT LOSING ACCESS TO OUR CURRENT COORDINATES...
PI
PI
PI
...WE SHOULD BE ABLE TO CONTINUE HEADING TOWARD THE COORDINATES SEVEN-SAN GOT FOR US...
...AND GET THERE EVENTUALLY!
NOW THAT THE REST OF US AREN'T ABLE TO SEE THE MAP...
...YOU'RE THE ONLY ONE WHO CAN CONFIRM OUR LOCATION, YUI...
WE'RE COUNTING ON YOU!
...!?
I'VE GOT US RIGHT WHERE WE WANT TO BE, PAPA!

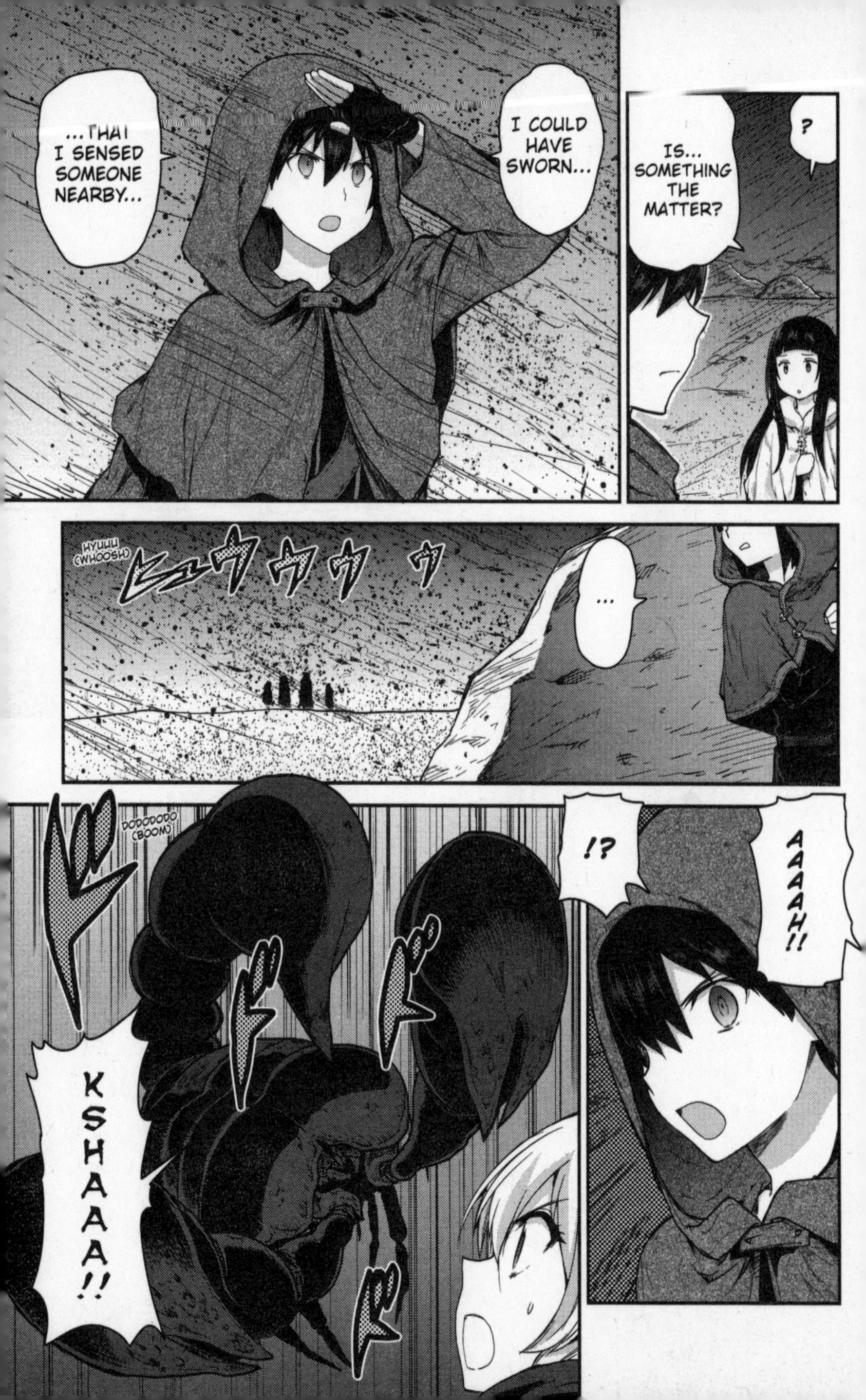
?
IS... SOMETHING THE MATTER?
I COULD HAVE SWORN...
...THAT I SENSED SOMEONE NEARBY...
...
HYUUU (WHOOSH)
AAAAH!!
!?
DODODODO (BOOM)
KSHAAA!!

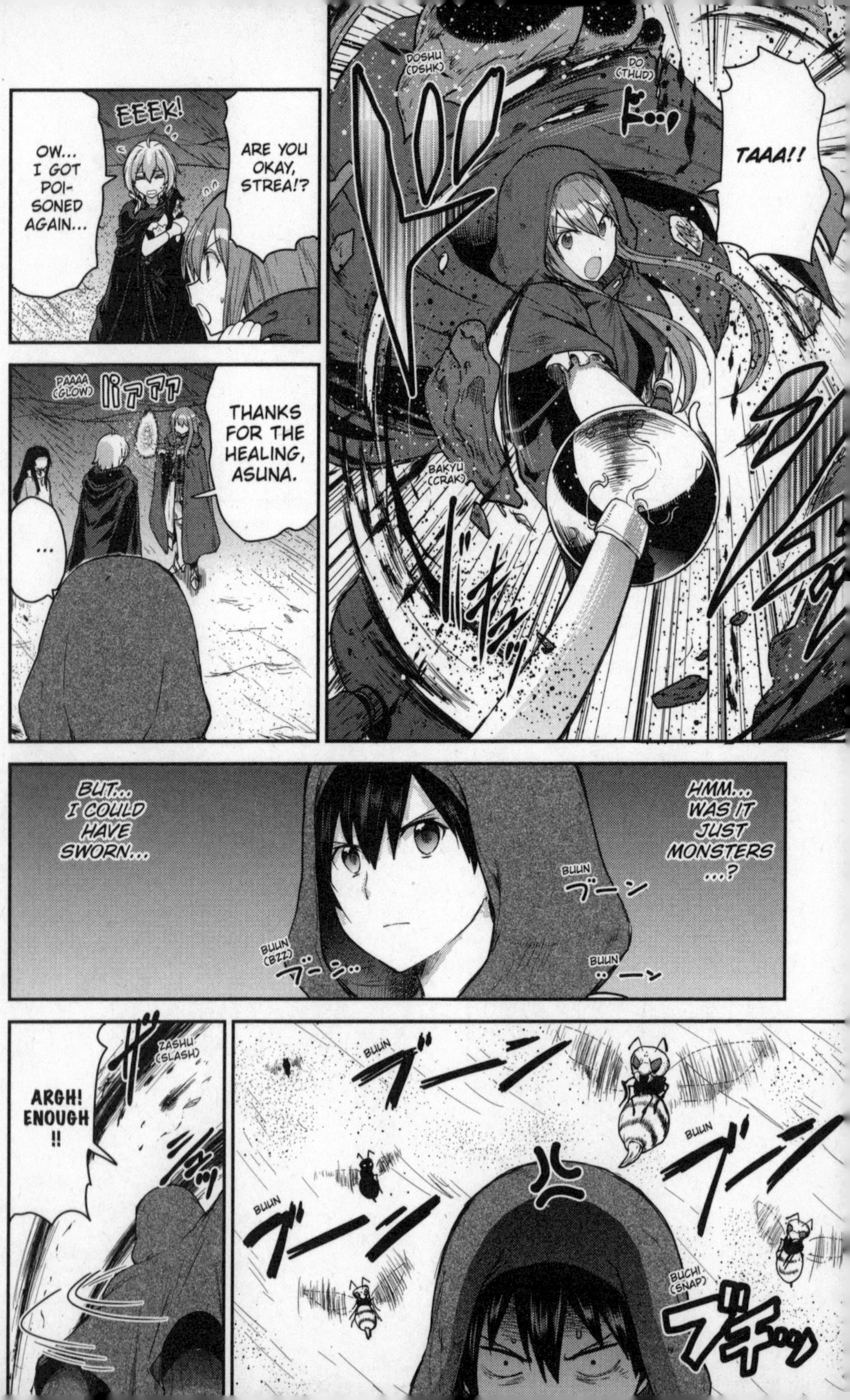
TAAA!!
DO (THUD)
DOSHU (DSHK)
BAKYU (CRAK)
EEEK!
ARE YOU OKAY, STREA!?
OW... I GOT POI-SONED AGAIN...
PAAAA (GLOW)
THANKS FOR THE HEALING, ASUNA.
...
HMM... WAS IT JUST MONSTERS ...?
BUT... I COULD HAVE SWORN...
BUUN
BUUN (BZZ)
BUUN
BUUN
BUUN
BUUN
BUCHI (SNAP)
ZASHU (SLASH)
ARGH! ENOUGH !!

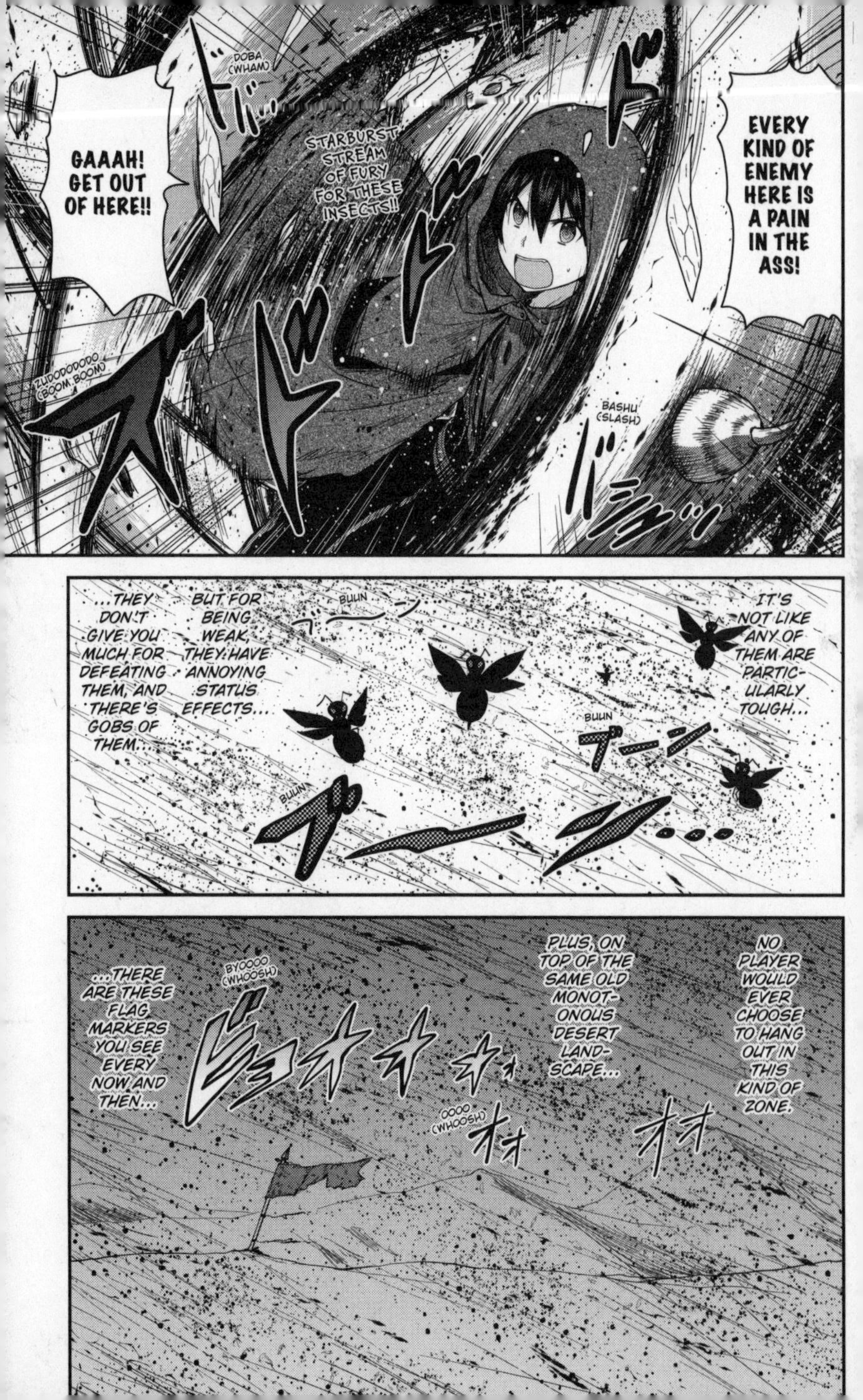
EVERY KIND OF ENEMY HERE IS A PAIN IN THE ASS!
DOBA (WHAM)
STARBURST STREAM OF FURY FOR THESE INSECTS!!
GAAAH! GET OUT OF HERE!!
BASHU (SLASH)
ZUDODODODO (BOOM BOOM)
IT'S NOT LIKE ANY OF THEM ARE PARTICULARLY TOUGH...
BUUN
BUT FOR BEING WEAK, THEY HAVE ANNOYING STATUS EFFECTS...
...THEY DON'T GIVE YOU MUCH FOR DEFEATING THEM, AND THERE'S GOBS OF THEM...
BUUN
BUUN
NO PLAYER WOULD EVER CHOOSE TO HANG OUT IN THIS KIND OF ZONE.
PLUS, ON TOP OF THE SAME OLD MONOTONOUS DESERT LANDSCAPE...
BYOOOO (WHOOSH)
...THERE ARE THESE FLAG MARKERS YOU SEE EVERY NOW AND THEN...
OOOO (WHOOSH)

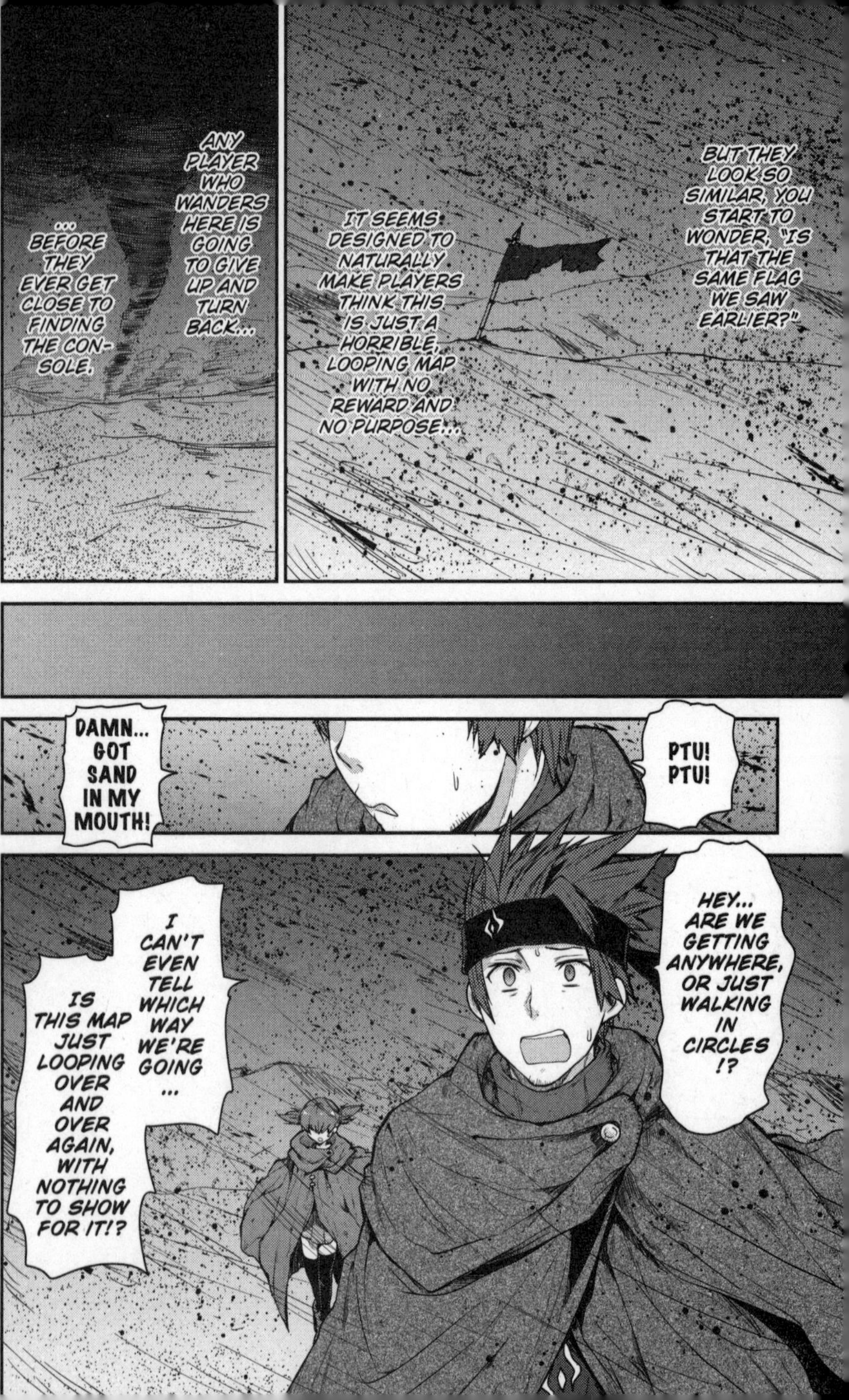

BUT THEY LOOK SO SIMILAR, YOU START TO WONDER, "IS THAT THE SAME FLAG WE SAW EARLIER?"
IT SEEMS DESIGNED TO NATURALLY MAKE PLAYERS THINK THIS IS JUST A HORRIBLE, LOOPING MAP WITH NO REWARD AND NO PURPOSE...
ANY PLAYER WHO WANDERS HERE IS GOING TO GIVE UP AND TURN BACK...
...BEFORE THEY EVER GET CLOSE TO FINDING THE CON-SOLE.
PTU! PTU!
DAMN... GOT SAND IN MY MOUTH!
HEY... ARE WE GETTING ANYWHERE, OR JUST WALKING IN CIRCLES!?
I CAN'T EVEN TELL WHICH WAY WE'RE GOING...
IS THIS MAP JUST LOOPING OVER AND OVER AGAIN, WITH NOTHING TO SHOW FOR IT!?

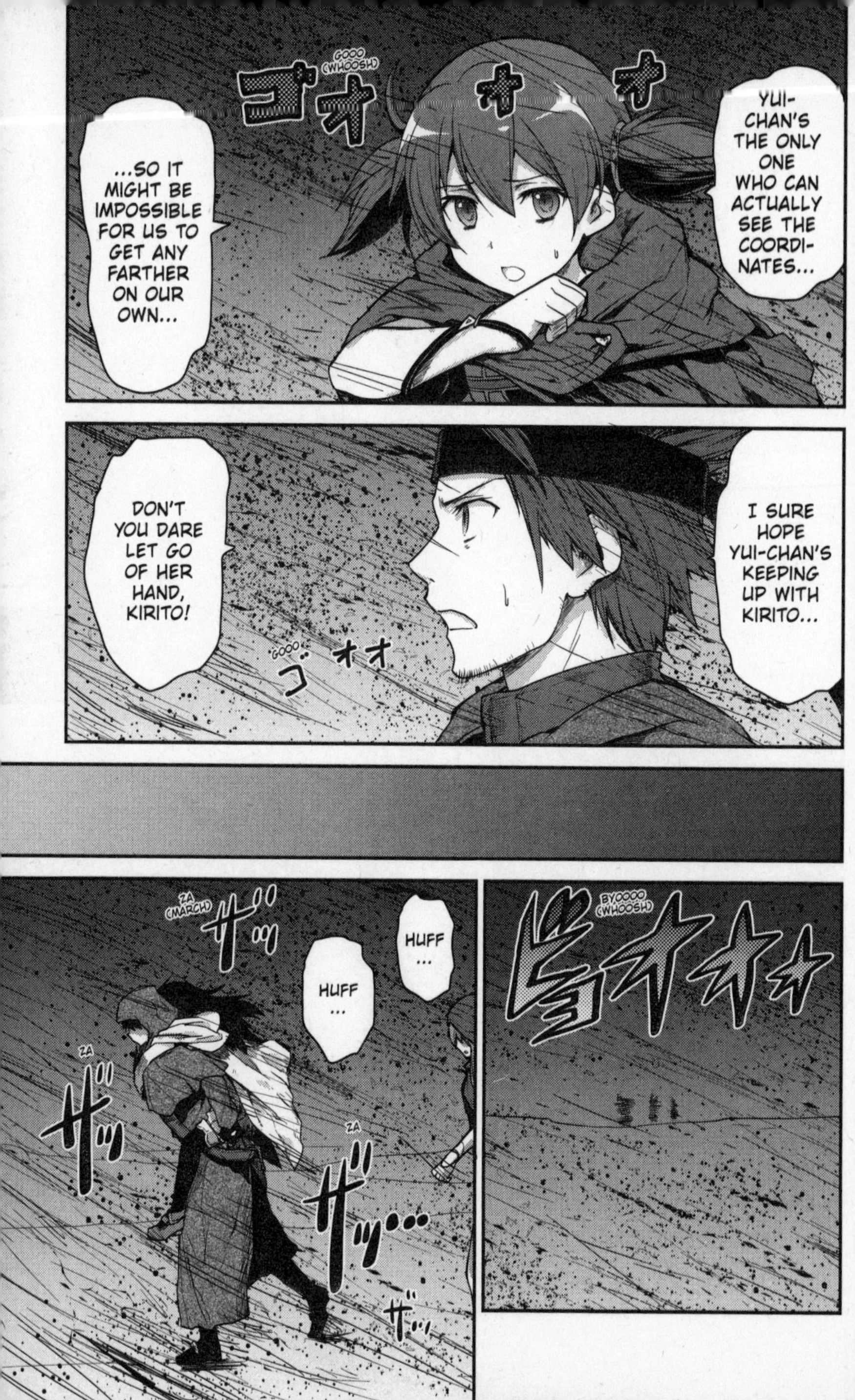
YUI-CHAN'S THE ONLY ONE WHO CAN ACTUALLY SEE THE COORDINATES...
GOOO (WHOOSH)
...SO IT MIGHT BE IMPOSSIBLE FOR US TO GET ANY FARTHER ON OUR OWN...
I SURE HOPE YUI-CHAN'S KEEPING UP WITH KIRITO...
DON'T YOU DARE LET GO OF HER HAND, KIRITO!
GOOO
BYOOOO (WHOOSH)
HUFF...
HUFF...
ZA (MARCH)
ZA
ZA

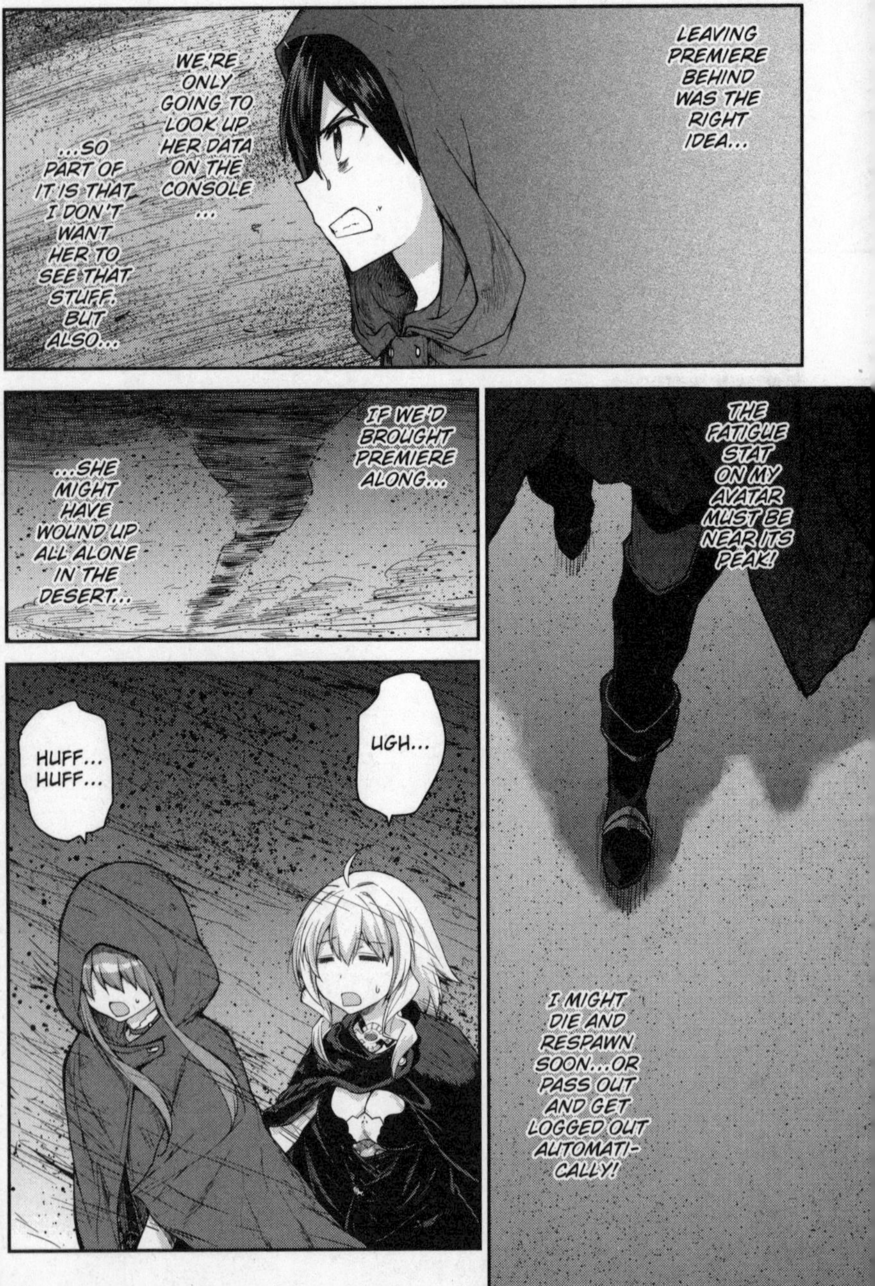
LEAVING PREMIERE BEHIND WAS THE RIGHT IDEA...
WE'RE ONLY GOING TO LOOK UP HER DATA ON THE CONSOLE...
...SO PART OF IT IS THAT I DON'T WANT HER TO SEE THAT STUFF. BUT ALSO...
THE FATIGUE STAT ON MY AVATAR MUST BE NEAR ITS PEAK!
I MIGHT DIE AND RESPAWN SOON...OR PASS OUT AND GET LOGGED OUT AUTOMATI-CALLY!
IF WE'D BROUGHT PREMIERE ALONG...
...SHE MIGHT HAVE WOUND UP ALL ALONE IN THE DESERT...
UGH...
HUFF... HUFF...

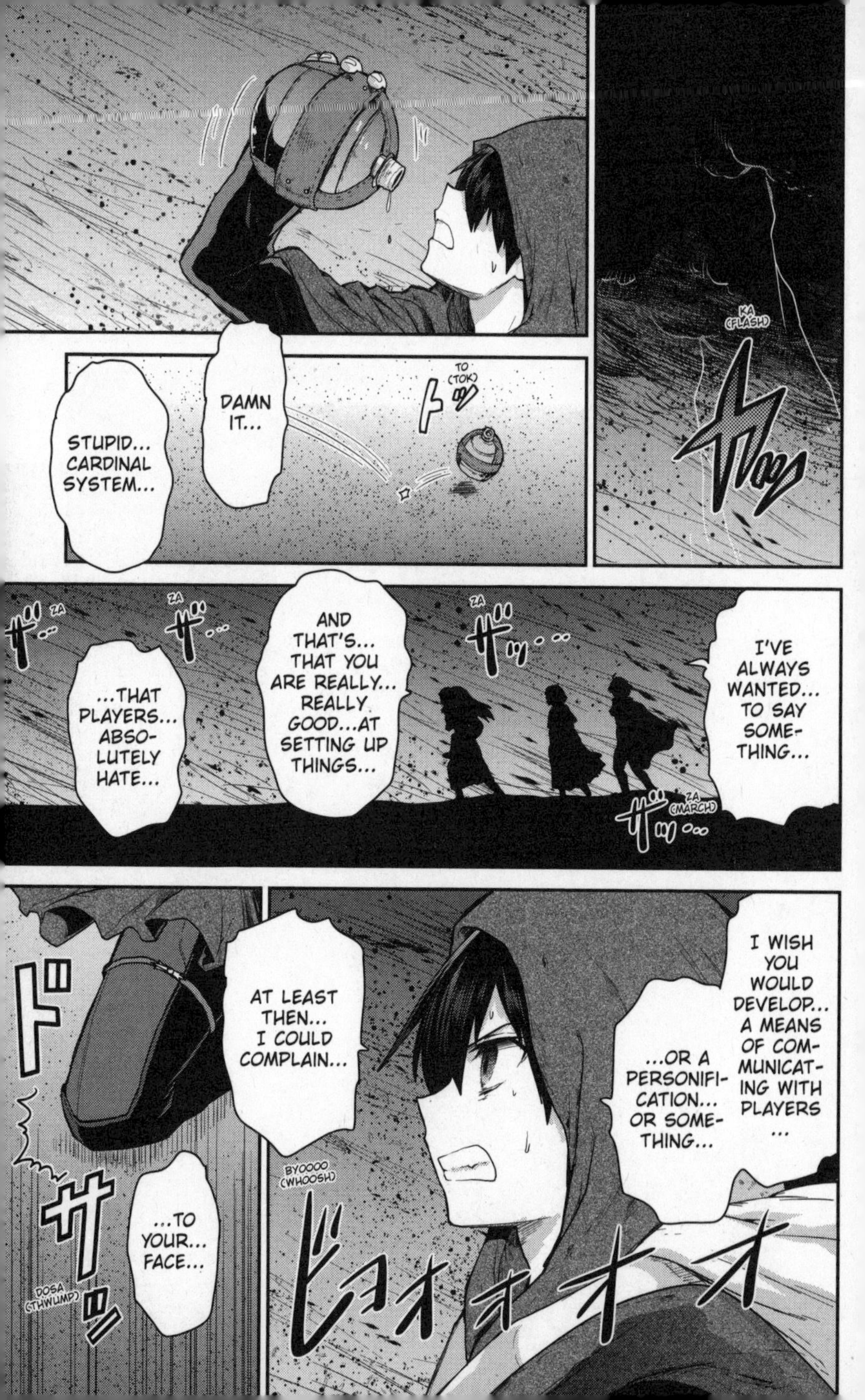
KA (FLASH)
TO (TOK)
DAMN IT...
STUPID... CARDINAL SYSTEM...
I'VE ALWAYS WANTED... TO SAY SOME-THING...
ZA (MARCH)
ZA
AND THAT'S... THAT YOU ARE REALLY... REALLY GOOD...AT SETTING UP THINGS...
ZA
...THAT PLAYERS... ABSO-LUTELY HATE...
ZA
I WISH YOU WOULD DEVELOP... A MEANS OF COM-MUNICAT-ING WITH PLAYERS ...
...OR A PERSONIFI-CATION... OR SOME-THING...
BYOOOO (WHOOSH)
AT LEAST THEN... I COULD COMPLAIN...
...TO YOUR... FACE...
DOSA (THWUMP)

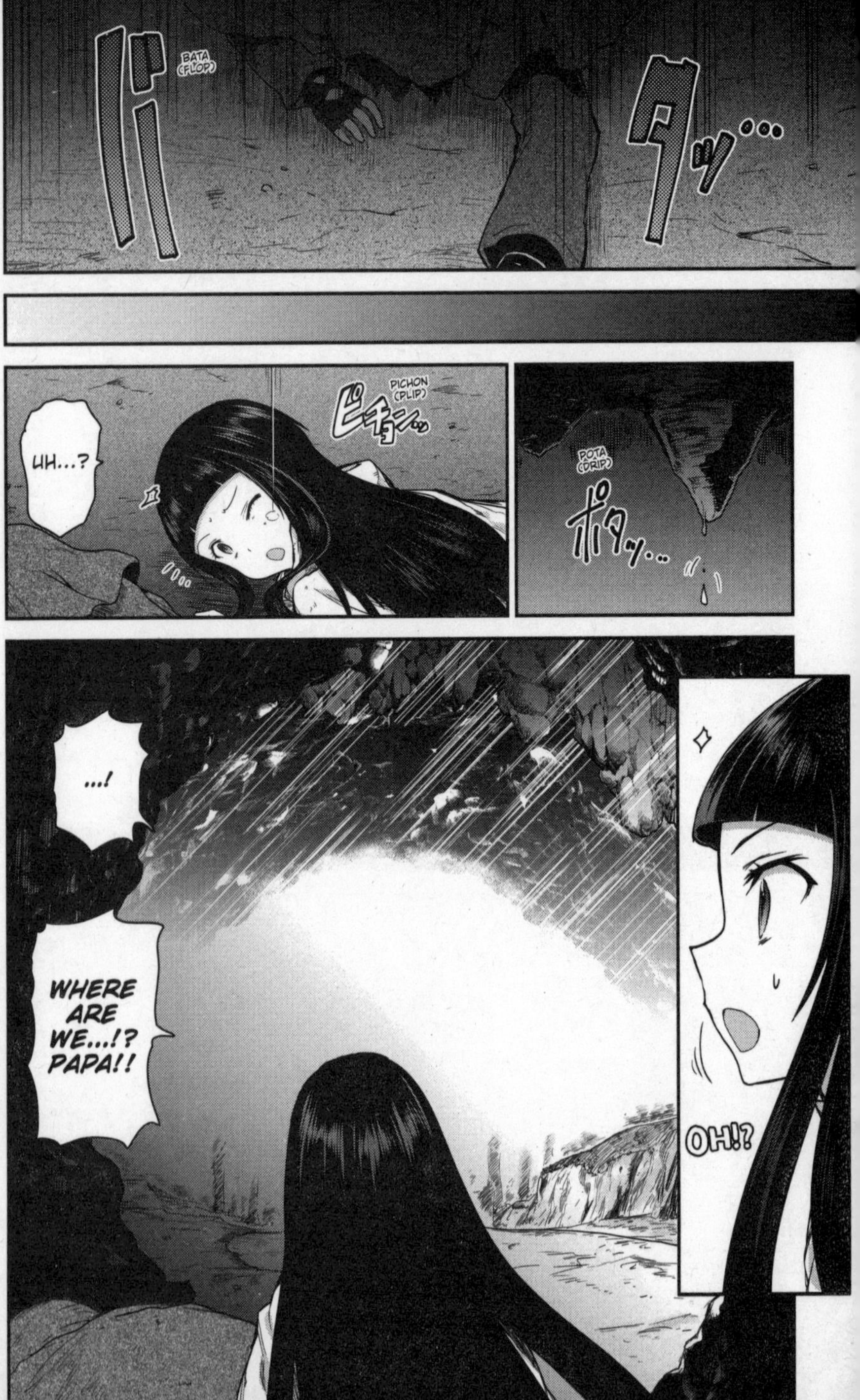
タッ…
BATA (FLOP)
バ
POTA (DRIP)
ポタッ…
PICHON (PLIP)
ピチョン…
UH...?
OH!?
...!
WHERE ARE WE...!? PAPA!!

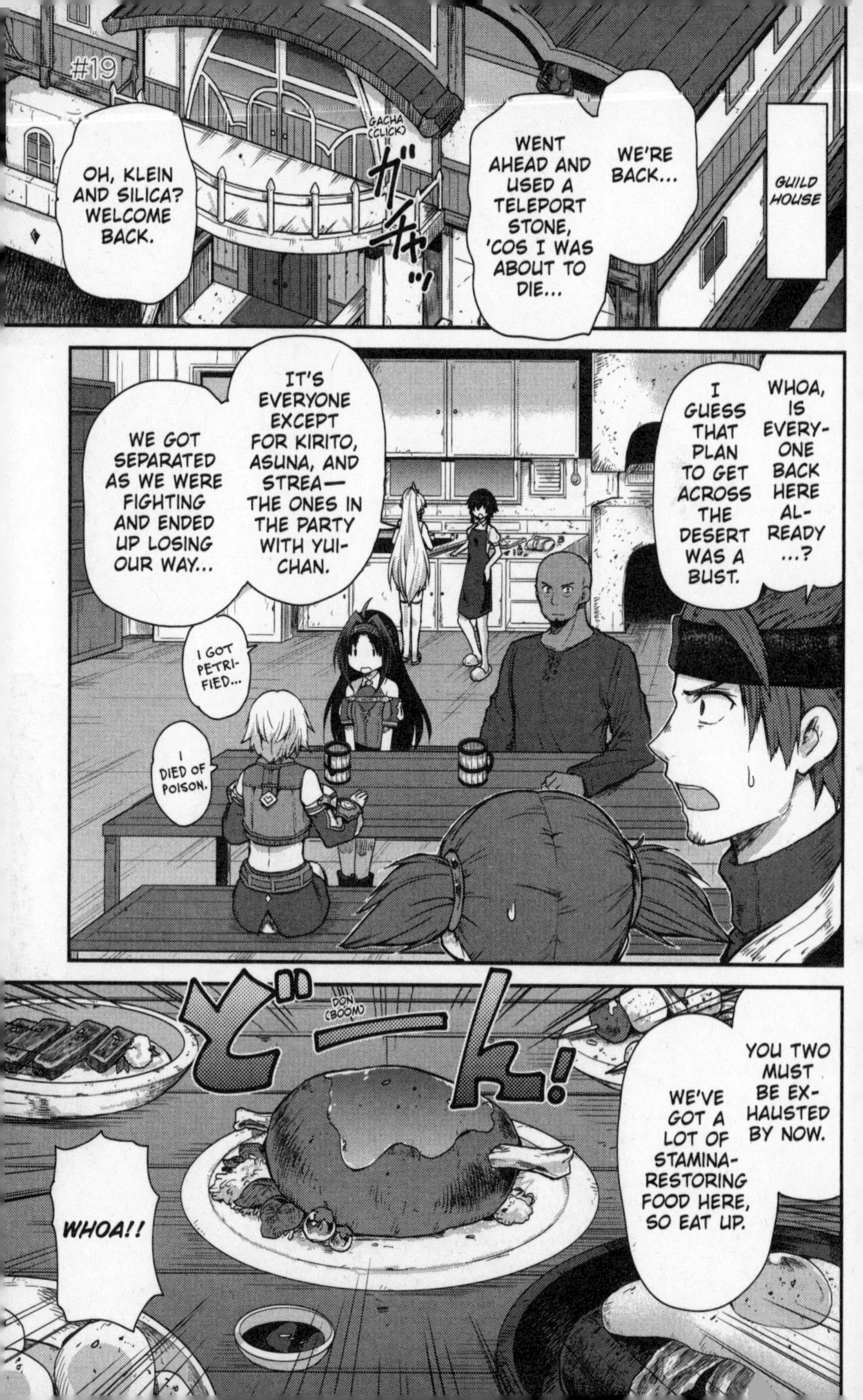
#19
GUILD HOUSE
WE'RE BACK...
WENT AHEAD AND USED A TELEPORT STONE, 'COS I WAS ABOUT TO DIE...
GACHA (CLICK)
ガチャッ
OH, KLEIN AND SILICA? WELCOME BACK.
WHOA, IS EVERYONE BACK HERE ALREADY...?
I GUESS THAT PLAN TO GET ACROSS THE DESERT WAS A BUST.
IT'S EVERYONE EXCEPT FOR KIRITO, ASUNA, AND STREA—THE ONES IN THE PARTY WITH YUI-CHAN.
WE GOT SEPARATED AS WE WERE FIGHTING AND ENDED UP LOSING OUR WAY...
I GOT PETRIFIED...
I DIED OF POISON.
YOU TWO MUST BE EXHAUSTED BY NOW.
WE'VE GOT A LOT OF STAMINA-RESTORING FOOD HERE, SO EAT UP.
DON (BOOM)
どーん!
WHOA!!

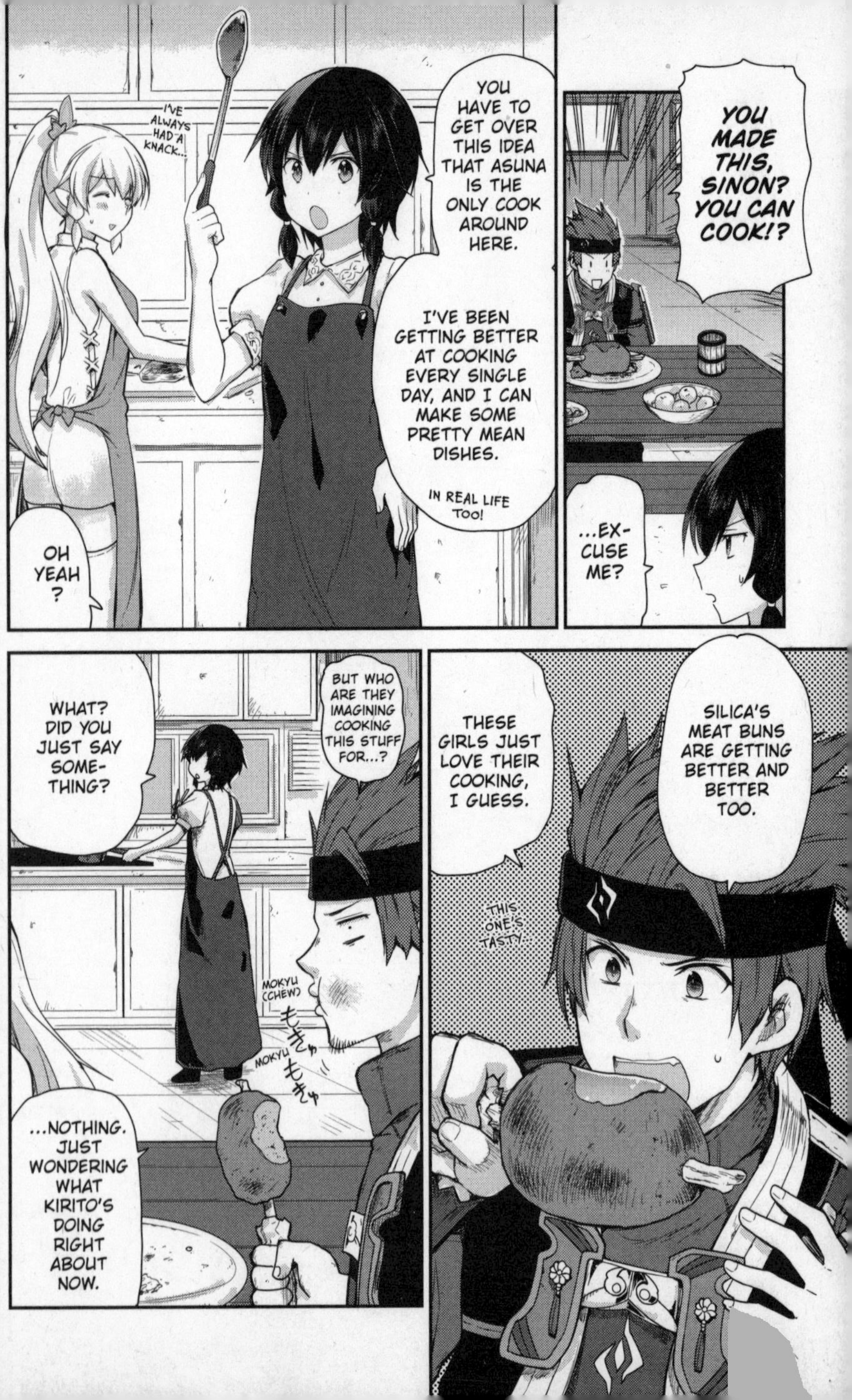
YOU MADE THIS, SINON? YOU CAN COOK!?
...EX-CUSE ME?
YOU HAVE TO GET OVER THIS IDEA THAT ASUNA IS THE ONLY COOK AROUND HERE.
I'VE ALWAYS HAD A KNACK...
I'VE BEEN GETTING BETTER AT COOKING EVERY SINGLE DAY, AND I CAN MAKE SOME PRETTY MEAN DISHES.
IN REAL LIFE TOO!
OH YEAH?
SILICA'S MEAT BUNS ARE GETTING BETTER AND BETTER TOO.
THESE GIRLS JUST LOVE THEIR COOKING, I GUESS.
THIS ONE'S TASTY...
BUT WHO ARE THEY IMAGINING COOKING THIS STUFF FOR...?
WHAT? DID YOU JUST SAY SOME-THING?
MOKYU (CHEW)
もきゅ
MOKYU
もきゅ
...NOTHING. JUST WONDERING WHAT KIRITO'S DOING RIGHT ABOUT NOW.

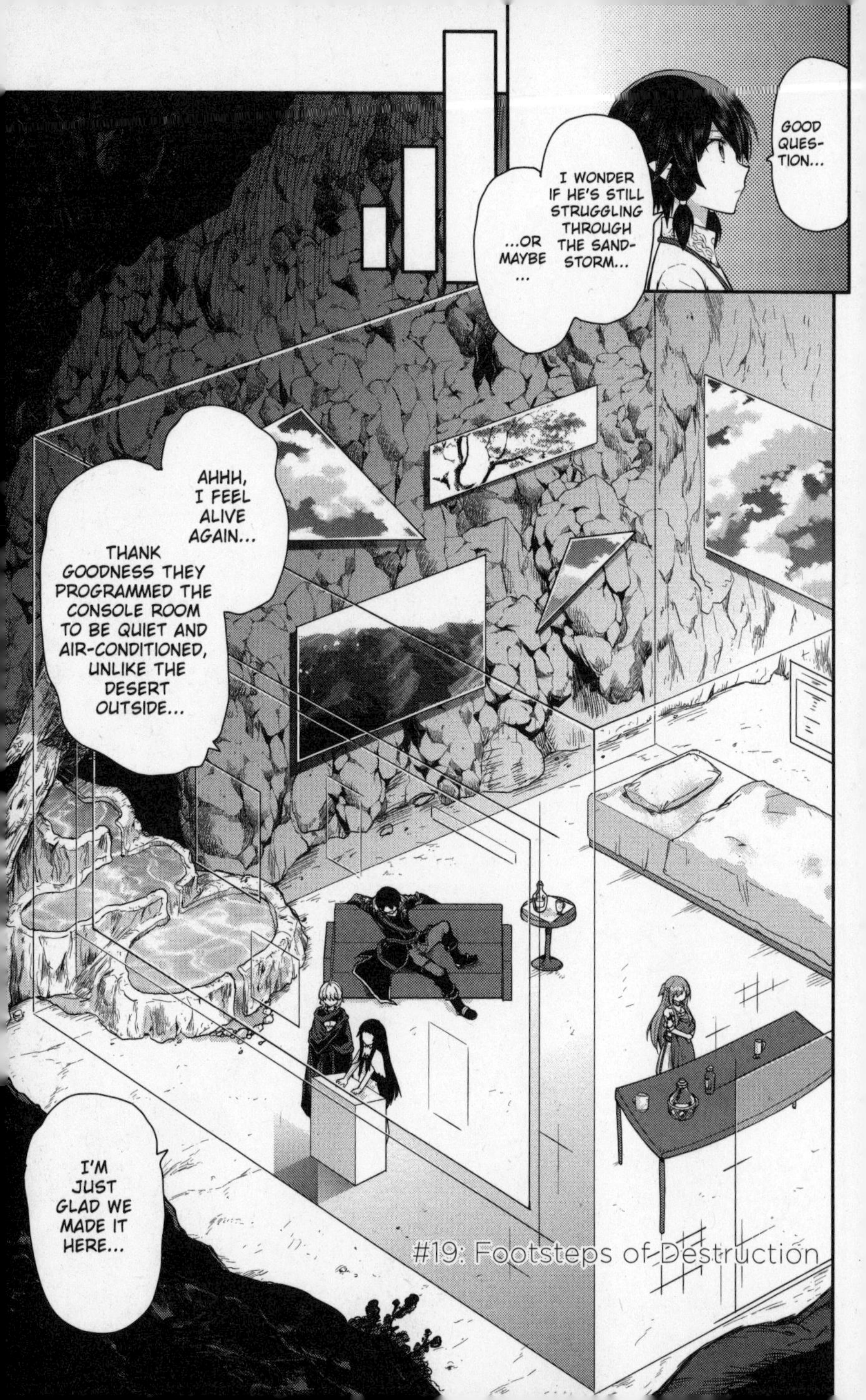
GOOD QUESTION...
I WONDER IF HE'S STILL STRUGGLING THROUGH THE SANDSTORM...
...OR MAYBE...
AHHH, I FEEL ALIVE AGAIN...
THANK GOODNESS THEY PROGRAMMED THE CONSOLE ROOM TO BE QUIET AND AIR-CONDITIONED, UNLIKE THE DESERT OUTSIDE...
I'M JUST GLAD WE MADE IT HERE...
#19: Footsteps of Destruction

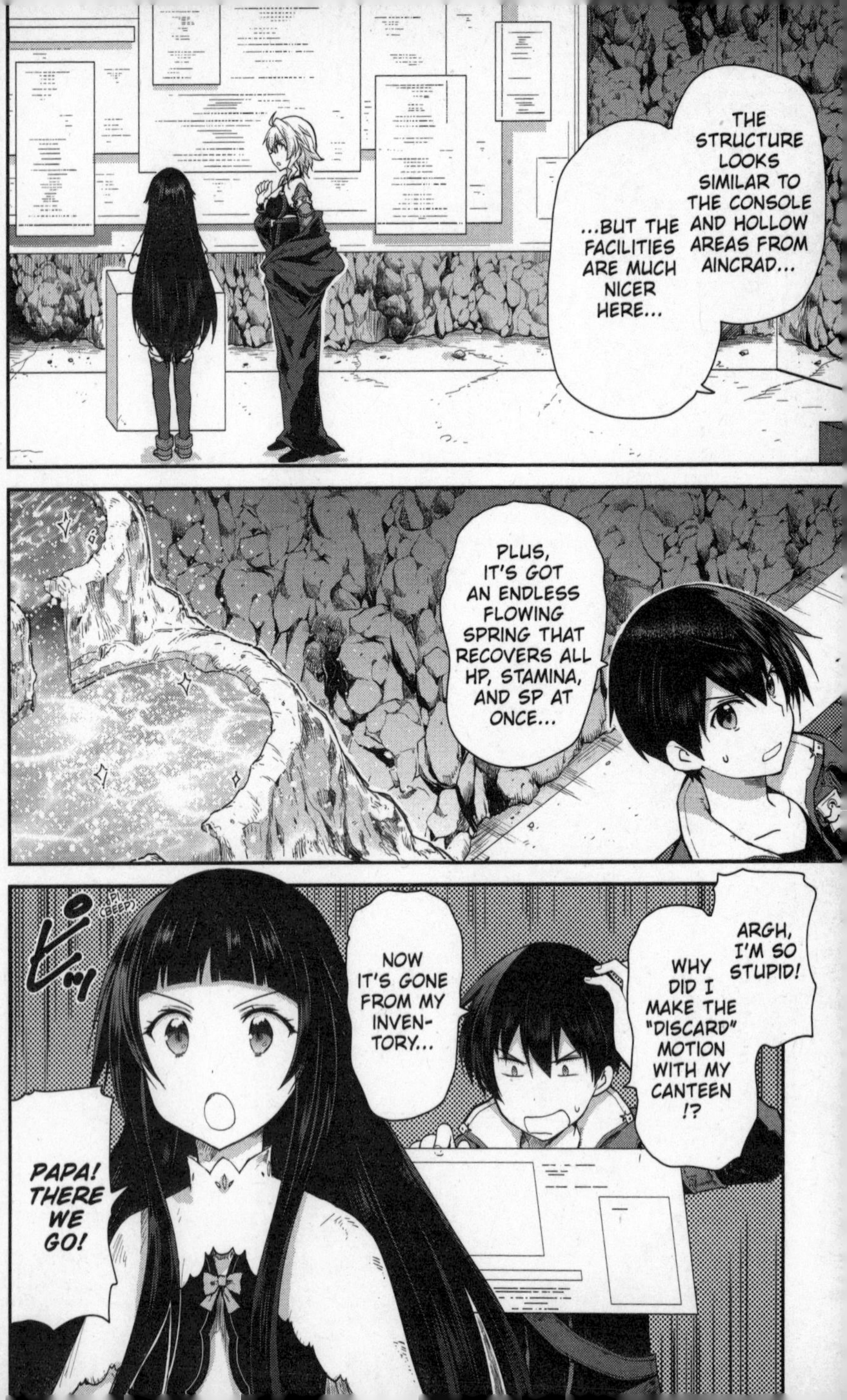
THE STRUCTURE LOOKS SIMILAR TO THE CONSOLE AND HOLLOW AREAS FROM AINCRAD...
...BUT THE FACILITIES ARE MUCH NICER HERE...
PLUS, IT'S GOT AN ENDLESS FLOWING SPRING THAT RECOVERS ALL HP, STAMINA, AND SP AT ONCE...
ARGH, I'M SO STUPID!
WHY DID I MAKE THE "DISCARD" MOTION WITH MY CANTEEN !?
NOW IT'S GONE FROM MY INVEN-TORY...
PI (BEEP)
PAPA! THERE WE GO!

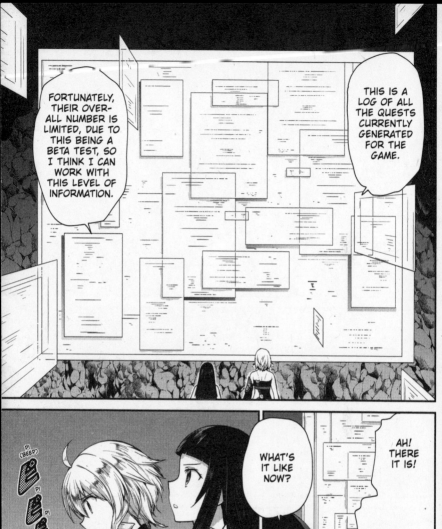

THIS IS A LOG OF ALL THE QUESTS CURRENTLY GENERATED FOR THE GAME.

FORTUNATELY, THEIR OVER-ALL NUMBER IS LIMITED, DUE TO THIS BEING A BETA TEST, SO I THINK I CAN WORK WITH THIS LEVEL OF INFORMATION.

AH! THERE IT IS!

THIS IS PREMIERE-CHAN'S QUEST LOG.

WHAT'S IT LIKE NOW?

HER CURRENT QUEST IS CLASSIFIED AS STILL ONGOING, BUT...

IS IT JUST ME, OR ARE THERE SOME ANOMALIES WITH THIS LOG?

PI (BEEP)

PI

PI

PI

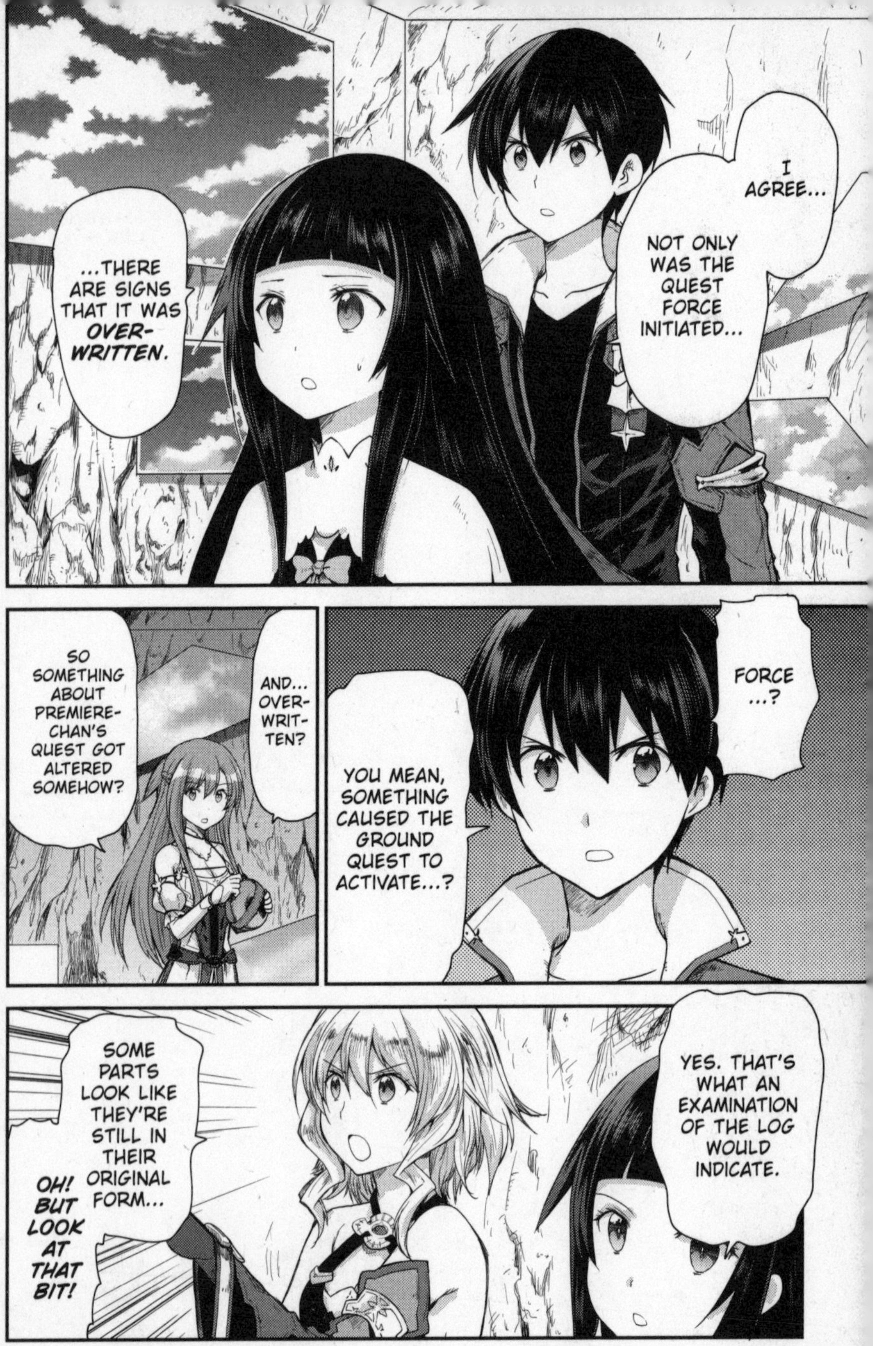
I AGREE... NOT ONLY WAS THE QUEST FORCE INITIATED...
...THERE ARE SIGNS THAT IT WAS OVER-WRITTEN.
FORCE ...?
YOU MEAN, SOMETHING CAUSED THE GROUND QUEST TO ACTIVATE...?
AND... OVER-WRIT-TEN?
SO SOMETHING ABOUT PREMIERE-CHAN'S QUEST GOT ALTERED SOMEHOW?
YES. THAT'S WHAT AN EXAMINATION OF THE LOG WOULD INDICATE.
SOME PARTS LOOK LIKE THEY'RE STILL IN THEIR ORIGINAL FORM...
OH! BUT LOOK AT THAT BIT!

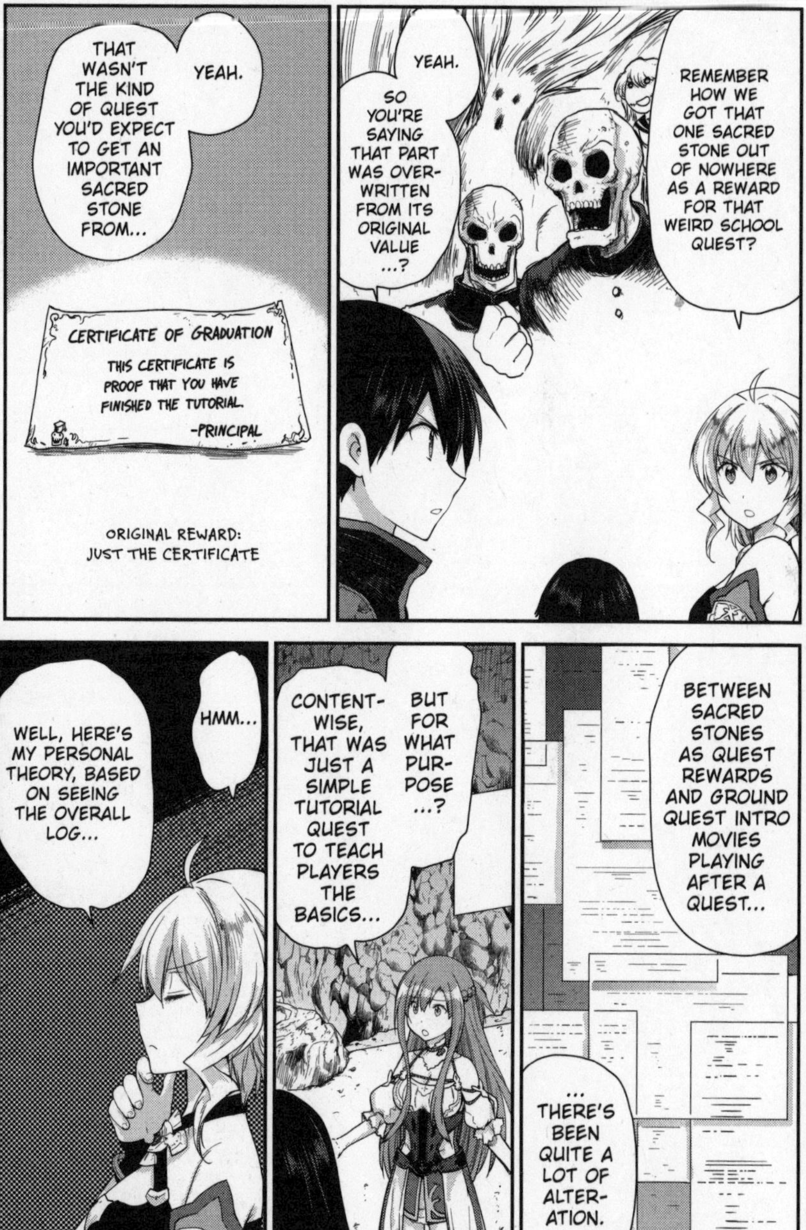
REMEMBER HOW WE GOT THAT ONE SACRED STONE OUT OF NOWHERE AS A REWARD FOR THAT WEIRD SCHOOL QUEST?
YEAH.
SO YOU'RE SAYING THAT PART WAS OVER-WRITTEN FROM ITS ORIGINAL VALUE ...?
YEAH.
THAT WASN'T THE KIND OF QUEST YOU'D EXPECT TO GET AN IMPORTANT SACRED STONE FROM...
CERTIFICATE OF GRADUATION
THIS CERTIFICATE IS PROOF THAT YOU HAVE FINISHED THE TUTORIAL.
-PRINCIPAL
ORIGINAL REWARD: JUST THE CERTIFICATE
BETWEEN SACRED STONES AS QUEST REWARDS AND GROUND QUEST INTRO MOVIES PLAYING AFTER A QUEST...
... THERE'S BEEN QUITE A LOT OF ALTER-ATION.
BUT FOR WHAT PUR-POSE ...?
CONTENT-WISE, THAT WAS JUST A SIMPLE TUTORIAL QUEST TO TEACH PLAYERS THE BASICS...
HMM...
WELL, HERE'S MY PERSONAL THEORY, BASED ON SEEING THE OVERALL LOG...

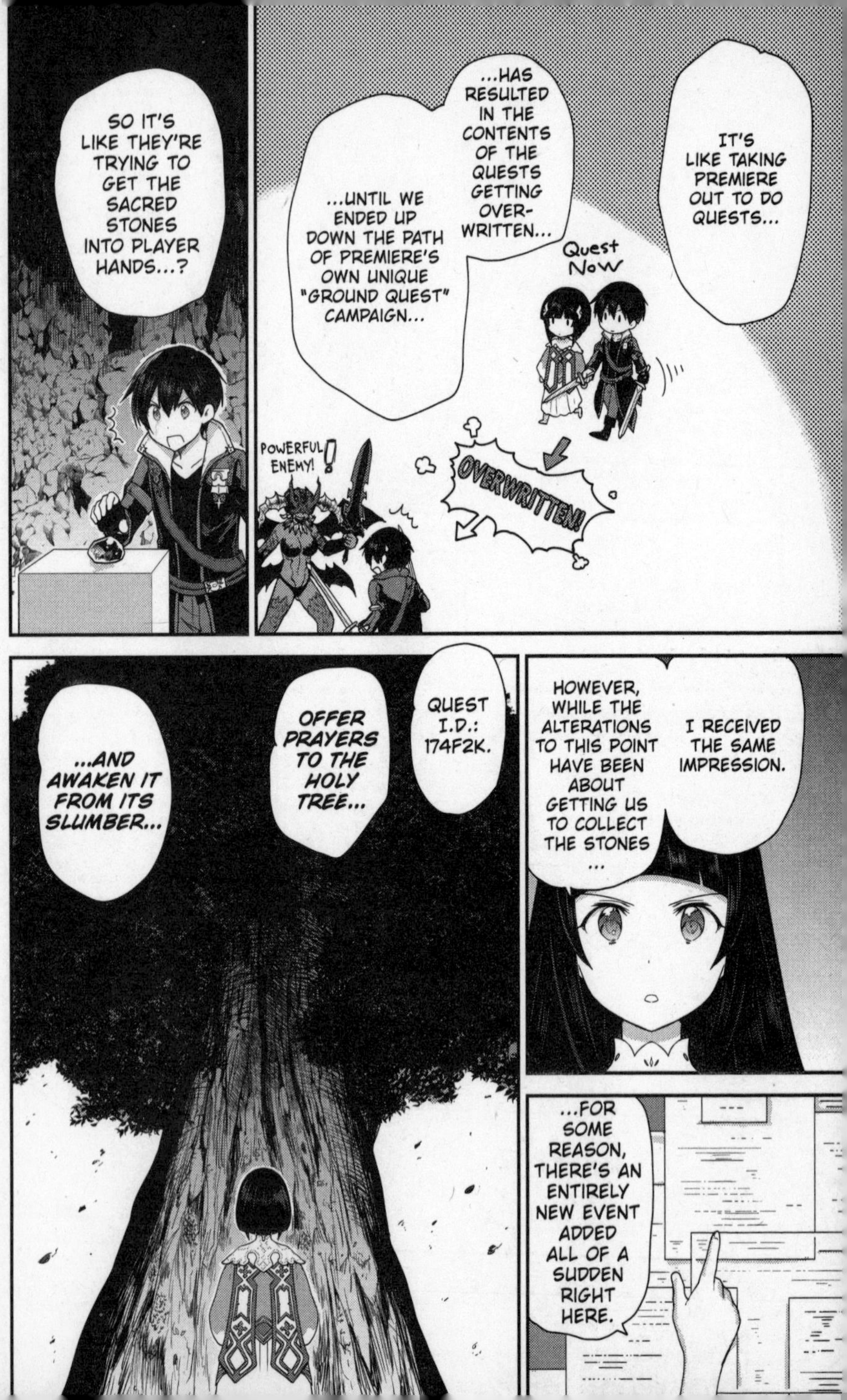
IT'S LIKE TAKING PREMIERE OUT TO DO QUESTS...
...HAS RESULTED IN THE CONTENTS OF THE QUESTS GETTING OVER-WRITTEN...
...UNTIL WE ENDED UP DOWN THE PATH OF PREMIERE'S OWN UNIQUE "GROUND QUEST" CAMPAIGN...
Quest Now
OVERWRITTEN!
POWERFUL ENEMY!
SO IT'S LIKE THEY'RE TRYING TO GET THE SACRED STONES INTO PLAYER HANDS...?
I RECEIVED THE SAME IMPRESSION.
HOWEVER, WHILE THE ALTERATIONS TO THIS POINT HAVE BEEN ABOUT GETTING US TO COLLECT THE STONES...
...FOR SOME REASON, THERE'S AN ENTIRELY NEW EVENT ADDED ALL OF A SUDDEN RIGHT HERE.
QUEST I.D.: 174F2K.
OFFER PRAYERS TO THE HOLY TREE...
...AND AWAKEN IT FROM ITS SLUMBER...

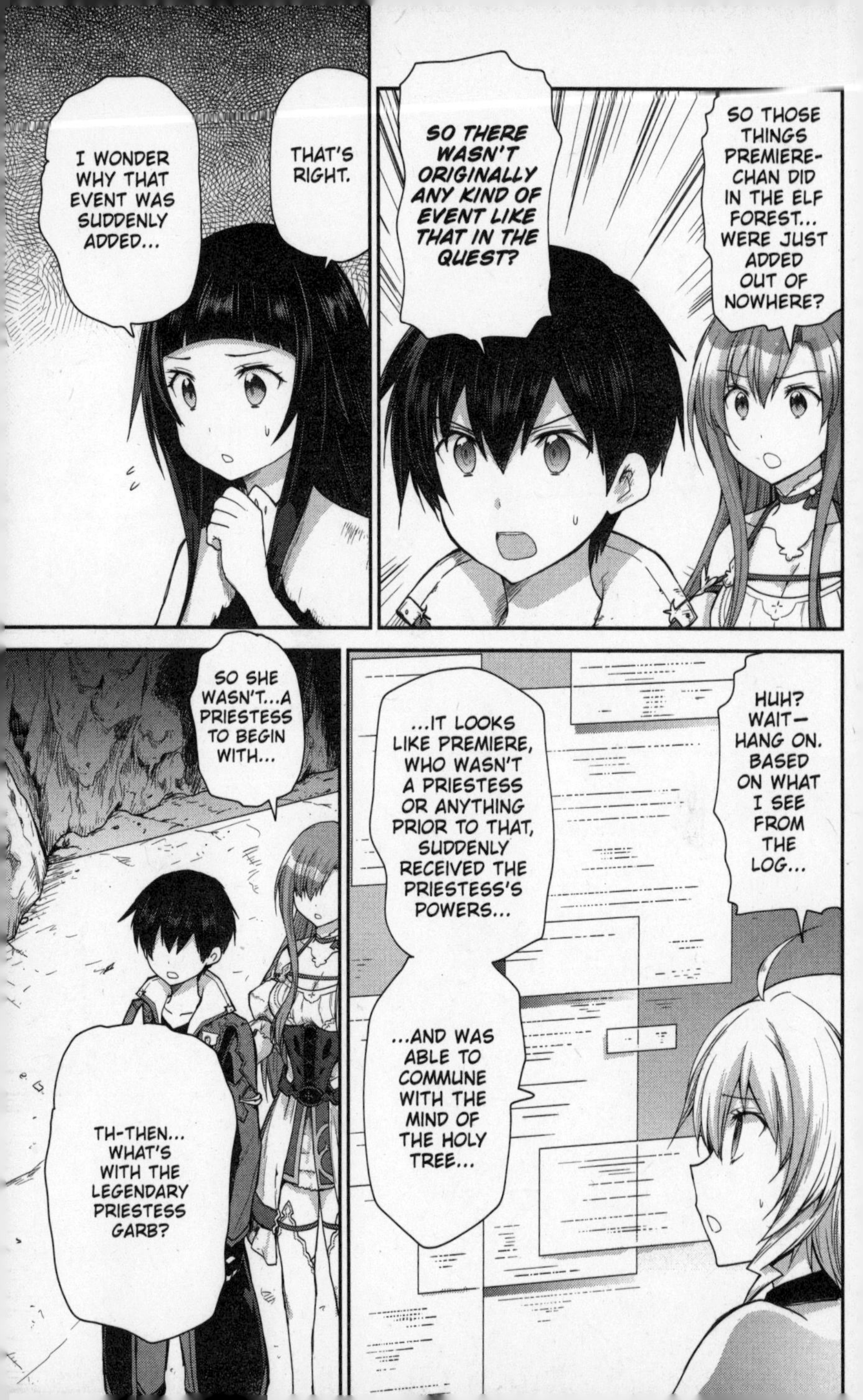
SO THOSE THINGS PREMIERE-CHAN DID IN THE ELF FOREST... WERE JUST ADDED OUT OF NOWHERE?
SO THERE WASN'T ORIGINALLY ANY KIND OF EVENT LIKE THAT IN THE QUEST?
THAT'S RIGHT.
I WONDER WHY THAT EVENT WAS SUDDENLY ADDED...
HUH? WAIT—HANG ON. BASED ON WHAT I SEE FROM THE LOG...
...IT LOOKS LIKE PREMIERE, WHO WASN'T A PRIESTESS OR ANYTHING PRIOR TO THAT, SUDDENLY RECEIVED THE PRIESTESS'S POWERS...
...AND WAS ABLE TO COMMUNE WITH THE MIND OF THE HOLY TREE...
SO SHE WASN'T...A PRIESTESS TO BEGIN WITH...
TH-THEN... WHAT'S WITH THE LEGENDARY PRIESTESS GARB?

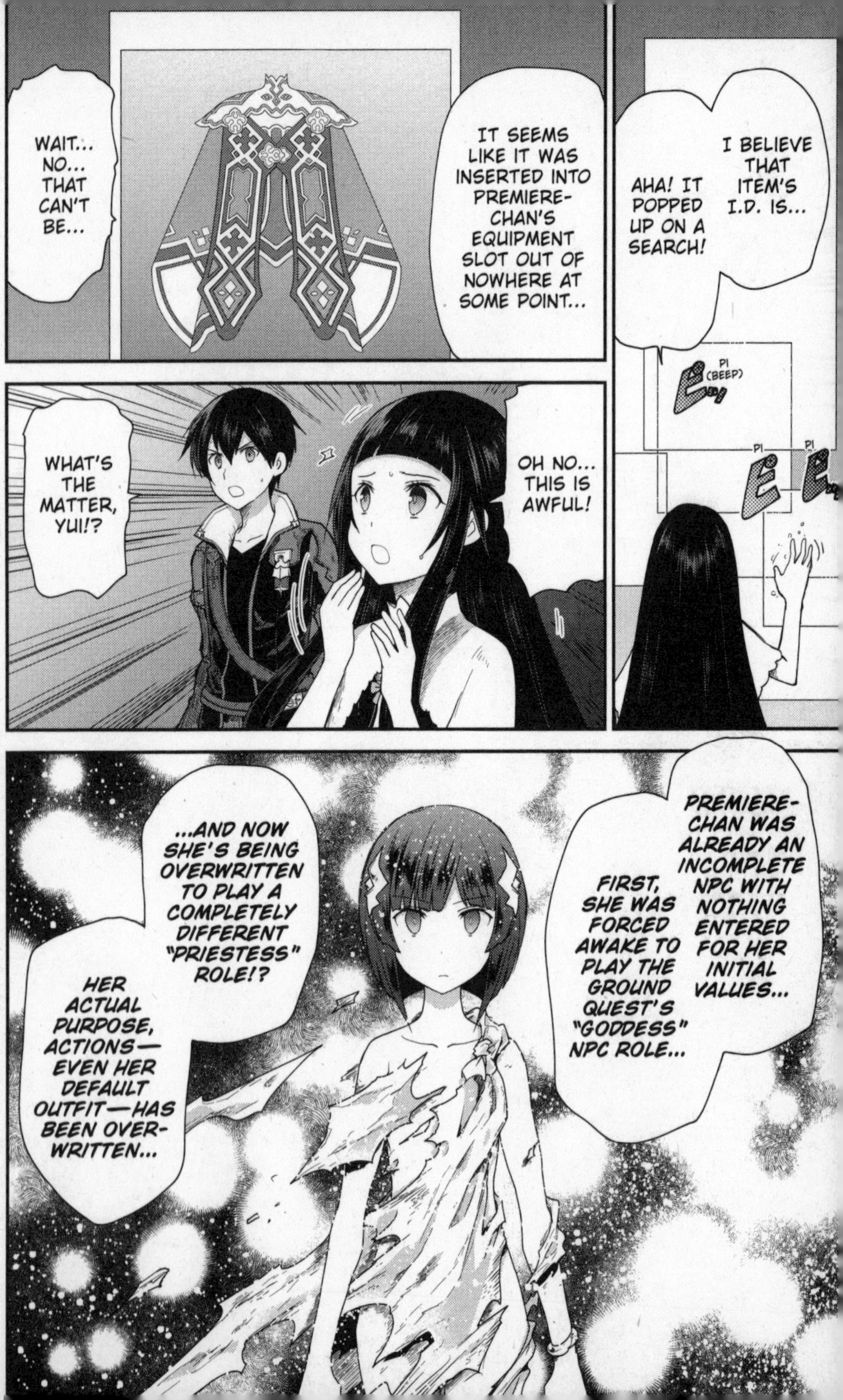
I BELIEVE THAT ITEM'S I.D. IS...
AHA! IT POPPED UP ON A SEARCH!
PI (BEEP)
PI
PI
IT SEEMS LIKE IT WAS INSERTED INTO PREMIERE-CHAN'S EQUIPMENT SLOT OUT OF NOWHERE AT SOME POINT...
WAIT... NO... THAT CAN'T BE...
OH NO... THIS IS AWFUL!
WHAT'S THE MATTER, YUI!?
PREMIERE-CHAN WAS ALREADY AN INCOMPLETE NPC WITH NOTHING ENTERED FOR HER INITIAL VALUES...
FIRST, SHE WAS FORCED AWAKE TO PLAY THE GROUND QUEST'S "GODDESS" NPC ROLE...
...AND NOW SHE'S BEING OVERWRITTEN TO PLAY A COMPLETELY DIFFERENT "PRIESTESS" ROLE!?
HER ACTUAL PURPOSE, ACTIONS—EVEN HER DEFAULT OUTFIT—HAS BEEN OVER-WRITTEN...

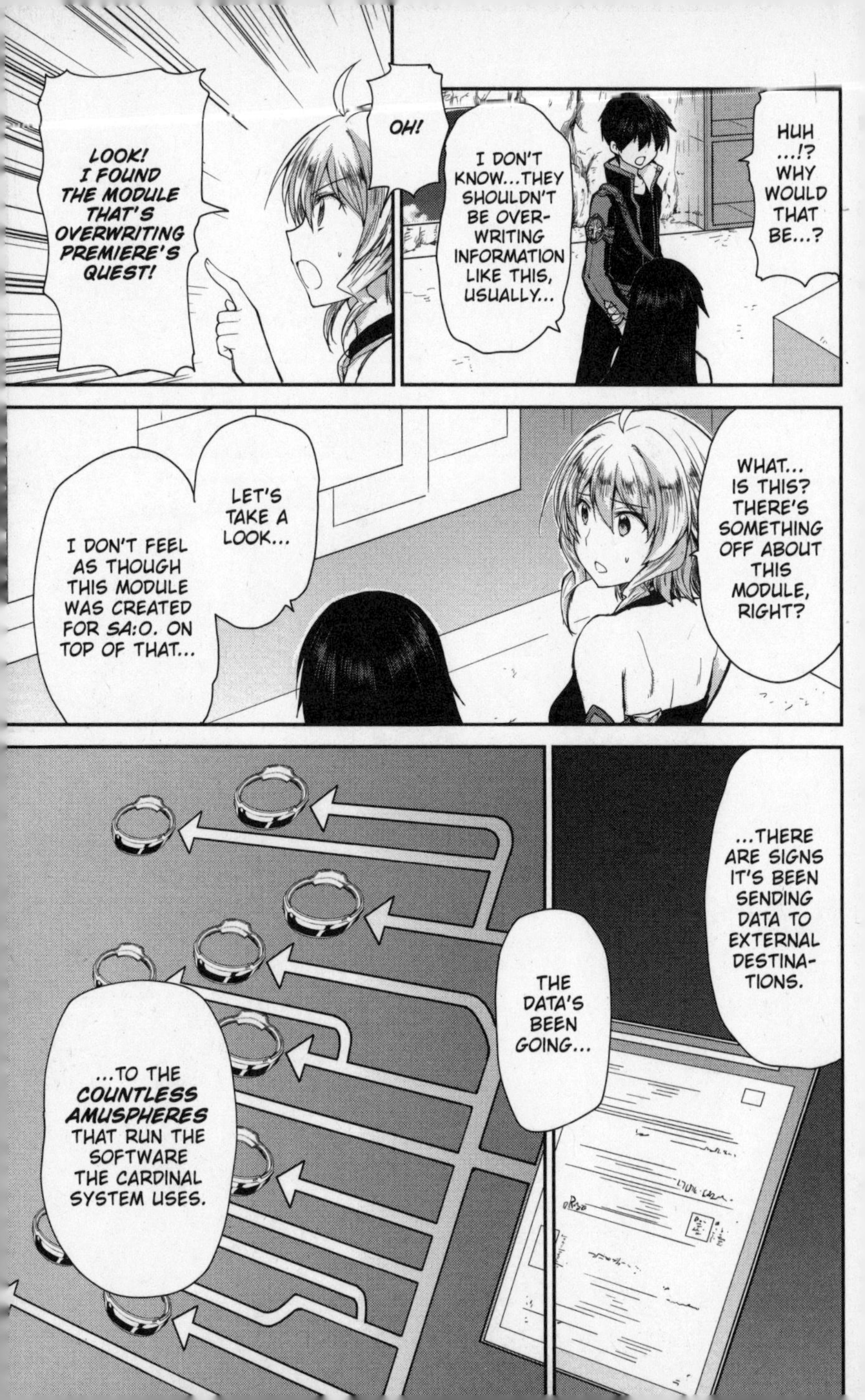
HUH...!? WHY WOULD THAT BE...?
I DON'T KNOW...THEY SHOULDN'T BE OVER-WRITING INFORMATION LIKE THIS, USUALLY...
OH!
LOOK! I FOUND THE MODULE THAT'S OVERWRITING PREMIERE'S QUEST!
WHAT... IS THIS? THERE'S SOMETHING OFF ABOUT THIS MODULE, RIGHT?
LET'S TAKE A LOOK...
I DON'T FEEL AS THOUGH THIS MODULE WAS CREATED FOR *SA:O*. ON TOP OF THAT...
...THERE ARE SIGNS IT'S BEEN SENDING DATA TO EXTERNAL DESTINA-TIONS.
THE DATA'S BEEN GOING...
...TO THE ***COUNTLESS AMUSPHERES*** THAT RUN THE SOFTWARE THE CARDINAL SYSTEM USES.

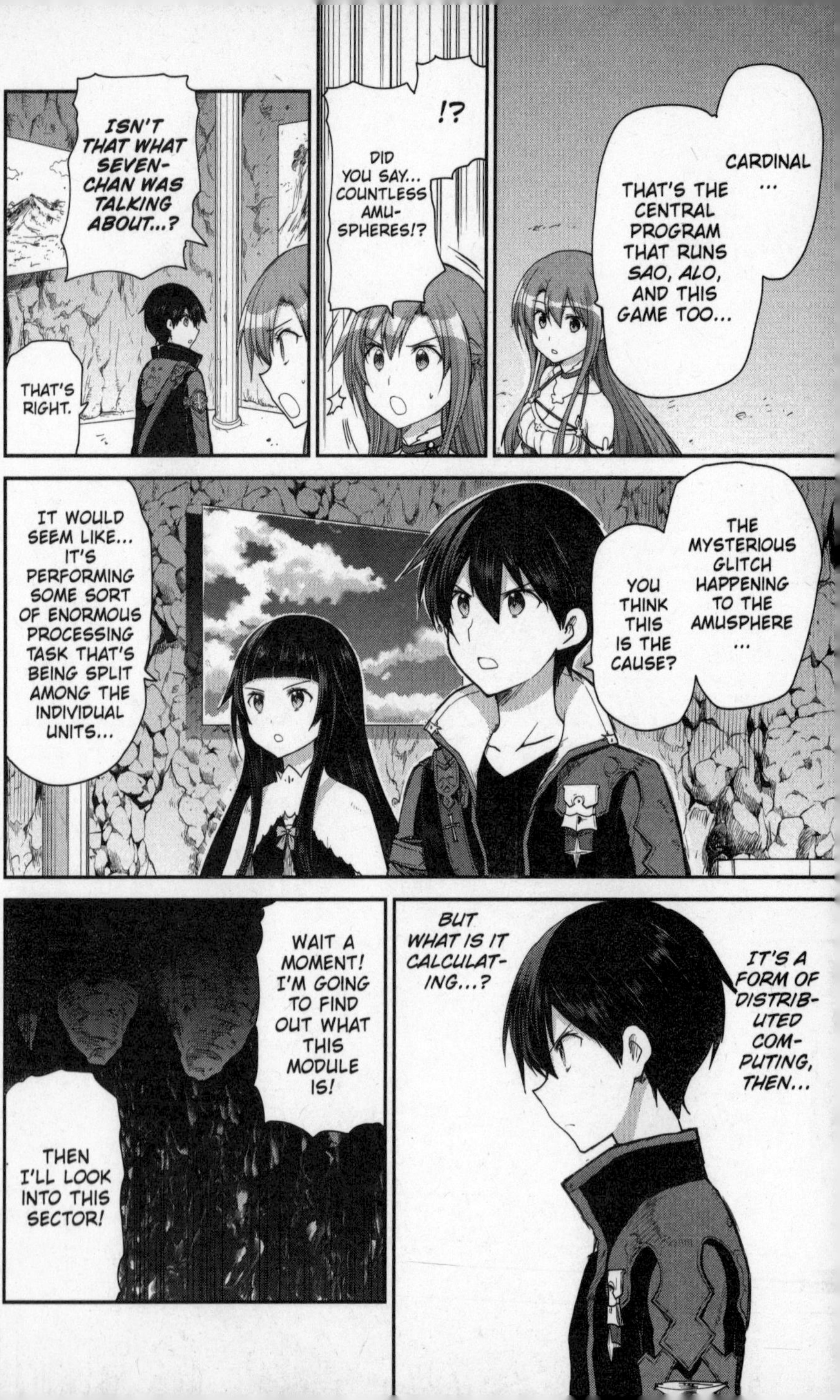
CARDINAL...
THAT'S THE CENTRAL PROGRAM THAT RUNS SAO, ALO, AND THIS GAME TOO...
!?
DID YOU SAY... COUNTLESS AMU-SPHERES!?
ISN'T THAT WHAT SEVEN-CHAN WAS TALKING ABOUT...?
THAT'S RIGHT.
THE MYSTERIOUS GLITCH HAPPENING TO THE AMUSPHERE...
YOU THINK THIS IS THE CAUSE?
IT WOULD SEEM LIKE... IT'S PERFORMING SOME SORT OF ENORMOUS PROCESSING TASK THAT'S BEING SPLIT AMONG THE INDIVIDUAL UNITS...
IT'S A FORM OF DISTRIB-UTED COM-PUTING, THEN...
BUT WHAT IS IT CALCULAT-ING...?
WAIT A MOMENT! I'M GOING TO FIND OUT WHAT THIS MODULE IS!
THEN I'LL LOOK INTO THIS SECTOR!

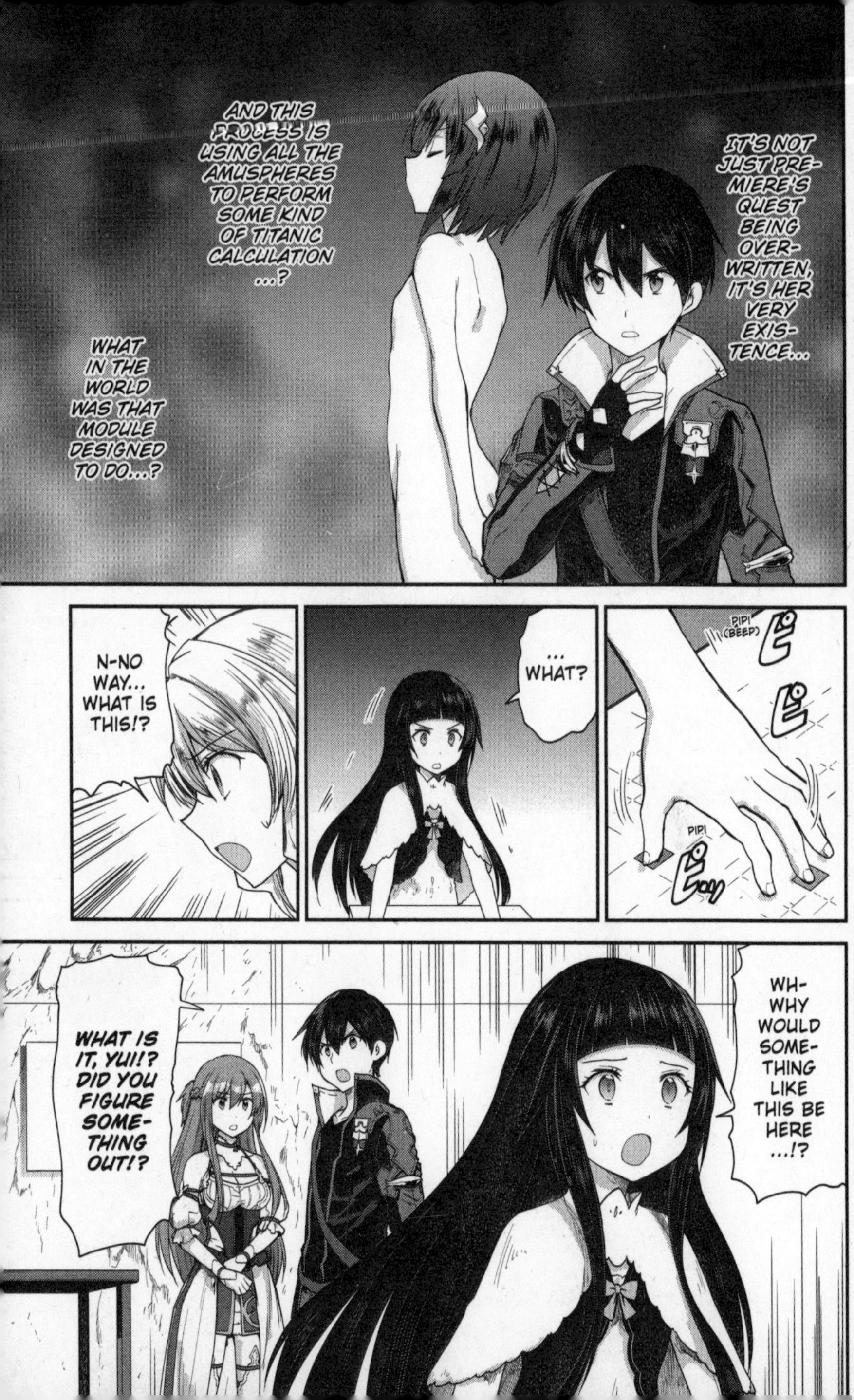
IT'S NOT JUST PRE-MIERE'S QUEST BEING OVER-WRITTEN, IT'S HER VERY EXIS-TENCE...
AND THIS PROCESS IS USING ALL THE AMUSPHERES TO PERFORM SOME KIND OF TITANIC CALCULATION ...?
WHAT IN THE WORLD WAS THAT MODULE DESIGNED TO DO...?
PIPI (BEEP)
PIPI
... WHAT?
N-NO WAY... WHAT IS THIS!?
WH-WHY WOULD SOME-THING LIKE THIS BE HERE ...!?
WHAT IS IT, YUI!? DID YOU FIGURE SOME-THING OUT!?

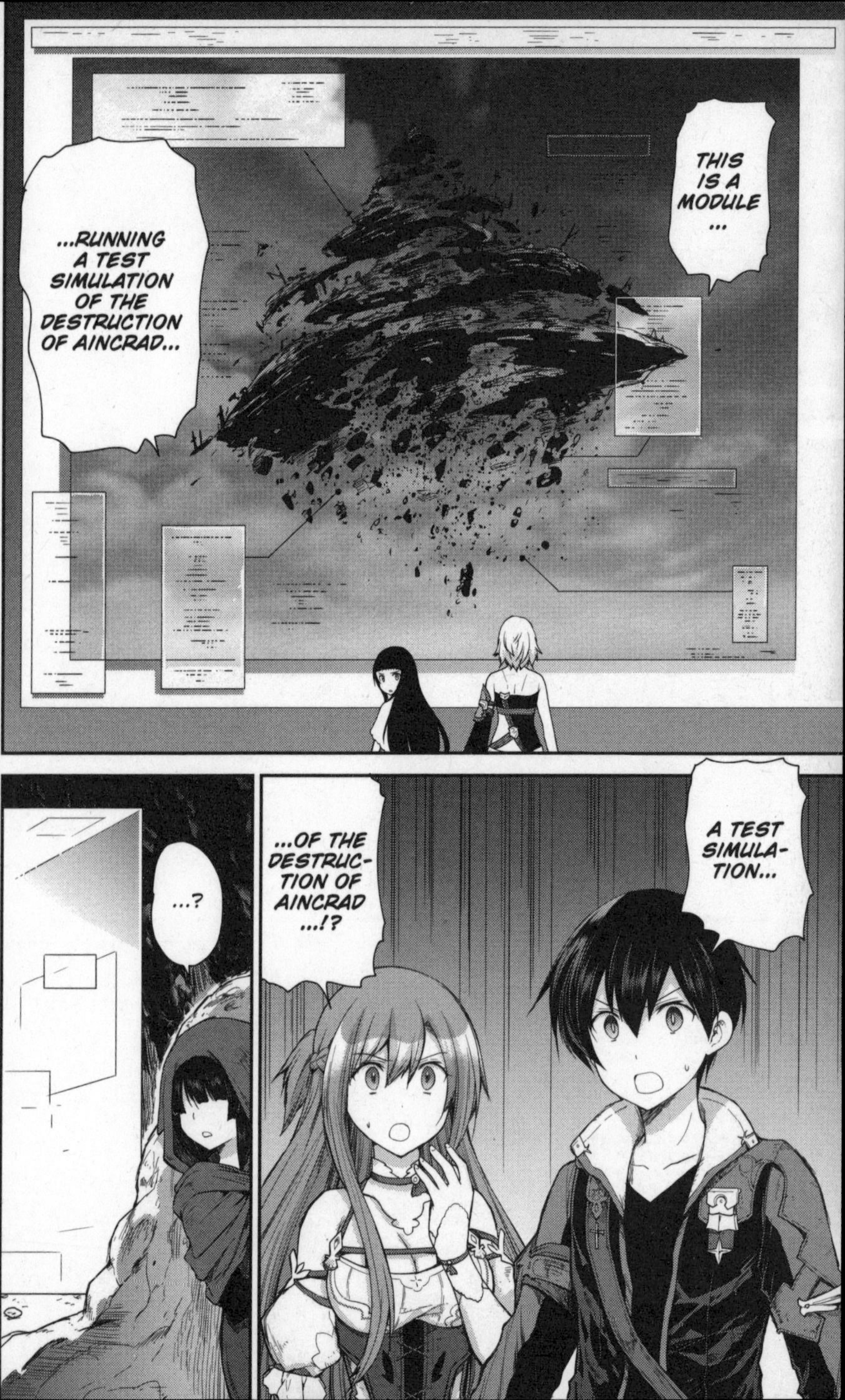
THIS IS A MODULE ...
...RUNNING A TEST SIMULATION OF THE DESTRUCTION OF AINCRAD...
A TEST SIMULA-TION...
...OF THE DESTRUC-TION OF AINCRAD ...!?
...?

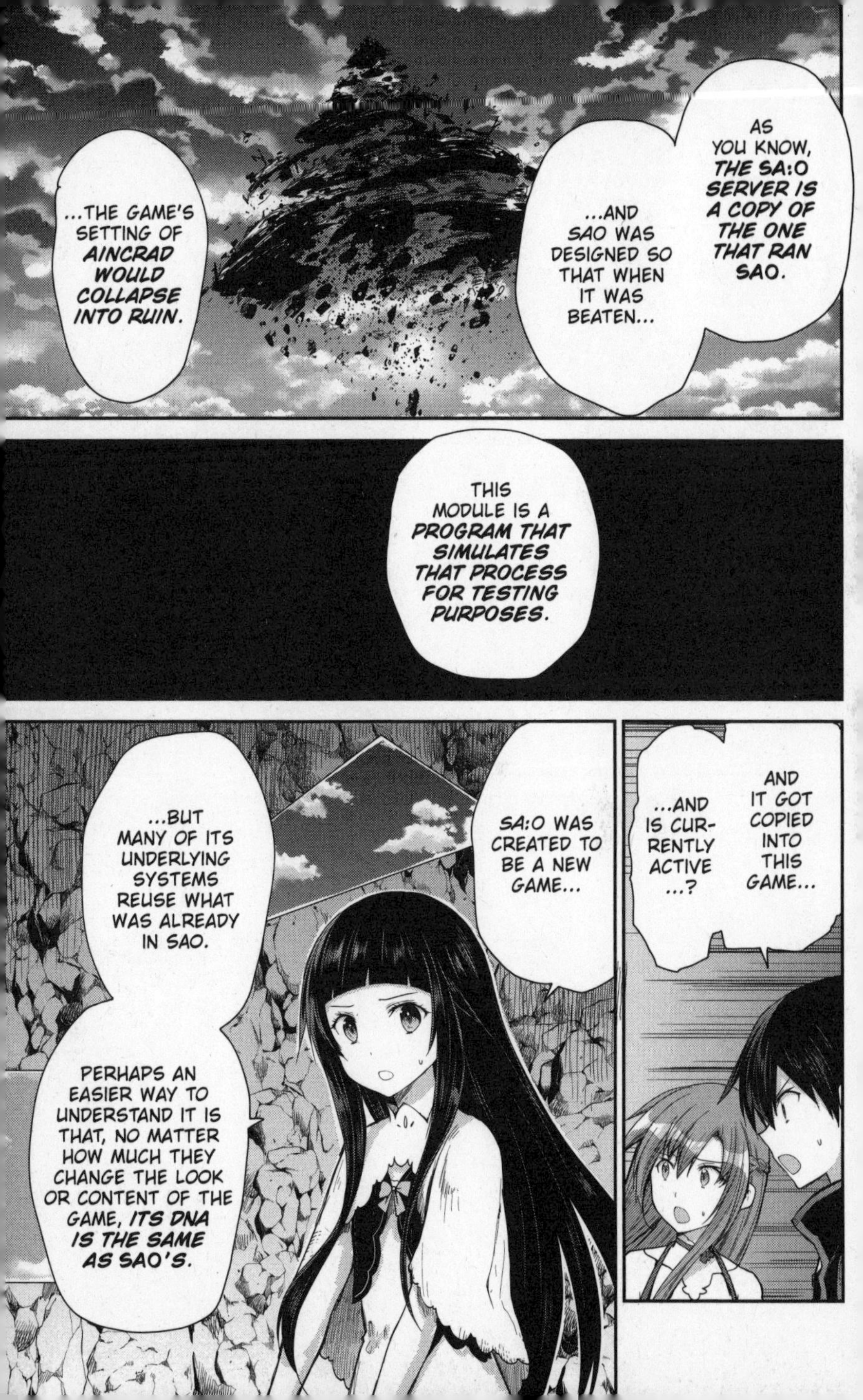
AS YOU KNOW, THE SA:O SERVER IS A COPY OF THE ONE THAT RAN SAO.
...AND SAO WAS DESIGNED SO THAT WHEN IT WAS BEATEN...
...THE GAME'S SETTING OF AINCRAD WOULD COLLAPSE INTO RUIN.
THIS MODULE IS A PROGRAM THAT SIMULATES THAT PROCESS FOR TESTING PURPOSES.
AND IT GOT COPIED INTO THIS GAME...
...AND IS CURRENTLY ACTIVE ...?
SA:O WAS CREATED TO BE A NEW GAME...
...BUT MANY OF ITS UNDERLYING SYSTEMS REUSE WHAT WAS ALREADY IN SAO.
PERHAPS AN EASIER WAY TO UNDERSTAND IT IS THAT, NO MATTER HOW MUCH THEY CHANGE THE LOOK OR CONTENT OF THE GAME, ITS DNA IS THE SAME AS SAO'S.

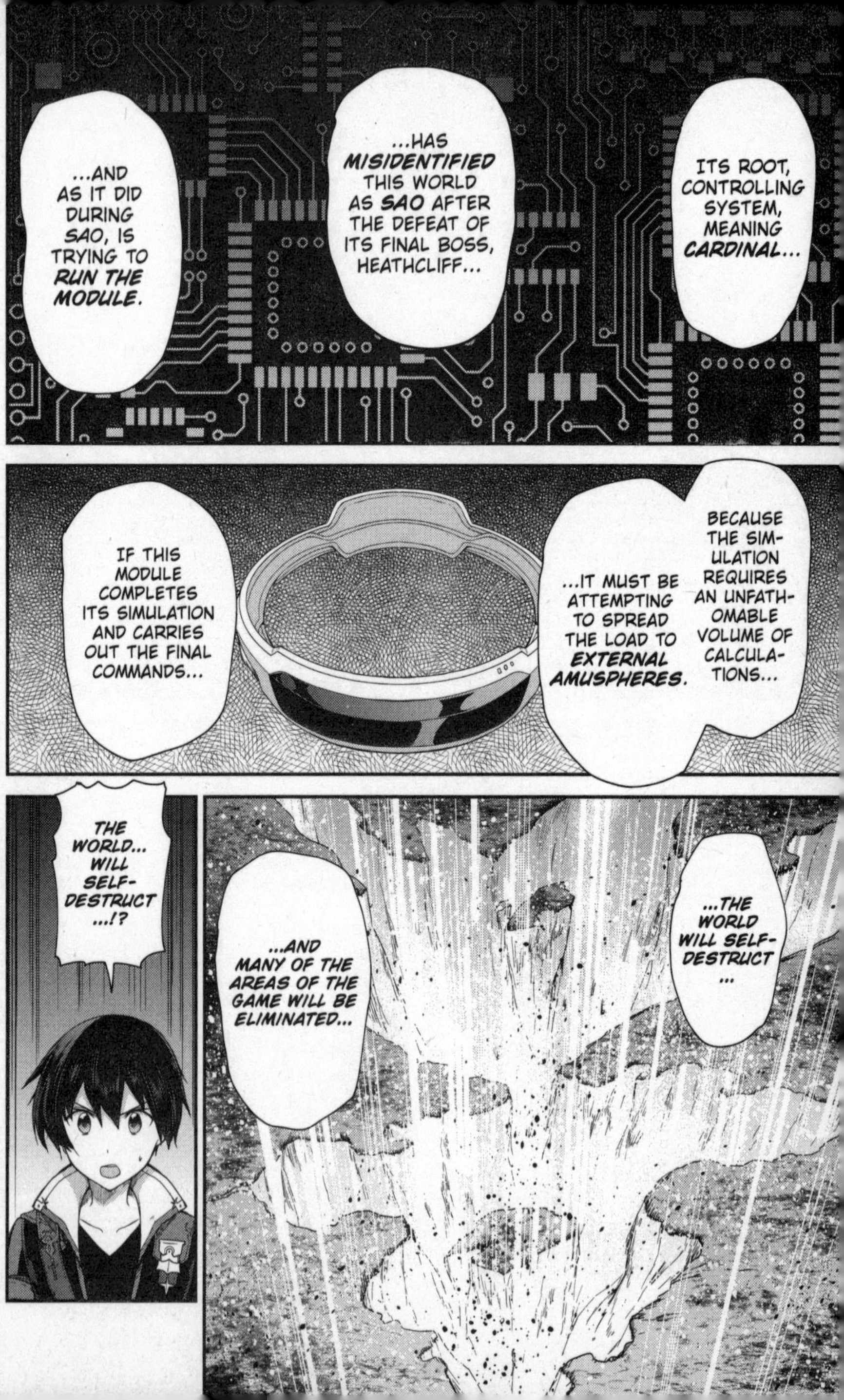
ITS ROOT, CONTROLLING SYSTEM, MEANING CARDINAL...
...HAS MISIDENTIFIED THIS WORLD AS SAO AFTER THE DEFEAT OF ITS FINAL BOSS, HEATHCLIFF...
...AND AS IT DID DURING SAO, IS TRYING TO RUN THE MODULE.
BECAUSE THE SIM-ULATION REQUIRES AN UNFATH-OMABLE VOLUME OF CALCULA-TIONS...
...IT MUST BE ATTEMPTING TO SPREAD THE LOAD TO EXTERNAL AMUSPHERES.
IF THIS MODULE COMPLETES ITS SIMULATION AND CARRIES OUT THE FINAL COMMANDS...
...THE WORLD WILL SELF-DESTRUCT...
...AND MANY OF THE AREAS OF THE GAME WILL BE ELIMINATED...
THE WORLD... WILL SELF-DESTRUCT...!?

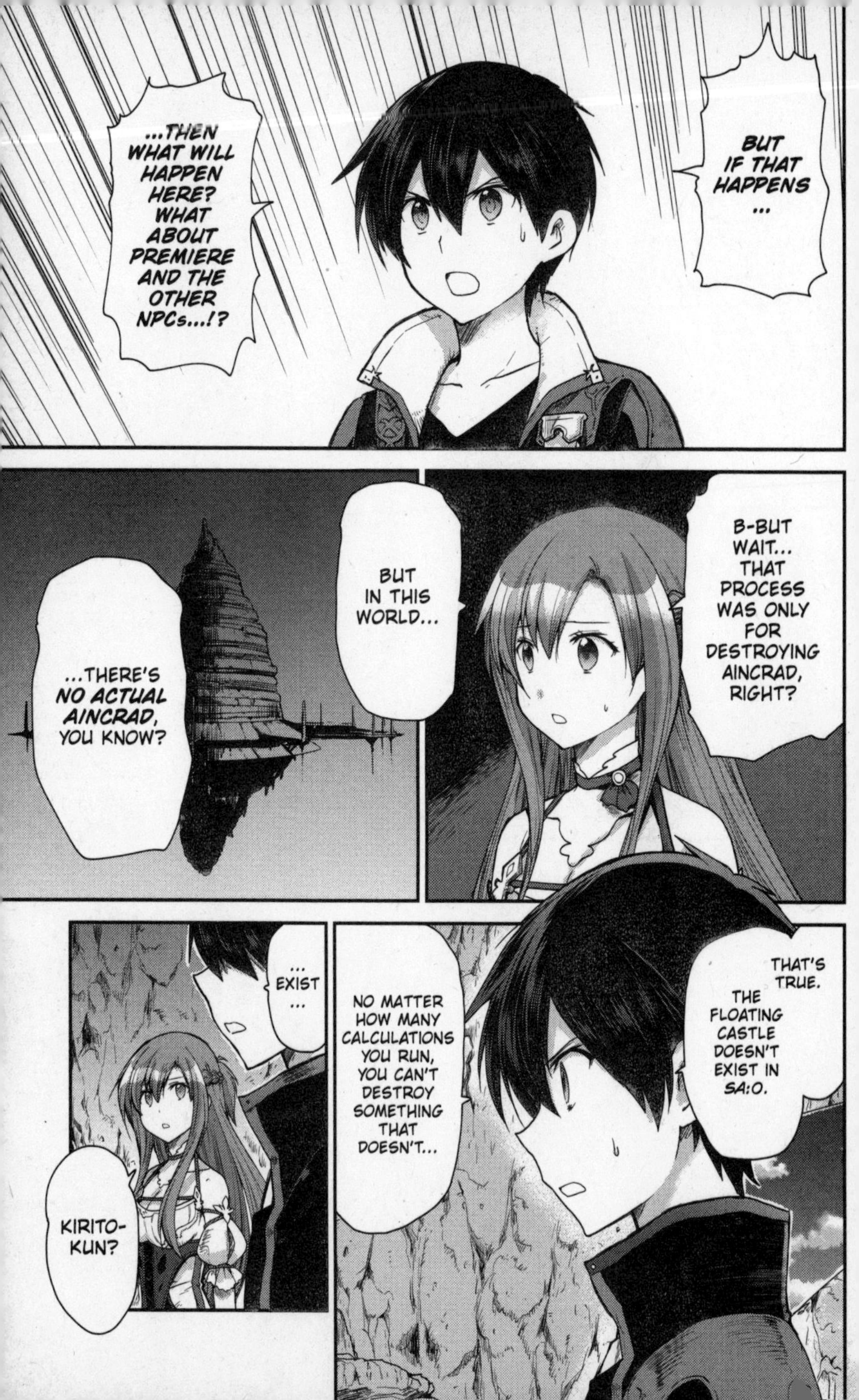
BUT IF THAT HAPPENS ...
...THEN WHAT WILL HAPPEN HERE? WHAT ABOUT PREMIERE AND THE OTHER NPCs...!?
B-BUT WAIT... THAT PROCESS WAS ONLY FOR DESTROYING AINCRAD, RIGHT?
BUT IN THIS WORLD...
...THERE'S *NO ACTUAL AINCRAD*, YOU KNOW?
THAT'S TRUE. THE FLOATING CASTLE DOESN'T EXIST IN SA:O.
NO MATTER HOW MANY CALCULATIONS YOU RUN, YOU CAN'T DESTROY SOMETHING THAT DOESN'T...
... EXIST ...
KIRITO-KUN?

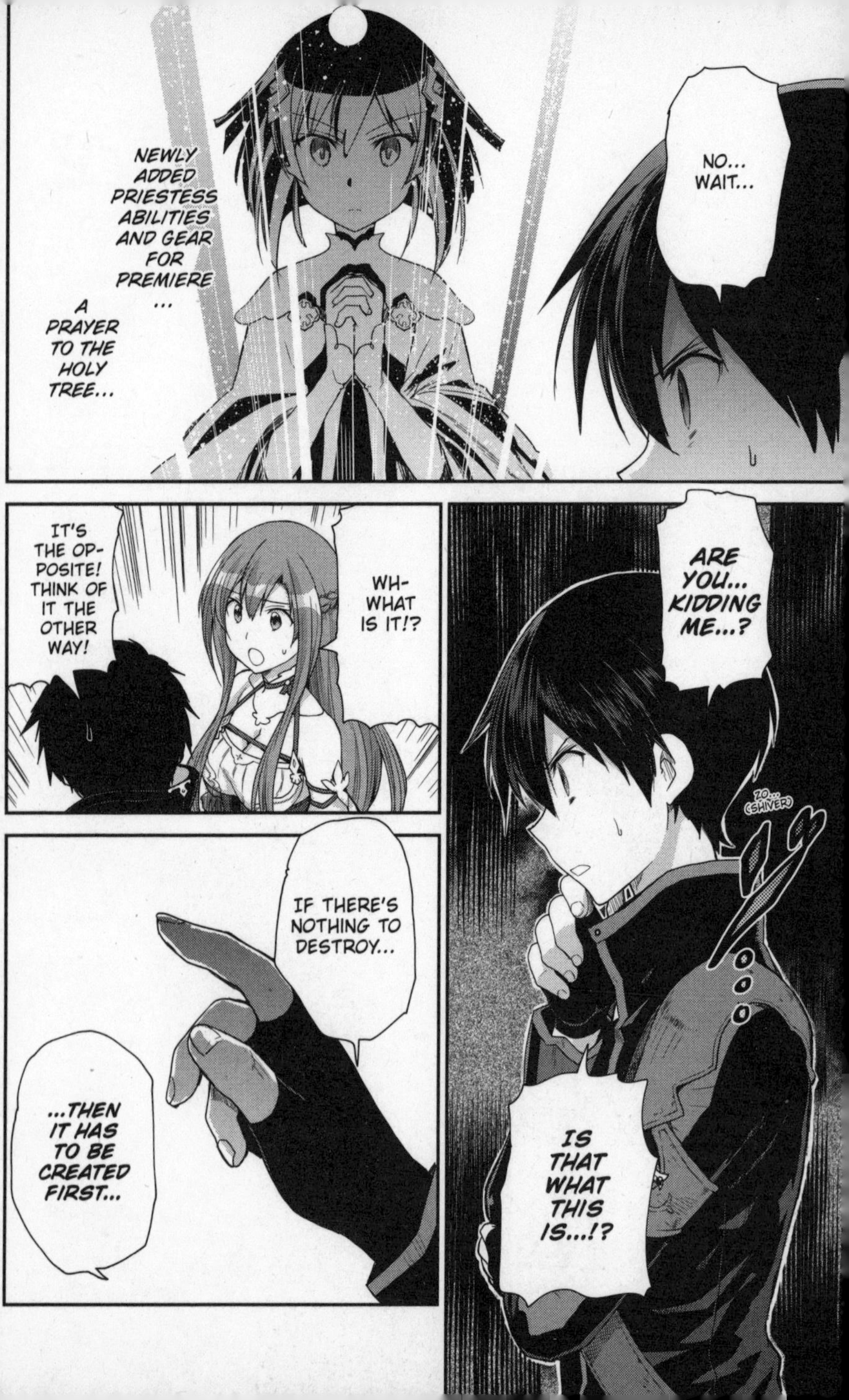
NO... WAIT...
NEWLY ADDED PRIESTESS ABILITIES AND GEAR FOR PREMIERE...
A PRAYER TO THE HOLY TREE...
ARE YOU... KIDDING ME...?
ZO... (SHIVER)
IS THAT WHAT THIS IS...!?
WH-WHAT IS IT!?
IT'S THE OP-POSITE! THINK OF IT THE OTHER WAY!
IF THERE'S NOTHING TO DESTROY...
...THEN IT HAS TO BE CREATED FIRST...

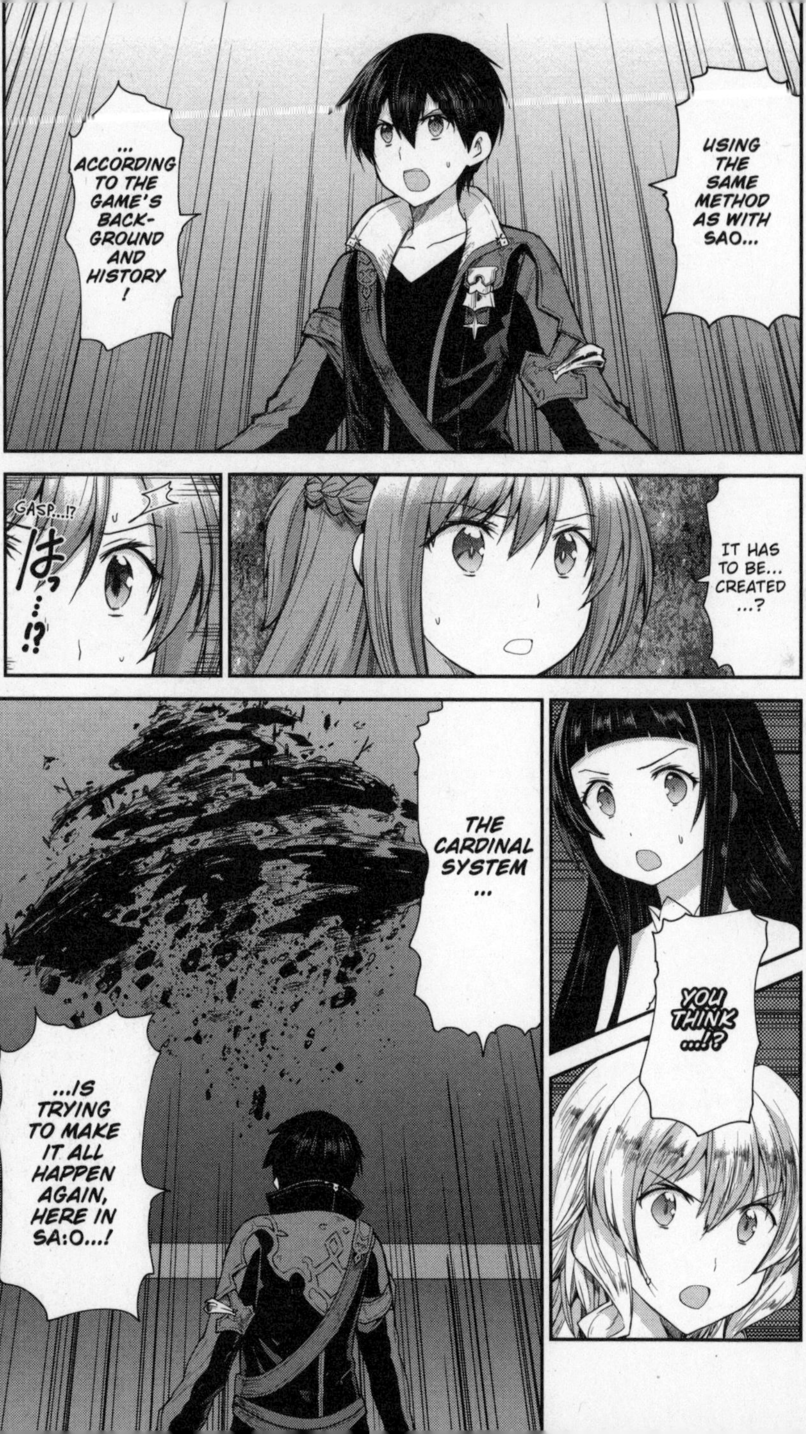
USING THE SAME METHOD AS WITH SAO...
...ACCORDING TO THE GAME'S BACK-GROUND AND HISTORY!
IT HAS TO BE... CREATED...?
GASP...!?
はっ…!?
YOU THINK...!?
THE CARDINAL SYSTEM...
...IS TRYING TO MAKE IT ALL HAPPEN AGAIN, HERE IN SA:O...!

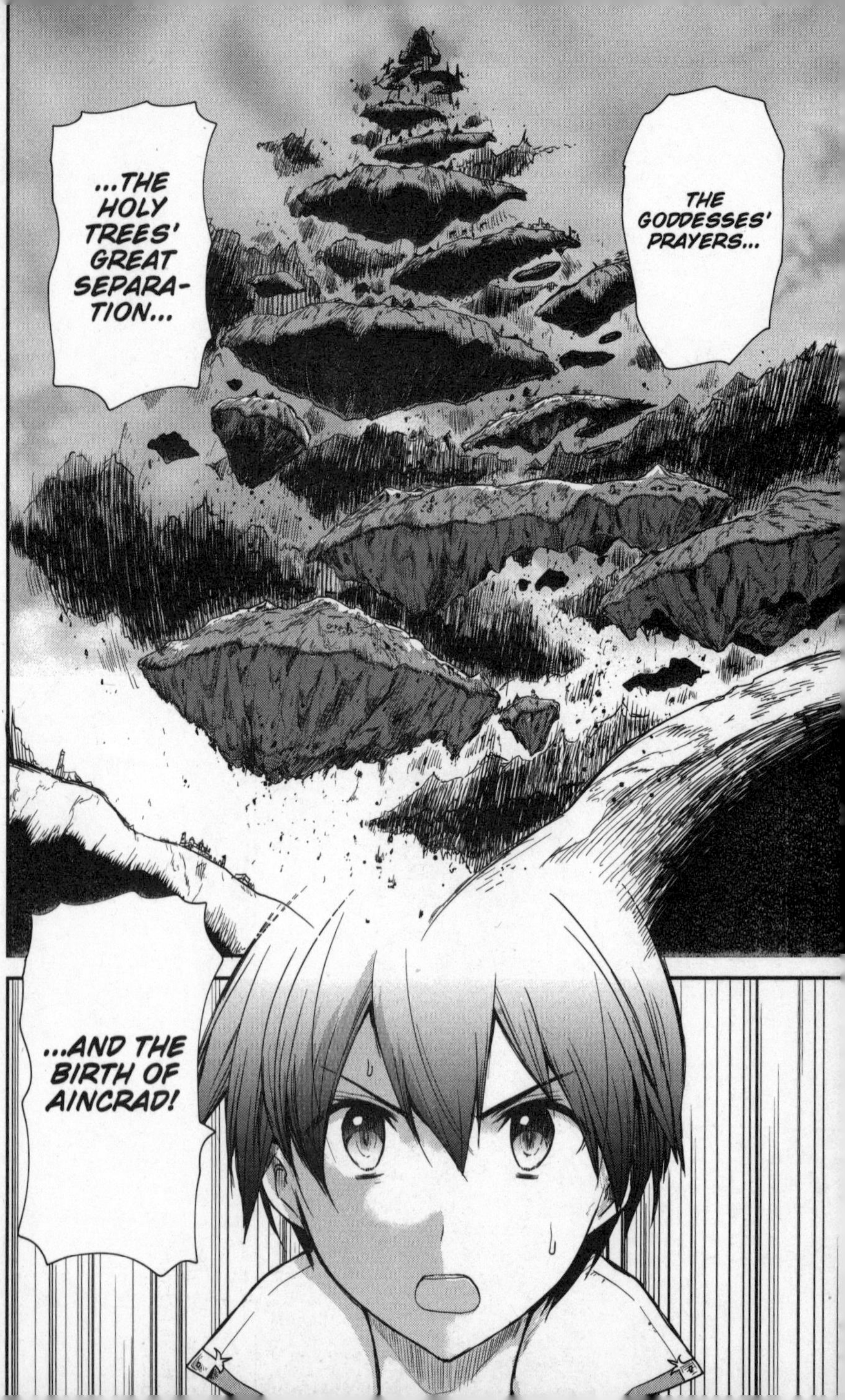
THE GODDESSES' PRAYERS...
...THE HOLY TREES' GREAT SEPARATION...
...AND THE BIRTH OF AINCRAD!

#20: Two Goddesses

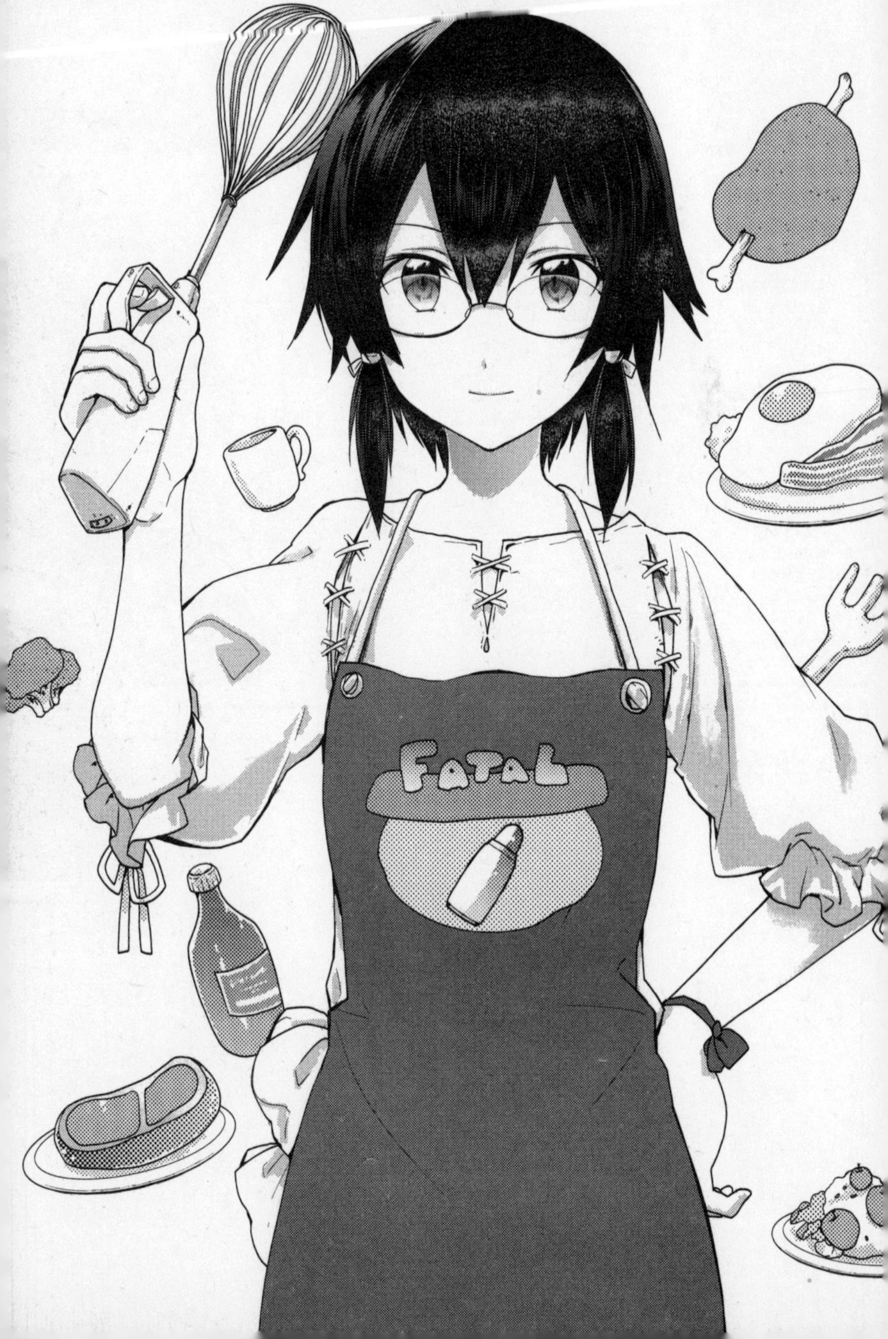

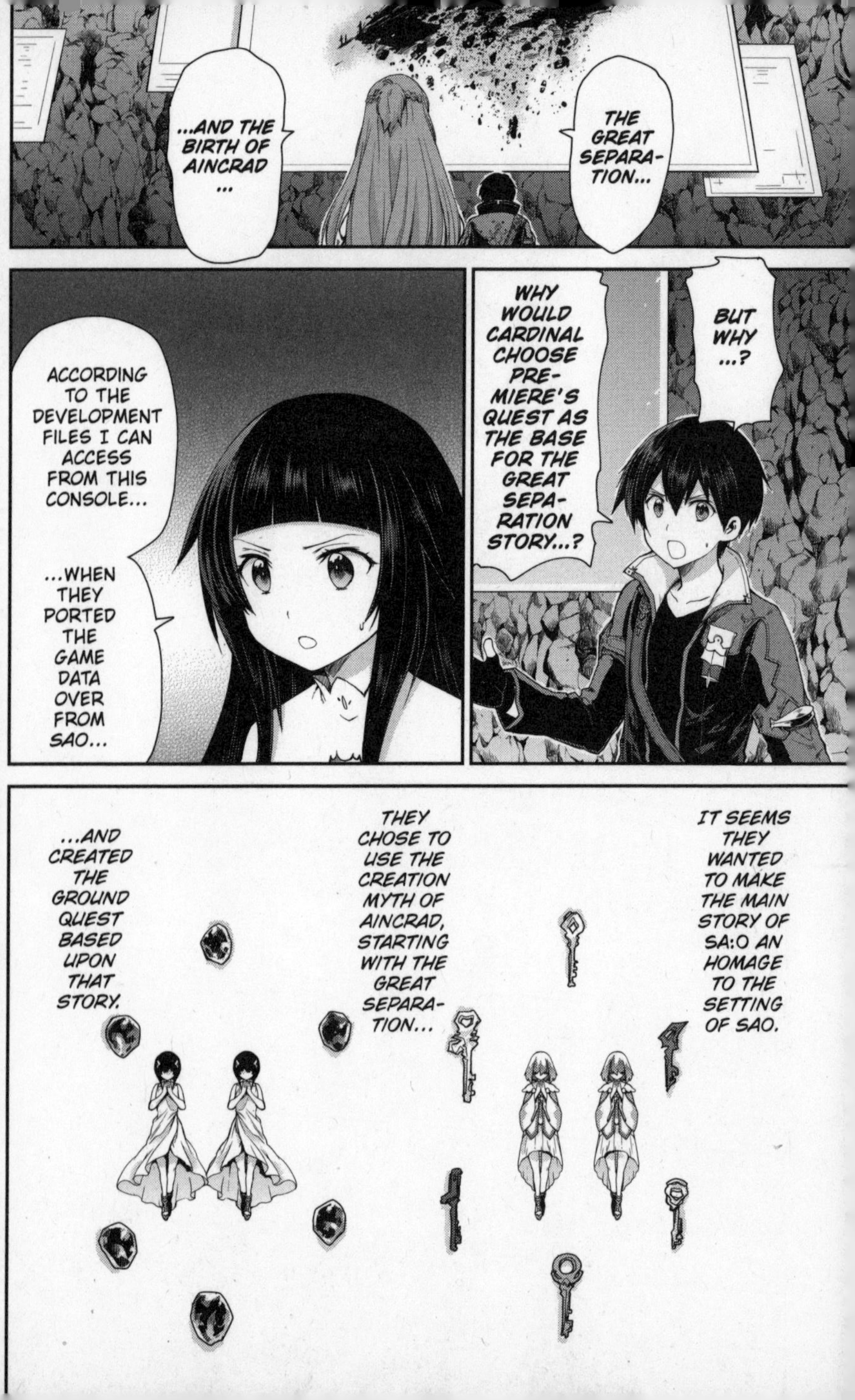
THE GREAT SEPARATION...
...AND THE BIRTH OF AINCRAD ...
BUT WHY ...?
WHY WOULD CARDINAL CHOOSE PREMIERE'S QUEST AS THE BASE FOR THE GREAT SEPARATION STORY...?
ACCORDING TO THE DEVELOPMENT FILES I CAN ACCESS FROM THIS CONSOLE...
...WHEN THEY PORTED THE GAME DATA OVER FROM SAO...
IT SEEMS THEY WANTED TO MAKE THE MAIN STORY OF SA:O AN HOMAGE TO THE SETTING OF SAO.
THEY CHOSE TO USE THE CREATION MYTH OF AINCRAD, STARTING WITH THE GREAT SEPARATION...
...AND CREATED THE GROUND QUEST BASED UPON THAT STORY.

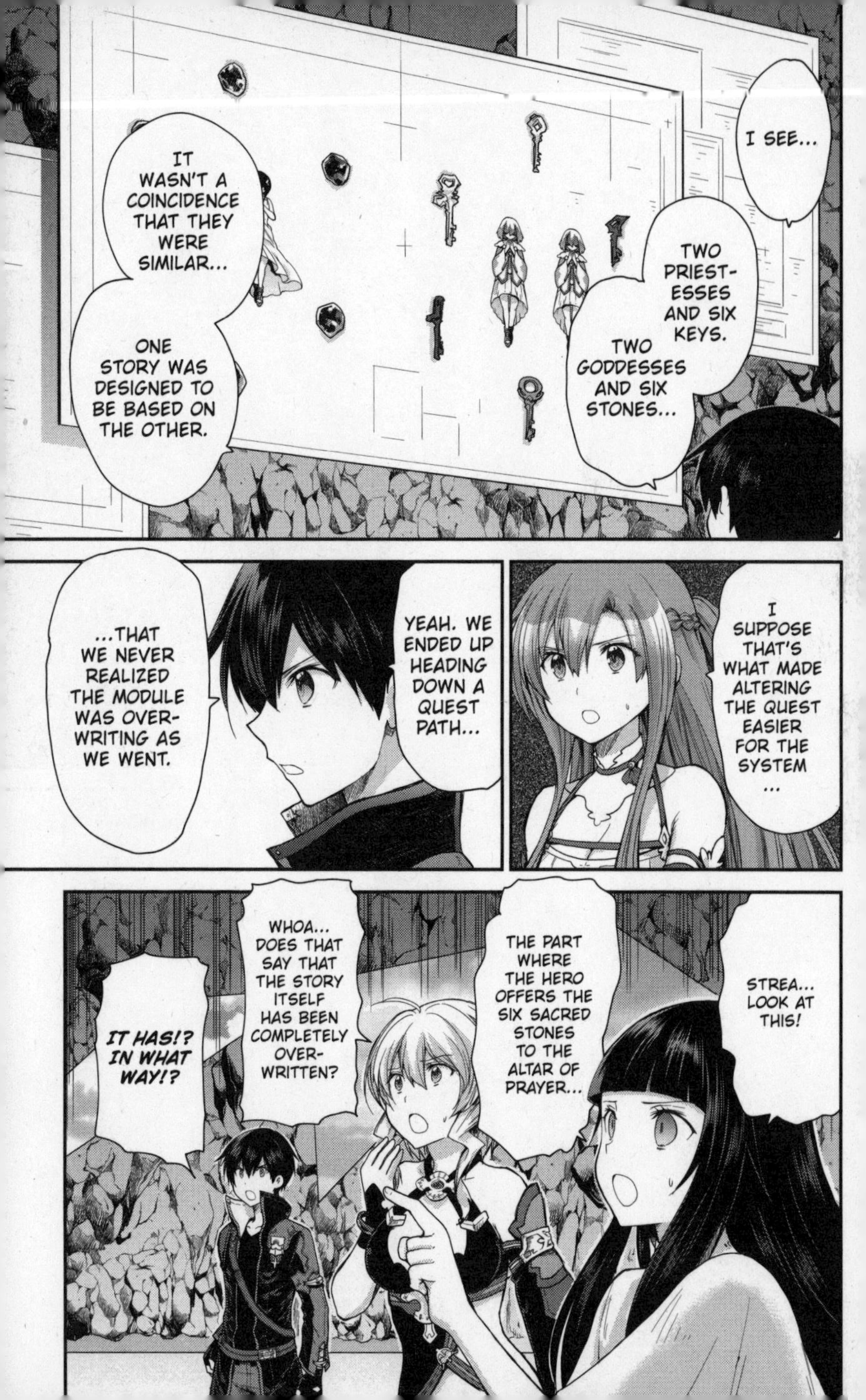
I SEE...
TWO PRIEST-ESSES AND SIX KEYS.
TWO GODDESSES AND SIX STONES...
IT WASN'T A COINCIDENCE THAT THEY WERE SIMILAR...
ONE STORY WAS DESIGNED TO BE BASED ON THE OTHER.
I SUPPOSE THAT'S WHAT MADE ALTERING THE QUEST EASIER FOR THE SYSTEM...
YEAH. WE ENDED UP HEADING DOWN A QUEST PATH...
...THAT WE NEVER REALIZED THE MODULE WAS OVER-WRITING AS WE WENT.
STREA... LOOK AT THIS!
THE PART WHERE THE HERO OFFERS THE SIX SACRED STONES TO THE ALTAR OF PRAYER...
WHOA... DOES THAT SAY THAT THE STORY ITSELF HAS BEEN COMPLETELY OVER-WRITTEN?
IT HAS!? IN WHAT WAY!?

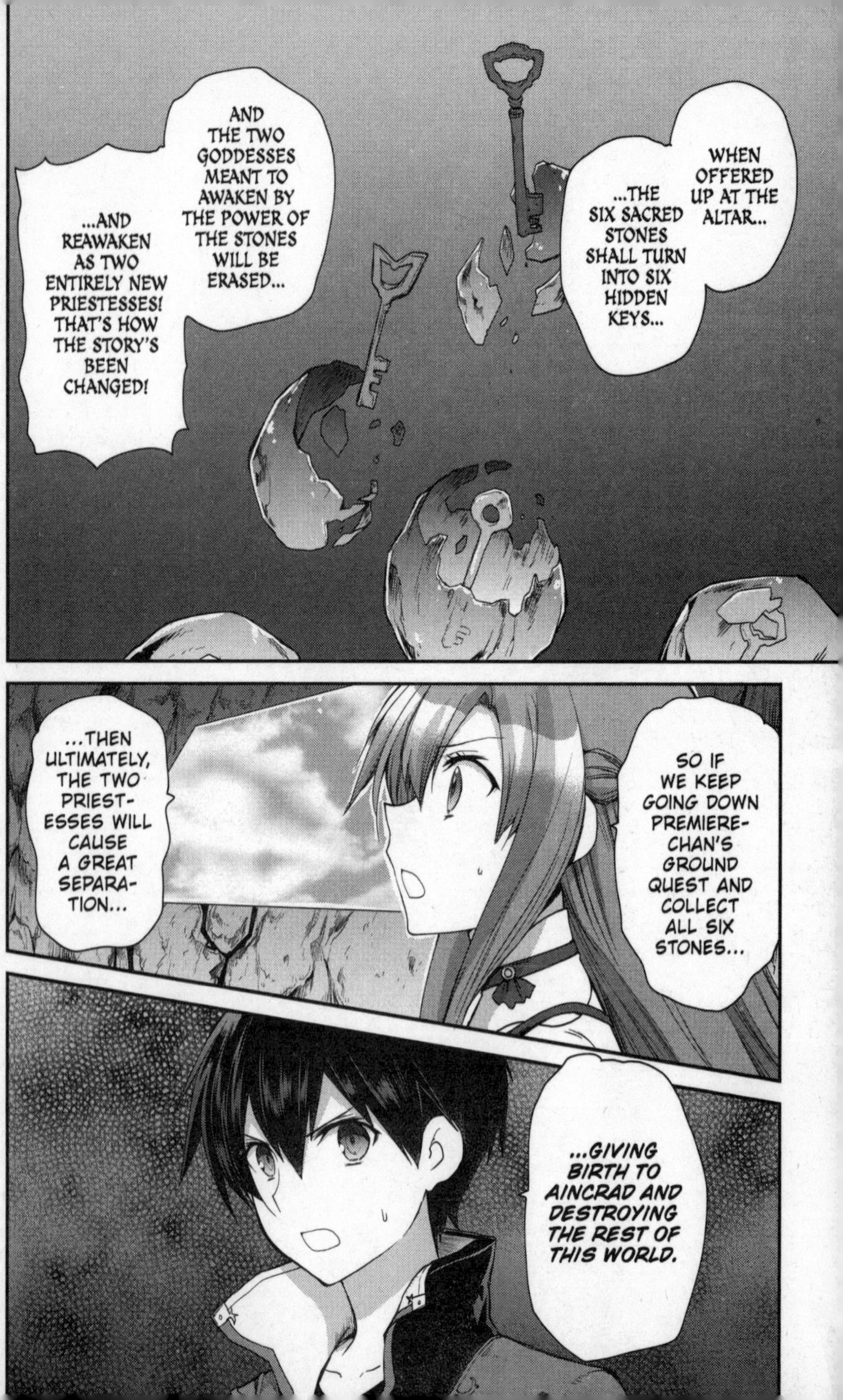
WHEN OFFERED UP AT THE ALTAR...
...THE SIX SACRED STONES SHALL TURN INTO SIX HIDDEN KEYS...
AND THE TWO GODDESSES MEANT TO AWAKEN BY THE POWER OF THE STONES WILL BE ERASED...
...AND REAWAKEN AS TWO ENTIRELY NEW PRIESTESSES! THAT'S HOW THE STORY'S BEEN CHANGED!
SO IF WE KEEP GOING DOWN PREMIERE-CHAN'S GROUND QUEST AND COLLECT ALL SIX STONES...
...THEN ULTIMATELY, THE TWO PRIEST-ESSES WILL CAUSE A GREAT SEPARA-TION...
...GIVING BIRTH TO AINCRAD AND DESTROYING THE REST OF THIS WORLD.

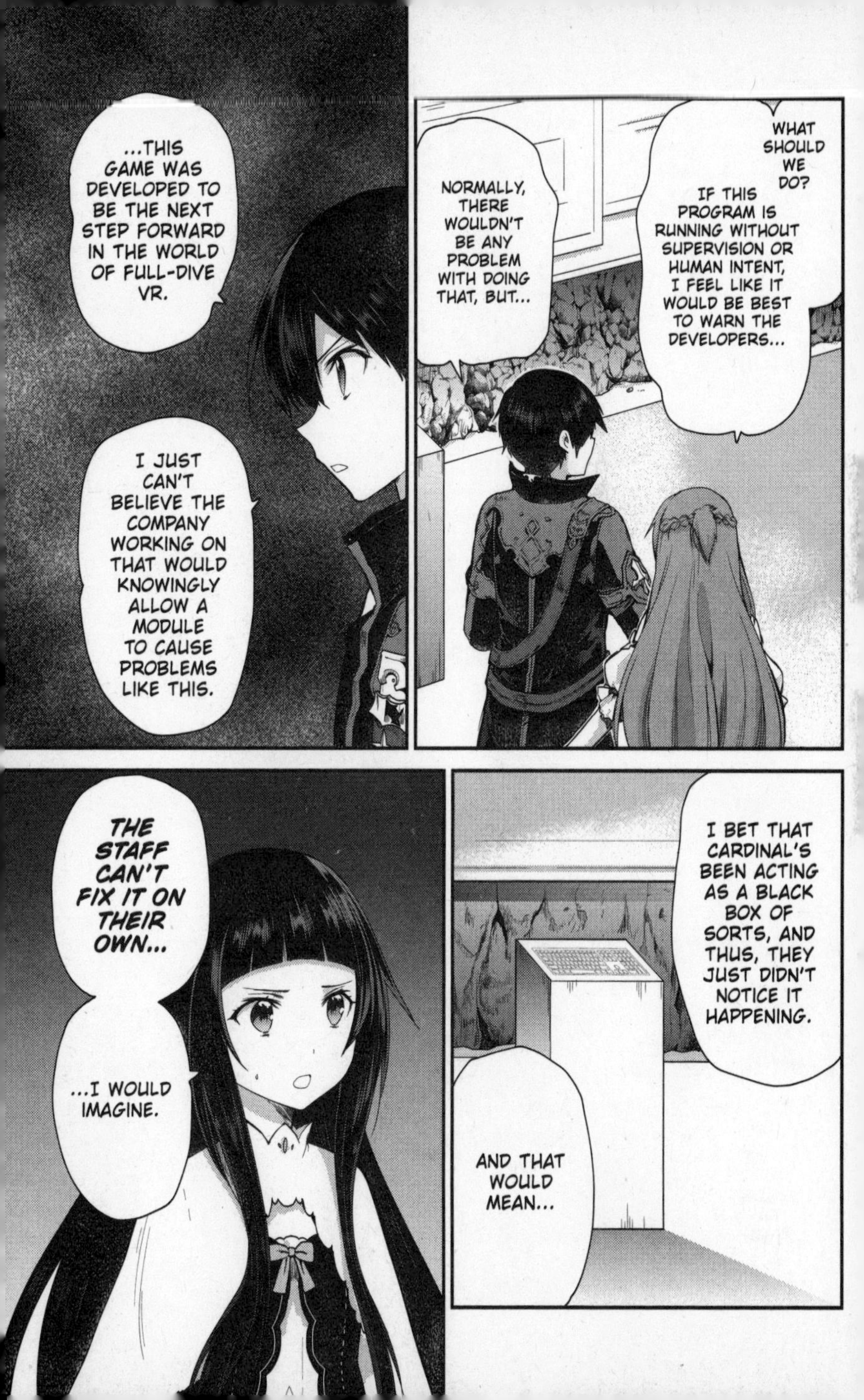
WHAT SHOULD WE DO?
IF THIS PROGRAM IS RUNNING WITHOUT SUPERVISION OR HUMAN INTENT, I FEEL LIKE IT WOULD BE BEST TO WARN THE DEVELOPERS...
NORMALLY, THERE WOULDN'T BE ANY PROBLEM WITH DOING THAT, BUT...
...THIS GAME WAS DEVELOPED TO BE THE NEXT STEP FORWARD IN THE WORLD OF FULL-DIVE VR.
I JUST CAN'T BELIEVE THE COMPANY WORKING ON THAT WOULD KNOWINGLY ALLOW A MODULE TO CAUSE PROBLEMS LIKE THIS.
I BET THAT CARDINAL'S BEEN ACTING AS A BLACK BOX OF SORTS, AND THUS, THEY JUST DIDN'T NOTICE IT HAPPENING.
AND THAT WOULD MEAN...
THE STAFF CAN'T FIX IT ON THEIR OWN...
...I WOULD IMAGINE.

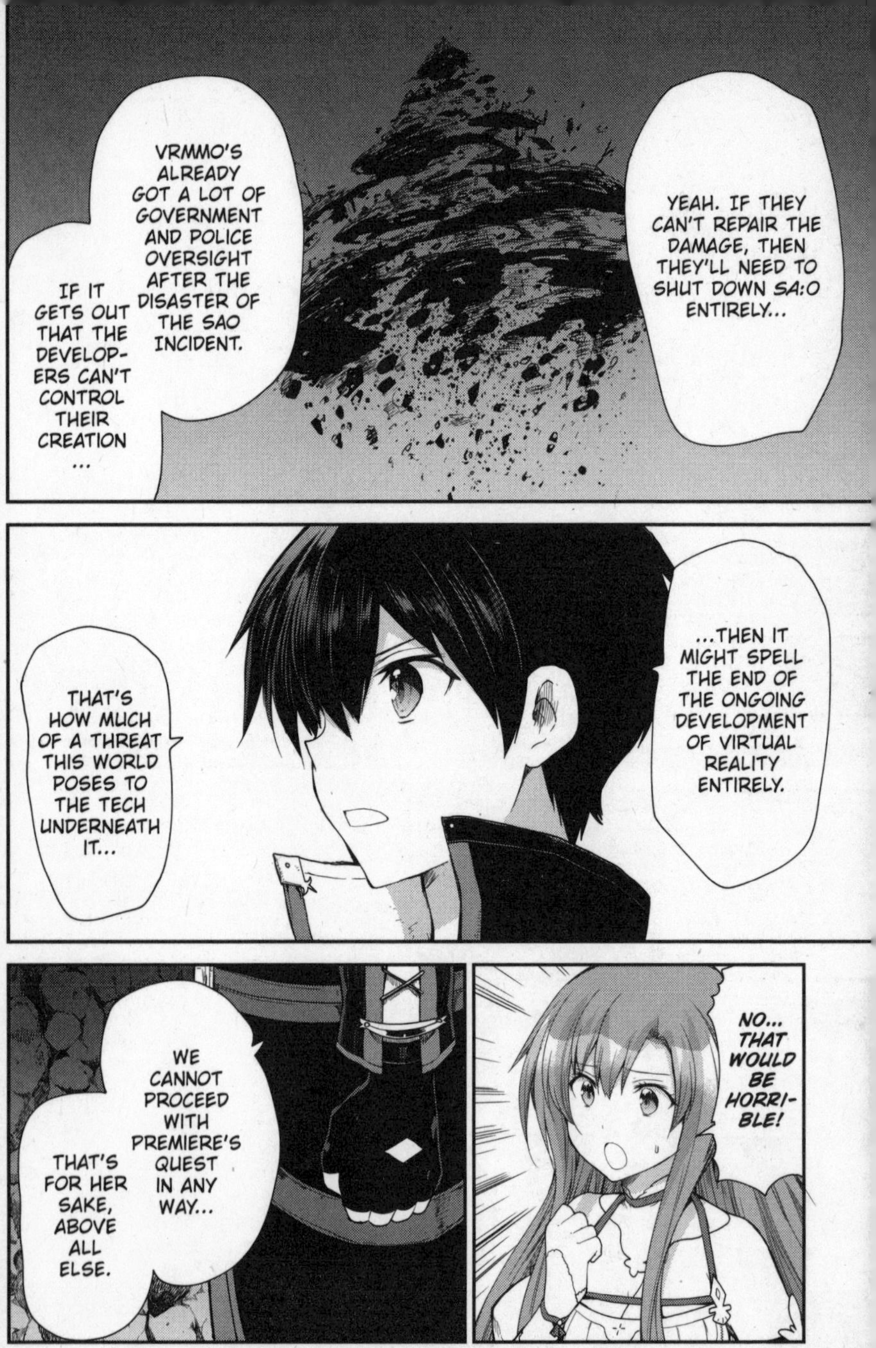
YEAH. IF THEY CAN'T REPAIR THE DAMAGE, THEN THEY'LL NEED TO SHUT DOWN SA:O ENTIRELY...
VRMMO'S ALREADY GOT A LOT OF GOVERNMENT AND POLICE OVERSIGHT AFTER THE DISASTER OF THE SAO INCIDENT.
IF IT GETS OUT THAT THE DEVELOPERS CAN'T CONTROL THEIR CREATION...
...THEN IT MIGHT SPELL THE END OF THE ONGOING DEVELOPMENT OF VIRTUAL REALITY ENTIRELY.
THAT'S HOW MUCH OF A THREAT THIS WORLD POSES TO THE TECH UNDERNEATH IT...
NO... THAT WOULD BE HORRIBLE!
WE CANNOT PROCEED WITH PREMIERE'S QUEST IN ANY WAY...
THAT'S FOR HER SAKE, ABOVE ALL ELSE.

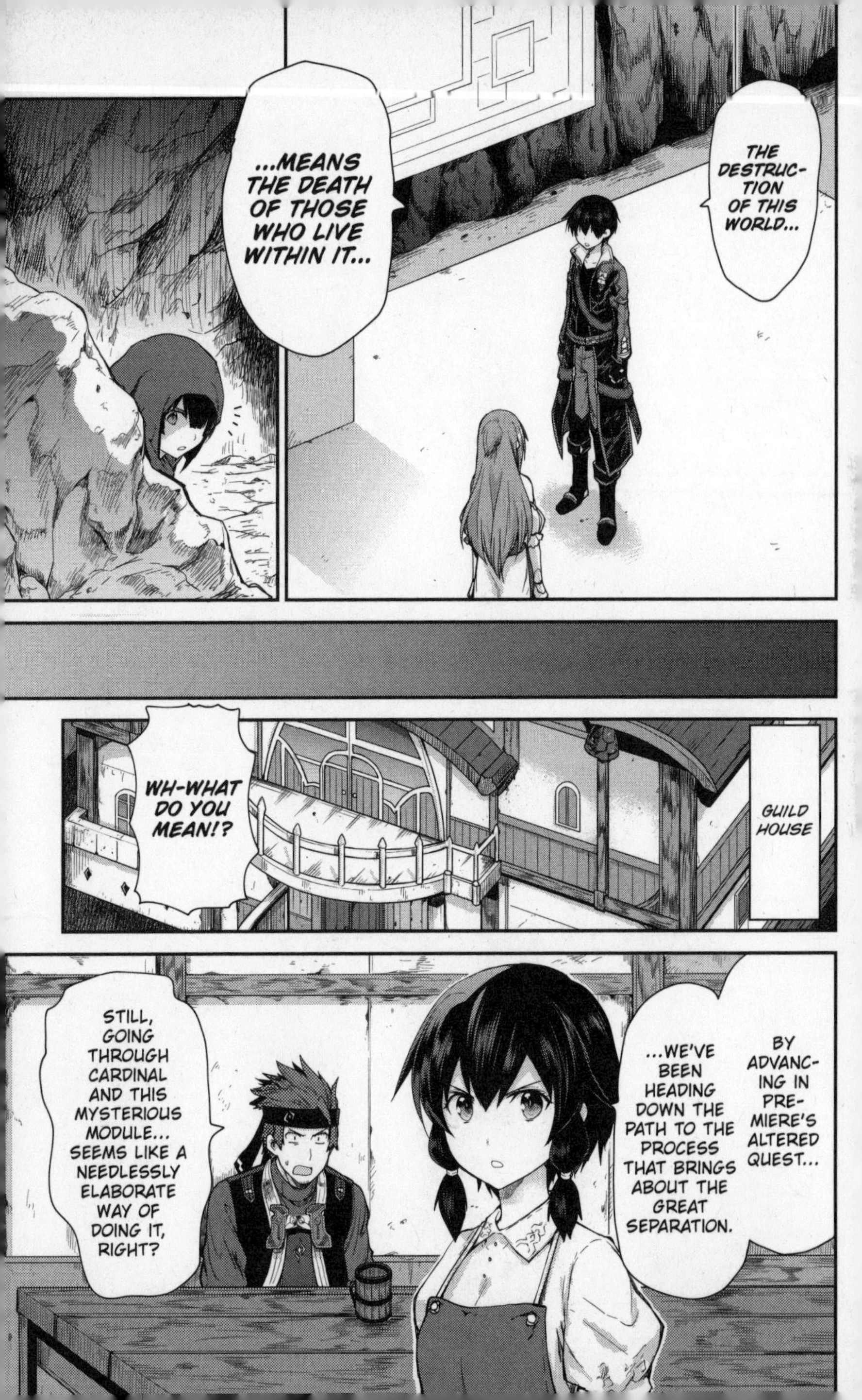

THE DESTRUCTION OF THIS WORLD...
...MEANS THE DEATH OF THOSE WHO LIVE WITHIN IT...
GUILD HOUSE
WH-WHAT DO YOU MEAN!?
BY ADVANCING IN PREMIERE'S ALTERED QUEST...
...WE'VE BEEN HEADING DOWN THE PATH TO THE PROCESS THAT BRINGS ABOUT THE GREAT SEPARATION.
STILL, GOING THROUGH CARDINAL AND THIS MYSTERIOUS MODULE... SEEMS LIKE A NEEDLESSLY ELABORATE WAY OF DOING IT, RIGHT?

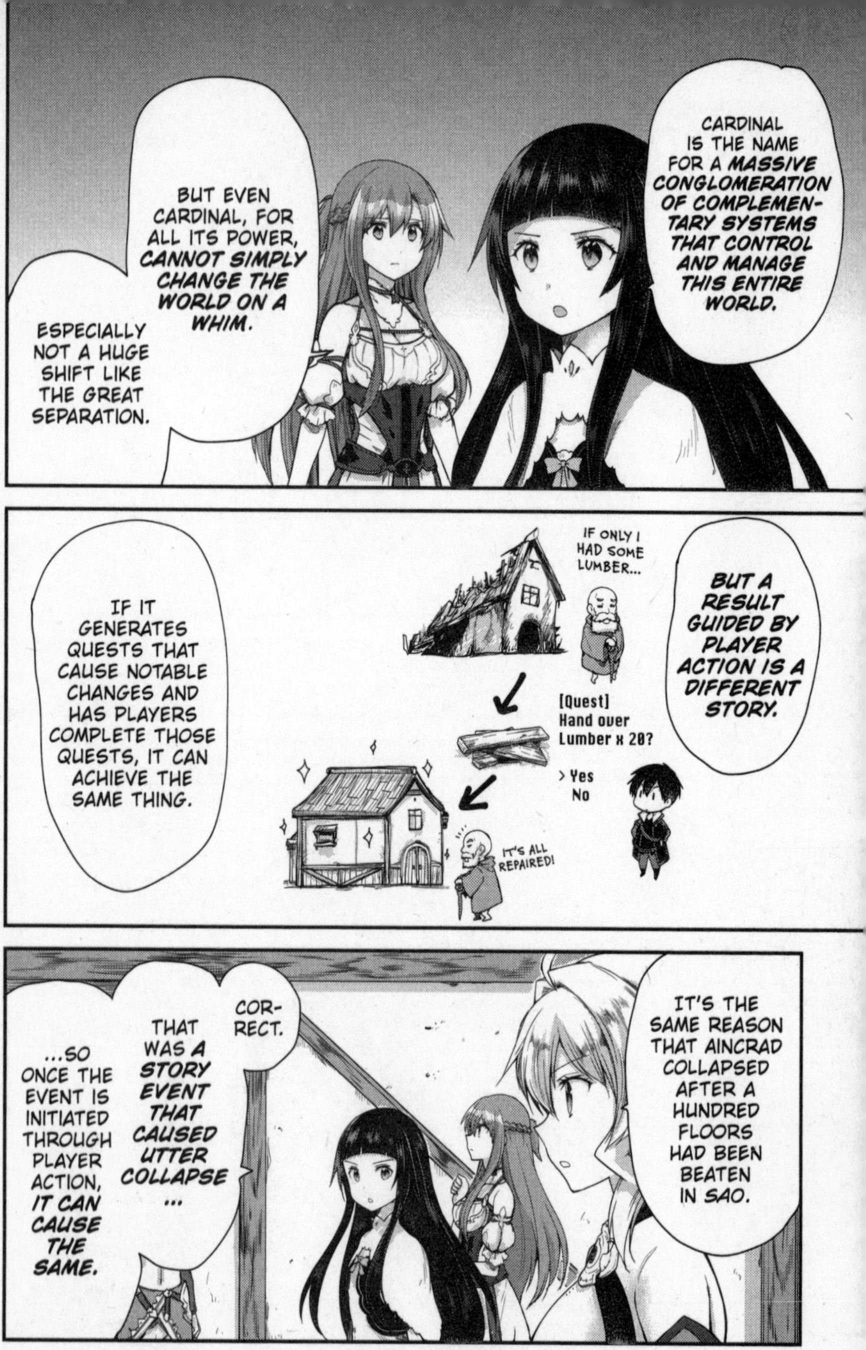
CARDINAL IS THE NAME FOR A MASSIVE CONGLOMERATION OF COMPLEMENTARY SYSTEMS THAT CONTROL AND MANAGE THIS ENTIRE WORLD.
BUT EVEN CARDINAL, FOR ALL ITS POWER, CANNOT SIMPLY CHANGE THE WORLD ON A WHIM.
ESPECIALLY NOT A HUGE SHIFT LIKE THE GREAT SEPARATION.
BUT A RESULT GUIDED BY PLAYER ACTION IS A DIFFERENT STORY.
IF ONLY I HAD SOME LUMBER...
[Quest] Hand over Lumber x 20?
> Yes
No
IT'S ALL REPAIRED!
IF IT GENERATES QUESTS THAT CAUSE NOTABLE CHANGES AND HAS PLAYERS COMPLETE THOSE QUESTS, IT CAN ACHIEVE THE SAME THING.
IT'S THE SAME REASON THAT AINCRAD COLLAPSED AFTER A HUNDRED FLOORS HAD BEEN BEATEN IN SAO.
COR-RECT.
THAT WAS A STORY EVENT THAT CAUSED UTTER COLLAPSE...
...SO ONCE THE EVENT IS INITIATED THROUGH PLAYER ACTION, IT CAN CAUSE THE SAME.

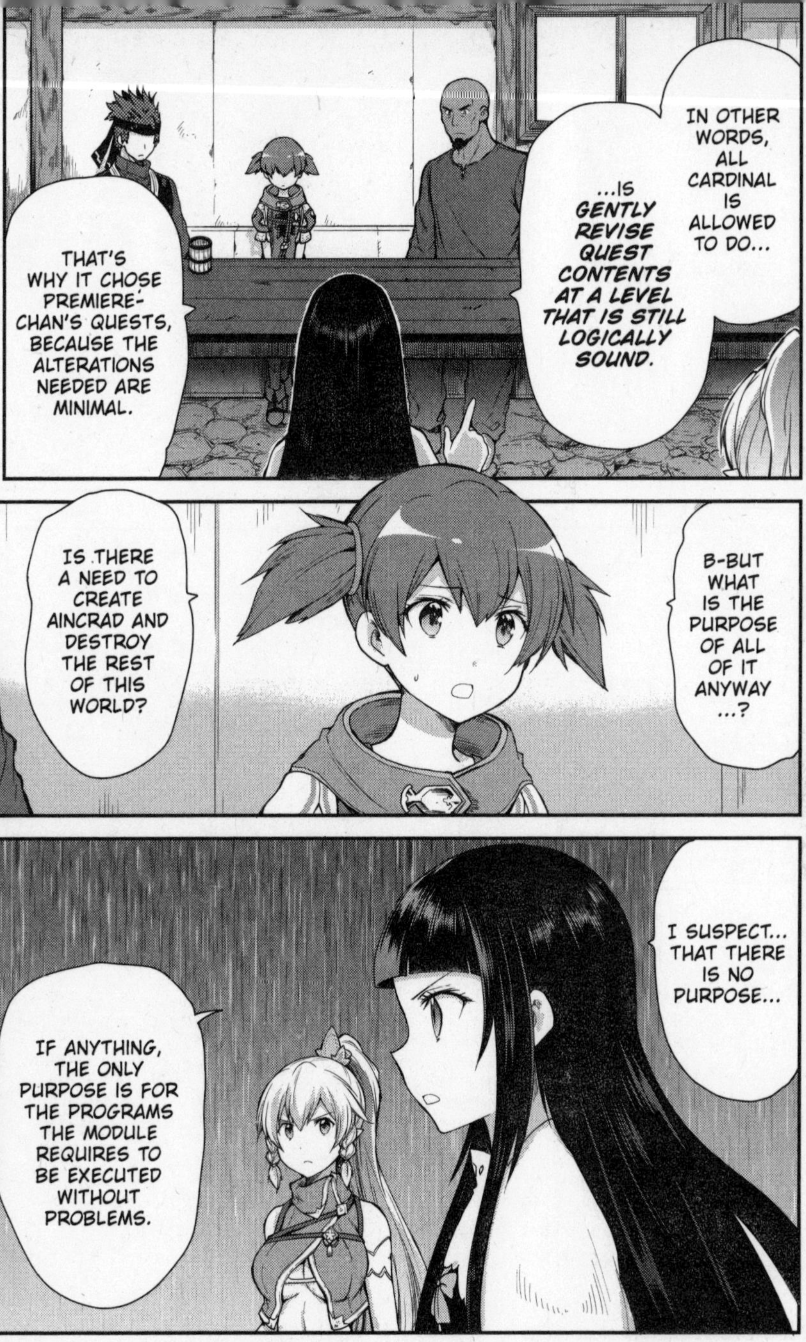
IN OTHER WORDS, ALL CARDINAL IS ALLOWED TO DO...
...IS GENTLY REVISE QUEST CONTENTS AT A LEVEL THAT IS STILL LOGICALLY SOUND.
THAT'S WHY IT CHOSE PREMIERE-CHAN'S QUESTS, BECAUSE THE ALTERATIONS NEEDED ARE MINIMAL.
B-BUT WHAT IS THE PURPOSE OF ALL OF IT ANYWAY ...?
IS THERE A NEED TO CREATE AINCRAD AND DESTROY THE REST OF THIS WORLD?
I SUSPECT... THAT THERE IS NO PURPOSE...
IF ANYTHING, THE ONLY PURPOSE IS FOR THE PROGRAMS THE MODULE REQUIRES TO BE EXECUTED WITHOUT PROBLEMS.

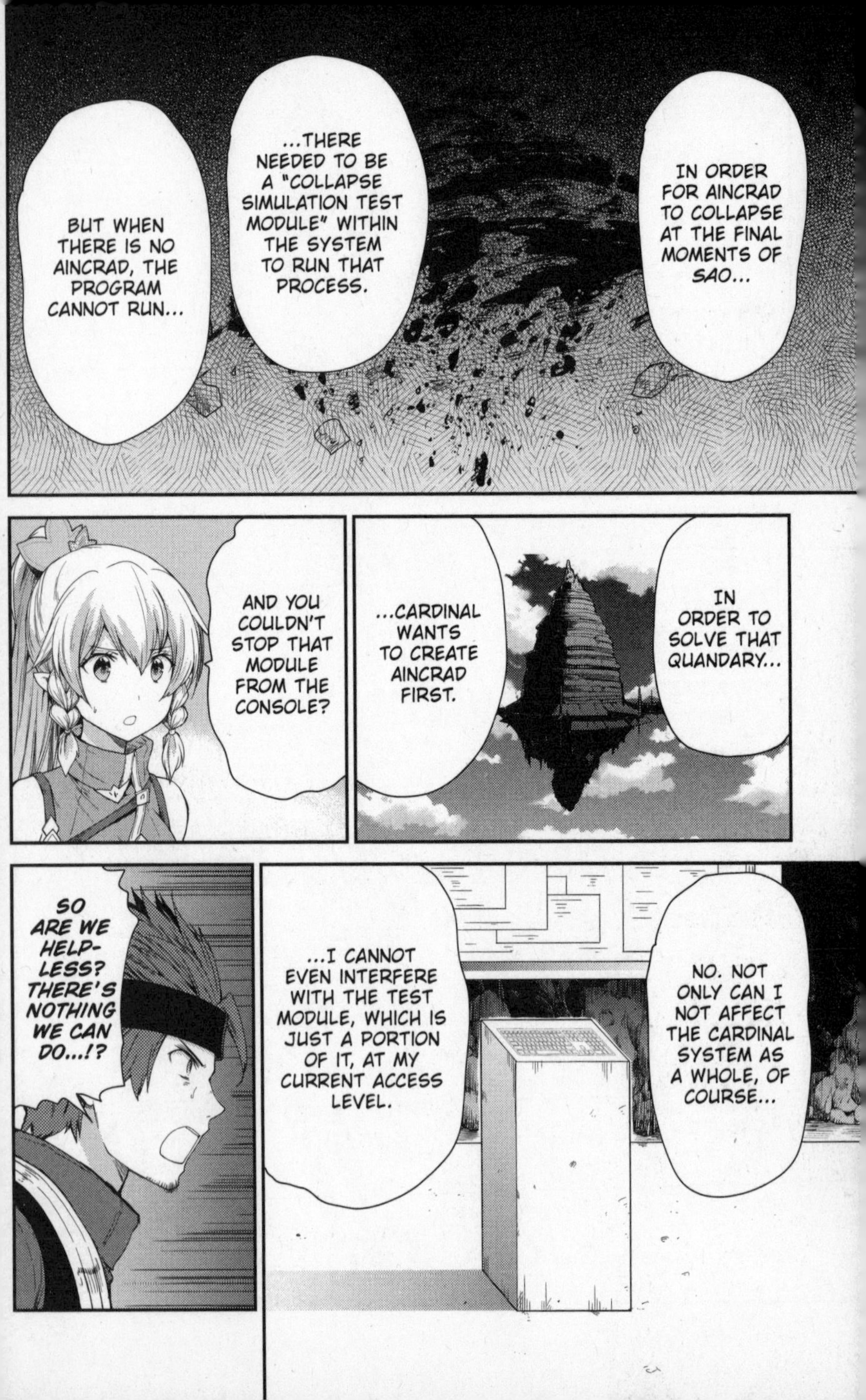
IN ORDER FOR AINCRAD TO COLLAPSE AT THE FINAL MOMENTS OF SAO...
...THERE NEEDED TO BE A "COLLAPSE SIMULATION TEST MODULE" WITHIN THE SYSTEM TO RUN THAT PROCESS.
BUT WHEN THERE IS NO AINCRAD, THE PROGRAM CANNOT RUN...
IN ORDER TO SOLVE THAT QUANDARY...
...CARDINAL WANTS TO CREATE AINCRAD FIRST.
AND YOU COULDN'T STOP THAT MODULE FROM THE CONSOLE?
NO. NOT ONLY CAN I NOT AFFECT THE CARDINAL SYSTEM AS A WHOLE, OF COURSE...
...I CANNOT EVEN INTERFERE WITH THE TEST MODULE, WHICH IS JUST A PORTION OF IT, AT MY CURRENT ACCESS LEVEL.
SO ARE WE HELP-LESS? THERE'S NOTHING WE CAN DO...!?

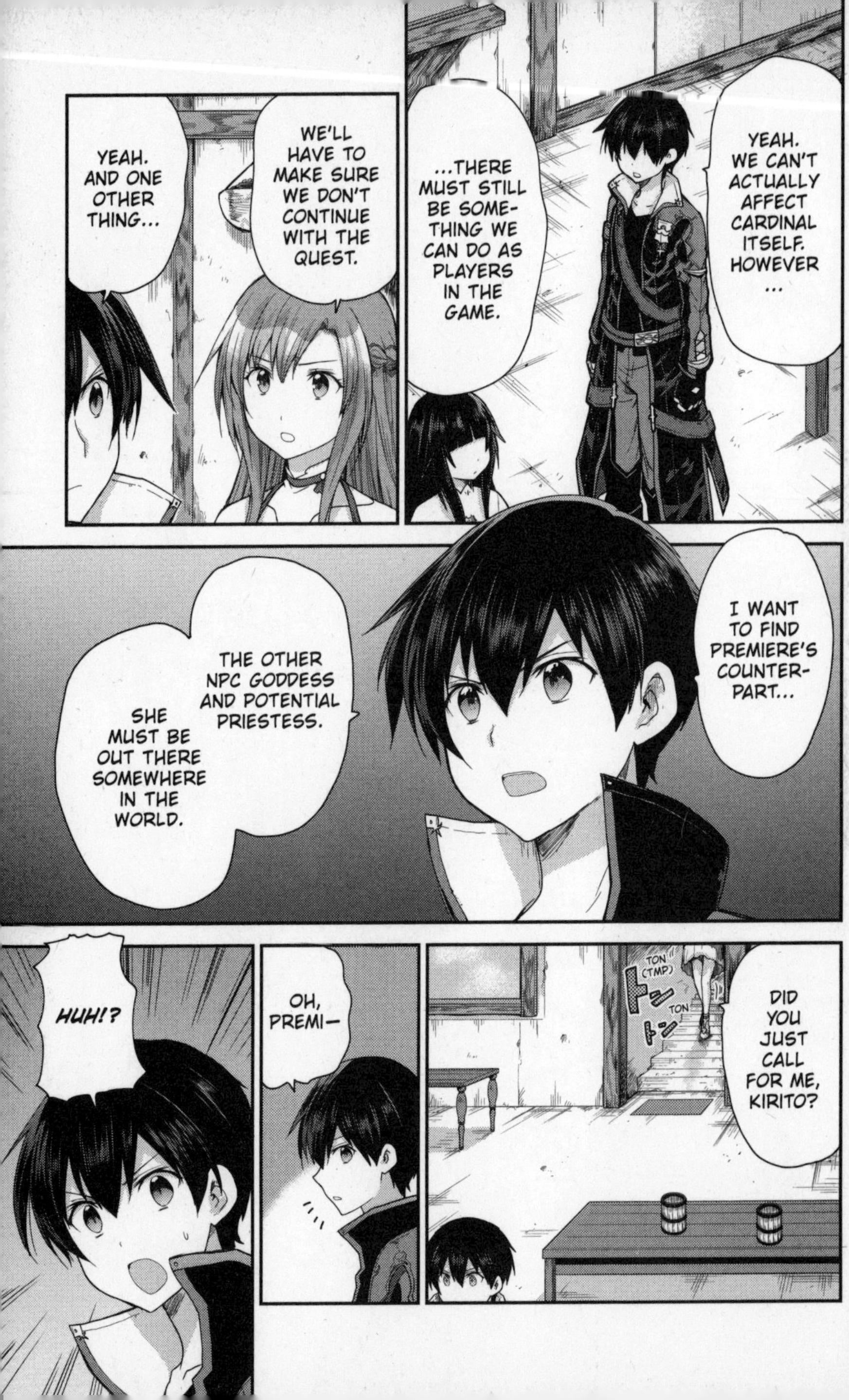
YEAH. WE CAN'T ACTUALLY AFFECT CARDINAL ITSELF. HOWEVER...
...THERE MUST STILL BE SOMETHING WE CAN DO AS PLAYERS IN THE GAME.
WE'LL HAVE TO MAKE SURE WE DON'T CONTINUE WITH THE QUEST.
YEAH. AND ONE OTHER THING...
I WANT TO FIND PREMIERE'S COUNTER-PART...
THE OTHER NPC GODDESS AND POTENTIAL PRIESTESS.
SHE MUST BE OUT THERE SOMEWHERE IN THE WORLD.
DID YOU JUST CALL FOR ME, KIRITO?
TON (TMP)
TON
OH, PREMI—
HUH!?

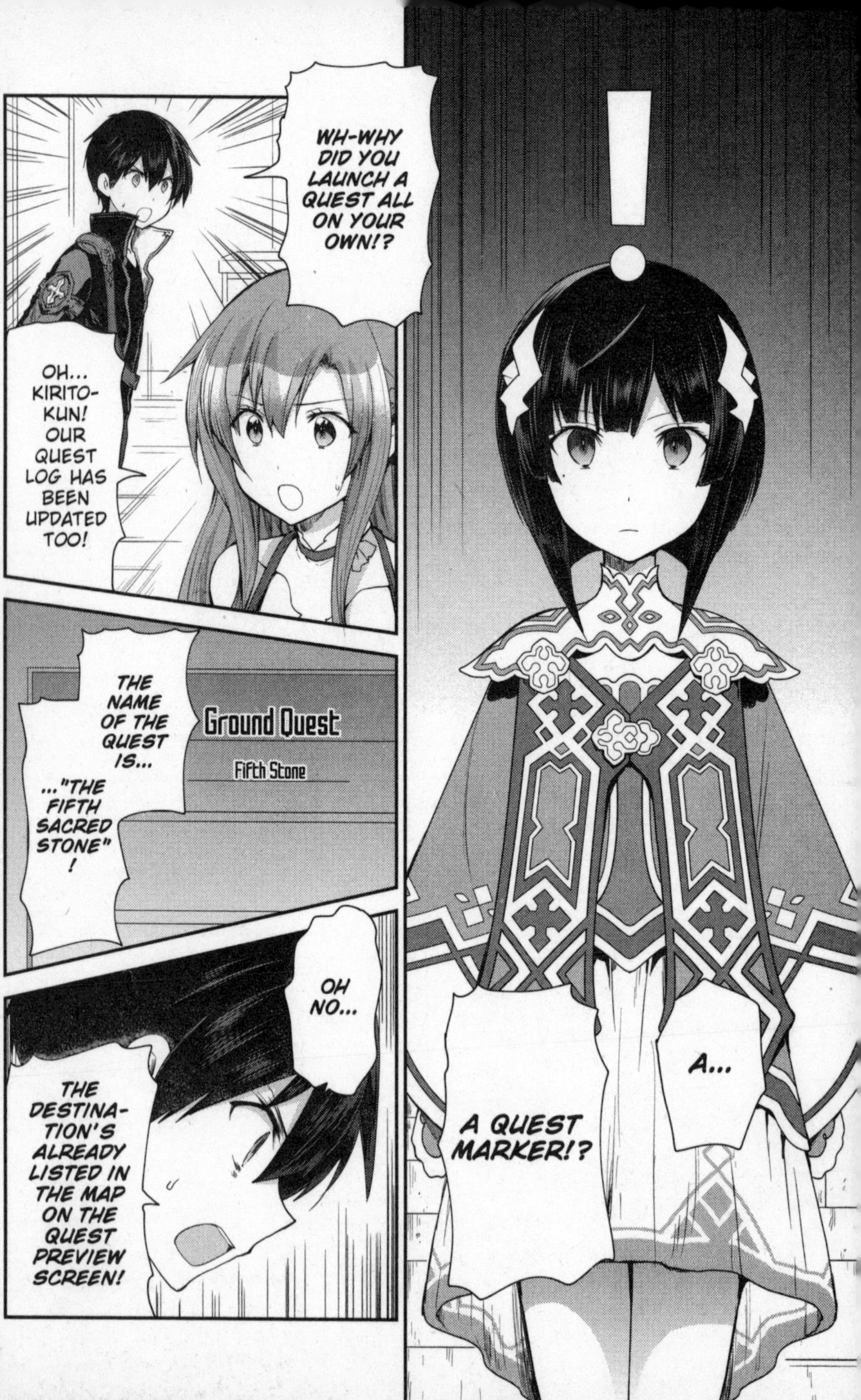
A...
A QUEST MARKER!?
WH-WHY DID YOU LAUNCH A QUEST ALL ON YOUR OWN!?
OH... KIRITO-KUN! OUR QUEST LOG HAS BEEN UPDATED TOO!
THE NAME OF THE QUEST IS...
Ground Quest
Fifth Stone
..."THE FIFTH SACRED STONE"!
OH NO...
THE DESTINATION'S ALREADY LISTED IN THE MAP ON THE QUEST PREVIEW SCREEN!

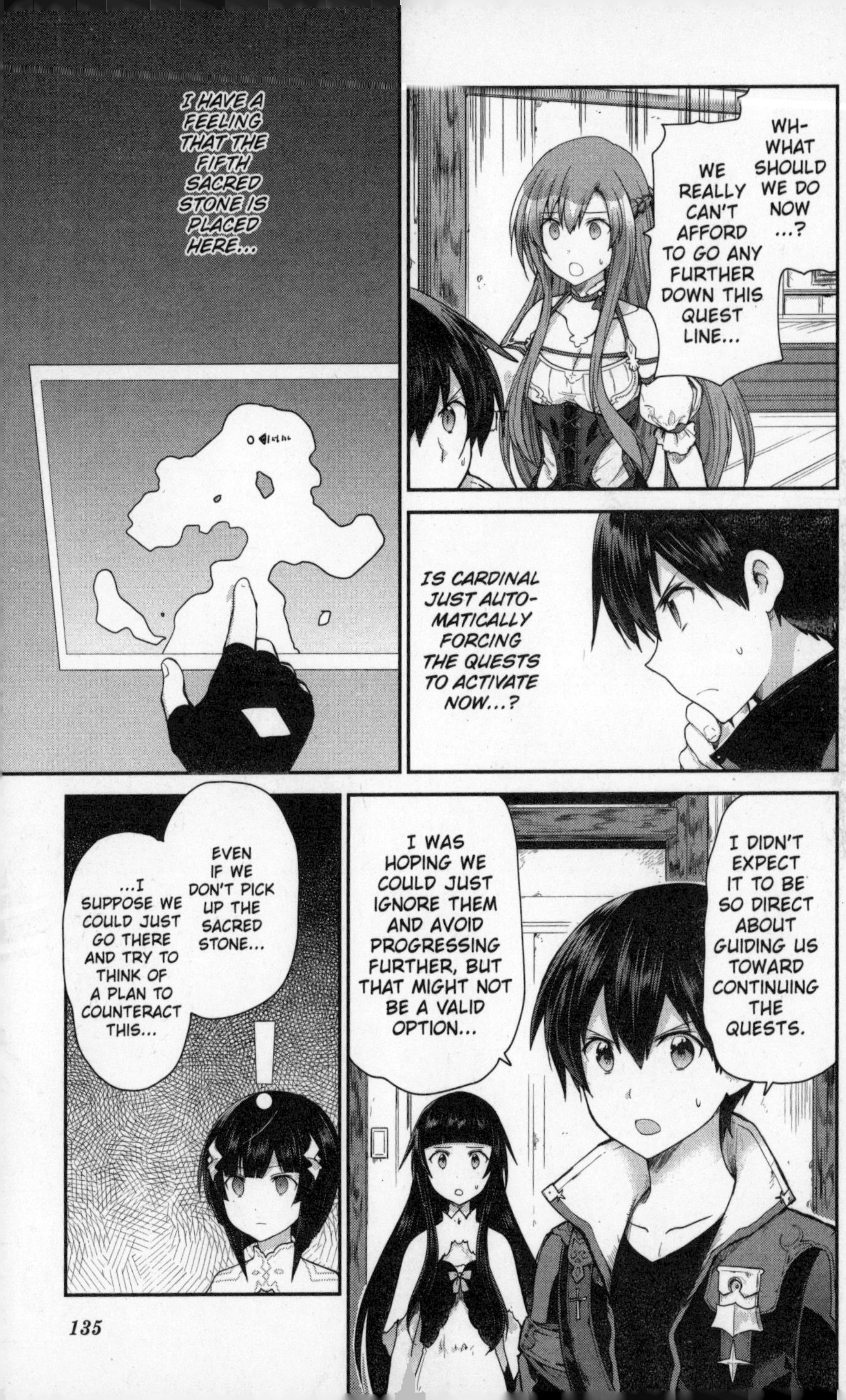
WH- WHAT SHOULD WE DO NOW ...?
WE REALLY CAN'T AFFORD TO GO ANY FURTHER DOWN THIS QUEST LINE...
IS CARDINAL JUST AUTO-MATICALLY FORCING THE QUESTS TO ACTIVATE NOW...?
I HAVE A FEELING THAT THE FIFTH SACRED STONE IS PLACED HERE...
I DIDN'T EXPECT IT TO BE SO DIRECT ABOUT GUIDING US TOWARD CONTINUING THE QUESTS.
I WAS HOPING WE COULD JUST IGNORE THEM AND AVOID PROGRESSING FURTHER, BUT THAT MIGHT NOT BE A VALID OPTION...
EVEN IF WE DON'T PICK UP THE SACRED STONE...
...I SUPPOSE WE COULD JUST GO THERE AND TRY TO THINK OF A PLAN TO COUNTERACT THIS...
!

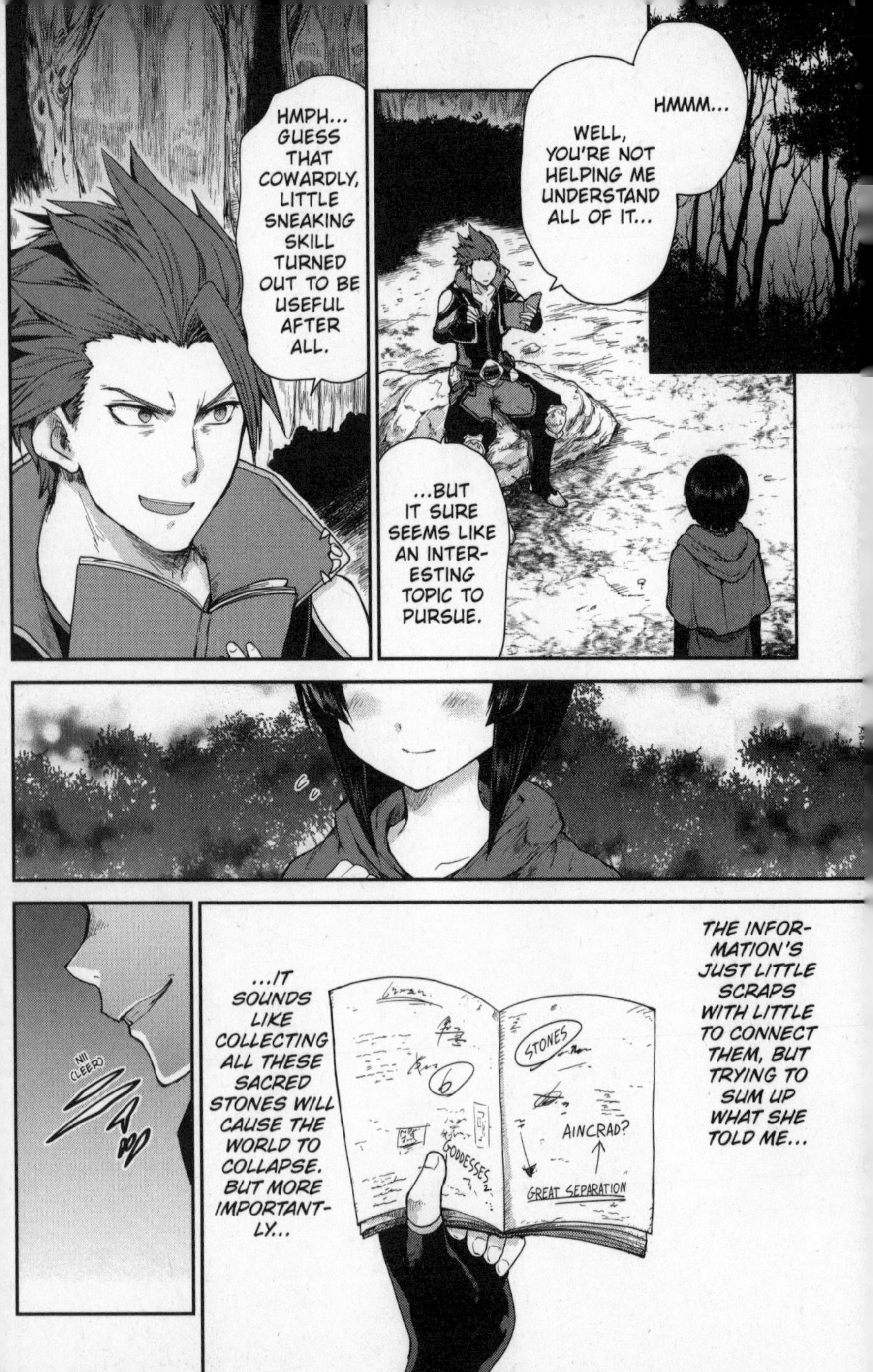
HMMM...
WELL, YOU'RE NOT HELPING ME UNDERSTAND ALL OF IT...
...BUT IT SURE SEEMS LIKE AN INTER-ESTING TOPIC TO PURSUE.
HMPH... GUESS THAT COWARDLY, LITTLE SNEAKING SKILL TURNED OUT TO BE USEFUL AFTER ALL.
THE INFOR-MATION'S JUST LITTLE SCRAPS WITH LITTLE TO CONNECT THEM, BUT TRYING TO SUM UP WHAT SHE TOLD ME...
...IT SOUNDS LIKE COLLECTING ALL THESE SACRED STONES WILL CAUSE THE WORLD TO COLLAPSE. BUT MORE IMPORTANT-LY...
STONES
6
AINCRAD?
GODDESSES
GREAT SEPARATION

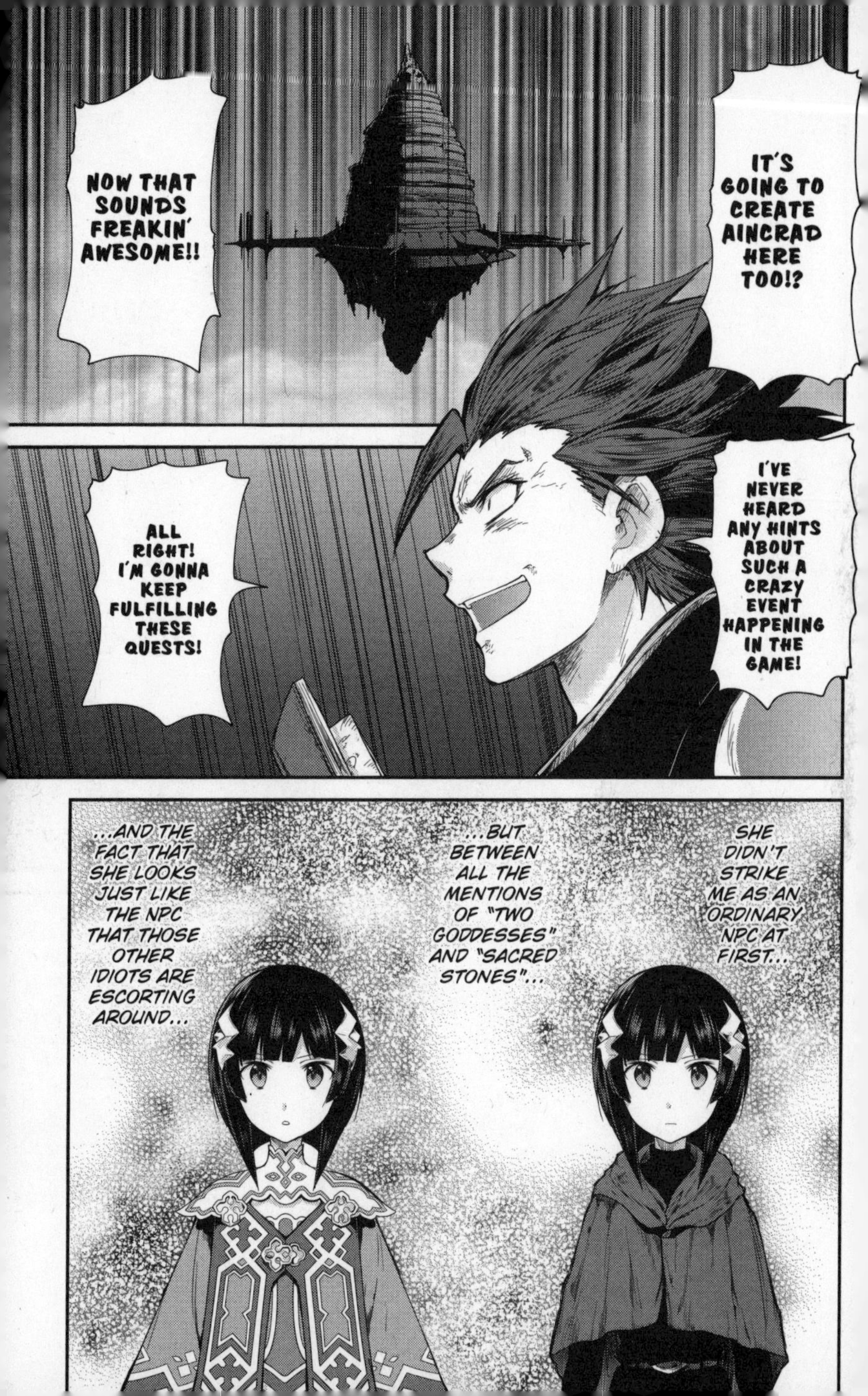
IT'S GOING TO CREATE AINCRAD HERE TOO!?
NOW THAT SOUNDS FREAKIN' AWESOME!!
I'VE NEVER HEARD ANY HINTS ABOUT SUCH A CRAZY EVENT HAPPENING IN THE GAME!
ALL RIGHT! I'M GONNA KEEP FULFILLING THESE QUESTS!
SHE DIDN'T STRIKE ME AS AN ORDINARY NPC AT FIRST...
...BUT BETWEEN ALL THE MENTIONS OF "TWO GODDESSES" AND "SACRED STONES"...
...AND THE FACT THAT SHE LOOKS JUST LIKE THE NPC THAT THOSE OTHER IDIOTS ARE ESCORTING AROUND...

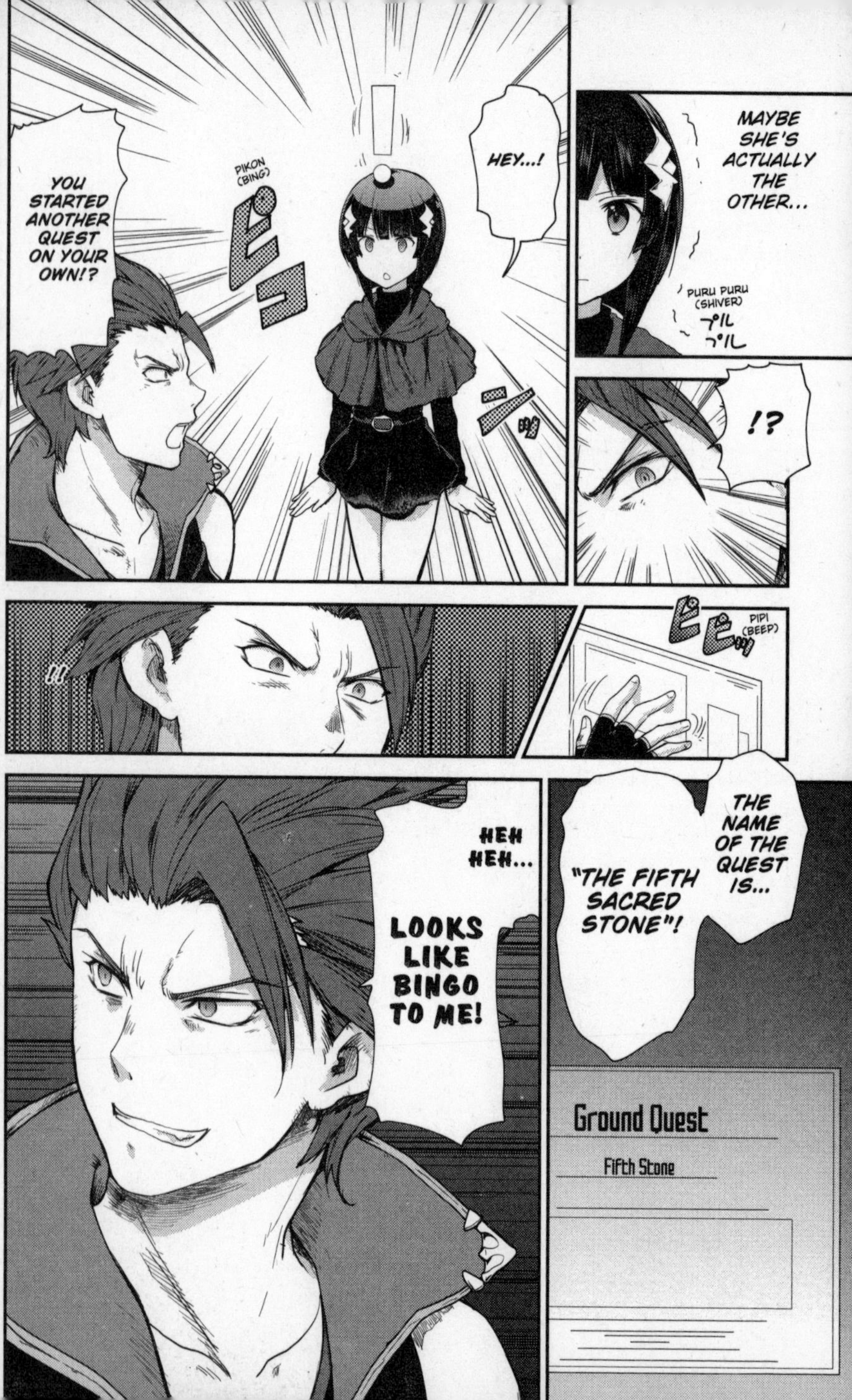

MAYBE SHE'S ACTUALLY THE OTHER...
PURU PURU (SHIVER)
!?
HEY...!
PIKON (BING)
YOU STARTED ANOTHER QUEST ON YOUR OWN!?
PIPI (BEEP)
THE NAME OF THE QUEST IS...
"THE FIFTH SACRED STONE"!
Ground Quest
Fifth Stone
HEH HEH...
LOOKS LIKE BINGO TO ME!

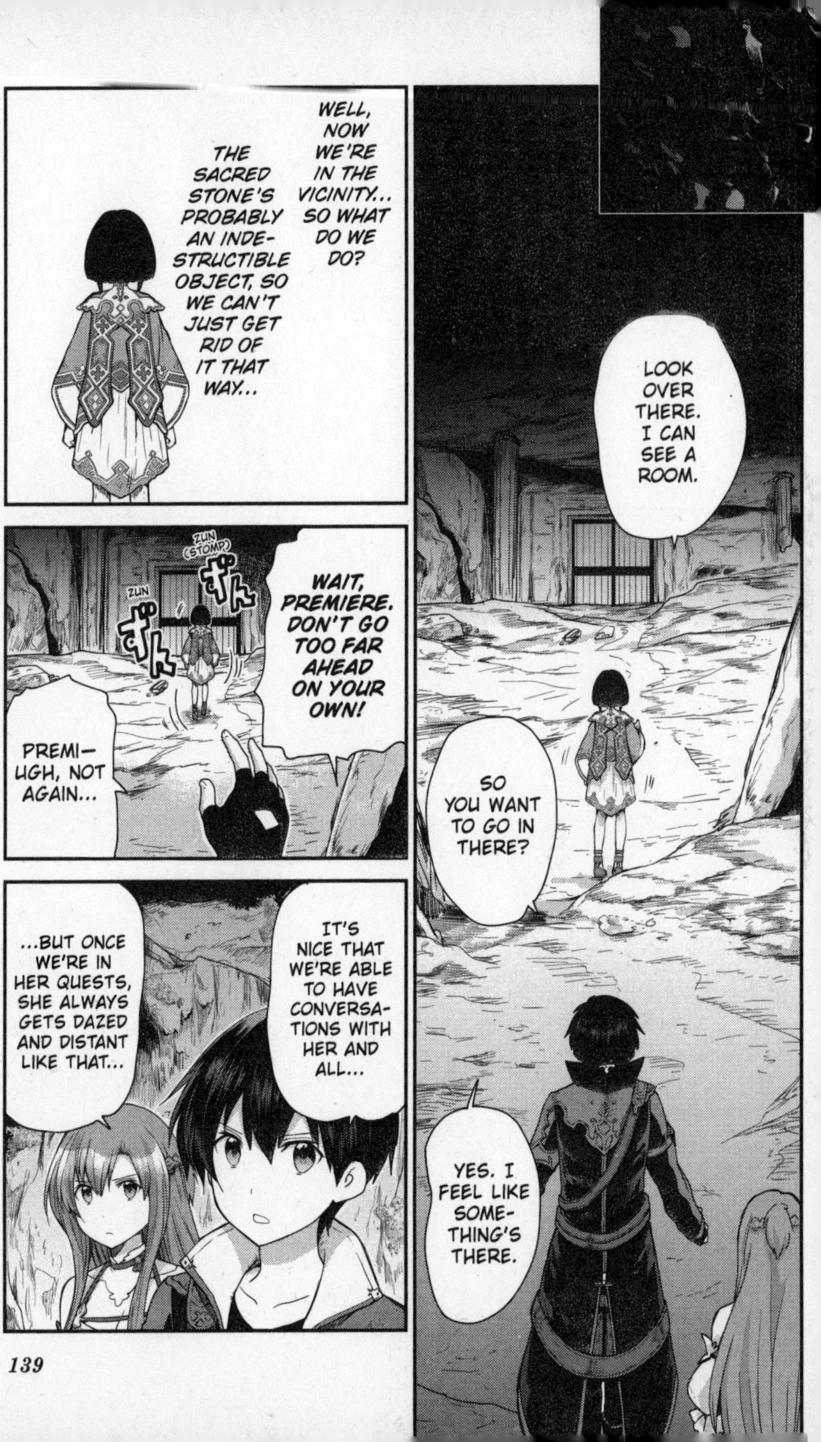
LOOK OVER THERE. I CAN SEE A ROOM.
SO YOU WANT TO GO IN THERE?
YES. I FEEL LIKE SOME-THING'S THERE.
WELL, NOW WE'RE IN THE VICINITY... SO WHAT DO WE DO?
THE SACRED STONE'S PROBABLY AN INDE-STRUCTIBLE OBJECT, SO WE CAN'T JUST GET RID OF IT THAT WAY...
ZUN (STOMP)
ZUN
WAIT, PREMIERE. DON'T GO TOO FAR AHEAD ON YOUR OWN!
PREMI— UGH, NOT AGAIN...
IT'S NICE THAT WE'RE ABLE TO HAVE CONVERSA-TIONS WITH HER AND ALL...
...BUT ONCE WE'RE IN HER QUESTS, SHE ALWAYS GETS DAZED AND DISTANT LIKE THAT...

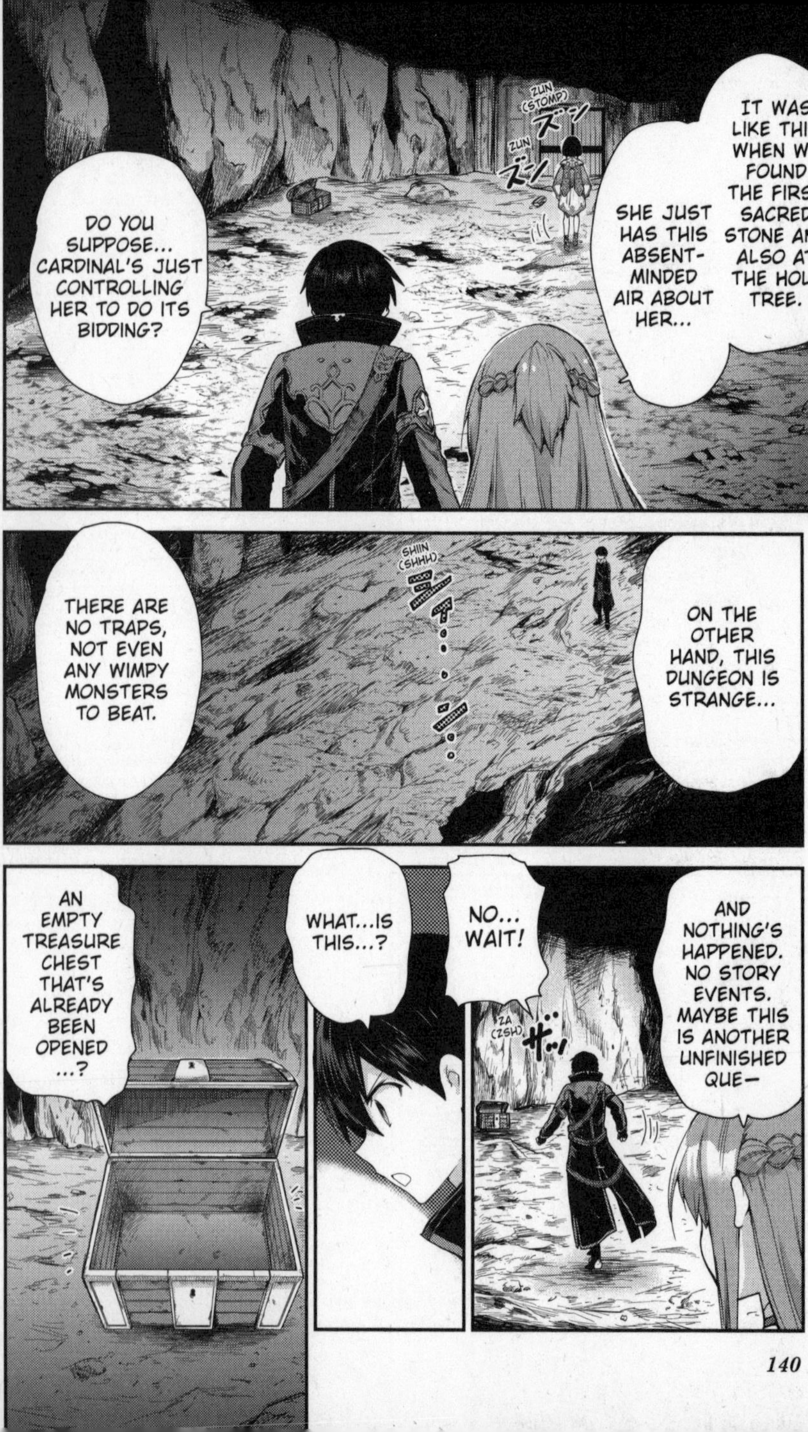
IT WAS LIKE THIS WHEN WE FOUND THE FIRST SACRED STONE AND ALSO AT THE HOLY TREE.
SHE JUST HAS THIS ABSENT-MINDED AIR ABOUT HER...
ZUN (STOMP)
ZUN
DO YOU SUPPOSE... CARDINAL'S JUST CONTROLLING HER TO DO ITS BIDDING?
ON THE OTHER HAND, THIS DUNGEON IS STRANGE...
SHIIN (SHHH)
THERE ARE NO TRAPS, NOT EVEN ANY WIMPY MONSTERS TO BEAT.
AND NOTHING'S HAPPENED. NO STORY EVENTS. MAYBE THIS IS ANOTHER UNFINISHED QUE—
NO... WAIT!
ZA (ZSH)
WHAT...IS THIS...?
AN EMPTY TREASURE CHEST THAT'S ALREADY BEEN OPENED ...?

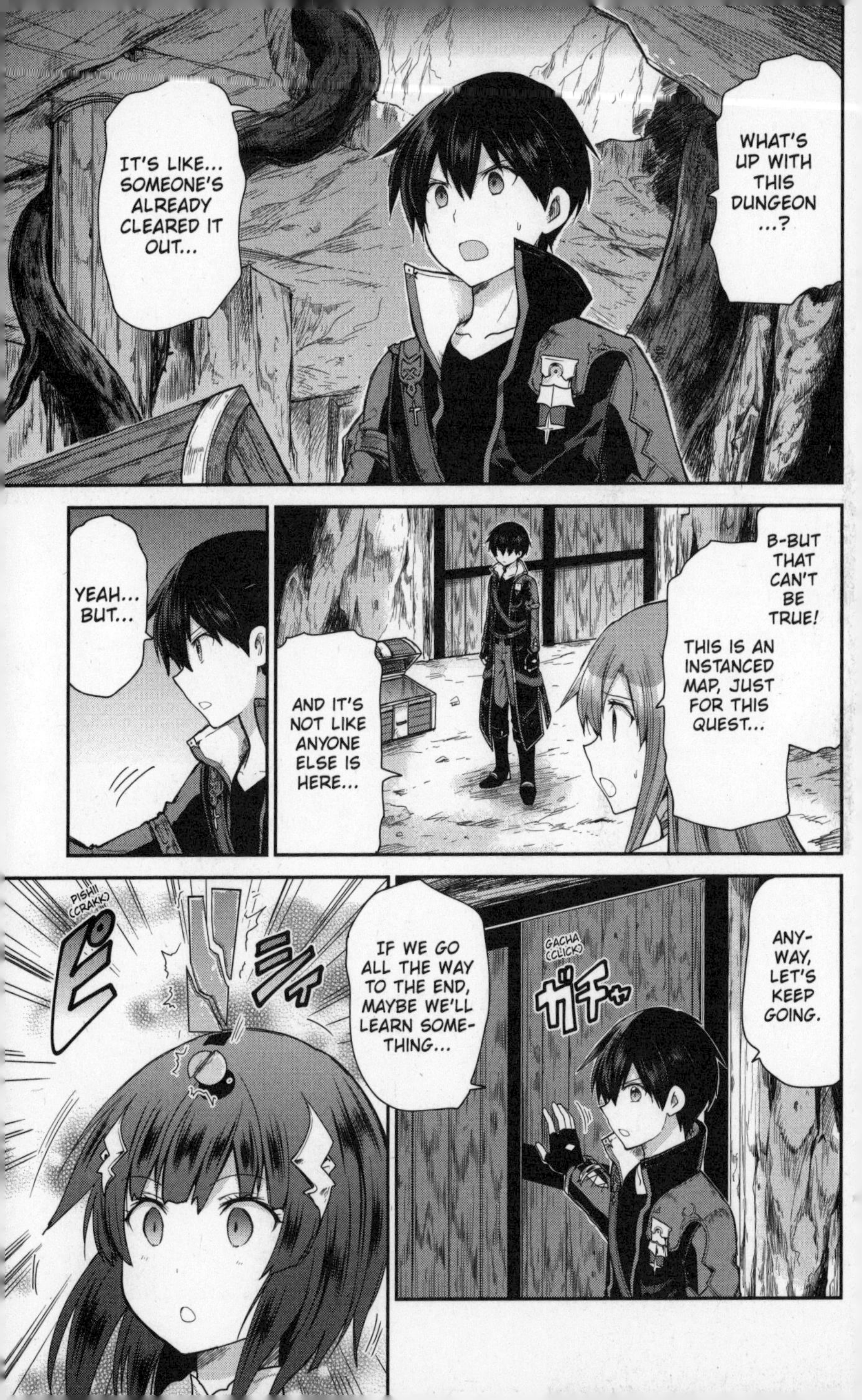
WHAT'S UP WITH THIS DUNGEON ...?
IT'S LIKE... SOMEONE'S ALREADY CLEARED IT OUT...
B-BUT THAT CAN'T BE TRUE!
THIS IS AN INSTANCED MAP, JUST FOR THIS QUEST...
AND IT'S NOT LIKE ANYONE ELSE IS HERE...
YEAH... BUT...
ANY-WAY, LET'S KEEP GOING.
GACHA (CLICK)
ガチャ
IF WE GO ALL THE WAY TO THE END, MAYBE WE'LL LEARN SOME-THING...
PISHII (CRAKK)
ピシィ

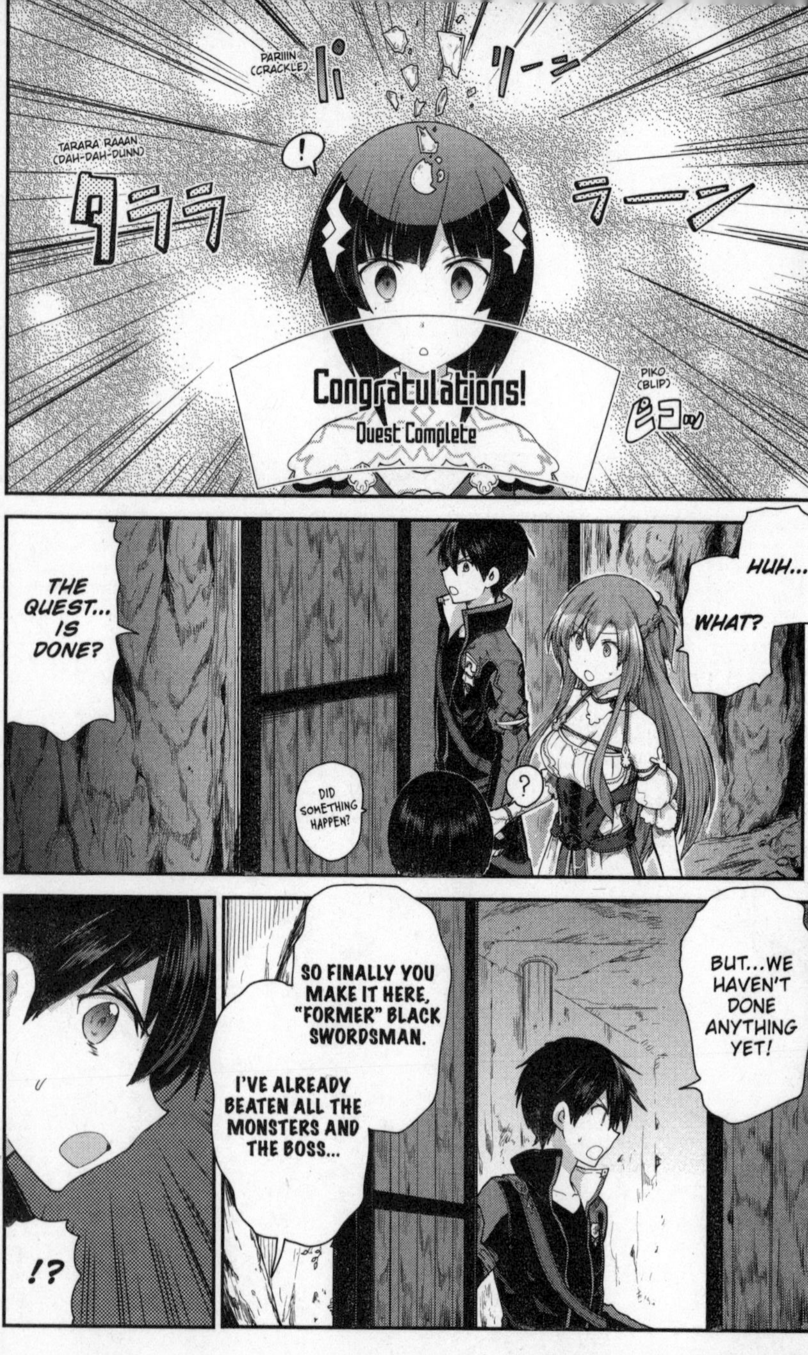
PARIIIN (CRACKLE)
パリーン
TARARA RAAN (DAH-DAH-DUNN)
タララ ラーン
!
Congratulations!
Quest Complete
PIKO (BLIP)
ピコッ
HUH...?
WHAT?
?
DID SOMETHING HAPPEN?
THE QUEST... IS DONE?
BUT...WE HAVEN'T DONE ANYTHING YET!
SO FINALLY YOU MAKE IT HERE, "FORMER" BLACK SWORDSMAN.
I'VE ALREADY BEATEN ALL THE MONSTERS AND THE BOSS...
!?

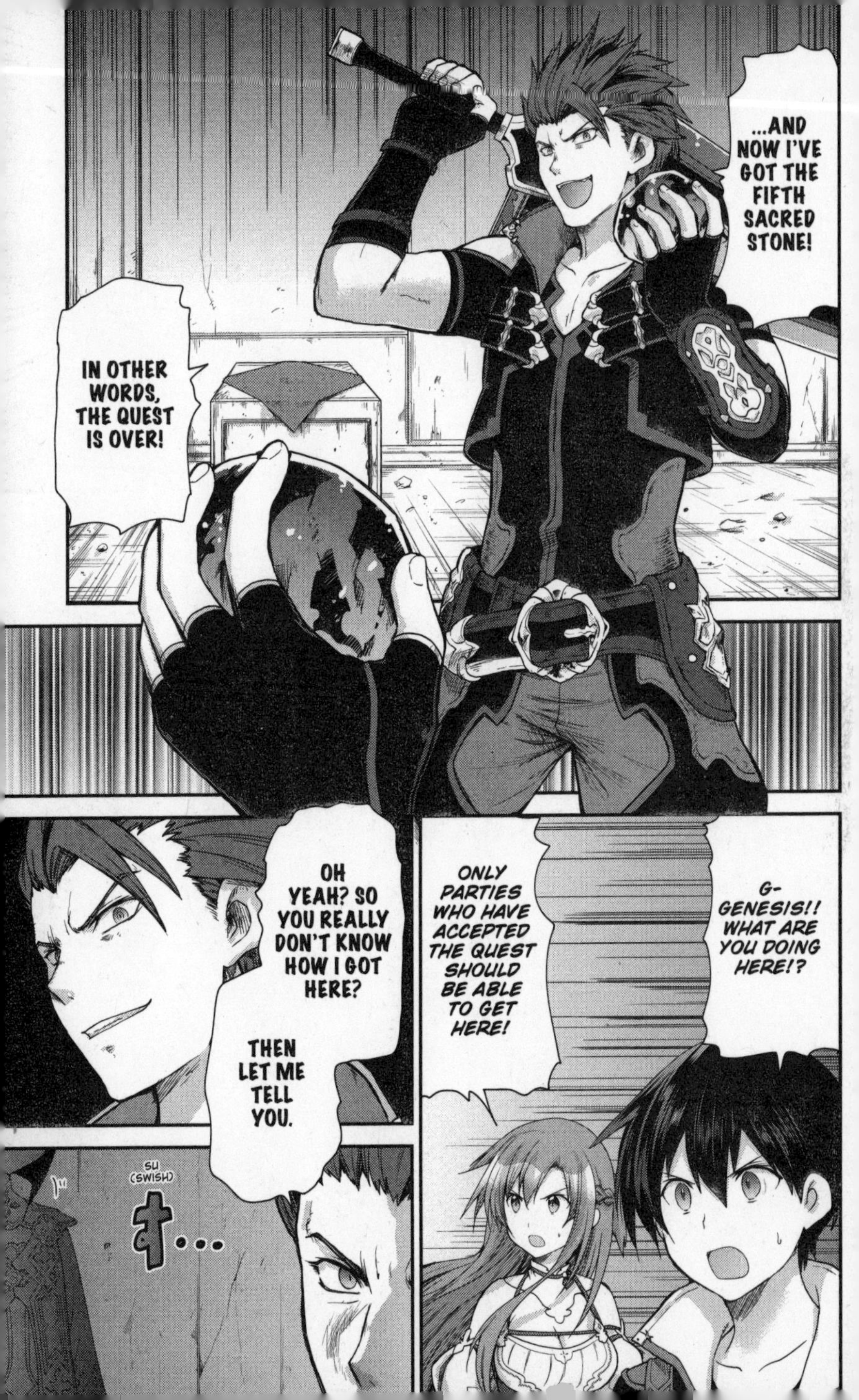
...AND NOW I'VE GOT THE FIFTH SACRED STONE!
IN OTHER WORDS, THE QUEST IS OVER!
G-GENESIS!! WHAT ARE YOU DOING HERE!?
ONLY PARTIES WHO HAVE ACCEPTED THE QUEST SHOULD BE ABLE TO GET HERE!
OH YEAH? SO YOU REALLY DON'T KNOW HOW I GOT HERE?
THEN LET ME TELL YOU.
SU (SWISH)
す...

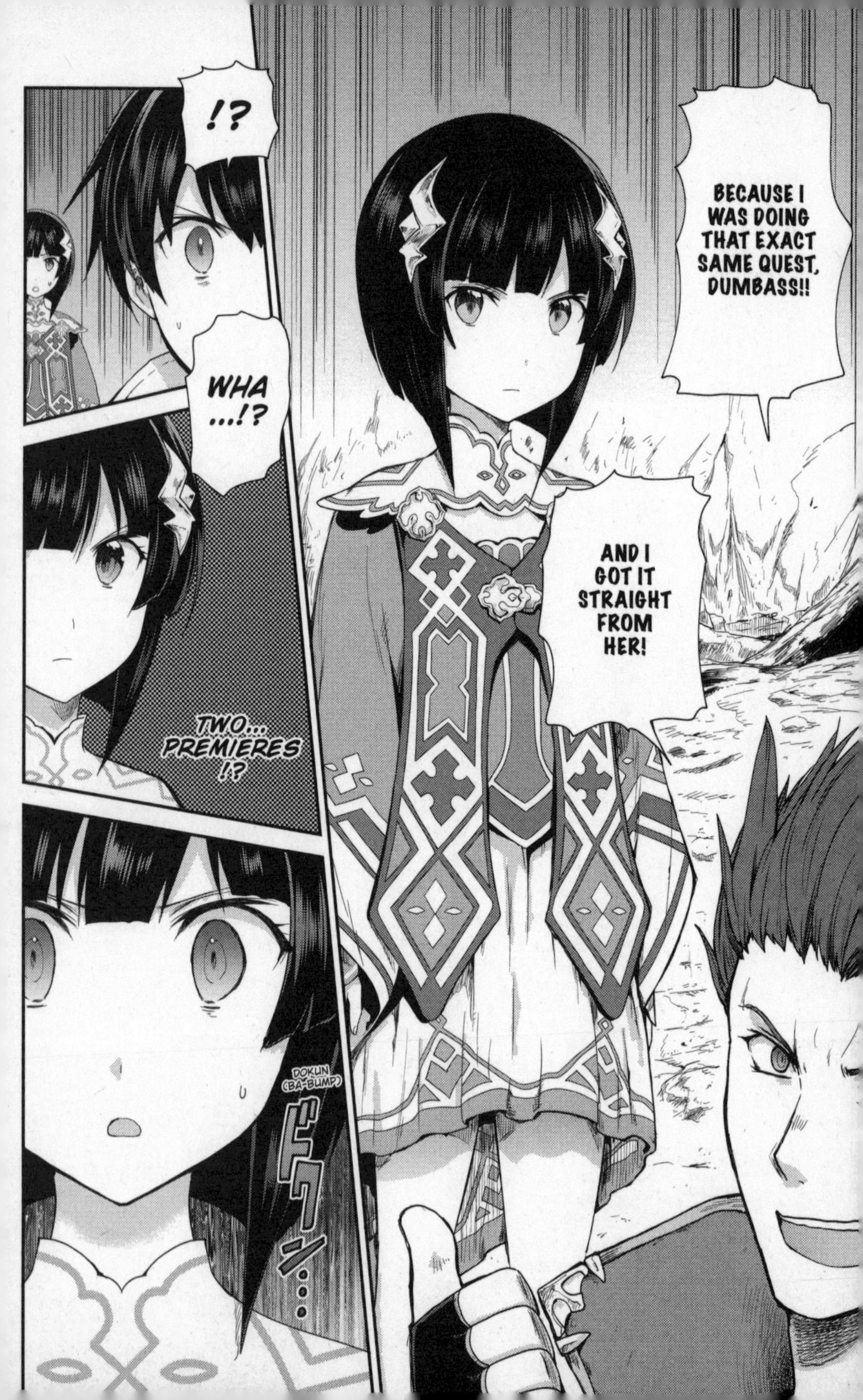
BECAUSE I WAS DOING THAT EXACT SAME QUEST, DUMBASS!!
AND I GOT IT STRAIGHT FROM HER!
!?
WHA ...!?
TWO... PREMIERES !?
DOKUN (BA-BUMP)

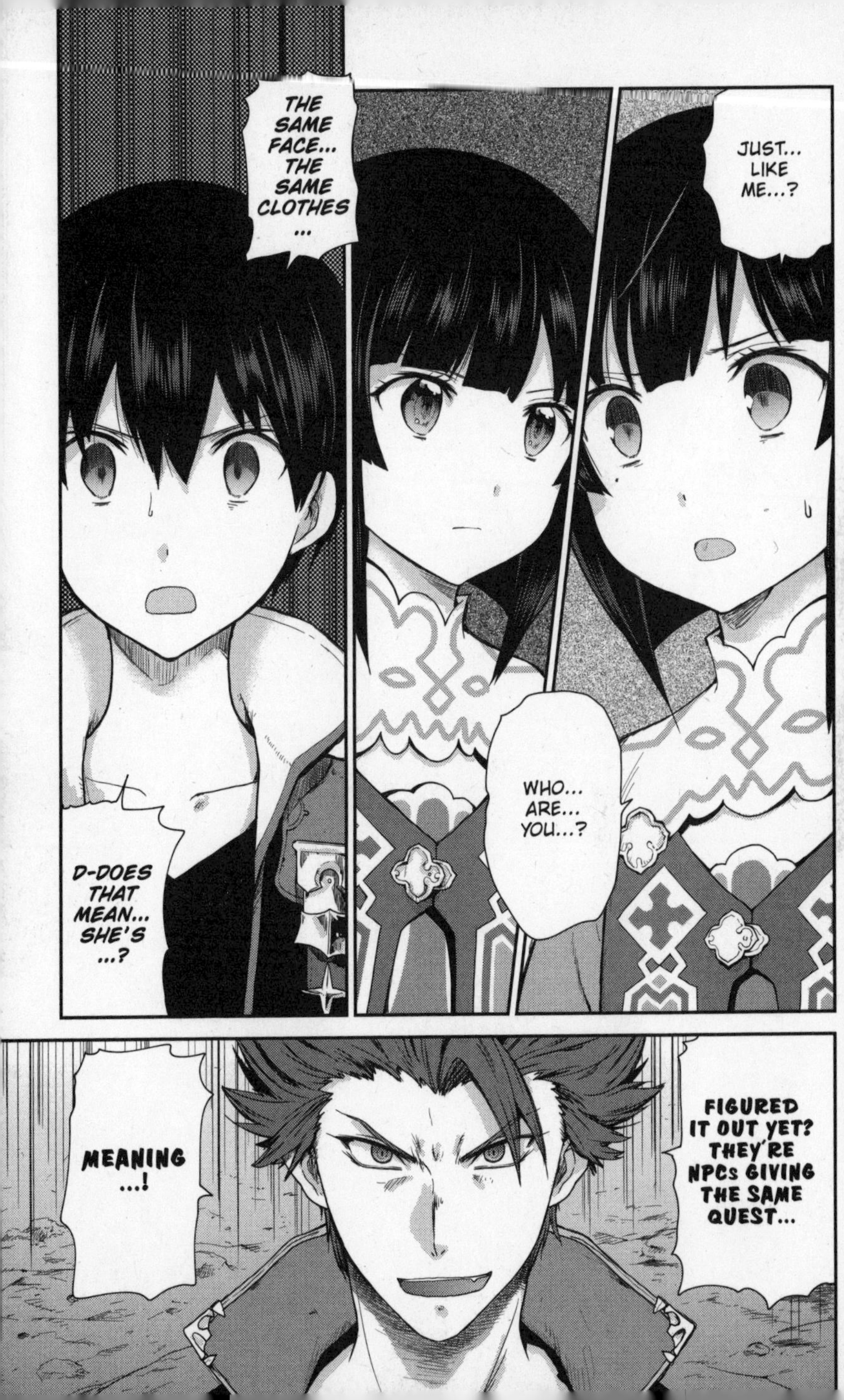
JUST... LIKE ME...?
WHO... ARE... YOU...?
THE SAME FACE... THE SAME CLOTHES...
D-DOES THAT MEAN... SHE'S...?
FIGURED IT OUT YET? THEY'RE NPCs GIVING THE SAME QUEST...
MEANING...!

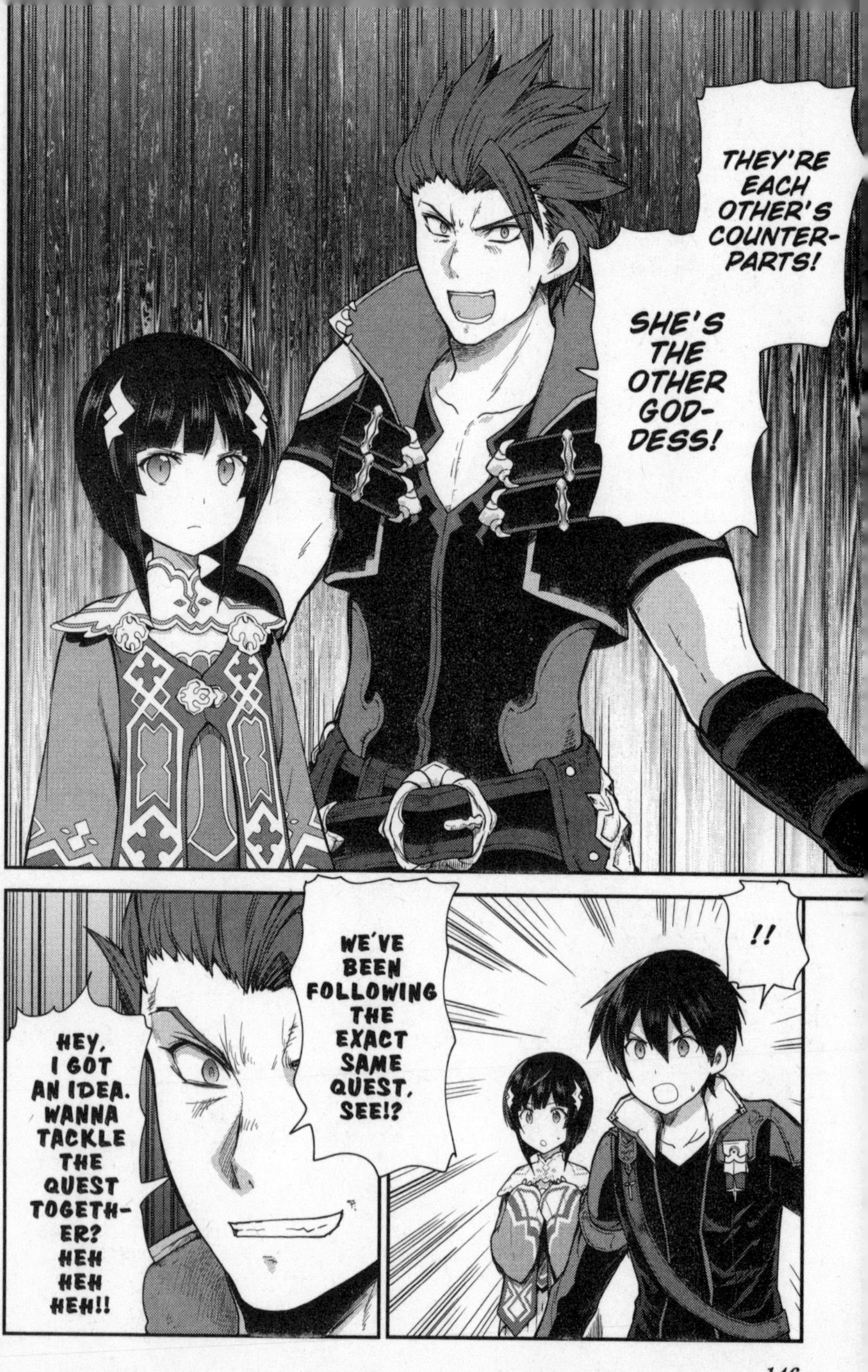
THEY'RE EACH OTHER'S COUNTER-PARTS!
SHE'S THE OTHER GOD-DESS!
!!
WE'VE BEEN FOLLOWING THE EXACT SAME QUEST, SEE!?
HEY, I GOT AN IDEA. WANNA TACKLE THE QUEST TOGETH-ER? HEH HEH HEH!!

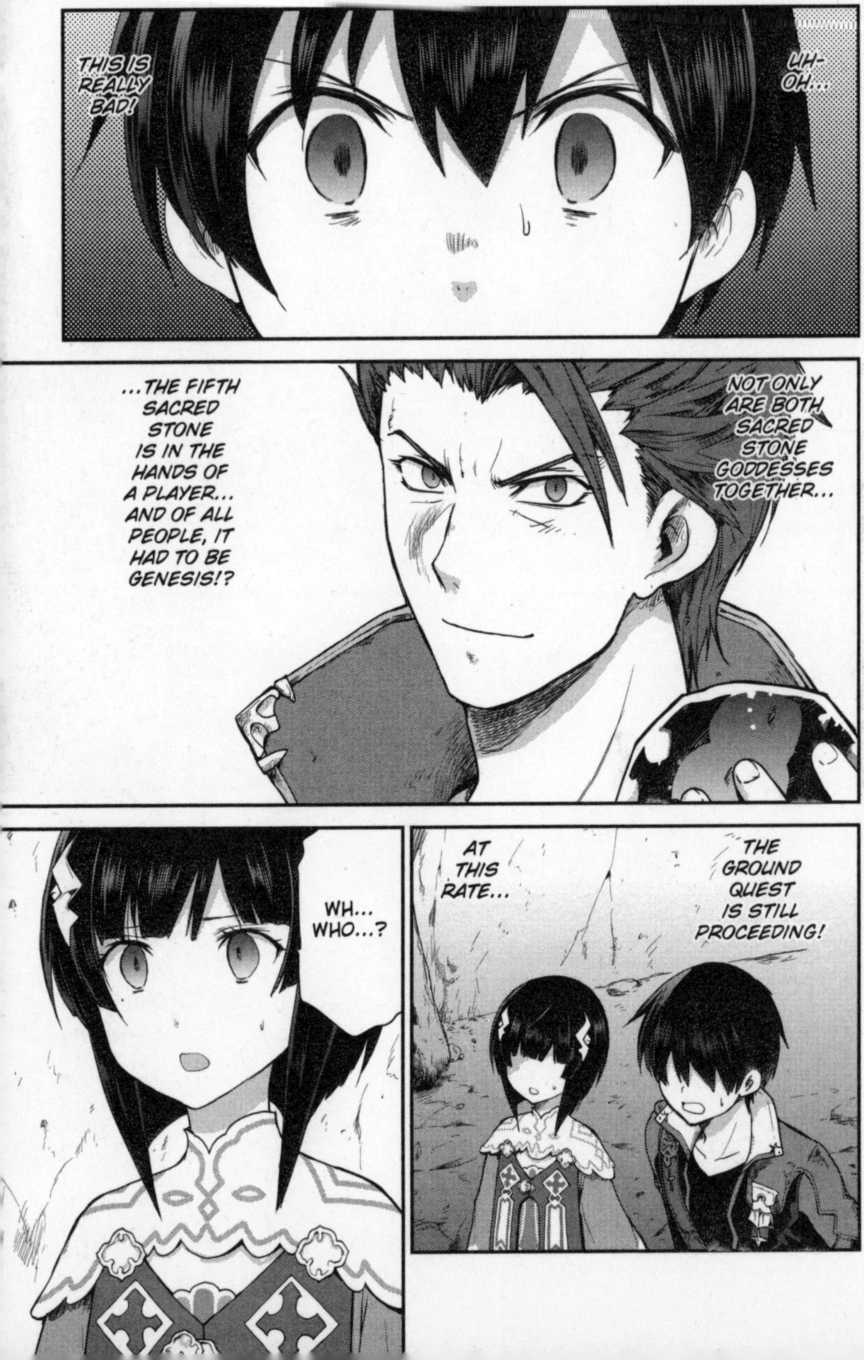
UH-OH...
THIS IS REALLY BAD!
NOT ONLY ARE BOTH SACRED STONE GODDESSES TOGETHER...
...THE FIFTH SACRED STONE IS IN THE HANDS OF A PLAYER... AND OF ALL PEOPLE, IT HAD TO BE GENESIS!?
THE GROUND QUEST IS STILL PROCEEDING!
AT THIS RATE...
WH... WHO...?

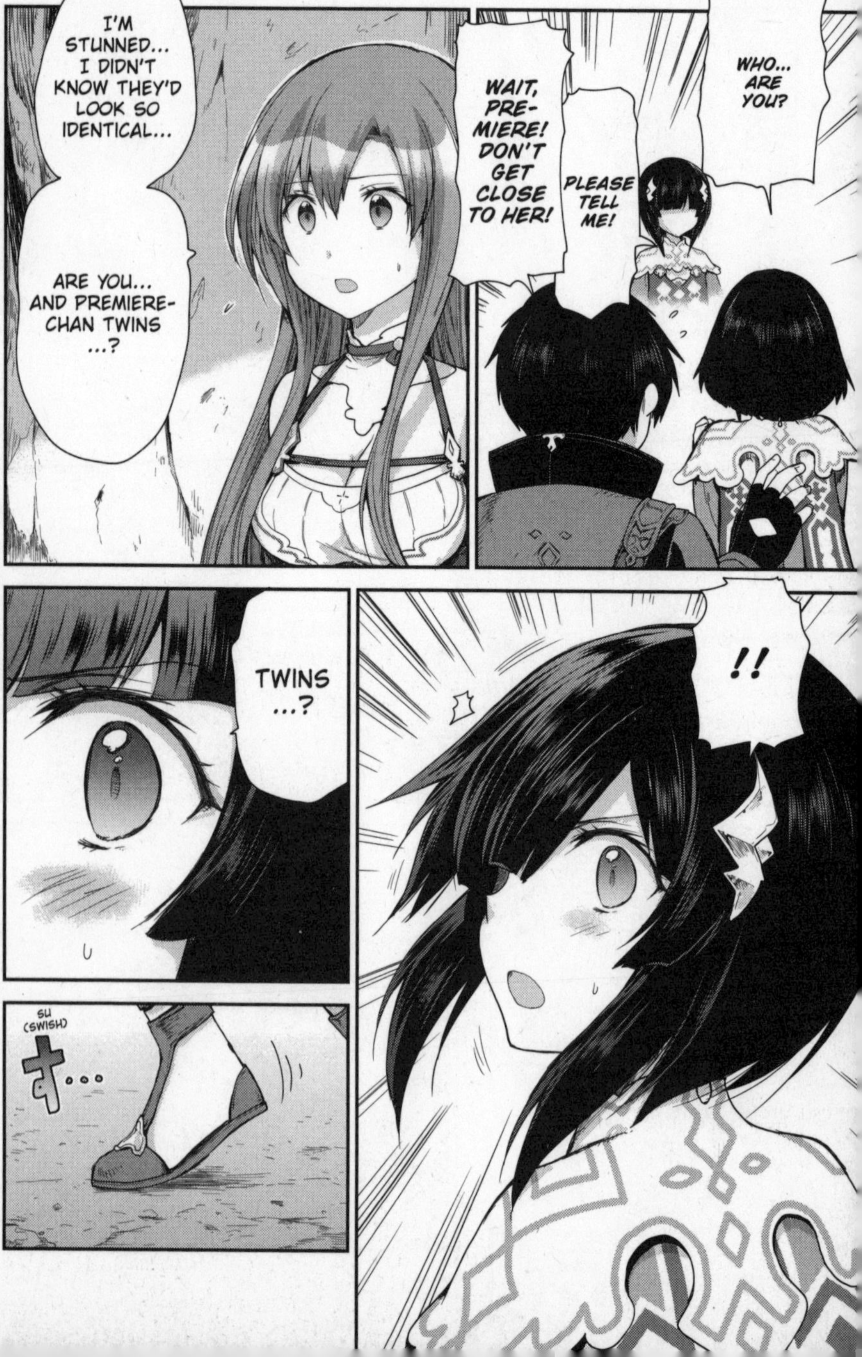
WHO... ARE YOU?
PLEASE TELL ME!
WAIT, PRE-MIERE! DON'T GET CLOSE TO HER!
I'M STUNNED... I DIDN'T KNOW THEY'D LOOK SO IDENTICAL...
ARE YOU... AND PREMIERE-CHAN TWINS ...?
!!
TWINS ...?
SU (SWISH)
す…

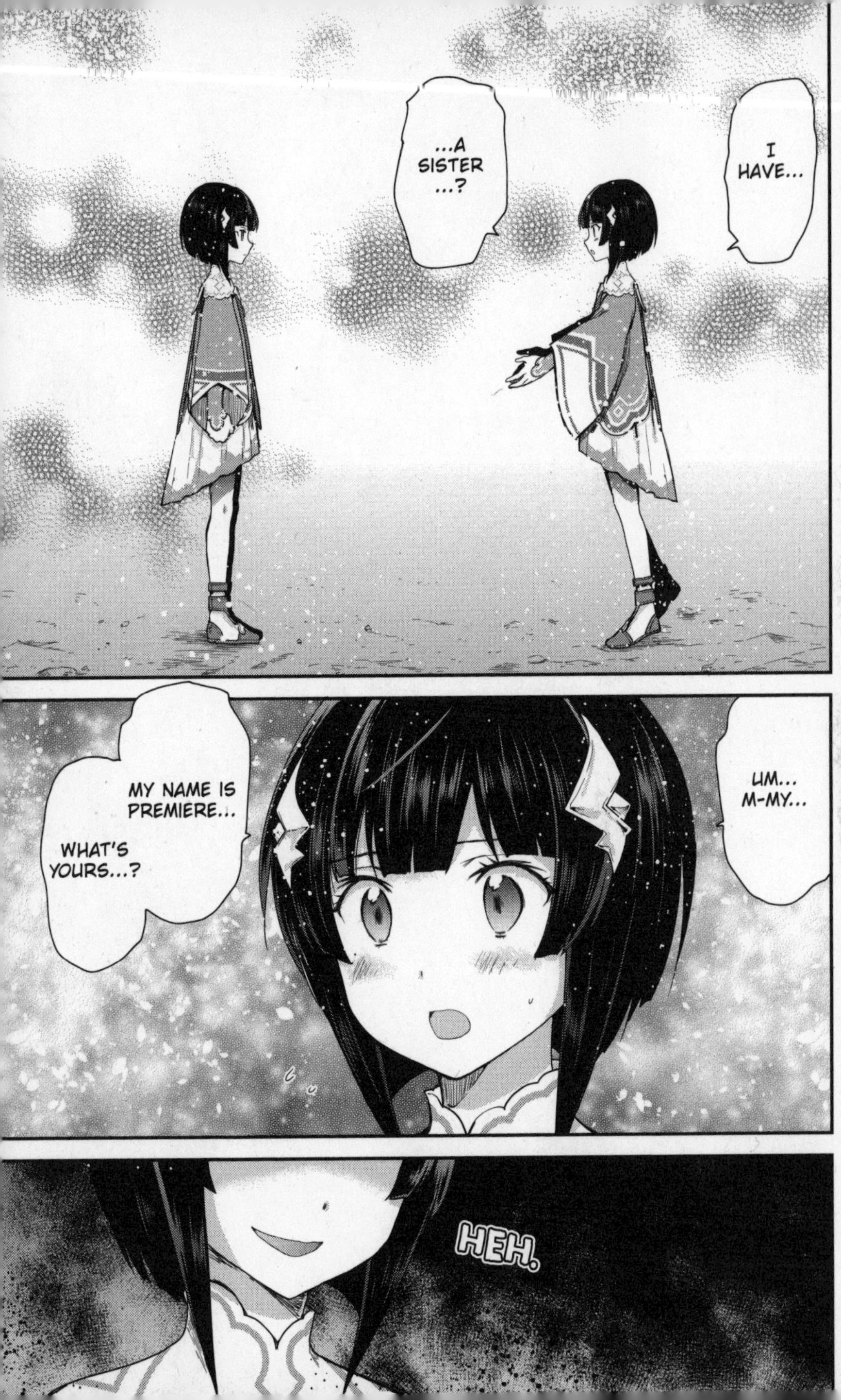
I HAVE...
...A SISTER ...?
UM... M-MY...
MY NAME IS PREMIERE... WHAT'S YOURS...?
HEH.

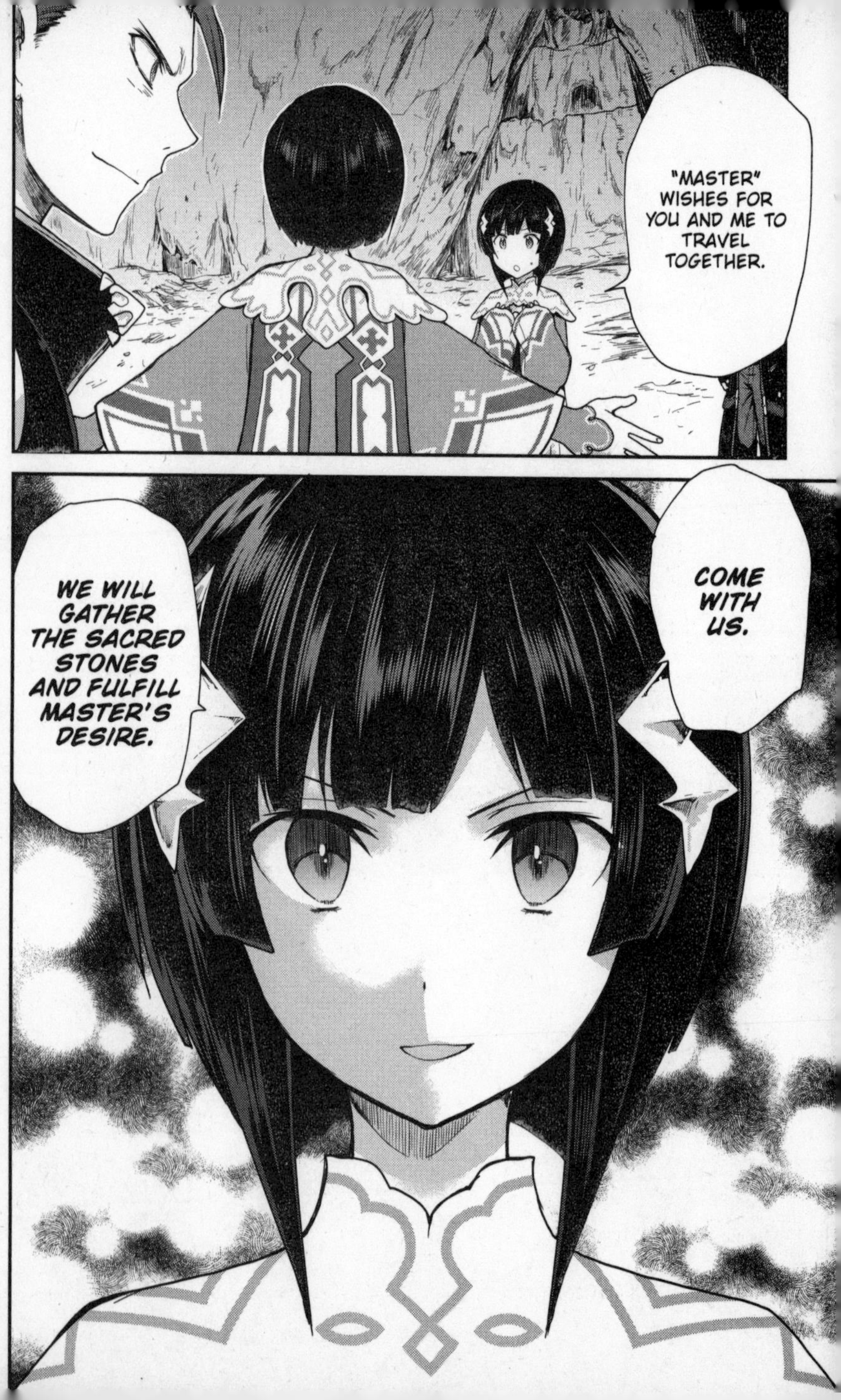
"MASTER" WISHES FOR YOU AND ME TO TRAVEL TOGETHER.
COME WITH US.
WE WILL GATHER THE SACRED STONES AND FULFILL MASTER'S DESIRE.

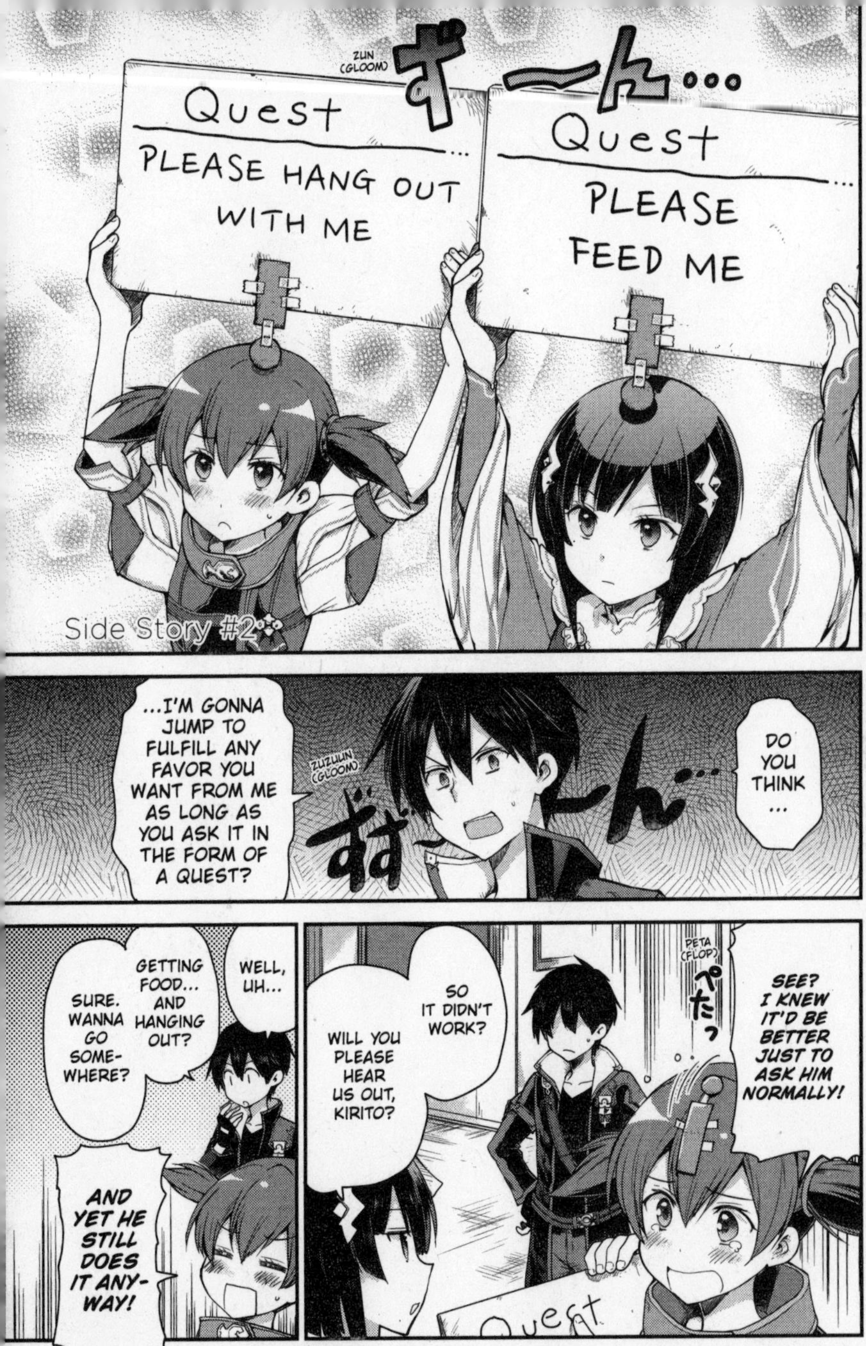
ZUN (GLOOM)
Quest
PLEASE FEED ME
Quest
PLEASE HANG OUT WITH ME
Side Story #2
DO YOU THINK ...
...I'M GONNA JUMP TO FULFILL ANY FAVOR YOU WANT FROM ME AS LONG AS YOU ASK IT IN THE FORM OF A QUEST?
ZUZUUN (GLOOM)
PETA (FLOP)
SEE? I KNEW IT'D BE BETTER JUST TO ASK HIM NORMALLY!
SO IT DIDN'T WORK?
WILL YOU PLEASE HEAR US OUT, KIRITO?
Quest
WELL, UH...
GETTING FOOD... AND HANGING OUT?
SURE. WANNA GO SOME-WHERE?
AND YET HE STILL DOES IT ANY-WAY!

Side Story #2: One Who Loves, Part II

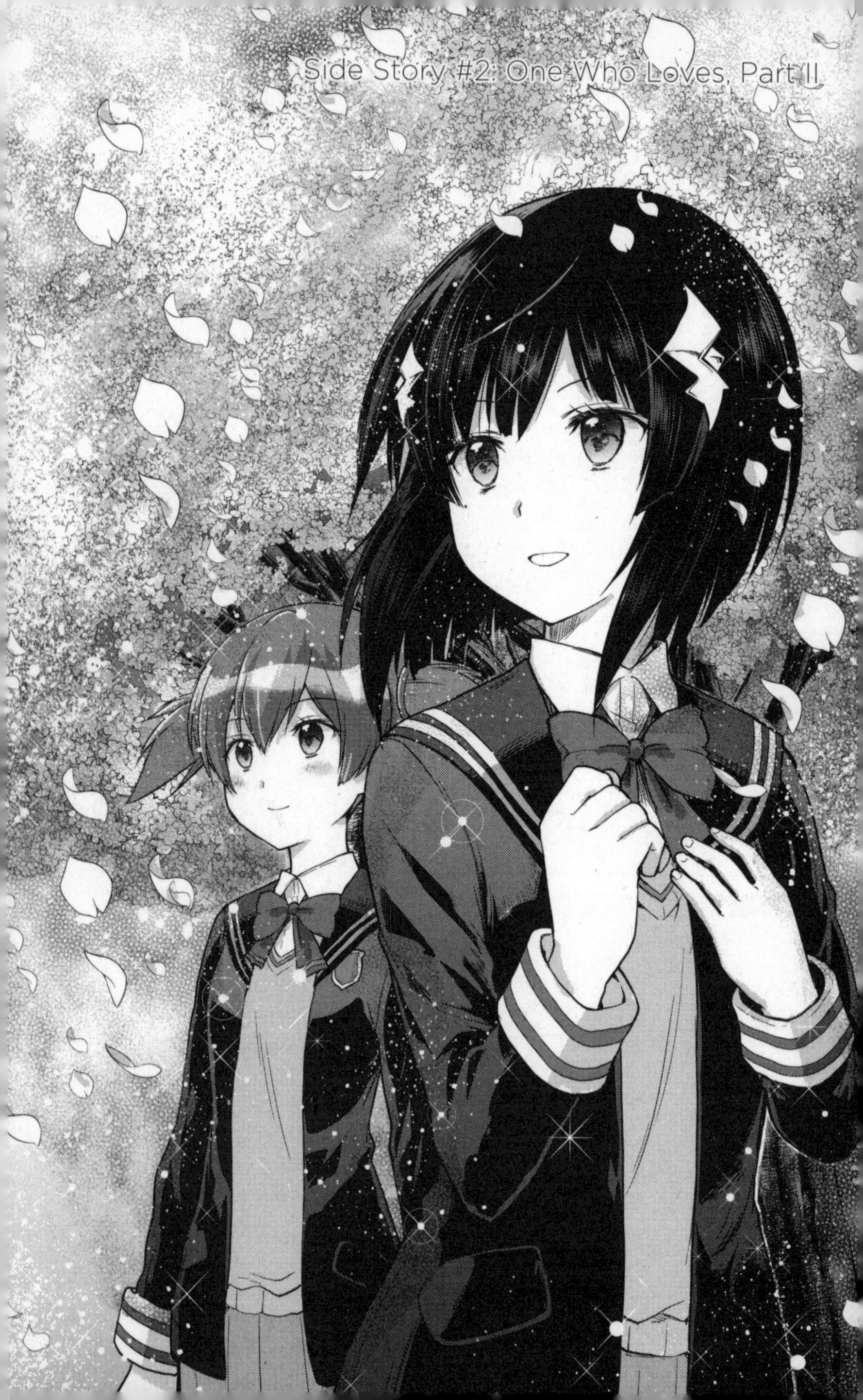

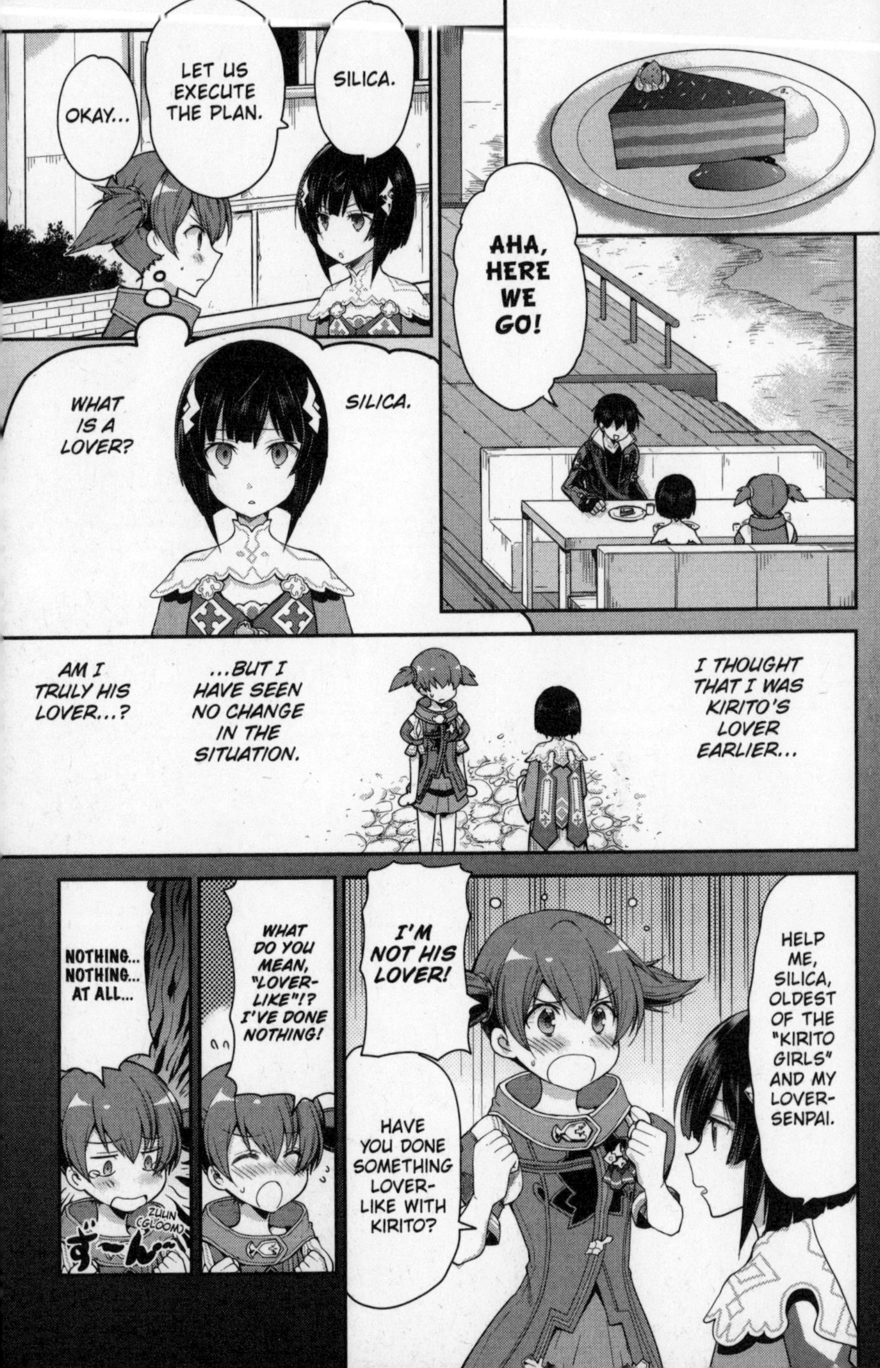

SILICA.
LET US EXECUTE THE PLAN.
OKAY...
AHA, HERE WE GO!
SILICA.
WHAT IS A LOVER?
I THOUGHT THAT I WAS KIRITO'S LOVER EARLIER...
...BUT I HAVE SEEN NO CHANGE IN THE SITUATION.
AM I TRULY HIS LOVER...?
HELP ME, SILICA, OLDEST OF THE "KIRITO GIRLS" AND MY LOVER-SENPAI.
HAVE YOU DONE SOMETHING LOVER-LIKE WITH KIRITO?
I'M NOT HIS LOVER!
WHAT DO YOU MEAN, "LOVER-LIKE"!? I'VE DONE NOTHING!
NOTHING... NOTHING... AT ALL...
ずーん
ZUUN (GLOOM)

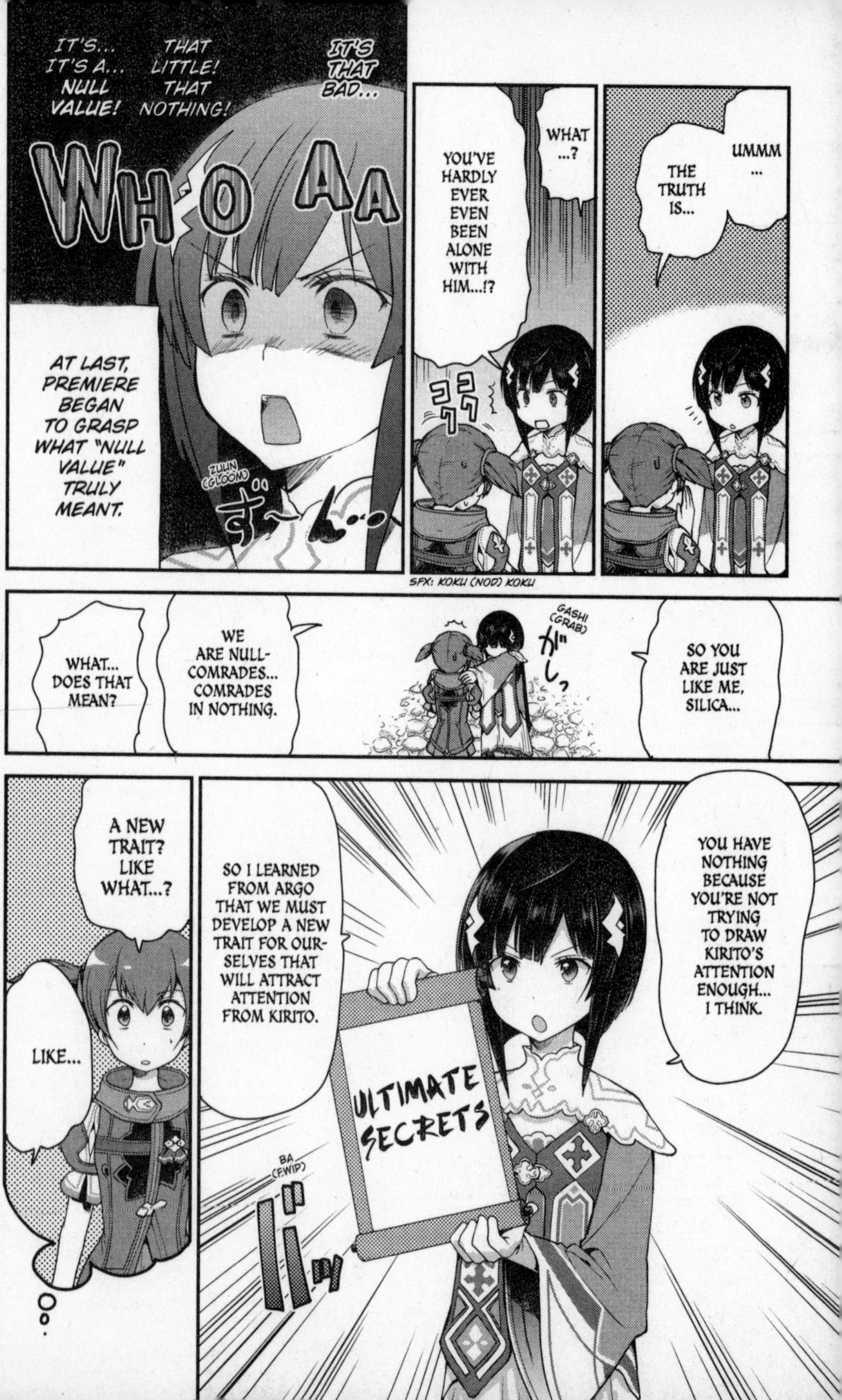
UMMM...
THE TRUTH IS...
WHAT...?
YOU'VE HARDLY EVER EVEN BEEN ALONE WITH HIM...!?
IT'S THAT BAD...
THAT LITTLE! THAT NOTHING!
IT'S... IT'S A... NULL VALUE!
WHOAA
AT LAST, PREMIERE BEGAN TO GRASP WHAT "NULL VALUE" TRULY MEANT.
ZUUN (GLOOM)
SFX: KOKU (NOD) KOKU
SO YOU ARE JUST LIKE ME, SILICA...
GASHI (GRAB)
WE ARE NULL-COMRADES... COMRADES IN NOTHING.
WHAT... DOES THAT MEAN?
YOU HAVE NOTHING BECAUSE YOU'RE NOT TRYING TO DRAW KIRITO'S ATTENTION ENOUGH... I THINK.
SO I LEARNED FROM ARGO THAT WE MUST DEVELOP A NEW TRAIT FOR OUR-SELVES THAT WILL ATTRACT ATTENTION FROM KIRITO.
ULTIMATE SECRETS
BA (FWIP)
A NEW TRAIT? LIKE WHAT...?
LIKE...

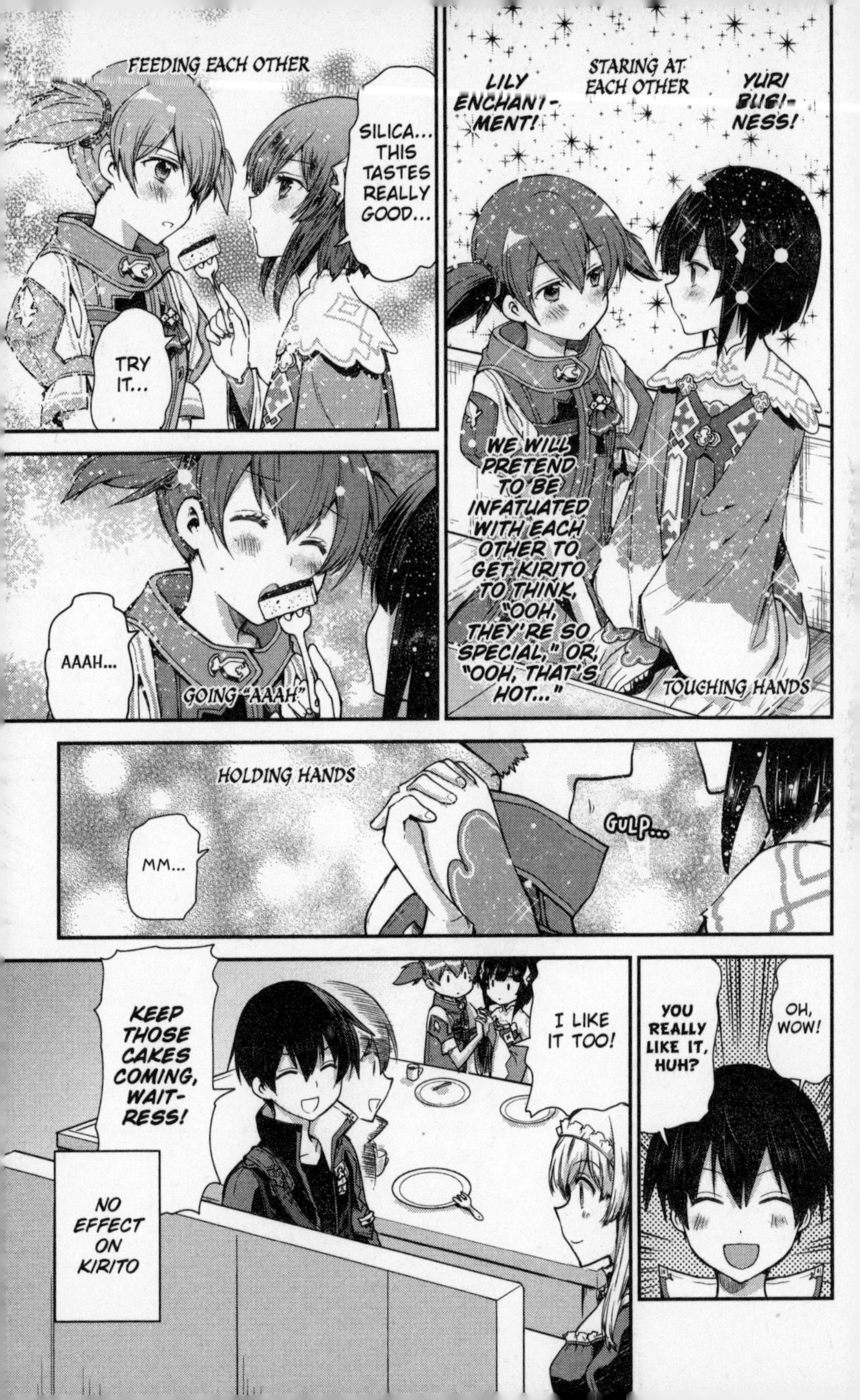
YURI BUSINESS!
STARING AT EACH OTHER
LILY ENCHANTMENT!
WE WILL PRETEND TO BE INFATUATED WITH EACH OTHER TO GET KIRITO TO THINK, "OOH, THEY'RE SO SPECIAL," OR, "OOH, THAT'S HOT..."
TOUCHING HANDS
FEEDING EACH OTHER
SILICA... THIS TASTES REALLY GOOD...
TRY IT...
GOING "AAAH"
AAAH...
GULP...
HOLDING HANDS
MM...
OH, WOW!
YOU REALLY LIKE IT, HUH?
I LIKE IT TOO!
KEEP THOSE CAKES COMING, WAITRESS!
NO EFFECT ON KIRITO

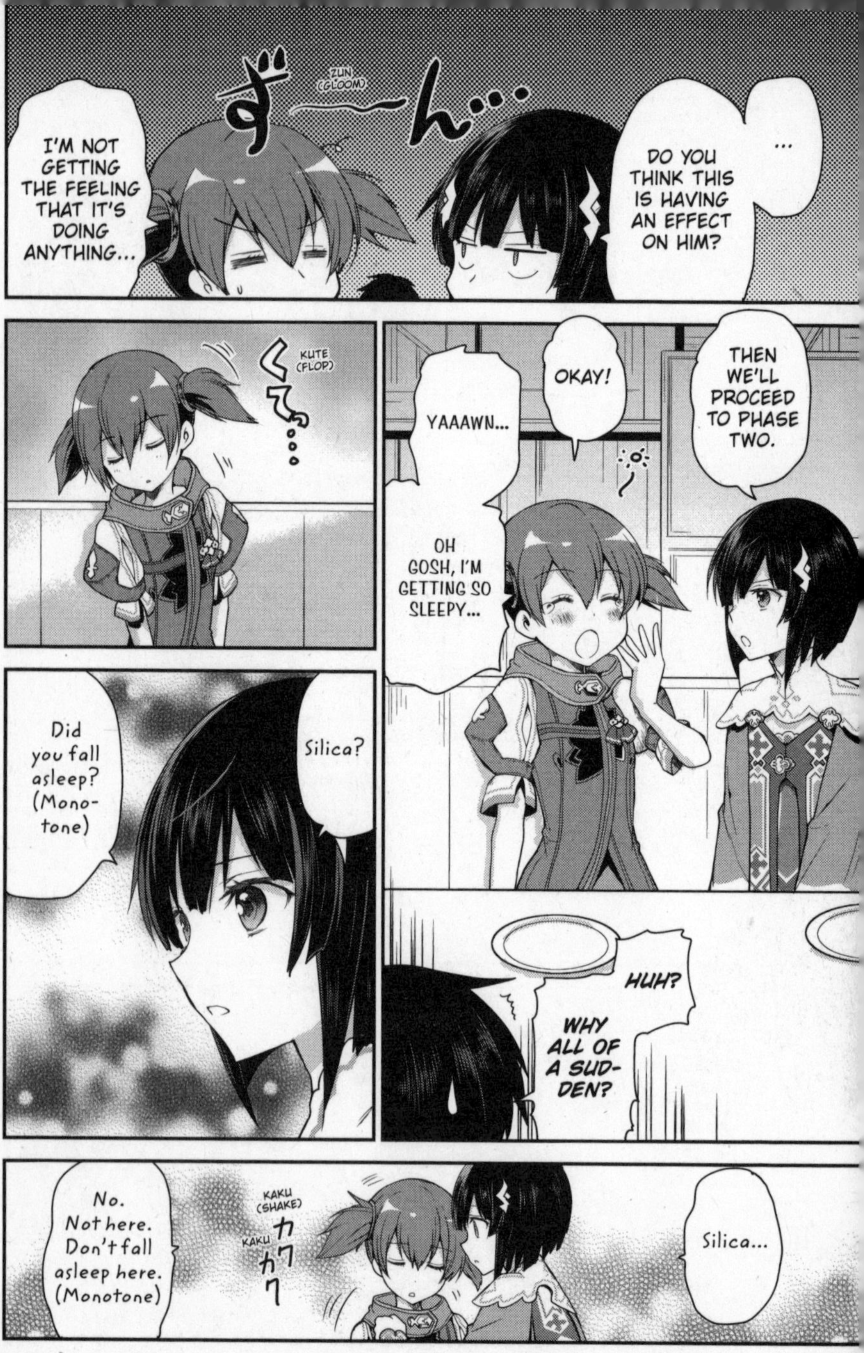
ず〜〜ん…
ZUN (GLOOM)
...
DO YOU THINK THIS IS HAVING AN EFFECT ON HIM?
I'M NOT GETTING THE FEELING THAT IT'S DOING ANYTHING...
THEN WE'LL PROCEED TO PHASE TWO.
OKAY!
YAAAWN...
OH GOSH, I'M GETTING SO SLEEPY...
くてっ…
KUTE (FLOP)
HUH?
WHY ALL OF A SUDDEN?
Silica?
Did you fall asleep? (Monotone)
Silica...
カクカク
KAKU (SHAKE)
KAKU
No. Not here. Don't fall asleep here. (Monotone)

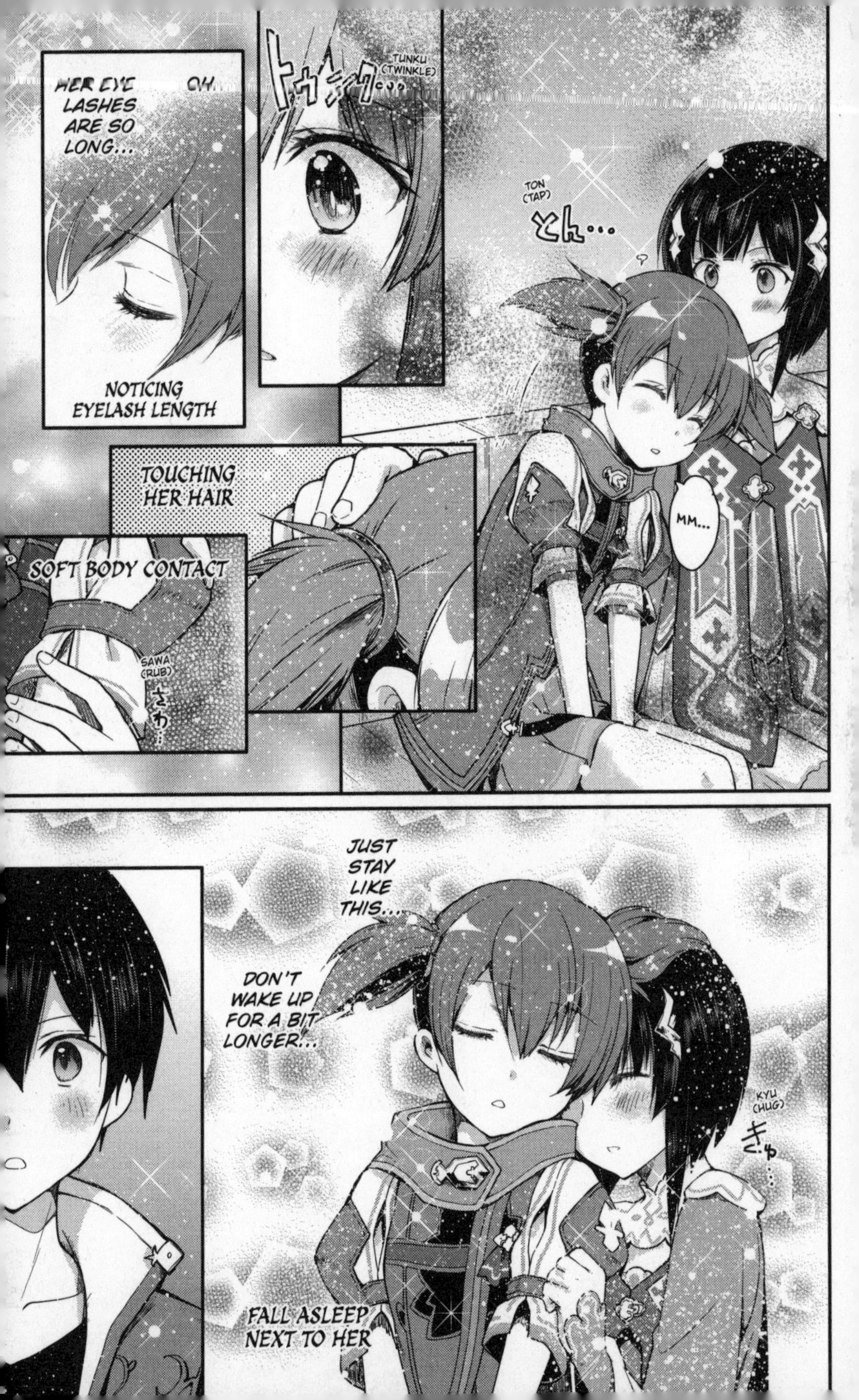
TON (TAP)
とん…
MM...
TUNKU (TWINKLE)
トゥンク
OH.
HER EYE LASHES ARE SO LONG...
NOTICING EYELASH LENGTH
TOUCHING HER HAIR
SOFT BODY CONTACT
SAWA (RUB)
さわ…
JUST STAY LIKE THIS...
DON'T WAKE UP FOR A BIT LONGER...
KYU (HUG)
きゅ…
FALL ASLEEP NEXT TO HER

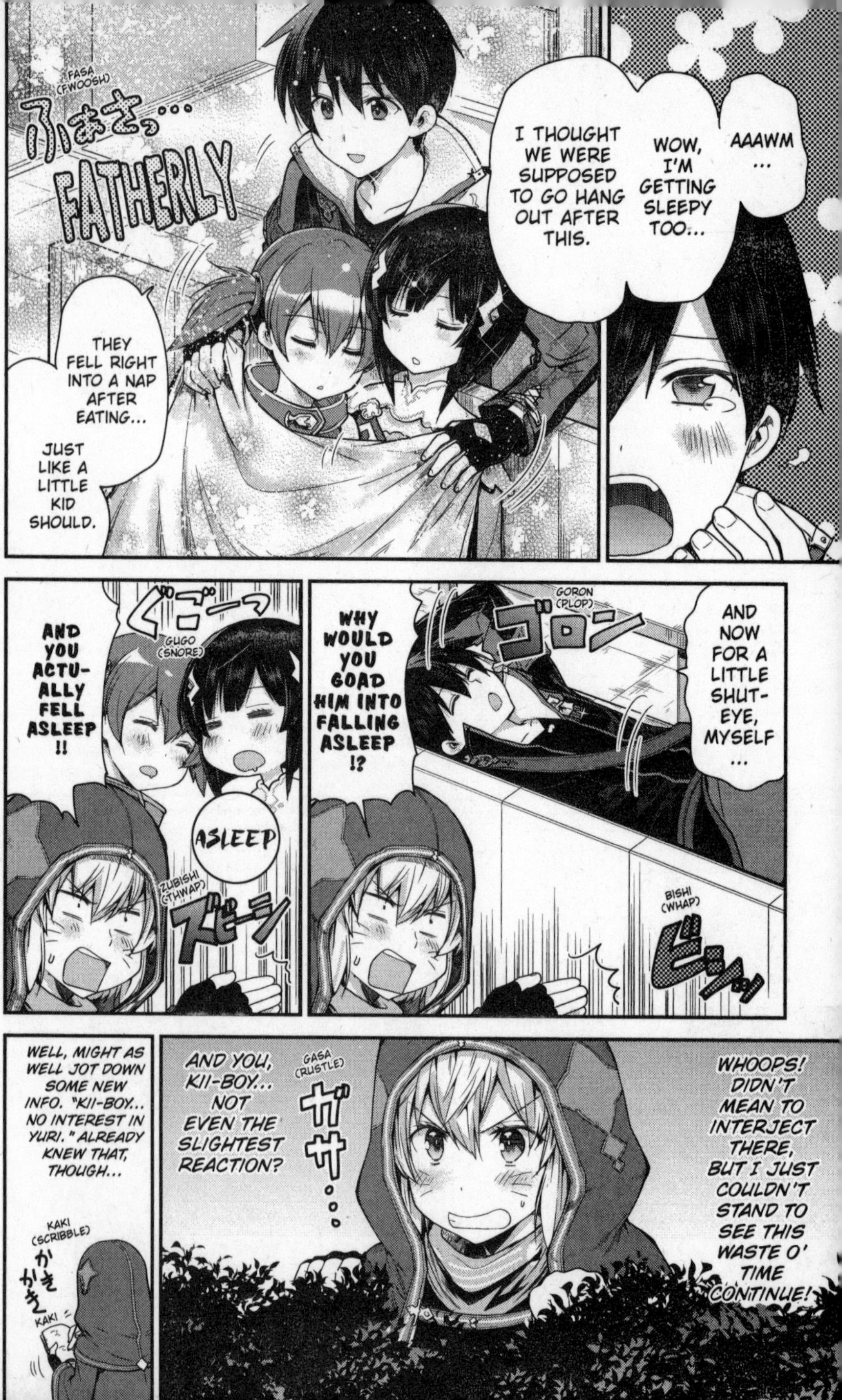
AAAWM...
WOW, I'M GETTING SLEEPY TOO...
I THOUGHT WE WERE SUPPOSED TO GO HANG OUT AFTER THIS.
FASA (FWOOSH)
ふぁさっ…
FATHERLY
THEY FELL RIGHT INTO A NAP AFTER EATING...
JUST LIKE A LITTLE KID SHOULD.
GORON (PLOP)
ゴロン
AND NOW FOR A LITTLE SHUT-EYE, MYSELF...
WHY WOULD YOU GOAD HIM INTO FALLING ASLEEP!?
BISHI (WHAP)
ビシッ
GUGO (SNORE)
ぐごーっ
AND YOU ACTUALLY FELL ASLEEP!!
ASLEEP
ZUBISHI (THWAP)
WHOOPS! DIDN'T MEAN TO INTERJECT THERE, BUT I JUST COULDN'T STAND TO SEE THIS WASTE O' TIME CONTINUE!
GASA (RUSTLE)
ガサ…
AND YOU, KII-BOY... NOT EVEN THE SLIGHTEST REACTION?
WELL, MIGHT AS WELL JOT DOWN SOME NEW INFO. "KII-BOY... NO INTEREST IN YURI." ALREADY KNEW THAT, THOUGH...
KAKI (SCRIBBLE)
かきかき
KAKI

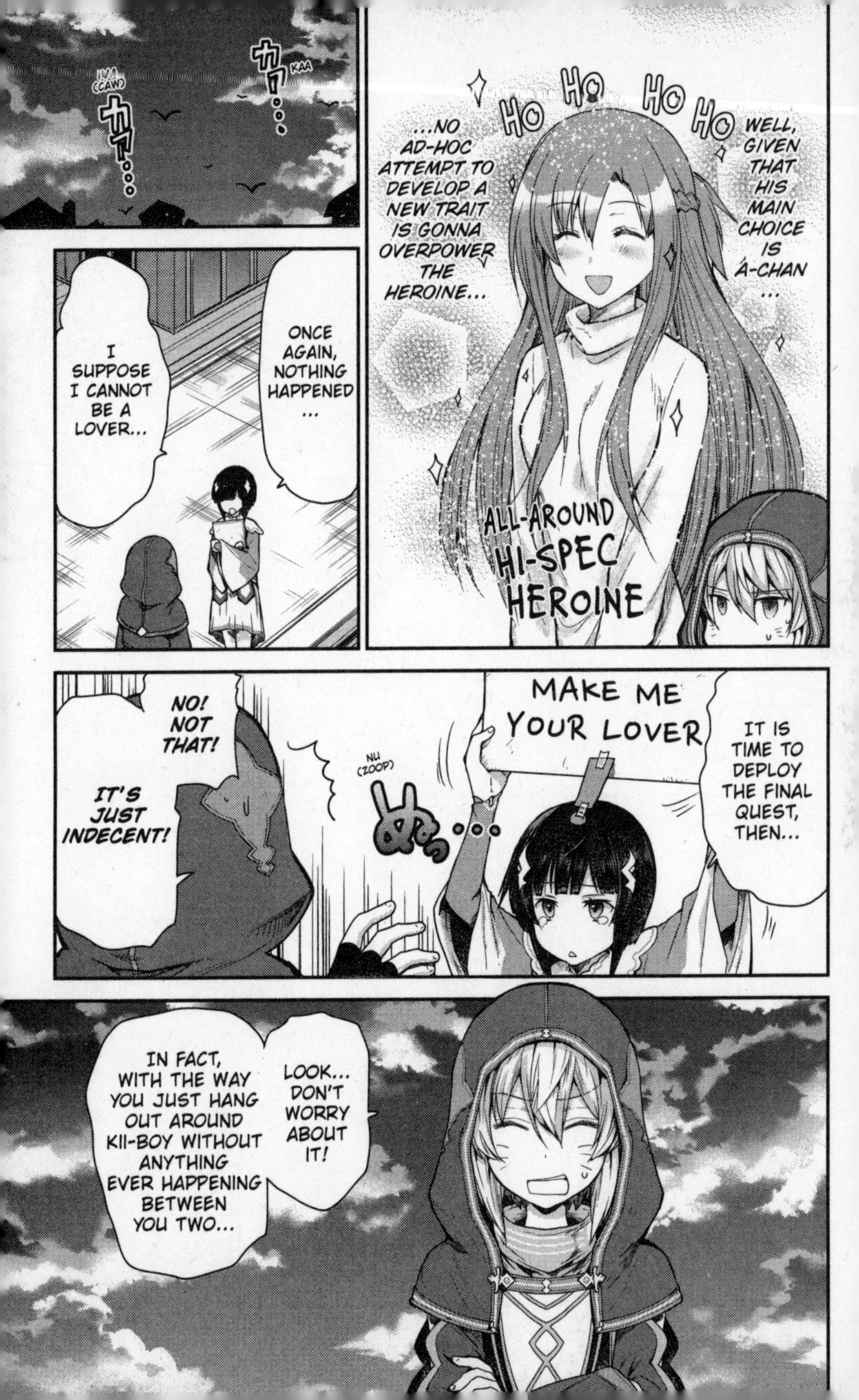
HO HO HO HO
WELL, GIVEN THAT HIS MAIN CHOICE IS A-CHAN...
...NO AD-HOC ATTEMPT TO DEVELOP A NEW TRAIT IS GONNA OVERPOWER THE HEROINE...
ALL-AROUND HI-SPEC HEROINE
カァ… KAA
カァ… KAA (CAW)
ONCE AGAIN, NOTHING HAPPENED...
I SUPPOSE I CANNOT BE A LOVER...
IT IS TIME TO DEPLOY THE FINAL QUEST, THEN...
MAKE ME YOUR LOVER
ぬっ… NU (ZOOP)
NO! NOT THAT!
IT'S JUST INDECENT!
LOOK... DON'T WORRY ABOUT IT!
IN FACT, WITH THE WAY YOU JUST HANG OUT AROUND KII-BOY WITHOUT ANYTHING EVER HAPPENING BETWEEN YOU TWO...

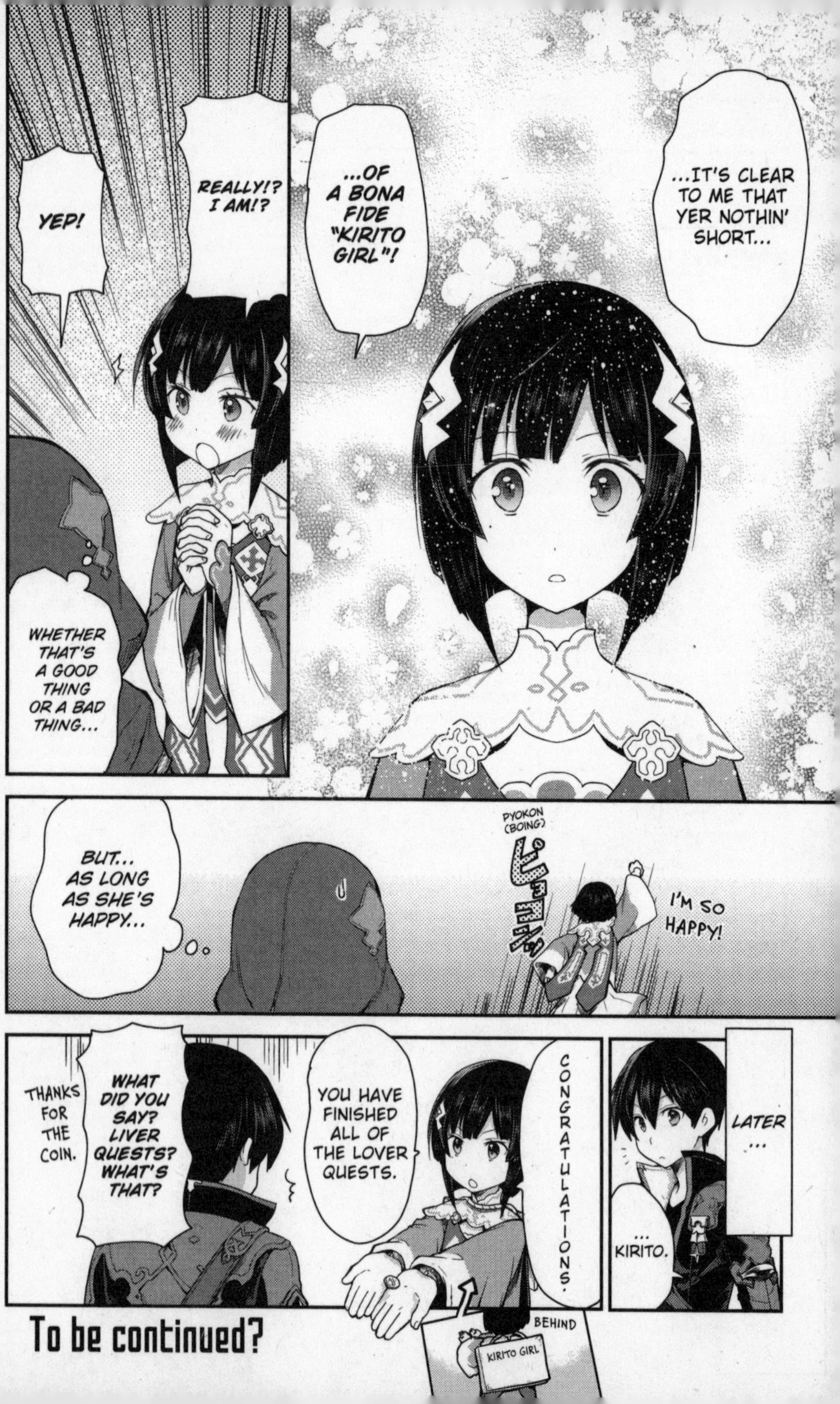
...IT'S CLEAR TO ME THAT YER NOTHIN' SHORT...
...OF A BONA FIDE "KIRITO GIRL"!
REALLY!? I AM!?
YEP!
WHETHER THAT'S A GOOD THING OR A BAD THING...
I'M SO HAPPY!
PYOKON (BOING)
BUT... AS LONG AS SHE'S HAPPY...
LATER...
...KIRITO.
CONGRATULATIONS.
YOU HAVE FINISHED ALL OF THE LOVER QUESTS.
WHAT DID YOU SAY? LIVER QUESTS? WHAT'S THAT?
THANKS FOR THE COIN.
BEHIND
KIRITO GIRL

To be continued?

VOLUME 4 AFTERWORD

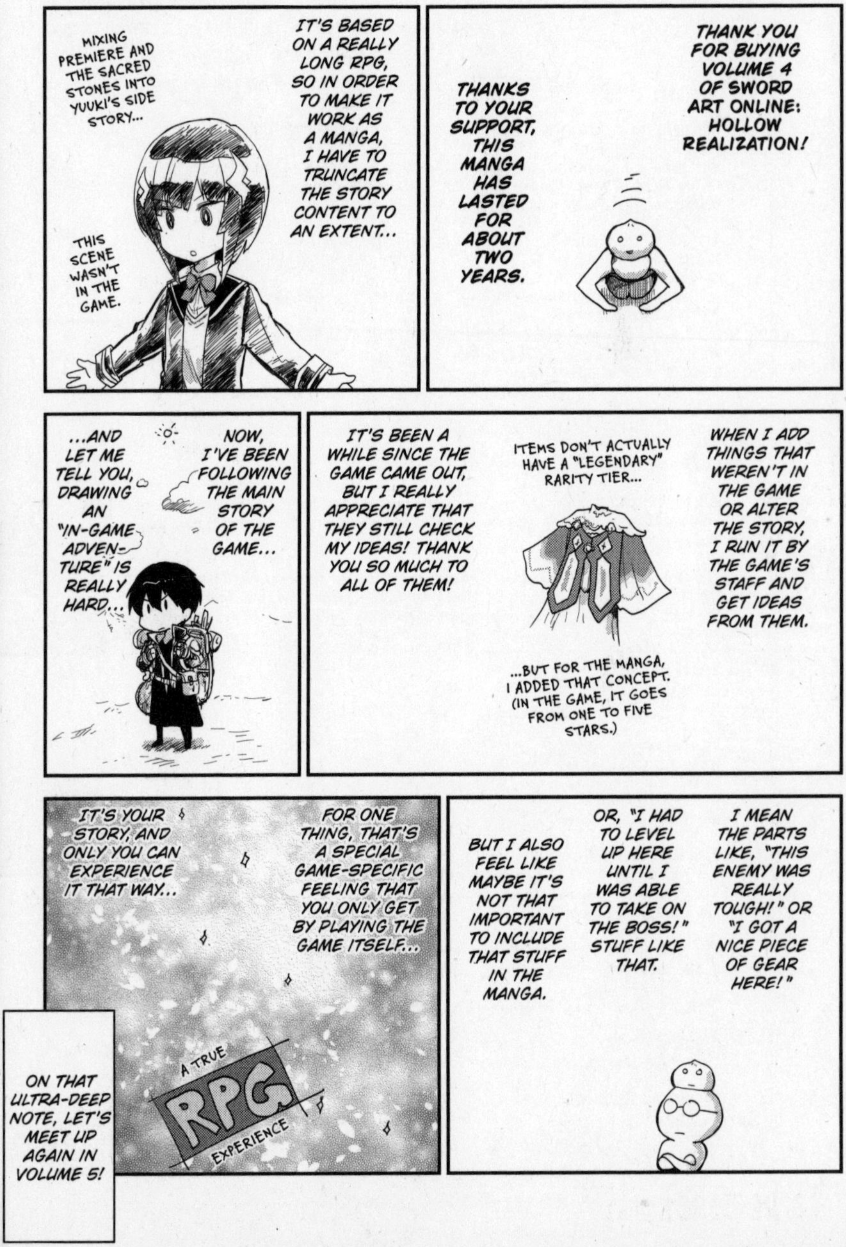
THANK YOU FOR BUYING VOLUME 4 OF SWORD ART ONLINE: HOLLOW REALIZATION!
THANKS TO YOUR SUPPORT, THIS MANGA HAS LASTED FOR ABOUT TWO YEARS.
IT'S BASED ON A REALLY LONG RPG, SO IN ORDER TO MAKE IT WORK AS A MANGA, I HAVE TO TRUNCATE THE STORY CONTENT TO AN EXTENT...
MIXING PREMIERE AND THE SACRED STONES INTO YUUKI'S SIDE STORY...
THIS SCENE WASN'T IN THE GAME.
WHEN I ADD THINGS THAT WEREN'T IN THE GAME OR ALTER THE STORY, I RUN IT BY THE GAME'S STAFF AND GET IDEAS FROM THEM.
ITEMS DON'T ACTUALLY HAVE A "LEGENDARY" RARITY TIER...
...BUT FOR THE MANGA, I ADDED THAT CONCEPT. (IN THE GAME, IT GOES FROM ONE TO FIVE STARS.)
IT'S BEEN A WHILE SINCE THE GAME CAME OUT, BUT I REALLY APPRECIATE THAT THEY STILL CHECK MY IDEAS! THANK YOU SO MUCH TO ALL OF THEM!
NOW, I'VE BEEN FOLLOWING THE MAIN STORY OF THE GAME...
...AND LET ME TELL YOU, DRAWING AN "IN-GAME ADVEN-TURE" IS REALLY HARD...
I MEAN THE PARTS LIKE, "THIS ENEMY WAS REALLY TOUGH!" OR "I GOT A NICE PIECE OF GEAR HERE!"
OR, "I HAD TO LEVEL UP HERE UNTIL I WAS ABLE TO TAKE ON THE BOSS!" STUFF LIKE THAT.
BUT I ALSO FEEL LIKE MAYBE IT'S NOT THAT IMPORTANT TO INCLUDE THAT STUFF IN THE MANGA.
FOR ONE THING, THAT'S A SPECIAL GAME-SPECIFIC FEELING THAT YOU ONLY GET BY PLAYING THE GAME ITSELF...
IT'S YOUR STORY, AND ONLY YOU CAN EXPERIENCE IT THAT WAY...
A TRUE RPG EXPERIENCE
ON THAT ULTRA-DEEP NOTE, LET'S MEET UP AGAIN IN VOLUME 5!

SWORD ART ONLINE: HOLLOW REALIZATION ④

Art: Tomo Hirokawa
Original Story: Reki Kawahara
Character Design: abec
Story Supervision: Bandai Namco Entertainment

Translation: Stephen Paul   **Lettering: Phil Christie**

This book is a work of fiction. Names, characters, places, and incidents are the product of the author's imagination or are used fictitiously. Any resemblance to actual events, locales, or persons, living or dead, is coincidental.

SWORD ART ONLINE -HOLLOW REALIZATION- Vol. 4
© REKI KAWAHARA 2018
© TOMO HIROKAWA 2018
© 2016 REKI KAWAHARA/PUBLISHED BY KADOKAWA CORPORATION
ASCII MEDIA WORKS/SAO MOVIE Project
© 2014 REKI KAWAHARA/PUBLISHED BY KADOKAWA CORPORATION
ASCII MEDIA WORKS/SAOII Project
© BANDAI NAMCO Entertainment Inc.
First published in Japan in 2018 by KADOKAWA CORPORATION, Tokyo.
English translation rights arranged with KADOKAWA CORPORATION, Tokyo,
through Tuttle-Mori Agency, Inc., Tokyo.

English translation © 2019 by Yen Press, LLC

Yen Press, LLC supports the right to free expression and the value of copyright. The purpose of copyright is to encourage writers and artists to produce the creative works that enrich our culture.

The scanning, uploading, and distribution of this book without permission is a theft of the author's intellectual property. If you would like permission to use material from the book (other than for review purposes), please contact the publisher. Thank you for your support of the author's rights.

Yen Press
150 West 30th Street, 19th Floor
New York, NY 10001

Visit us at yenpress.com
facebook.com/yenpress
twitter.com/yenpress
yenpress.tumblr.com
instagram.com/yenpress

First Yen Press Edition: August 2019

Yen Press is an imprint of Yen Press, LLC.
The Yen Press name and logo are trademarks of Yen Press, LLC.

The publisher is not responsible for websites (or their content) that are not owned by the publisher.

Library of Congress Control Number: 2018950180

ISBNs: 978-1-9753-0554-3 (paperback)
       978-1-9753-8648-1 (ebook)

10 9 8 7 6 5 4 3 2 1

WOR

Printed in the United States of America